THIS
STRANGE ADVENTURE

by

MARY ROBERTS
RINEHART

MCMXXIX

DOUBLEDAY, DORAN & COMPANY, INC.

GARDEN CITY

N. Y.

CONTENTS

BOOK I
Stella

Chapter I

THE house was very small. There was a narrow hall, a frigid parlour, a dining room and kitchen on the first floor. On the second there was a front bedroom, behind it the one the little girls used, and a rear room, a sort of storeroom, which in times of affluence was used by a maid of all work, called the hired girl, and in all times, good and bad, housed the trunks, the broken chairs, the oil lamps in case the gas company turned off the gas—which was not infrequently—and all the other flotsam and jetsam of that curious heterogeneous group which was the Colfax family.

Missie was always afraid of that back room. Its door stood at the turn of the stairs, and after dark she held her breath as she raced by it. About it she built up gradually a superstition of horror. It contained ghosts; at any time its door might open and some bony hand protrude itself to clutch at her. And after a long time, she knew that it contained *a leg*.

Neither she nor Ellen was supposed to go into it.

"You girls keep out of that room," was their mother's order. "You're not going in there to open trunks and mess things up."

But one day the door was open, and Missie looked in and saw the leg. It was deadly white and very horrible. She never spoke of it. She was quite sure that no one knew about it but herself. But after that it was not a hand that threatened her, but a dead white foot.

Not for a long time did she know that it was only a plaster cast, from the time her father had broken his leg when a horse ran away with him. She never did know why it had been preserved.

3

She was a highly imaginative child. Ellen, the step-sister, was matter of fact in the extreme. Ellen would stop on the landing in the dark, on her way to bed, and look longingly back and down into the lights below, and Missie would stand inside their small bedroom waiting to hear a shriek. But Ellen never shrieked.

Later on Missie was to realize that this quality of practicality in Ellen, her ability to see things as they were and not as she imagined them, had enabled her to organize her life securely, to turn things to her own account. Missie had no such ability. She was too romantic, too imaginative, too little self-absorbed. Ellen took, Missie gave. Ellen dominated, Missie was a creature of circumstance.

"Don't be such a little silly," Ellen would say. "Look here, I'll open the door. Give me a match."

"I'll tell Mother if you do," she would threaten, terrorized.

The parlour was seldom used. It was furnished with rosewood upholstered in black horsehair, and on the top of each chair-back was a carved rose surrounded by leaves. There was an old square piano, also, and between the two windows a long gilt mirror, with a marble slab a foot or so from the floor. The furniture, Missie knew, had been bought by her father at an auction sale, and she knew too that her mother hated it.

"It has no style," she would complain.

"It's real, at least, my dear," her father would say, and smile that strange smile of his which even then Missie resented. It was a patronizing, superior smile, and it seemed to be reserved for her mother. He never used it to Missie. Missie was his own child. It appeared that there was this odd difference between Ellen and Missie; it was puzzling, for Missie had a father and Ellen had none.

"But where is your father?"

"I don't know. Dead, most likely."

"But why don't you ask her?"

The mother was often "her" between them.

Ellen looked at her with candid practical eyes.

"She says he's dead. But maybe she's lying."

Gradually there sprang up in Missie a fierce loyalty to her mother.

Her father she knew very little about. He was tall and fair, and the small household served him almost cringingly. He was never awakened in the morning, and it was necessary to keep everything very quiet until he roused. Sometimes Missie could see him in bed, the sheet drawn over his head to keep the light out of his eyes. He was so long that he extended from one end of the big walnut bed to the other, and he lay almost in the center.

When he did rouse, everything was instant excitement. Ellen watched the breakfast, Missie carried up the hot water, for there was no bathroom in the house, and her mother went upstairs and laid out his fresh clothes and put the studs and buttons in his shirt. Sometimes she would call down for Ellen to put an iron on the fire, and while he ate his breakfast she would iron his high silk hat. When he finally started down the street to that mysterious spot called the office he was handsome, resplendent, even amiable.

Even then Missie realized that the house revolved around her father. Such pinching as took place, and there was much of it, was never suffered to touch him. The cream from the top of the milk was saved for his coffee, the best of the beefsteak if he was late, as he often was. And however slovenly she might be during the day, her mother was always dressed for his return. She would lace herself into her long highbreasted corsets, do her heavy hair in great coils on top of her head, powder her face—although the little girls were not supposed to know that she used powder. Then she would tie her bustle around her waist over her long cambric petticoats, and over that would go the voluminous skirt, the basque which fitted close to her lovely figure.

She was a very handsome woman, was Stella Colfax in those days; a common woman in many ways, given to quick angers when she would slap the two children or show an unexpected knowledge of the vernacular to some cringing servant girl. A passionate woman, too, hot blooded, jealous, possessive. There was undoubted provocation behind Lambert Colfax's desertion of her later on.

That she was passionately in love with him until the day of her death there is no doubt. From what depths he had taken her neither one of the girls was ever to know. There had been some obscure first marriage—Lambert always insisted that Ellen was legitimate—but Stella's past was locked in a trunk in the room at the head of the stairs, a vast square trunk from which, when times were parlous, she occasionally brought some queer exotic fabric which she made, skillfully enough, into frocks for the children.

They had had the trunk in the boarding house, before they moved to the little house on Grove Street. Only there it was covered with a cloth and had served as a table.

Even the neighbours, who did not speak to her, admitted that Stella Colfax was a handsome woman. Missie was never to have her beauty, although Ellen had inherited some of it. She must have been thirty-six or so when they moved into the little house, and her figure was still fine according to the standards of the time; her breasts were high and firm, her waist, in spite of her childbearing, laced in to the nineteen inches above which it was never allowed to creep. One of Missie's earliest memories was of her mother with a tape measure, carefully measuring her waist with a sort of fixed intensity.

Her clothes were designed to show every line of her contour. Her basques fitted her as though she had been poured into them. When she moved, there would be soft quivering ripples over her bosom, and although when Missie and Ellen dressed up as ladies they could reproduce her contours, they were never able to reproduce that seductive softness.

She was neat about herself, almost fastidious. The heavy muslin undergarments of the time were as attractive as she could make them. Her corset covers were run through with ribbon, her petticoats elaborately frilled. But she was no housekeeper. Servants came and went; they slept in the back room among the lumber, crept down at dawn to a frigid kitchen, and while they were there a sort of order prevailed. But there were long intervals when there was no servant; when soiled clothes piled up, and dishes were fitfully washed, and the food Stella prepared came to the table almost unfit to eat.

During these periods Lambert stayed away from home as much as possible. He was a fastidious man, and the infatuation which had brought about his wild marriage was long over. Stella was his slave, his servant, occasionally his mistress, but never in the best sense of the word his wife. There were no confidences between them. At the best, his attitude toward her was one of affectionate contempt; at his worst, he became a sneering jibing monster, riding roughshod over her pride and her small vanities, turning even her love for him into a low and degraded sensuousness.

It was a queer preparation for life for the little girls; periods of enough varied by longer periods of semi-privation. Weeks of coldness between the man and woman, and then brief passionate days when, for some reason beyond the children's understanding, the bond between husband and wife was re-established and peace entered the little house.

Lambert's family had cast him off, except for one member. Now and then, generally on summer evenings when they were "sitting out" and could not escape, there would come pompously down the street the handsome elderly and immaculate figure of a man, his soft hat in his hand, the ends of his white lawn tie fluttering in the breeze. And Stella would say:

"Here's that old sponge again! If you give him anything, Lambert Colfax . . ."

"Colonel Archibald Kennedy is my uncle," perhaps Lambert would say, in his suave jeering voice. "What do you know of the ties of blood, my dear?"

"I know a lot about rent and grocery bills. And as to blood —the Colfaxes have no blood; they have skimmed milk in their veins."

But when old Archibald went away he generally carried with him a banknote or two, and sometimes the rent had to "go over."

Until she was a grown woman, the word "rent" had a connotation of drama for Missie. In good months she or Ellen, and sometimes both, walked into Mr. Elliott's grocery store down on the corner—the same grocery one went to to telephone for the doctor—and handed him the bills and said: "Mother wants a receipt, please." Then Mr. Elliott went to the back of the store to his dusty littered desk, and finally found his pad of blank receipts and filled one out.

The floor of the store was neatly spread each day with sawdust, and in the morning the assistant sprinkled yesterday's sawdust with water and then swept it out with a broom, preparatory to the new dressing. All around were open barrels and boxes, and on the good days Mr. Elliott would cut them a slice of bologna sausage, or dip into a barrel with a large hairy hand and give them each an enormous very sour pickle.

The bad days were different, however. Then it was a note they carried, written in an uncertain hand by Stella on thin paper, which was thin so that the heavily ruled sheet she slipped underneath to keep the lines straight would show through. And Mr. Elliott would scowl and spit on the floor and give them until the next Tuesday.

There always followed, to Missie, a sense of impermanence. Indeed, it hovered over the entire feminine portion of the household. Only Lambert remained the same as ever, dressed as carefully, slept as late, poured the cream as lavishly, and went down the street to the horse cars as debonairly as ever.

Only once there was very nearly a débâcle. Tuesday came, or whatever the day was, and Mr. Elliott rang the door bell that evening and said he had stood as much as flesh and blood could bear.

"I'm a hard-working man," he said, eying Lambert. "I get up early and I work late, and what I can't pay for I do without. Which is more than I can say for a lot of folks."

And Lambert heard him through, still with that queer patronizing smile, and then reached down in his trousers pocket and brought out the money.

It was after he had gone that the scene occurred, with Stella crying that he was hard and cruel, and that he might have told her he had the money, and Lambert imperturbable as ever.

"And that's what comes of my little surprise for you, my dear!"

"Surprise! You let me worry myself into the grave, and about nothing."

"Precisely," said Lambert. "About nothing. Jehovah-Jireh, my dear. But I forget; you don't know your Bible as well as you should. It means 'The Lord will reveal himself.' Provide, in other words."

And Stella looked at him with the sort of helplessness Missie was always to remember in connection with her father, and turned and went out of the room.

Outside of the casual contacts of the public schools they had no friends. Old Archibald Kennedy was the only member of the Colfax family who ever visited the little house, and Stella apparently had neither family nor friends. Life for Missie until she was ten was limited to the little house. There were few books. The private libraries of the seventies and early eighties were largely limited to dingily bound editions of the classics and ponderous theological works, but even these were lacking. But once, when Missie was nine and Ellen twelve, there came into the back room a servant named Annie who brought in, each Saturday night, a copy of the *Fireside Companion*. The little girls pored over it; always the heroines were poor but beautiful, with long lashes and large brown or violet eyes; and always there was a heroic hero and a villain of unalloyed villainy. They were filled with sickly, cloying sentiment and red-hot romance, and in many of Missie's early dreams she was the heroine, finally triumphant, and sweeping down a marble staircase in trailing black velvet and pearls.

But one night Stella missed the big yellow cake bowl, and when Annie was discovered bathing her tired feet in it she had to go.

"In the cake bowl!" shrieked Stella. "Of all the impudence!"

"I'll wash it."

"What's your washstand basin for?"

"I haven't any. It's broken."

"Then you broke it, you dirty slut!" said Stella furiously.

So Annie left, without notice and minus one dollar, deducted for breakage, of the two dollars a week for which she had washed, ironed, scrubbed, baked, swept, cooked, and emptied into the small out-house at the end of the yard the family slops. And with her departed her violet-eyed heroines, and those stories of high romance which were subconsciously to influence Missie for so many years.

She was highly imaginative. One day a child in the neighbourhood died, and holding tight to Ellen's hand they went in to look at the small corpse, neatly laid out and surrounded by flowers. It was after that that Missie arranged a tableau, admission one penny, and Ellen being the corpse.

When Stella came home that afternoon—it was her custom after the mid-day dinner to dress herself carefully, and slowly to promenade the principal streets—she found the cold parlour filled with children, Ellen laid out like a corpse on a table beneath the mantelpiece, and perched on that narrow shelf two quivering angels, clad only in sheets and covered with goose-flesh.

She turned the mourners out, and spanked and dressed the little girls. But when she told Lambert he threw back his handsome head and laughed.

"I'll bet it was Missie's idea!" Then he stopped smiling

and looked at her. "And where were you while this was going on?"

"I was out," she told him defiantly.

"So I suppose. You're out a good bit, my dear. Do you think it is necessary for my wife to parade the streets, like a common street walker?"

"It's necessary for your wife to do a good many things. And to stand for a good many more."

For Stella had begun to be suspicious.

Chapter II

IT WAS a strange, irregular household, isolated in the midst of an otherwise friendly neighbourhood. There were evenings when Lambert came unsteadily on his long fine legs up the street, and when Stella sat sullen and red-eyed across the table from him. And as time went on there were nights when he did not come home for supper, and the little girls, studying their lessons under the gas light at the dining-room table, could hear Stella upstairs, moving restlessly about, or rocking doggedly back and forth in her rocking chair.

"I wish she would stop that," Ellen would say, fretfully. "What's she worrying about, anyhow?"

Ellen was three years older than Missie. She was a pretty child, blonde and with lovely calculating blue eyes; a prettier child than Missie, with her straight hair, her faintly irregular features, her candid look. Stella, who worshipped beauty, dressed Ellen carefully if oddly. But it was on Missie that Stella lavished such maternity as she had. Missie was her love child.

"I know. She's worrying about Father."

"I wish he'd stay away for good."

The little girls were not unhappy. The impending tragedy between the two adults did not touch them. Around them moved the deliberate, unhurried life of the early eighties. Their life was the life of the street; the huge horses with hairy fetlocks drawing over the cobbles the brewers' wagons, the ice and coal wagons, and stopping at the watering trough to lower their great heads and drink deeply; the icemen, dropping the ice on the pavement and moving on, and housewives hurrying out to get it before it melted in the sun; the milkman, with his great copper boiler beside him on the seat. He rang a gong and people went out with pitchers and said: "A quart, please." Or a pint, maybe. The milkman put a measure under the tap and there was a delicious gurgling, but when they wanted cream he reached back for a can, and poured it carefully.

The earth between the cobblestones was slightly sour and ammoniacal, and in dry weather bits of manure flew about. After a rain the children floated paper boats in the gutter, following them until they disappeared in that strangest of all mysteries, the sewer drop. In caterpillar season they tied hairy caterpillars to paper wagons, and Missie wept when Stella stepped on one and killed it. She was a gentle child, filled with pity for small creatures, already maternal, cuddling her dolls with a fierce protective passion.

Once she broke a doll and Stella beat her.

"I'll teach you to go dropping things," she said vindictively.

And Missie cried herself to sleep that night, not because of the beating, but because of the broken doll.

Stella's nerves were going back on her during those years. Ellen bore with her slaps, her raised voice, with a sort of cold disdain, but Missie suffered. Her small smile was not so ready, not so sure. She developed the habit of obliterating herself at times, sitting in a corner with a doll or some small cherished thing, until the storms were over and peace descended again. Just how much that uncertainty influenced her later life she never knew. There was, she felt, always an element of fear in her. In her happiest moments she was to know it, and to be subconsciously waiting for the happiness to end. She could take nothing for granted; she must look and watch and question it.

But she developed a small philosophy of her own. She made no protests when the mothers of the neighbourhood called in the little girls who stopped to look at the caterpillar wagons.

"Nellie, come here. I want you."

Because the Colfax children had a gift for inventing their own small amusements, the children left unwillingly. But they always went.

"Stuck up thing," Ellen would mutter. But Missie would go quietly on with her playing. She was learning to ask for nothing and to expect very little. She blamed nobody. Once —this when she was seven or eight—Ellen told her that the reason the neighbours hated them was because their mother was a divorced woman; but she did not explain that, and Missie watched her mother after that to see if there was anything strange about her.

"For mercy's sake, Missie! What are you staring at?"

"Nothing, mom," said Missie, politely. She was a polite child.

"Then go ahead and eat your supper."

Dinner was in the middle of the day. Lambert came home to it from the office, which was never for long the same office, but something different. Sometimes he was amiable, sometimes not. Occasionally in the spring and summer there would be a Ladies' Day at the baseball grounds. Baseball was supposed to be a prerogative of the male, but once a week women were admitted free of charge. Then indeed was Stella in her glory. She would spend hours over her dressing, lacing in her stays, curling her heavy hair, fastening on her enormous bustle, adjusting her polonaise and her long pointed basque. Her gay little bonnet was tied coquettishly under her chin with ribbons, and she would sit upright in the seats, aware that the men around knew she was a fine woman. Aware of their maleness, of her own allure; looking casually right and left to catch their eyes, glancing down demurely, possibly showing an inch or two of well-formed ankle.

And nothing of this by-play was lost on Lambert Colfax. He knew her and he knew her type. He would sit, ostensibly absorbed in the game, with a faint sneer on his handsome mouth. He knew it was only a game, that this woman was

his, body and soul, that the very game was designed to show
him that she was still attractive to men, and thus to enhance
her charms for him. But his fastidiousness was revolted.
There came a time when he refused to take her again.

"And why not?"

"Because I'm sick at my stomach of watching you, my
dear."

"Watching me! You've got a dirty mind, Lambert Colfax.
And what's more . . ."

There followed one of the usual bitter quarrels, with Stella's voice raised until Mrs. Wilkinson next door pounded on
the thin party wall.

A queer preparation indeed for life for the children in
that house. Ellen came out of it hard, practical, ambitious; on
Missie it was to impose certain qualities which were never to
leave her, a certain gravity and tolerance, a feeling of the
impermanence of any happiness, and a tendency during any
strain to a trembling of the hands.

"Mom, Missie's broken another cup."

"You be careful, out there, or I'll break a switch over you."

But in spite of Stella's violent temper Missie was passionately devoted to her mother. Ellen had no devotion for any
of them. And it is probably due to this that as time went on it
was Missie who became Stella's confidant. She was twelve by
that time, wearing a surreptitious little bustle of her own to
school, a bustle made of newspapers tied with a string; a
wistful appealing child, not pretty, but slim and with the Colfax fine sensitive hands.

True, much that Stella told her passed over her head. She
was entirely innocent. But the sense of impending tragedy
was clear enough to her. There was one cold fall day when,
after a quarrel, Stella walked out of the house and took
Missie with her. They walked a long time, and finally fetched
up on a bench in the new park along the river bank. At first
Missie was content to sit and be quiet; the river was busy in
those days. Great stern-wheeled white packets travelled up

and down, and smaller, dingier tow-boats, pushing ahead of them long lines of barges loaded with coal. Whistles sounded, bells rang, mysterious figures came and went, and these figures Missie fitted into stories of her own invention, and was content.

But as dusk fell she grew cold; her small hands were red and blotched, and still Stella sat and stared at the river.

"Aren't we going home soon, mom?"

"We're not going home," said Stella stonily.

"Not ever?"

"Never. Now listen to me. Stop that crying and listen. Your father's a bad man; he's hard and cruel and bad. He's got another woman."

Missie was stunned and puzzled.

"What for?"

Stella laughed bitterly.

"You'll know some day," she said. "You'll have to know some time. There are bad men and bad women in the world, Missie." She turned on her fiercely, "Promise me you'll never be a bad girl, Missie. You promise that and I'll feel better."

She promised, obediently enough. She had no idea of what it was all about; at the worst she saw the probable defection on the rent money, and they had lived through that before.

"Who's the other woman, mother?"

"Never mind about that," said Stella shortly.

It was long after dark when they left, and Stella's gesture had been a vain one after all. For when they got back—where else could they go?—they found that Lambert had not been back to supper, and that Ellen was crouching over the kitchen stove reading a book.

After that they were alone, the three of them, more than ever. There was no longer a servant, even at intervals, and Mr. Elliott was increasingly gruff about the notes in the fine slanting hand. Ellen was doing most of the cooking, and was showing a certain practical efficiency in it. But there were more and more evenings when the supper dried up on

the stove, and when Stella, sitting down at last, ate little and
sullenly. She must have begun to age at that time, for in the
pitiless glare of the gas jet over the table even Missie noticed
fine wrinkles at the corners of her handsome mouth.

It was this aging which ruined her one genuine attempt to
get away. She refused to acknowledge it to herself, fought it
to the best of her ability. Missie could always remember, in
a day when soap and water and Providence were supposed
to care for a woman's skin, Stella sitting before the walnut
dresser with its marble top and rubbing cream into her face.
When she had finished she wiped it off carefully, and then
powdered. She used no rouge; that was the badge of the
women of the town, and whatever her faults may have been,
Stella clung to the respectability her marriage had brought
her. But she carefully brushed and dressed her abundant
hair, and her care of her body became almost a passion with
her.

Did she hope that Lambert would come back to her? What
did she think of, in the long wakeful nights when she lay
alone in that wide bed, suffering those agonies of jealousy
which left their signs written on her face? Her children never
knew. She remained to the end unfathomable. They had no
background for her, outside of the little house; Ellen did
not remember her own father, and when the time came for
them to wonder, Stella had carried the past with her where
no questioning was of any avail.

There was but one bit of illumination; and that was when
she started out one day, taking Missie with her. Lambert
had not been at home for two days, and although the fare
on the horse cars was only a nickel, they walked into the
business part of the town.

Stella had made an unusually careful toilet. It was winter,
and she wore a long black velvet cloak, rather shabby but
showing every line of her still opulent figure. Over her shoulders was one of the very short tight fur capes of the period,
and her hands were thrust into a tiny muff. Her small bonnet

sat high on top of her hair, and from beneath it came a heavy bang twisted into a row of small flat curls. Even Missie noticed that men on the streets looked at her with interest.

But Stella was not looking for carnal admiration, not that day at least. Missie was breathless when at last they reached an alley way and turned into it. There was a door there, and a man on guard, but he let them in.

"Hardly knew you at first," he said. "Miss Beaumont's expecting you."

"Have I changed like that?" said Stella, suddenly arch.

"Handsomer than ever, *I'd* say," said the door-man, and there was a bit of colour in Stella's face as they went in.

It was a queer place in which Missie suddenly found herself. The wings of a theatre during a burlesque show of the 80's; a gas-lighted untidy place, filled with men in working clothes and women with no clothes at all. At least so the child thought at first, and she felt breathless and panicky. Even the discovery that they wore tights did not greatly reassure her. They were big women mostly, full of figure, bewigged, made up for the footlights into grotesque masks which fairly startled Missie. Under cover of the blare of the band she tugged at Stella.

"Mom!" she said. "Mom! They're not dressed!"

Stella was impatient.

"They're covered," she retorted. "Don't stare like that. And get this into your head, my girl. There's nothing sinful about the human body unless you make it sinful."

Poor Stella! With what she had in mind that horror of Missie's must have been a rather dreadful thing. One has to think back to the 80's to realize just what it meant. Burlesque was still confined to theatres frequented only by men; the woman in tights was being thundered at from every pulpit; poor Amazons of the stage, exhibiting their rather portly charms at a minimum wage, they were supposed to be sending a degenerating America to decadence and perdition. And to this life Stella was proposing to return.

But it was not to be. When Miss Beaumont, seemingly larger, more curved and blonder than any of the others, came into her dressing room, it was to show decided shock at Stella's appearance.

"Why Stell, you poor thing!" she said. "Whatever have you done to yourself? You haven't been sick, have you?"

"No," said Stella, dully.

"Well," said Miss Beaumont, philosophically, "I suppose you can't have everything." Then she looked at Missie. "My God, don't tell me this is yours!"

"You knew I had her."

"I guess I forgot how time was going. Sit down, dearie. Don't mind me if I have to change a bit."

As she gave every indication of stripping then and there, however, Stella turned to Missie. "You get behind that screen," she said.

So it was from behind the screen that Missie overheard the rest of that conversation. Not all of it registered. She sat on a low stool and looked about her. There was a trunk like the one in the back room, and on a shelf below a brilliantly lighted mirror were innumerable pots and jars. She was filled with curiosity; she wished that she might grow large, with vast breasts and big swelling hips; that her hair would turn yellow. Then, when she swept down the marble staircase in black velvet and pearls . . .

"But what about Bertie? What does he say?"

"I don't know, and I don't care."

"Don't tell me he's left you?"

"Just about. There's somebody else."

Miss Beaumont gave a long sigh.

"Isn't that the way it goes?" she demanded. "They get you, and you bear their children and lose your figure, and then they up and run."

"I haven't lost my figure," Stella put in stoutly. "I measure exactly what I did when——"

She checked herself and called to Missie.

"You go outside," she called. "Sit on the stairs. Don't you go wandering around, either. You hear me?"

So that brief bit was all that Missie ever knew of Stella's one attempt to break her now useless chains. She sat on the iron staircase, and after a time a man went into Miss Beaumont's room, an authoritative sort of a man, in a loud checked suit and a still louder waistcoat. He stayed only a short time, and then Stella came out and they went home.

Missie saw that she had been crying.

She did not tell Ellen about that visit. Ellen was a big girl now, sixteen. After school hours—she was in the high school —she would tidy Stella's disorderly house with a sort of detached efficiency. She hated disorder. But that night, drying the dishes for her, Missie said out of a clear sky:

"I hate men."

"Why?" said Ellen, scraping at a frying pan.

"Men and boys too."

"You'll get over that. Some of them are all right."

Lambert did not come home that night, and when Missie went in to her mother's room to say good night, she found her before her mirror. She was standing in her long tight heavily boned stays, with the high cusps which supported her breasts, surveying herself from under swollen eyelids.

Missie lay in bed that night sleepless. Men were cruel, hard and cruel.

You worked for them; you put in their studs and cufflinks, and ironed their hats, and saved the cream for them, and you watched when the steak was cut to see if it pleased them or not. And then they turned on you, and you could do nothing. Her father, Mr. Elliott, the man in the checked suit, the principal at the school, with his rattan standing in a corner, all of them were cruel. She hated them. And most of all she hated her father.

Chapter III

NOTWITHSTANDING the increasing irregularities of the household, Missie was a cheerful child. With the philosophy which children learn so much more readily than adults, she took life as it came. When there was peace and comparative plenty she sang in a thin little pipe, and when matters were very bad, when Lambert had not been at home for days and Stella left off her stays and went around like a woman in a trance, she was quiet, watchful, and wary.

"What do you want for supper, mom?"

"I don't care. You might open a can of tomatoes."

Ellen's air of detachment was increasing. It was when she was settled at the dining table with her school work that Stella would open her door and call:

"Missie! Come on up. I want to see you about something."

And Missie would go heavily. She feared those hours when Stella, unable to keep her troubles to herself, poured out to her her jealousies and her suspicions. Young and ignorant as she was, it was only in her later life that she realized fully what they meant, but she began to learn that there was something shameful and dreadful between men and women. All men, but not all women. There were women who were good. But others were bad. They took the rent money and any other they could get, and they went around in mother-hubbard wrappers and sat inside windows and called men to come in.

Only once Ellen made a protest. She was a methodical person, absorbed in her own affairs. Every night when she sat down at the table to work she sharpened a row of lead pencils and then washed her hands. The figures she made were beautiful, and her writing was neat and according to the best Spencerian method. Also she had a gift for silence. In that house where Stella talked and Missie sang she was mostly silent.

But that night when Stella called she put down her pencil impatiently and went to the foot of the stairs.

"Missie's got lessons to do, mom."

"She can go right down again."

"But she won't." Then something seemed to break in Ellen. "Why don't you let her alone?" she demanded. "If you've got to talk, talk to me. What's the use of filling her up with a lot of stuff, anyhow?"

Stella was outraged.

"You mind your business, Ellen," she said sharply. "And that's not true. All I want is to know where she put my scissors. Missie!"

"They're in the sewing box," Missie quavered. She was alarmed. Ellen was white and shaking, and she had caught her by the shoulder. There was a brief silence; then Stella's door slammed and Ellen relaxed.

After that Stella was more careful, but sometimes when Ellen was out of the house she hinted at dark matters. She had no friends, no confidants; possibly she selected Missie instead of Ellen because Ellen would have understood, while Missie did not. And to do her credit, these outpourings of hers did not affect the child's inner life. Certainly not at the time.

"Mom, here's the organ grinder. Can I have a penny for the little monkey?"

Or:

"Mom, here's the umbrella man! Where's your umbrella?"

And while the umbrella man mended the umbrella, he would talk. Business was not as good as it used to be.

"Umbrellas are gettin' too cheap," he would grumble. "Used to be folks took care of them; handed them down. Now they go and buy a new one. There's one umbrella I look after's been in one family for twenty-five years. Seen a whole family grow up, it has."

There was a dramatic story of how a staunch old umbrella had acted as a sail in a wind-storm.

"Carried that girl—and she was as big as you, maybe bigger—carried her about a block and set her down, nice and easy, right on her front door step."

"Didn't it turn inside out?"

"It turn? You don't know a real umbrella! Why say, I bet you could take that umbrella and sail down the river in it to the sea."

She had a great admiration for the umbrella man. Not so for the tattered individual who on Saturday mornings drove down the back alley, yelling in a stentorian voice: "Rags, old iron, paper. *Rags, old iron, paper!*" He was a dirty man and a miserly. He would pull a scale with a hook out of his pocket and weigh the sack carefully.

"Three cents," he would say.

"Make it five," she would coax.

"Three cents is a big price," he would retort, and hand back the sack. Then he would pick up the reins of his bony horse and prepare to drive on. "Rags, old iron . . ."

"All right," Missie would call hastily, and pocket the pennies. The rag money was hers.

Lambert came back, of course. There would be a quarrel and then, instead of the old reconciliation, a truce of sorts. Stella would dress carefully, but she was moody and taciturn, and Lambert would be sulky and silent also. After supper he would put on his hat—he was wearing a derby now—and call to Stella:

"I'm going to play some pool at Conroy's."

"That's what you say."

"If you don't believe it you can send the girls to find out."

"I'm likely to do that!"

Nevertheless, in her loneliness and despair once she did that very thing.

It was a hot night. Ellen was washing the dishes, and
Stella and Missie were on the front steps when old Archibald
Kennedy once more came down the street. He had not been
around for a year or two; the pickings had been too lean. But
now he came, a fine tall old hulk of a man, his white beard
flowing in the breeze, his cane tapping the pavement author-
itatively. When he saw Stella he swept off his hat in the
grand manner.

"Good evening, Stella. And I hope I am seeing you well?"

But there was a little fear in his eyes. He had always been
afraid of this common woman his nephew had married. In
that world of pretense in which he lived she had a vulgar
habit of tearing away the shams. But when Missie was older
she often thought of old Archibald Kennedy. That fear in
his pale blue eyes, the slight tremor of his knotted aristocratic
old hands, were they all caused by fear of her mother? Was
there not some greater fear behind them? The fear of desti-
tution, fear of finding his white head shelterless, fear of—
dreadful to think of that now—fear of actual hunger?

This evening, however, Stella was kinder.

"I'm all right," she said. "Bert's not here. Maybe you'd
care to sit down."

He sat still, holding the large soft hat which had been his
affectation ever since the Civil War.

"So this is Missie! She's growing. But she'll never be as
handsome as her mother."

Perhaps this mollified Stella, perhaps she had her own
reasons.

"Would you like a glass of beer?"

"My dear lady, I couldn't possibly trouble you."

Stella got up and called Missie in the house after her.

"Get ten cents and a pail," she said, "and go to the Ladies'
Entrance at Conroy's. Mrs. Conroy'll give it to you. And. . . .
Missie!"

"Yes, mom."

"You might just glance in the pool room and see if your father's there."

Lambert was there, and old Archibald got his beer. But nothing else. When Missie came back she knew Stella had been talking to him.

"It's the way of the world, Stella," he was saying. "Men must work and women must weep."

"He doesn't work. Not any more than he can help. And I'm about through with weeping."

Over his beer old Archibald waxed garrulous.

"We're a curious family," he said. "The women are too cold and the men are too hot. Good blood often works that way. It makes ladies out of its girls, not women." The word "suppression" in its later connotation was unknown then; Archibald considered over his glass. "We teach them that what is natural in the males is original sin in them. And then we expect——"

He sighed. His voice trailed off. He finished his beer and got up. His hands were steadier.

"You tell Lambert for me," he said, "that if I had a wife and a girl like his I'd be taking care of them. It's a bad world for women. Well, good night, and thanks."

He was a widower, and his two sons had drunk themselves to death. Now he had only his pension and an iron determination not to die in the Soldiers' Home. Long ago he had severed relations with his family, and he lived alone in a shabby room somewhere, immaculately clean and increasingly shabby. Once every week, winter and summer, through rain and snow, blistering heat and summer dust, he climbed the hill to the cemetery and visited his graves. Rumour said that he had been an unfaithful husband and a bad father, but time had softened his memories of those long-ago days. Now save in flashes he saw himself as bereaved, a victim and not a triumphant survivor.

Life went on somehow, the primitive life of an inland

American city in the 80's. Sometimes Ellen and Missie went on Saturday afternoons to the Dime Museum, where the freaks sat in rows: fat ladies, bearded ladies, tattooed men, the dog-faced boy. In another room a man sang an illustrated song, and a little girl who was dying in a white nightgown on the stage developed wings and rose on wires to heaven. Missie sobbed as though her heart would break.

Culture as such had not left the coast. The inland cities were built along narrow streets, as though after the long loneliness of the wilderness these pioneers craved companionship. They had as yet no music, no art, no recreation. The struggle for survival was still going on. Religious bigotry and intolerance ran high, and side by side with the churches stood the saloons, each with its long bar, its mirror back of it, its cuspidors, its brass rail, its swinging door, its Ladies' Entrance. Men got drunk on Saturday night and went to church on Sunday morning.

Missie's early life, then, was primitive in the extreme. In hot weather, when the flies came, Stella would sweep the table languidly with a whisk made of strips of newspaper fastened to a stick. Ellen and Missie both bathed and washed at a wooden washhand stand, behind which Stella had crookedly nailed a splasher. At night both the children could hear the rumble of excavating wagons; they emptied the outhouses of the neighbourhood and then carried their loads of night soil out into the country, or to the river. In the daytime they could watch herds of cattle driven through the city streets, and now and then a steer got loose and the cry would go up: "Wild bull! Wild bull!"

The butchers had a portion of the town for themselves, and over it always hung the odour of stale blood.

Not far away was the Drovers' Hotel. Here stopped the men who were driving cattle through town to the local slaughter houses. Here also came the farmers, driving through the night to sell their butter, eggs, chickens and vegetables at the market. Their wives sat beside them on the wagons; they unloaded at the market, left the women, drove their teams to the great yard behind the hotel, and unhitching them, tied them in the sheds which lined its sides. The tired women sat nodding in their stalls, the men sometimes stretched out in the wagons and slept. About the yard, about all the streets indeed, was a faint ammoniacal scent and the heavier odour of manure. And the yard and the streets—all travelled streets— were paved with cobblestones, with rounded gutters also of cobbles to carry off the rains.

Sometimes, when money was plentiful, the children were allowed to use the horse cars. One dropped a nickel in a slot behind the driver, and he heard it and was satisfied. But once Missie forgot to drop her nickel, and the driver turned a red angry face, and hammered with his fist on the glass. She loved the cars, however. The driver cracked his whip, the passengers jerked, then one moved along. In summer the drivers tied wet sponges on the horses' heads, and in winter there was straw on the floor, to keep one's feet dry and warm. She thought the drivers, who looked so fierce, were really kind.

That was her world, the street and beyond it the narrow track of the horse cars. However, life beat and surged on that narrow street as everywhere else, and even Missie did not miss contact with it. Children were born, people were sick, sometimes died. She learned in time to recognize the quick beat of the doctor's horse on the cobblestones.

"Ellen, the doctor's gone into the Whalen's!"

And sometimes, when he left there would be a baby. It was just like a miracle. First there was no baby and then there was one. It never occurred to Stella to explain these neighbourhood phenomena to her. She was fourteen before she knew that the doctor did not carry the baby in his satchel.

And the knowledge was a hideous shock to her. It took years of living to rebuild that castle of dreams of hers, to enable her once more to see that childbirth was a beautiful and a holy thing. But all her life, indeed, Missie was to learn that this building, tearing down and slow painful rebuilding

was to be her lot. No sooner had she accepted a thing than it
was changed; love, loyalty, fidelity, even marriage, one built
up a concept of each of them only to have it destroyed. Then
one built again, better and stronger and truer, and perhaps
something permanent was achieved. Any girl, any woman,
perhaps; but most certainly Missie.

Sometimes death came to the little street. There would be
a hush over it; the parlour organs and the pianos would be
stilled, the children would walk by the house silent and awed,
and the house itself would have its shades drawn and a black
or a white or a lavender crape hung to the doorbell. Men
would take off their hats on the front steps and tiptoe inside,
and then on the third day a decorous crowd would go in and
a line of hearse and carriages draw up at the door.

It was a long time before Missie could dissociate any shining black carriage from a funeral.

Stella had a morbid interest in funerals. She would bow
the shutters of her bedroom and sit inside peeping out.

"Eleven carriages," she would say. "A lot they'll have left
of the insurance money!"

But these deaths only dismayed Missie. They did not touch
her. Some one no longer walked home from the horse cars
at the corner, or sat out on the steps on summer evenings, but
that was all. Then one morning she started to school, and
there was a lavender crape on the Wilkinsons' bell next
door.

She had never thought of Mr. Wilkinson dying. True, he
had not worked for a long time. That was how Missie knew
him so well. He had to walk a great many blocks every day,
and as he said it made no difference which way he walked,
he went around the block he lived in.

"Then, you see, I've got a place to sit down every now and
then," he explained to her in his panting voice.

They had talked quite a lot together. Sometimes in the
evenings she had even accompanied him on his walks. He
seemed lonely. Mrs. Wilkinson was a big woman eternally

busy with her house; everything in it was polished and scrubbed. She "turned out" every room once a week, and even at night Missie occasionally heard the sound of her broom.

"Some people think more of their houses than of their husbands," Stella darkly hinted. "If she doesn't watch out——!"

Mr. Wilkinson told Missie about the stars, and about a number of other things.

"Now you take this piece of land here," he would pant. "Some day that's going to be a regular playground for children. Swings and all sorts of things. I'll not see it, but you will, Missie. Maybe your children will play on it. And a lot of this waste land will be parks. There's a lot to be learned about city living, only we're too soon. I am, anyhow."

He had no children of his own, and in his own way, remote because he knew that he had almost finished with life, or life with him, he loved Missie and tried to counsel her. Probably he knew or suspected that things were all wrong in the house next door.

"Take them by and large," he said, "people are better than we're likely to think they are. I don't know as I've ever known a real bad person; bad all through, that is. Get them the right way and you'll see that what looks like badness maybe isn't so at all. Folks get to thinking wrong, that's all. And when they think wrong . . ."

Often he had to stop and cough. It was a terrible rattling cough, and he would break into a sweat that ran down his face. But he would not take off his overcoat, even in the hottest weather.

"Perspiration's good for you," he would say. "Get's the poison out."

Three times a week he got on the cars and went to a slaughter house on the edge of town. There he drank fresh warm blood, and there was surely a new vitality in his step when he came back.

"It's not pleasant," he confided to Missie, "but it stands

to reason it's helpful. I've been running a little short of blood for a year or two."

And now he was dead. Missie did not go to school that day. All day long she lay on the sagging bed in the room she shared with Ellen, crying as if her heart would break. Stella tried to reason with her.

"I'd be ashamed if I were you. He's better off anyhow. I'll bet that woman is figuring now about how to clean up after the funeral."

When fresh sobs greeted this she tried argument.

"If you carry on like this about some one who doesn't belong to you, what would you do if anything happened to some one of your own? It's wicked, that's what it is. You get right up and come down to supper."

Missie dutifully got up; she was an obedient child. But she ate nothing, and when sobs threatened to overtake her she sipped at a glass of water.

It was months afterwards, the next spring indeed, that Missie went out into the backyard to put up string along the fence so the morning glories would cover its stark ugliness, and that Ellen found her huddled in a small heap on the cold ground, crying desperately and silently.

"What on earth's the matter? Of all the queer girls . . . !"

"I hit my thumb with the hammer," Missie lied.

She could not say that she and Mr. Wilkinson had put up the strings together the year before. Nor that the sound of Mrs. Wilkinson cheerfully beating a carpet in the next yard had seemed to her the epitome of all the tragedy of life.

Chapter IV

MISSIE was fifteen when Lambert finally severed his connection with his family.

Mr. Wilkinson's dying had made a lasting impression on her. Her young philosophy of acceptance failed her before death, her fear of life was accentuated. Perhaps it was rather a suspicion of life. It could do dreadful things to you, whether you were good or bad. If you loved people, either they hurt you or they died. The thing then was not to love; not too much anyhow. And if you did, because you couldn't help it, then you had to keep a stiff upper lip. Stella's words.

Sometimes she watched Ellen. Ellen was a young lady now with beaus. On the day she was expecting a "caller" she would clean out the parlour, scrubbing and polishing everything. Then at a quarter to eight she would light the oil lamp on the table and turn down the gas. Or instead of calling, on warm evenings a half-dozen youths would sit on the doorstep late, and with mandolins and guitars serenade the second-story windows.

Stella enjoyed this.

"Some night I'll stick my head out and tell them to go into the backyard where you can hear them."

"If you ever do, mom!"

They still called her "mom."

They were an undistinguishable lot, these serenaders: a young mechanic named Wilkins, whose father kept a junk yard; a clerk from Elliott's grocery store; a youth who drove a laundry wagon. Strange to think what the years were to do to them, especially to Tommy Wilkins. Strange indeed to

31

think of what the years were to do to all of them, to Missie, to Ellen, to Stella. To Stella.

But once Lambert came home when they were there. He stood on the pavement, feeling for his latch key, his high-held face derisive, his voice a little thick. He had been drinking.

"I daresay my wife is enjoying this little—er—treat," he said, "but I shall want to get some sleep. Also I would like to get to my front door, so if you will move on . . ."

They did move on, slipping off abashed in the darkness, and that was the last time Ellen was serenaded.

Even Missie knew by that time what Stella had meant by his having another woman. It sickened her. And that it was not just another woman. It was women. He had not even loyalty to them, such as they were. They came and went, poor drabs, maybe caring for him after their own fashion, succumbing to that patrician streak in him, to his good looks, his surface urbanities. And when he was tired of them he left them as he would have left a dead dog, never looking back.

Stella's dreadful confidences had destroyed all of Missie's illusions. It took her long years to re-build them, to see that the relationship between a man and a woman could be, like childbirth, a beautiful thing; that the human heart is a lonely heart, craving union to escape its spiritual isolation. But she saw nothing of that then. She watched Ellen. Did she know? Could she bear to put herself in the power of some man, to be hard to her, unfaithful, and—when that last break came—coldly brutal?

There had been no fresh quarrel, so far as she knew. He walked out one morning and did not come back. Stella, however, had herself well in hand. After all, she had had years to recognize her defeat. Her passion for Lambert had been, probably still was, the strongest influence in her life. She had been utterly his creature. What maternity she had was for his child, not for Ellen. But the fight had been hopeless.

It had aged her. In the mornings her face looked ravaged.

But her figure was still good, and her hands soft and white. Although for years now there had been no servant in the back room, which had gradually filled with lumber, the girls had taken over the cooking and the dishwashing. Stella's part was the making of the beds, a task generally performed by a perfunctory drawing up of sheets and blankets.

But Missie knew that when, as occasionally she still did, Stella set out for one of those aimless afternoon promenades of hers, there was now a touch of rouge on her face. Also that her small waist had broadened with years and indolence, and that the long cuirasslike corset was a thing of torture when she wore it. She would come in, get it off, draw a long breath and survey herself anxiously in the mirror.

"I don't look any fatter, do I?"

"Not much, mom. Just a wee bit around the waist. If you'd get some exercise . . ."

"Exercise! It's bearing children that's done it! If men had to lose their figures there'd be mighty few children born, I'm telling you."

She was almost apathetic then when Lambert left. She stood on the stairs, fully dressed at that hour, a thing in itself remarkable, and watched him below her as he went through his routine of straightening his tie before the glass in the hat rack.

"That's all, is it?"

"Well, I've told you about the rent," he said.

"Never mind about that. I'll attend to it."

He seemed to hesitate, put on his hat, adjusted it carefully, drew up the corner of his handkerchief. He did not look at her.

"I'll send an express wagon around."

"When? I suppose I'll have to pack for you. This afternoon would be best."

"All right."

Ellen was not there. Missie was standing inside the kitchen door, with her heart beating fast. She had a sense of drama rather than tragedy; she felt that this was the end, and because she was afraid he might come to say good-bye to her she hurriedly wiped her hands on her kitchen apron.

But the next thing she heard was the closing of the front door. When she went into the hall Stella was sitting quietly on the staircase.

"I want to get your father's clothes in order, Missie," she said. "We have to get his trunk ready by this afternoon." She rose somewhat heavily, steadied herself by the banister. "I guess you and I can get it out of the storeroom. I asked him to, but he forgot it."

Together they carried it into the front room, Missie bearing the brunt of the weight, Stella panting. Not once did her composure break. Missie, counting collars and handkerchiefs, hastily sewing on a button here and there, was aware of a new admiration for the woman sitting there in her rocking chair. She felt a glow of love, a surge of sympathy. Suddenly she bent over and laid her young cheek against her mother's raddled one.

"Poor old mom," she said. "We'll get along fine. You'll see."

Stella continued to rock somberly.

"They're all alike," she said. "You can't trust them. They take everything and give nothing. That's men for you."

With the departure of the trunk a strange quietness settled on the house. Whatever his failings, Lambert had brought vitality with him; the heavy tread of masculine feet, the smell of tobacco and Peau d'Espagne, the clutter of newspapers, all had been a part of him. Even during that period of intermittent returns, there had been the drama of waiting for him. Days would go by, and then there would be the sound of his key in the lock, the opening and closing of the front door. And although quarrels and bickerings would follow, the vitality had been there.

Now it was gone.

With all her faults, Stella had a certain stoical courage.

What memories she had as she sat in that upper room Missie never knew, but years later she was to wonder how they compared with the drab present; if time had not covered with the glamour of all lost things the struggles of her earlier days. That she had been on the burlesque stage was clear; when, two years or so after Lambert left, the two girls opened the trunk in the back room, they found photographs of her in the costumes of a Gaiety girl of the late 70's and early 80's. They showed her in tights, mostly with velvet shorts over the swelling curves of her hips; they showed considerable beauty, also.

Ellen was shocked and outraged. There was very little forgiveness in Ellen. But Missie, remembering that visit to Miss Beaumont, took one of the best of them and kept it.

"What do you want with it? You can't show that as your mother's picture!"

"I don't intend to show it."

"And you're never to tell about her. Do you hear that?"

"I suppose she had to get money somehow."

"There were decent ways to get money."

But before she was married Missie burned the picture. It was too hard to explain.

The house settled down into a grim routine of supply and demand. Ellen took a clerical position, and every morning at six Missie went downstairs and lighted the fire, for those were the days of early openings, and Ellen had to be at work at seven-thirty. She cooked the breakfast, got Ellen off, straightened the lower floor, and went to school. At nine or thereabouts Stella came down, drank some coffee, and then made the beds. She seemed to have no plans, no hopes. Sometimes, but not often, she went to the market. She carried a basket on her arm, and the touch of rouge under her veil was increasingly evident.

But the trips to market were disquieting to the girls. She spent too much, for one thing, and also there was something

vaguely mysterious about them. She had never marketed in
the old days. One day Ellen's office was closed, and she followed Stella at a distance. She saw her do her buying, and
then take up her position at the curb as though waiting for
something or somebody.

Ellen waited, and Stella stood there until an ancient carriage drew up, driven by a negro coachman, and there descended a tall thin old woman in a jet dolman and a high
black bonnet. A boy ran out to hold the horses, the coachman
descended with a market basket, and followed his mistress
inside. Stella was about to follow her when Ellen touched
her on the arm.

"What are you waiting for, mom?"

Stella started.

"I'm not waiting for anything," she said sharply. "What
are you doing here?"

She went home very quietly, Ellen carrying the basket, but
inside the door she called for Missie and caught her to her in
a storm of tears. Ellen never told Missie about that incident,
or that the old woman was her grandmother, Mrs. William
Colfax.

No letters came from Lambert. Curious to remember that
no letters ever came of any sort. Once inside the house they
seemed to be cut off from the active world around them, that
strangely intolerable world of the 80's, with its family prayers
and grace before meat, its hypocrisies and evasions, alluding
to legs as limbs, whispering of pregnancies as of something
shameful, and yet insisting on voluptuous curves in its
women, padding flat breasts and accentuating hips; cutting
off Stella for a past it only suspected, and condoning Lambert because he was a Colfax. He had left the city. That was
all they knew, and his promises had been as unreliable as always.

For three or four months a lawyer in town named Mac-
Donald paid the rent. Then he notified Stella that the funds

in his hands were exhausted, and pending receipt of others
the payments would cease. Stella made an elaborate toilet—
corset, rouge and all—and went to see him. But he could do
nothing. He was a gray-haired taciturn man who had lost an
arm in the war, and he lived not far away. He was a Scot,
and every April, on his birthday, or perhaps on some national holiday in his native land, he employed a piper in the
MacDonald plaid to walk up and down the pavement in front
of his house, bare knees and all, and to wail deliriously for
an hour or so.

One of Missie's earliest memories was of that piper.

But his sentiment was apparently limited to the bagpipes.
He disapproved of Stella, of her reputed history, of her em-
phasized figure, of her unfortunate attempt to charm him.
He sat fingering the safety pin which fastened his empty
sleeve across his breast.

"You are a strong woman. Can't you find anything to do?
Why let your child support you?"

"Why shouldn't my husband do that? He *is* my husband,
you know."

"I don't even know where he is."

"*They* know."

"Possibly. They have not confided in me."

"And they'll do nothing?"

"They have very little. Yes, I know," he said, as Stella
made a scornful gesture. "They keep a carriage and all that.
But they have a certain position to keep up."

And then Stella forgot herself.

"Position hell!" she said. "Look at my position. I'm likely
to be turned out on the streets!"

Perhaps it was in his mind to intimate that the streets were
nothing new to her, but he refrained. Instead, wincing under
an oath from a woman, and especially from a woman legally
bearing the sacred name of Colfax, he made a practical suggestion.

"I don't know much about these matters, but with what is still an excellent figure . . ."

"I'm too old," said Stella, thinking of the theatres. "My body's all right, but even with stage make-up my face——"

Mr. MacDonald lifted a horrified hand.

"My dear lady!" he said. "I was alluding to a store. Don't they have women of——er——good figure in certain departments? Cloaks and so on. It seems to me——I could give you a letter, possibly."

To give him his due he did give her a letter. He was a Covenanter and a rigid churchman. He had fought for years against the installation of a parlour organ in the church loft. He regarded dancing and cards as devices of the devil, and Stella as a scarlet woman; but he gave her a letter. What else could he do? There was no vast eleemosynary machinery yet devised to help dependent women, not even an aroused public conscience to recognize them. They lived their narrow despairing lives, died and passed on, unremembered and ungrieved.

Stella walked out with her letter in her hand, but she did not go home at once. She walked, in her tight stays, to an old and handsome part of the town. Here, each within its own property, shut off from the vulgar by an iron fence, lived the aristocracy of the city; their brick or stone houses lineal descendents of the log cabins of their grandfathers. At such a property Stella went in. Her head was high, her eyes dangerous. She jerked the bell viciously.

"I would like to see Mrs. Colfax."

The same coloured man who had driven the carriage had opened the door. He stood gazing at her; he knew her, and she knew that he knew her.

"Mrs. Colfax is not receiving, mam."

"She'll receive me or I'll know why. Tell her Mrs. Lambert Colfax is here."

He wavered, turned, leaving her to stand in the vestibule.

But Stella was aroused; she stepped inside and slammed the front door. When he came down again she was at the foot of the stairs.

"Mrs. Colfax can't see you, mam."

"Then I'll see her. Stand out of my way, you—nigger."

But old Ishmael had the bottom step of the stairs and he held his position.

"I'm going up, I tell you."

"Beg pardon, but you're not, mam. The ladies aren't receiving."

"They'll receive plenty from me when I see them," shouted Stella. But once more she knew she was beaten, and once more there was a certain dignity in her retreat. She went down the steps, along the gravelled drive and out of the gates, quietly and without looking back, although she knew that cold and hostile eyes were staring at her from the window behind her.

Stella kept her letter for a week. Then, Mr. Elliott becoming urgent, she decided to present it.

It was Missie who stood over her while she dressed for that visit, Missie who suggested the black dress, and who hid the rouge pot before Stella could get to it.

"You look fine, mom. Quiet and nice."

Stella eyed her, but she said nothing.

She secured the position. There were no mannequins then, slim bits of girls delicately made up, on whom even ordinary garments reflected a part of the glamour of youth. "Fine" women were in demand, full-figured, not too young. They both sold their wares and exhibited them.

"Let me slip this on and you can see."

And the heavy coats and capes went on, the bosoms well filled, the hips accentuated.

"I won't fill it out like that, I'm afraid."

"Downstairs at the corset counter they are selling——"
Stella's voice would fall to a whisper. What Nature had failed

to supply could be bought, stuffed with the best hair. Bustles, breast pads, hip pads. "Some people just sew stiff ruffles into their dresses, but they are apt to flatten. Personally I think . . .

Missie left school. She was not sorry to leave. Her clothes had been shabby for a long time; her spring-heeled shoes were worn. And with the frank cruelty of youth the other pupils had increasingly left her alone. She felt timid and shy with them, self-conscious. When on Decoration Day each child took a plant to decorate the soldiers' graves in the cemetery on the hill, her plant was always the smallest and cheapest. Yet the lines of veterans in procession never failed to bring tears to her eyes, while the other girls giggled and laughed.

"Look at that rag of a flag! Wouldn't you think they'd mend it?"

She did not know why she wept. The war to her meant only a series of dreary dates in a dreary history book, and Mrs. Kelch, who came in now to do the washing, insisted that with all the niggers it had turned loose, it was as much as an honest white could do to keep body and soul together. Yet the sound of the fifes and drums, the sight of the men who had fought for those tattered flags, affected her profoundly. The tears rolled down her cheeks. She knew nothing of America, its hopes and aspirations, its enormous potentialities; later on she was to learn, to suffer and almost die in the learning, and out of that, as out of all pain, something fine was to come. But not then. Not until years had gone by.

She was alone all day, after that. Sometimes she sat, after her work was done, and tried to puzzle things out. They seemed to have no meaning for her. Men were hard and cruel, and yet they fought wars and died for their country. Strange inconsistency! Children were born, in pain and sometimes they died. Then why have to suffer and bear a child? To what end? Women loved men, bore their children, did the best they knew how, and lost them anyhow. Why should that be? Or there were good men, like Mr. Wilkinson, and one day there was a crape on the door and they were gone, and their wives went on cheerfully beating carpets in the yard.

She would never marry. She would look after Stella the rest of her life, make up to her if she could. A wave of passionate love for her mother, of passionate resentment for what life had done to her, would fairly shake her.

Chapter V

MISSIE was sixteen when she fell in love, a slim wistful-eyed girl, with a sensitive mouth, a delicate colour that came and went, and hands reddened with housework. She had put away her dolls and the long button string which had represented almost every dress made in the neighbourhood in a dozen years, big buttons and little buttons, buttons of glass and of metal, of shell and of bone.

"I guess I can find you some. Mary, run and bring the button box. And there's that old blue basque of yours. I don't reckon you'll wear it again."

That was old Mrs. Seiden, across the street.

She read in her small leisure. She had discovered the public library, and the world outside the house and the street was developing in her consciousness. She began to see it, not as a series of orange and blue and pink areas in the school maps, but as a vast background against which human beings like herself were born, fought and endured, wept and were happy. She thought about them, dreamed about them. One evening she went out into the yard and looked up at the moon. Queer to think that that same moon shone down on so many different people, people like herself; speaking different languages, different even in colour, but like herself nevertheless.

"Come on in, Missie," Stella called fretfully. "What with Ellen shut up with that Wilkins fellow and you star-gazing, I never have a soul to talk to."

She sighed and went in, but there was no resentment in her face. And Stella would talk, on and on.

"And I said to her, I said: 'Well, if you're going to take

that attitude I have nothing to say. I've never done a thing to attract his attention, and if you say I have . . . .' "

"She's jealous of you," Missie would say sagely. "Of course you'd never look at him."

The "him" was the floor-walker on the third floor of Carter's store. His name was Taylor. Missie had no opinion of him whatever. He was a tall lean man with a gold tooth, hair parted in the middle and a long walrus moustache. He had a habit of standing stroking this moustache with one hand, the other thrust into the breast of his Prince Albert coat, which Missie considered affected; but it was the way he watched her mother that she resented.

"You wouldn't look at him, would you, mom?"

"Me? He's an old fool, that's what he is."

Nevertheless, there was a certain unction in these recitals of Stella's. And Missie recognized it. Perhaps it was good for her. She no longer on entering the house cast that quick stealthy glance toward the hat rack for letters. There were fewer and fewer occasions when Missie, wakening in the night, would hear the steady creak of her mother's rocking chair. For the time at least her passion for Lambert was in abeyance.

But she had aged. Missie could see that. Often at night when she came home Missie helped her out of her shoes and her torturing stays, and sometimes carried up a tray to her.

"You just sit still, mom. I'll be up in a jiffy."

She would hurry down, deftly poach an egg, clear the coffee with its shell, make toast, get marmalade. Ellen would watch her scornfully.

"Let her come down. I'm working all day, and nobody fusses over me."

"She's old. She's too old to have to be on her feet the way she is."

Small wonder that Missie felt that her falling in love with Harry Sloane savoured of disloyalty.

The two girls had never figured in the life of the neighbour-

hood, and even had things been other than they were, the
fact that both Stella and Ellen were working would have
militated against them. There was still a definite line drawn;
the supported woman looked down on the one unsupported,
and men were opposed to women in business for various
reasons, one being that "they could not smoke or take off their
coats if there were women around." So when a number of
the young people of better class in the ward rented a vacant
lot and built a tennis court, neither Missie nor Ellen was approached. Missie was philosophic about it.

"Where would we get the money?" she asked.

But Ellen was resentful. She was ambitious even then.
She was definitely engaged to Tommy Wilkins by that time,
and wore an infinitesimal diamond set high in a mass of gold.

"Some time I'm going to show this neighbourhood something," she said angrily. "You mark my words. Tommy isn't
much to look at, but he's got brains. He'll get on, and a lot
of these people will be crawling on their knees to get into my
house some day."

Thus Ellen: ambitious, prophetic Ellen.

The tennis court was behind the yard, that yard where
Missie and Mr. Wilkinson had strung the morning glories,
and where now Mrs. Wilkinson lustily and cheerfully beat
her carpets; and on summer evenings from the back window of the kitchen Missie could see them there, the girls in
their long white skirts, the boys self-conscious in their flan-
nels. Sport had only just come to America. Up to that time
horses for men, archery and croquet for women, had com-
prised the outdoor play of the wealthier classes. There was
often a line of jeering small boys outside, their noses pressed
against the wire.

From the window of the kitchen Missie watched the play-
ers as she worked. She felt no resentment. She watched them
as she would have watched creatures from another world,
the ball flying, the sharp impact as it hit the net, the girls
pretty and flushed, the boys moist, protective, teasing. When

dusk fell they would go away, and sometimes they would pass the front of the house on their way to the ice-cream parlour around the corner. She could stand, hidden by the dark vestibule, and watch them go by.

Long after Ellen was asleep Missie would lie in the dark and stare at the ceiling. There was no particular bitterness in her thoughts. Some day she would be pretty and well dressed, like these girls. There would be a miracle, and it would happen. And when at last she slept it was to dream that she was beautiful, that her straight hair curled, that the rather pathetic hollows above her collar bones were filled out, that her small breasts were full and rounded.

It was inevitable, then, that Missie's first love should be by way of the tennis court. It is only curious that it should have lasted as it did, that it should somehow have impressed itself on so much of her later life; it was as thin, as tenuous throughout, as the stuff her dreams were made of; it was built almost entirely in her own imagination, more a rallying point for her romantic dreams and an escape from her drab existence than anything else. Yet for years the name of Harry Sloane was to bring about a queer constriction about her heart, a trembling of the hands that she could not control.

She was in love with him before she even knew his name. He was a tall boy with dark hair that slightly curled, and he was a cheerful boy. He laughed a great deal, showing strong white teeth, and when he passed the house, swinging his racket, on the way to the ice-cream parlour, he was often smiling. He was a good-looking boy, but to Missie he was a young god. She knew nothing about him; all she knew was that her heart beat faster when she saw him. When she was able to look back on that affair without pain, she wondered how age could take so lightly those heart-burnings, despairs, and fleeting joys of adolescent love; it was so hopeless, so futile, so poignant. A day lifted above its fellows by a chance meeting, a word or two, to be cherished and dreamed over, a touch of the hand, a smile.

About this boy, then, Missie built her first dreams. It was no small part of that early tragedy of hers that she knew they would never come to fruition. She was a fatalist, although she had never heard the word, and she had no belief whatever in active happiness, nor any acquaintance with it. Even Ellen, hemming towels at night for her modest new home, seemed expectant rather than happy. Tommy had gone into the bicycle business; he was making money, had left the junk yard. He said the bicycle was going to sweep the country. Missie wondered, when she saw him go into the parlour, with his narrow sloping shoulders, his pale blue eyes and straw-coloured hair, his machinist's hands, if he and Ellen talked bicycles when they were alone.

So Missie watched this boy surreptitiously from the kitchen window, lay in wait and watched him again from the front door. When he glanced in her direction she would shrink back, her heart beating, her face flushed.

Then one day she learned that his name was Harry. Aye, and spoke to him face to face. She was in the yard, and he was looking for a lost ball. She heard somebody open the gate.

"Hello! Seen a tennis ball hiding anywhere around here?"

"No, I haven't," she said, breathlessly.

"Little devil! I told it if it ran off again what I'd do to it." She looked at him shyly.

"What would you do?"

"Stick a pin in it. That's all you *can* do. They're used to spanking."

Then somebody called: "Harry! Har*eee!*"

That was how she knew his name was Harry.

After that, if he saw her, he waved his racket to her, and she took to inventing small businesses in the yard, so she could look at him. She began to feel less lonely. Often she sat on the steps to see him go by after the evening games, and he would look for her and smile and take off his cap. Once or twice he came alone, and one wonderful evening he sat down on the doorstep and talked to her. But Stella heard the voices and came creaking down the stairs. She was in a loose wrapper.

"That you, Missie? Who's there?"

Missie's heart sank.

"I'll be in in a minute, mom."

But Stella was curious, curious and perhaps a little jealous. "I'm coming out. It's dark; nobody can see me, and it's hot inside."

She slumped down on the shallow doorstep, gathering her wrapper about her, and favoured Harry with a long look.

"And what's your name? Missie seems to think I'm a mind reader."

His name was Sloane, it turned out, and Stella warmed a bit. It developed that Stella knew his mother; had indeed sold her her winter coat. "She wanted something quieter, but I said to her, 'Now, Mrs. Sloane, you take my advice and take that one. Once a lady always a lady, and a bit of colour can't change that.'"

Harry was his mother's own son. He listened politely, and at the first lull in her loquaciousness he picked up his racket.

"Well, I guess I'll be going on."

"Give my regards to your mother," Stella called after him, airily.

He never failed to wave at Missie after that, but he did not stop at the steps again. Nor did Missie wait for him. She had her own intuitions, her own delicacies. But never once did she admit to herself that Stella had unwittingly destroyed something that had been very precious to her; never once, then or later, did she acknowledge that through all those early years her mother had borne down on her with a crushing weight, and that the weight was growing greater day by day.

For something queer was happening to Stella. Not Mr. Taylor. Mr. Taylor was only a mirror, before which she proved to herself that her attraction for men still existed. This was something else, something that would hardly bear thinking about.

There were things coming into the house which Stella's pay envelope could not account for. Not much; a bolt of ribbon, a pair of fine lisle stockings, gloves occasionally. And now that Ellen was filling a hope chest, a towel or two, or a pair of linen pillow cases. After the free and easy manner of those days, saleswomen could take preferred customers through the store, and Missie knew it.

The small tragedy of Harry Sloane was almost wiped out in her anxiety. She had almost decided to go to Ellen, when one night it flashed on her that Ellen knew, knew and was saying nothing.

Stella came down after supper and laid some yards of lace before Ellen.

"There," she said, "put that on your pillow slips. Let those Wilkinses see that you've got decent things, too."

"Thanks," said Ellen calmly.

But when Tommy rang the doorbell she hastily thrust the lace into a drawer of the old walnut sideboard. There was something furtive about it, something that made Missie want to jerk the drawer open again, confront them both, rend them in her anger, to say:

"It's stealing, mom, stealing and nothing else. And you, Ellen, you're as bad as she is. You know she hasn't any money. You——"

Stella had sat down heavily. There were bags under her eyes, she had let down the moist masses of her hair.

"My feet are killing me, Missie," she groaned. "Suppose you heat a kettle of water and let me soak them. I'm too tired to live."

She said nothing, got the water and the basin, knelt and rubbed Stella's swollen feet. Something in her, new and desperate, was longing for escape. "I want to get away. I'll never live at all if I stay here, just she and I. Ellen going and just she and I." And at the same time she felt a passionate tenderness for her mother. She would never go. She would see her through. Poor mom.

"Are they better now?"

"Yes. They don't ache so much. If you'll turn down my bed I'll crawl in."

"Maybe if I fan your hair . . ."

"All right. My head's hot."

No, she would never go.

Chapter VI

In the early fall of that year Stella came home one night with her face set and her manner tense. Ellen was not in yet, and Missie was in the kitchen. There was something ominous in the way Stella opened the kitchen door.

"Come on upstairs, Missie. I want to talk to you."

Missie sighed, put back her frying meat and obeyed. She found Stella pacing the floor in her stocking feet, her hat still grotesquely on her head and two bright spots of colour on her cheeks.

"Your father's back in town," she said, without preliminary. "I saw him on the street to-day. He didn't see me, but I saw him all right."

"Are you sure?"

"Sure? Don't you suppose I know the man I lived with for seventeen years? If old MacDonald lies until he's black in the face, I'll get the truth out of him. You get out my other dress. I'm going there now."

She began feverishly to throw off her clothing. She had never had any of the usual reserves before either of her daughters, but Missie slipped out before she had stripped. When she returned Stella was almost dressed again, and it was all Missie could do to force her to drink some coffee. All the time she was talking, excited and angry. And all the time Missie was conscious that the excitement was not entirely rage; that some vague, pitiful hope underlay it. Young as she was, she was old and wise where Stella was concerned. Stella still loved her father, madly, tragically, hopelessly. This middle-aged woman, with her coarsening figure and the puffs beneath her eyes, could still love, could still hope, could still dream.

Her heart was heavy when she let her out and watched her down the street.

But Stella's return was quieter, more cheerful. Lambert was in town, and Mr. MacDonald would arrange a meeting. Lambert had apparently settled down, done well in the West. Mr. MacDonald was sure some sort of arrangement could be made, financial of course. Not a great deal, perhaps, but something. It would probably be the day after to-morrow. What could she wear? Everything she had was in rags.

"Wear your rags and show him," advised Ellen, always practical.

Missie, however, saw that the excitement, if allayed, was still there. Stella talked quietly enough, but her hands shook and her eyes glittered.

"You wouldn't lend me your new coat, would you, Ellen?"

"It wouldn't go halfway round you."

"I needn't button it."

But the coat was the pride of Ellen's heart, and she refused to lend it. Stella was resentful, injured. She went upstairs, sent for hot water, carefully washed her heavy hair, and rubbed and greased her face. When Missie went to bed she was still puttering about her room, manicuring her nails, examining her small stock of clothing; and late in the night she heard her go heavily into the back room and open her trunk. In the morning there was a long and gaudy feather on her old marble-topped bureau.

Stella came home early that day, under pretext of a headache. She had a bundle under her arm, and she locked herself into her room. All afternoon, however, Missie heard the sewing machine rumbling overhead almost without cessation. She came down to supper, looking fagged but cheerful, and hurried up again to her mysterious sewing. Ellen came back once to protest against the noise.

"What on earth is she doing?"

"She's making something."

"Well, I didn't suppose she was playing the piano," said Ellen, irritably, and went back to the parlour.

Late that night Stella came rustling triumphantly down the stairs. From head to foot she was clad in shining elegant black silk, and on her head was a black bonnet, from which curled down over her ear a bright blue feather.

"How does it look, Missie?"

"You look wonderful. Do you mean to say——?"

"I've worked, I'll say that. Am I all right?"

"Fine. But I wouldn't wear that feather, mom. You look best in black. Plain black."

"And look as though I was in mourning for him?" Stella jeered. "If he thinks I'm as easy as that, he can think again."

Somehow, it was clear, in that day or two Stella had managed to build her house of dreams into a castle. It was to her no mere meeting to discuss financial arrangements by that time. With the age-old faith of all women who have once been loved, she believed that the sight of her, her mere physical presence, could make a dead thing live again.

Missie helped her to dress the next morning.

"I don't look so bad now, do I?"

"You look great, mom. Fine."

Curious that it was Stella now who was so credulous, Missie who was the sceptic.

"Don't you let him think all he's got to do is to raise his finger, and you'll sit up and beg, mom."

"What am I telling you? He's the one who'll have to crawl."

Missie watched her down the street. She herself had no faith whatever in a reconciliation; no hope. And she was justified, as events proved, for Stella crept back to the house an hour or two later a crushed and broken thing. Missie in the kitchen, hearing that slow closing of the front door, the furtive way in which she crept up the front stairs, started out impulsively, ran after her, only to have Stella's door slammed in her face and locked and then silence, complete and utter silence; no creak of the rocking chair, no anything. The hours going by; the delivery boy from the grocery store that Ellen had telephoned she would not be home to supper; fixing the old black japanned tray and carrying it up, only to be sent away; darkness falling and Mrs. Wilkinson's heavy steps beyond the partition wall; Mary Selden practising Paderewski's Minuet over and over down the street,—"Te tum tum, tiddle ee um tum, tiddle ee um tum, tiddle ee um tum."

At eight o'clock there came a ring at the doorbell, and a wild leap of Missie's heart. Perhaps it was her father. Perhaps he had been sorry, after all, and had come back to fix things. But when she opened the door it was Mr. Taylor, the floor-walker from the store, and another man who stood outside under the trees in the shadow.

"You can't see her. She's sick. She didn't eat any supper."

Mr. Taylor turned to the man at the curb.

"I'll go in, Jim. She'll see me."

"I don't think she will, Mr. Taylor."

"I'll have to try, Missie."

And there was something heavy and dejected in his voice. There was something unreal in it all, in Mr. Taylor, going up the stairs ponderously, frock coat rather shiny in the gas light, boots creaking; and coming down again, just as shiny but rather less ponderous, having met only with stubborn silence up above. Something portentous in the whispered consultation outside, in Mr. Taylor's mopping his forehead with his handkerchief, stepping in again, assuming a confidential air.

"You give her this message for me, and don't forget it, Missie. Tell her I'll fix everything all right. Tell her she's not to worry. And she'd better just stay quiet to-morrow morning. I'll come around at noon."

Suddenly Missie liked Mr. Taylor. There was worry in his light gray eyes, but there was kindness, too.

"And don't you worry either, Missie. You go to bed and get your sleep."

She felt when she closed the door behind him that she had shut out the only friendliness within reach.

She went to Stella's door again.

"He says you're not to worry, mom. Not to worry about anything."

And at last she heard Stella's voice, thick and muffled.

"Tell the old fool to go away," she said.

They were the last words she ever spoke.

For two hours or so Missie sat in the dark in her room, waiting for Ellen, for some movement from the front room. After a long time she lay down on the top of the bed dressed as she was, and fell asleep.

Just when Stella crept into the back room Missie never knew. She remembered Ellen coming in and waking her, and that she drowsily undressed and crawled into the bed. The next thing it was morning, and Ellen was shaking her by the arm.

"Where's mother?"

"In her room. She locked the door and wouldn't let me in."

"She's not there. She's not in the house."

But Stella was in the house. She was in the room at the turn of the stairs, with the battered gas bracket on the wall turned on full and the windows closed. She had been dead for hours. She had left no scrap of writing, nothing. Somehow, some time that night, she had given up the struggle. Before that, maybe. Perhaps on that dreary trip back to the house from the lawyer's office, where Lambert had sat with folded arms and impassive face, a stranger to her; where her stolen finery had failed of all effect. Limping home in her tight shoes, her bright feather blowing, her laced stays making her short of breath; fumbling for her keys and letting herself in, crawling upstairs and into her nightgown, and then the lonely haven of her bed. The crash had come, Missie felt, long before Mr. Taylor had creaked up the stairs and down again.

Perhaps her strongest feeling, outside of her shocked grief, was hatred for her father. She needed no Stella to confide in her: "And there he sat, frozen-faced, and what do you think he offered? To get a divorce and pay me alimony! To pay me for letting him go! I said 'You've got another woman you want to marry; that's you all over. Well, you get no divorce. You deserted me. And you've got nothing on me, either. I've been a true and faithful wife to you.'"

Yes, Missie knew.

She was cold and still under the ministrations of the neighbours, now suddenly kind. It seemed to her that no sooner had they found Stella than the house was filled with them. Mrs. Wilkinson moved in bodily and set to vigorous scouring, Mary Selden wandered back and forth. It was she who was constantly practising the Minuet, and now she was offering to play hymns for the funeral. Hymns for Stella's funeral. Stella was dead, and they were going to have a funeral.

"I'll run over and see if she's all right. I'm always afraid she'll try to go downstairs and fall."

"She" was Mary's mother, an aged paralytic. People said Mary would have married, but she couldn't leave her. And now she was living on and on, and Stella was dead.

Food came from unknown sources, was cooked and eaten. People wandered in and out. On the evening of that first day Mary Selden took the girls in to see Stella, and Missie saw that they had put on the black silk dress.

"Doesn't she look as though she's asleep?"

Ellen was crying decorously, but Missie stood white and still by the bed.

"What's it all about?" she said at last. "What's it all for, anyhow?"

Then she turned and went out.

Sometime in that black period before the funeral Harry Sloane came in. She found him standing in the hall, but there was no room in her mind for him. He was only one of the shadowy figures who came and went, people who had ignored

or disliked or sneered at Stella, and now that she was dead
could afford to praise her.

"Is there anything I can do?"

"I don't think so."

"I'm awfully sorry."

"Why? She's through with worrying, anyhow."

Probably that shocked him. Probably he thought she was
hard. Well, let him think so; what was he to her? "Don't you
ever get crazy about any of them, Missie. They're all alike."
And she was hard. Mary Selden thought she ought to cry.
Ellen was crying a lot. Missie had had to wash and iron some
handkerchiefs for her, while she sat in the parlour with her
head on Tommy's shoulder.

BOOK II

The Colfax Family

Chapter VII

LAMBERT did not appear for the funeral, but for once there was no difficulty about money. It came freely, as though released by the happy accident of Stella's death, with Mr. MacDonald as its bearer. And there was a smugness about the one-armed lawyer, a relief behind his decorous behaviour, that Missie resented furiously.

"Just keep him out of my sight. That's all I ask."

"Don't be a little fool. What on earth would we have done without him?" said Ellen impatiently.

He took charge, that is certain. He seemed experienced in such matters, and when at last that strange assortment of pall-bearers carried Stella to her grave he was among them. So too was Mr. Taylor, Mr. Elliott, who for once was not worrying about the rent, and Tommy's father called in at the last moment. And Stella would have been gratified, had she known, that the people who had ignored her during her life made what amends they could at the end, and attended the funeral.

It was as well for Lambert that he did not come back. All that last day Missie stood on guard beside the undertaker's man at the front door. There was in her a terrible smouldering anger. She would have struck him dead if she could. In vain Ellen begged her to retire to the correct seclusion of the second floor.

"You let me alone," she said. "He's not coming into the house, not unless he knocks me down."

But Lambert was in Chicago and intended to remain there. Years later she was to learn that he had left town before it happened, that while Stella was agonizing in that upper room he had been blithely facing West toward that new life which was not to include her; also—but it was many years before he told her this—that he had lost considerable money on the train that very night at poker. She felt her throat tighten when he made that airy confession.

"And you felt nothing? You had no regrets when you abandoned her?"

"You want me to say that I had, my dear, don't you? Well, I am no hypocrite. God forbid that I should speak ill of her now, but you have lived your life and made your own mistakes. No, I had no regrets. Of course, when I heard . . ."

She looked down at him, so tidy, so unregenerate in his soft bed, and she wondered. What had he done when he heard, what had he thought?

"Of course," he said, "it was a relief to learn why she did what she did. There was a man at the store who was pretty well cut up about it; I gather from MacDonald that this fellow had precipitated the whole thing; went to the house that night and scared her."

She watched him. "And you think that's why she did it?"

"What else? The fact that I wanted a separation was nothing new to her."

Well, maybe that was life, to evade facts that hurt, to build up a defensive mechanism against the truth. How real was any one? Strip off the armour of self-delusion, the shams and self-hypocrisies, and what was left? A cringing soul, unable to bear the truth about itself, desperately drawing about its nakedness imaginary virtues, and covering itself fiercely with denials.

But that was years later, when Missie had made her own mistakes and had ceased to judge any one.

They went back, the two girls, to that empty house, its dominating personality gone, a strange silence and order pervading it. It was odd how Stella's going had changed it, as though its heart had ceased to beat. Ellen moved about it, plan-

ning to escape; Missie did the work and then sat, her rough-
ened hands folded in her lap, stricken, dazed, defiant. She
did not dare to look back, and there was nowhere to look
ahead.

And then on the second day the doorbell rang, and Ellen
after a glance at Missie went to answer it herself. When she
came back to the dining room she closed the door behind her.

"It's your grandmother."

"What are you talking about?"

"It's your father's mother," Ellen explained briefly.
"You'd better brush your hair."

Missie had never known her father's mother was living.
It came to her as a blow. She stiffened, straightened.

"I'm not going to see her."

"Certainly you are going to see her. And behave yourself,
for heaven's sake. She hasn't done anything to you. And
she's a lady. There's a carriage at the door."

Suddenly Missie laughed hysterically.

"A carriage!" she said. "She comes in a carriage, after
letting Mom work and struggle the way she did! You go in
and tell her to take herself and her carriage away from here,
or I——"

"Hush, Missie! Hush, I tell you."

"When I think of her poor feet at night——"

"Now listen to me. If you shout like that I'll shake you.
Mom would want you to see her. She often said so. She
wanted you to be friends."

Missie began to cry. She stood dabbing at her eyes with a
soiled handkerchief, her face twisted with grief, and Ellen
stood by, tense and watchful.

"You're going in, and you're going to behave like a lady.
I've stood all the nonsense I'm going to. What are you going
to do, anyhow? If you act properly maybe she'll help you.
I can't ask Tom to support you, with your grandmother
driving around in a carriage while he walks!"

There was something harsh and strident in Ellen's voice.

For the first time Missie saw her as she was, a little hard, more than a little selfish. All that day, sewing quietly, she had not been grieving. She had been planning, thinking, contriving.

"Did you send for her?"

"I told MacDonald she ought to do something for you."

Missie looked at her, opened the door, went out. In the narrow hall she hesitated. Then she squared her shoulders and went into the parlour. Mrs. Colfax was sitting stiffly on one of the hard rosewood chairs. She made no move, and Missie surveyed her coldly.

"You are Marcella?"

Missie nodded. She could not speak. She felt *gauche* and untidy before this old aristocrat, so cold of voice, so erect of body, but there was bitter resentment in her. Her eyes were hostile.

"I am your father's mother. I am Mrs. Colfax. I daresay your sister told you."

"Yes. But I don't want any help from you. Don't think that. I can work. I want to work. I don't want—charity."

"Charity and duty are not the same."

"What duty do you owe me that you didn't owe to my mother?" Missie demanded uncompromisingly.

Mrs. Colfax winced.

"It has not been easy for me to come here. I must ask you not to make it any more difficult. I realize that you have had a shock, a great shock. Perhaps I should have waited a day or two. Please sit down. I find it hard to talk to you when you are standing."

Missie sat down. There was something compelling about the thin high voice, and something pathetic about the trembling of the high jet trimming in Mrs. Colfax's bonnet. Outside the carriage horses were moving restlessly on the cobblestones, and down the street Mary Selden was once again practising the Minuet. Never in all her life was Missie to hear that music without being transported back again to that small stiff parlour, with the plaster statue of Eve on the piano decorously draped by poor Stella with a "throw" of pale green satin, with the crocheted lambrequin on the mantel, the gilt mirror with its cracked plaster frame between the windows. And to Mrs. Colfax, her long hands carefully gloved, her high buttoned shoes carefully blackened and shining, and the jet aigrette in her bonnet trembling and quivering.

She was frightened, afraid of this tall old woman and all she stood for. Walls seemed to be closing in on her, new walls, without association, without love. She could almost hear Stella's voice.

"These grand people, their lives are just one don't after another. 'Always a lady.' Well, God knows I'm a lady, but I'm a woman, too."

She roused and flushed. She had crossed her knees, and Mrs. Colfax was gazing at them.

"I'm sorry," she said. And as if there was some reflection on Stella implied: "Mom—Mother never let me do it. She was very particular."

"I'm glad to hear that," said Mrs. Colfax, without great conviction. "First of all, I must explain that my son—that your father could not get back. Not in time."

"It's a good thing he didn't," said Missie darkly.

And then, as though she had been listening outside, as indeed she had been, Ellen came in. It was to Ellen that Mrs. Colfax made her proposal to take Missie home with her. In vain Missie wept, fought the very idea, appealed to Ellen. Ellen ignored her. It was to Mrs. Colfax that she spoke, in a voice fully as high as that lady's, and rather affected.

Certainly it was the best thing. It was wonderful of Mrs. Colfax to suggest it. Missie was young, too young to realize how wonderful it was. Of course she would miss her sister, but she must not stand in her way. She was going to be married herself very soon. She looked self-conscious at that. Naturally there would always be a home for Missie with her, but they were young too. Just starting. She did not like to ask Mr. Wilkins. . . .

"I can work," Missie almost shouted.

"Your dear father would never permit that."

"He's not my dear father."

Mrs. Colfax only looked pained, and turned again to Ellen, and at last Missie could only sit back and stare at her with angry disparaging eyes, at the black silk dolman trimmed with jet, at her tightly gloved hands, at the cameo pin at her collar and the gold chain to the watch tucked into her flat bosom, between the buttons of her dress.

"She would not be entirely alone. My daughter, her Aunt Adelaide, is still with me."

"I am sure she would be very happy."

Happy, shut up in a house with two old women! Stick out your little finger while you eat. Don't slouch in your chair. Turn your toes out when you walk. Don't swing your arms; keep your elbows in. Never blow your nose in public. Oh, my God!

Against her dogged obstinacy little was accomplished that first day. Ellen was sulky after Mrs. Colfax had gone.

"You're sixteen. It's time you showed some sense."

"I haven't asked you for anything, have I? You or your Tommy either."

The one thing about that visit that stood out to Missie, beyond its object, was that Mrs. Colfax had not touched anything. True, she had sat on the edge of a chair, but there had been no other contacts. She had not shaken hands; in going through the narrow doors she had seemed by some miracle of evasion not to touch the lintels. Her very entrance into her carriage had been a *tour de force* of detachment.

It was soon after that visit that old Archibald came again. He had attended the funeral, but for the past year the family had seen little of him. The pickings had been too lean, and he was no fool; he knew Stella disliked him.

He found the small household demoralized, Ellen nagging,

Missie wretched, and with his shrewd not unkindly old eyes on the two girls he listened to the proposition.

"So she wants you, eh?" he said to Missie. "Now why?" He reflected, running his fingers through his long patriarchal white beard. "It's sixteen years since we've exchanged any conversation, but she's my own sister, and unless she's altered considerably she has a reason for it."

He contemplated many things, sitting there stroking his knees with his blue-veined hands. He had no love for his sister, never had had. But he eyed Ellen and then Missie, still grieving, still red-eyed and not too tidy, and drew his own conclusions.

"Well," he said at last, "it's not a life sentence anyhow. Not necessarily. You could try it, and if it gets too strong for you you could run away, I reckon." He chuckled at some ancient memory. "It's in the blood, running away. We're not a patient family, Missie. We all run away. But we all get caught, too, and we come back. Yes, we all come back in the end."

Before he left he said something that touched the girl, and perhaps gave weight to the compromise he suggested.

"I just wanted to say that, if I can manage it, I'll look after —up there," he said. "I go up once a week myself anyhow, and it's sometimes a comfort to know they're being looked after."

She lay in her dark room after he had gone—Ellen had moved into Stella's—and debated the question with more calmness than before. She would have to do something. Tommy and Ellen were planning to marry soon. She did not resent that. She could see their viewpoint. That was always Missie's difficulty. When she was old enough to think about it she lamented it as a weakness, this ability to see both sides of the shield. She had an uncanny gift for putting herself into the other person's mind and seeing why he did this or felt that. It made it difficult for her to feel resentment, even to make any definite stand, except on a principle. And even there! She herself called it being muddle-headed; looking back, she had "muddled" through her life.

But it was evident that they intended to force her hand. But then, why not? They had a right to their life together without her. Also, both of them felt that to be recognized by her father's family was a step up in the world.

"You'll be riding in your carriage when the people on this street are hunting a nickel for the cable cars," was one of Ellen's arguments. The cable cars had come by that time; streets were torn up and in between the new heavy tracks ran the long slot that carried the cable. There was a "grip" under the car, and it caught hold of the moving cable and the car went along. It was amazing.

Or Tommy, heavily humorous, would stroke his small blond moustache and tease her.

"Will you speak to us when you're riding in state, and we're out on the tandem?" Yes, Tommy had a new tandem bicycle for Ellen and himself; it was one of the first in the city.

Missie would sit, eying first the one and then the other. She did not much care what she did, only she rather wanted to be alone. She was never alone, somehow. They were always dragging her into the parlour with them, so they could argue with her.

After all, she might try it. It was not a life sentence, as old Archibald had said. If she didn't like it she could run away.

She did not know that that very night old Archibald had a conversation with his sister. He sat alone in his small room, with the vital noisy life of the slums going on underneath his window and a bottle of whisky beside him—his pension had just come—and held high converse with her. She was not there, but that did not matter.

"I understand you want to take Bert's girl."

"That's my affair, Archibald."

"It's hers, too. Why are you doing it?"

"Because I've got what you never had, a sense of duty."

"Good God!" he bawled. "If that's all, let her alone. If you're taking her because Bert's acted like a dirty scoundrel and you want to make up to the girl for it, that's one thing. Duty's another. And there's something else, too."

"And what is that?"

"Don't you take her and freeze her. Do you hear that? That woman who killed herself, she had red blood in her veins. This girl has it, too, or I don't know women. And I've never been accused of that!"

"You may be insulting in my house, but need you be vulgar?"

That pleased him. He chuckled over it.

"A little vulgarity would have been valuable to you, Sarah, at a good many times in your life. But that's neither here nor there. Take this girl in if you will, but give her something more than duty. If you don't give her love she'll go outside for it. That's what Bert did."

And here the imaginary dialogue ceased, and he smote his knee with a mighty thump.

"Bert!" he said. "By God, that's it! She's holding onto Bert through the girl! Well, much good may it do her!"

He took another drink or two before he put on his long nightshirt and crawled into his bed. Indeed, he was quite pleasantly tight; he forgot to turn out the gas, and he lay back on his pillows and looked at the pictures on the walls. His wife, the boys; queer old daguerreotypes, his wife's breastpin touched with gold paint. But his eyes strayed from them to other photographs, not so staid, some rather disreputable; himself in the clothes he used to wear to the races at Saratoga, a picture or two of women in tights, a horse he had run years ago.

He smiled faintly and sank agreeably into sleep.

Chapter VIII

IT WAS a small thing which finally decided Missie. It was to be like that with her, always; it was as though there was a complete absence of design in her particular weaving, as though that fortuitous and casual concourse of atoms which was Missie Colfax was meant to be the sport of every circumstance, the victim of any chance wind that blew.

One night she went out for a walk to get away from Tommy and Ellen. The streets were dark, save for an occasional gas lamp, and under a tree she came across a boy and a girl. The girl was giggling self-consciously, the boy talking in a low tone. She had passed them by when the boy laughed, and she knew it was Harry Sloane.

He had not seen her. She wandered on, the dead leaves of autumn eddying about her, and her own heart and mouth as dry as they. The streets were empty and quiet, the tired horses of the day's traffic were in their stables, the wagons in the stable yards. Now and then an occasional carriage went by, its matched team trotting, its harness shining, its coachman erect on his box. Inside were women, women in enormous picture hats and evening gowns on their way to the theatre, their short full capes covering their décolleté; or on their way to dinners, or balls, their long trains carefully gathered into their laps, their heads garnished with wreaths or feathers, their satin slippers with their sharply pointed toes resting in carriage warmers or clad in fur-topped carriage boots.

The wind penetrated her coat, whipped her soft hair around her face. She walked along, stumbling over the uneven bricks of the pavements. After all, why not go to her grandmother?

Nobody else wanted her. They were all busy with their own affairs, Ellen and Tommy back there in the parlour, Harry Sloane——

She went back to the little house and opened the parlour door. They had not expected her, and Ellen was sitting on Tommy's knee. She slid off, flushed and irritable.

"I do think you might knock, Missie."

"Don't you suppose I knew you sat on his knee?" She looked at them. She felt a sharp repulsion just then, an actual physical loathing. She shivered. "I just came to tell you that I've made up my mind. I'll go. We can sell this stuff, Ellen. You won't want it, and I never want to see it again."

Then she went out and slammed the door.

They were greatly relieved. They had not meant to be cruel, and with her problem off their minds they began after that to make much of her.

"Just think how grand you will be. You'll get fatter, too. She'll be really pretty when she's fatter, Tommy, won't she?"

"Nothing to frown at now," Tommy would say gallantly.

They were married three weeks later, a church wedding but a quiet one; a few neighbours, two or three of Ellen's office associates, Tommy's family and some of his friends. Ellen sent a note to Mrs. Colfax, telling her that Missie would be ready the day after the ceremony, and inviting her and "Miss Adelaide" to the church. In reply Adelaide Colfax wrote that the carriage would call for Missie at four o'clock of the day designated, and did not refer to the marriage at all.

"Why should you care?" asked Tommy. "They're not your people."

"Well, they are in a way," said Ellen. Already she was building on that Colfax connection.

Daylight weddings in Protestant families had as yet no vogue. So it was that Missie, in a white organdy dress which was supposed to resemble *mousseline de soie,* found herself one evening walking down a church aisle, with a scattering of people on either side. She felt awkward and self-conscious, but for once she knew that she was pretty. That helped her. And duly Tom and Ellen were married. Missie had never heard the marriage service; it startled her with its finality. "Whom God hath joined together let no man put asunder."

That was what people promised at the altar. They made a solemn covenant with God, and then they did all sorts of dreadful things and God punished them. Only He mostly punished the innocent.

She scarcely noticed Tom's best man when they walked side by side down the aisle. He was the youth who drove the laundry wagon.

Mrs. Wilkinson spent that night with her. She was a heavy Rabelaisian type of woman, and she hinted not too delicately at Ellen's change of status, but Missie turned on her eyes at once so frank and so puzzled that she desisted.

"Upon my soul," she considered. "I wonder what the child thinks marriage is?"

Stella's confidences, her dark hints, had not served to destroy Missie's innocence. They had made her wretched, but she had never understood them. When in later years she did understand, it was to find that she distrusted herself, was ashamed of her honest emotions, her even honester passions. There were inhibitions in her that could not be broken down.

The next day the second-hand man came with his wagon and backed it to the curb. When he had gone Missie swept out the empty rooms and burned the trash in the yard; that yard where she and Mr. Wilkinson had strung their morning glories. Harry Sloane was playing tennis across the alley, and she knew that he was watching her. But she paid no attention. She was dirty and untidy, but she did not care. Let him flirt with girls on the dark streets. She would live her life and he could live his.

She went into the house, washed and dressed, closed and locked her trunk, the trunk which had been Stella's, and sent it off. And at half-past five came old Ishmael and the carriage, and Missie got in. There were a few good-byes, old Ishmael waved his whip, the horses moved off.

She cried quietly all the way to her new home.

Afterwards she could smile at that home-coming of hers, but not for years. The carriage turning in at the drive, the elderly woman in black and white who opened the door, her grandmother and her Aunt Adelaide sitting silent in the enormous front parlour, with its gigantic plush chairs and sofas, its marble-topped tables, its dreadful felt lambrequin on the mantel, painted with peacock feathers, and over that, looped up in the centre and at both corners with large bows, a "drape" of blue surah silk. On top of that a gargantuan clock of black marble, black marble urns flanking it.

Missie walking in, her feet sinking in the deep pile of red velvet carpet, her knees shaking, her hands trembling; and a squat ugly woman with prominent moles on her face rising awkwardly.

"Here she is, mother. I am your Aunt Adelaide."

Adelaide had been making spills. Her lap had been full of long strips of newspaper, a corner of which she moistened between thumb and forefinger, and delicately rolled. As she got up the strips fell to the floor. She seemed uncertain whether to pick them up or to shake hands. There was a queer indecision about her.

"Pick them up," said Mrs. Colfax. "Come here, Marcella."

She held out a thin hand and Missie took it. Adelaide was on her knees on the floor. Mrs. Colfax searched the girl's face for something she failed to find, sighed, withdrew her hand and wiped it with her handkerchief.

"Adelaide will show you your room. You will want a bath, too. Adelaide——"

Missie flushed.

"I've had a bath."

"Still, you will want to be fresh when you change for dinner."

"I've had a bath, and I can't change for dinner, or for anything else. I have only this one black dress."

There was a silence. Mrs. Colfax drew a long breath. A maid came in. She had a long gas lighter with a wax taper in it, and a slot; with the slot she turned the keys of the high chandelier, with the taper she lit the gas and then turned it down. The effect was funereal, appalling.

"Katie, tell Norah to draw a bath for Miss Marcella."

Then abruptly, with unexpected vigour, Mrs. Colfax left the room. Missie, being led upstairs by Adelaide, saw her at the washstand under the stairs, washing her hands.

She was frightened and dispirited. The two women, one old, one elderly, the sepulchral lights, the silence, the smell of old dust from heavy carpets long unlifted; even a musty odour from Adelaide's dress, as though it had been worn too long; the frightful overwhelming atmosphere of gentility were almost too much for her. And when she was alone in her high-ceilinged room, with its vast bed and its hideous walnut wardrobe, she could hear the bath water running, and suspected that Adelaide was lurking outside, to be sure that none of the dust from Stella's house be allowed to linger in this sacrosanct stronghold of Colfax pride.

She took her bath, the first time in her life she had entirely immersed her thin young body. The tin tub shone brightly, the water was hot, the towels large and heavy. She relaxed somewhat. After all, they were doing their best by her. She must not mind. And maybe some young life would help them. They must be lonely, there alone with their pride. There would be things she could do for them, like the things she had done for Stella.

Her eyes filled, her chin quivered.

She dressed quickly, for the autumn night was cold. When she went downstairs again Adelaide was there alone. There was a coal fire going, and a scuttle beside it. Each piece of coal in it was wrapped in paper. Missie was absorbed by it, fascinated. Adelaide had changed her dress, but it looked exactly like the one she had taken off, and a bit of gray alpaca petticoat was showing. She was very ugly. No one had prepared Missie for Adelaide Colfax, but then no one had prepared her for anything. Adelaide was a squat, heavy woman of fifty or so, with coarse heavy features and small furtive dark eyes. Here and there on her face and neck were large fleshy moles, and at first it was difficult not to look at them. Except to her mother, who was slightly deaf, she spoke in a low voice; there was indeed always something rather stealthy about Adelaide, the secretiveness of a highly nervous woman who was never able to call her soul her own.

And now Adelaide was even more nervous than usual. Missie was to grow accustomed to her incoördination, her jerking head, the hands that dropped almost everything they held, but then it shocked her. She was twitching now violently.

"Before your grandmother comes down," she began and stopped. "Before mother comes down, Missie, I want to ask you something. Please don't speak of your mother before her."

Missie stiffened.

"Why not? I am not ashamed of her."

"It is an old trouble," said Adelaide, jerking more than ever. "And she is an old woman. You owe her that. Your father is different. She will like to hear about him."

"Not what I have to say!" said Missie, and was instantly sorry. But to her surprise she saw a quick gleam in Adelaide's eyes, as if the speech had pleased her.

Dinner. Dinner in the evening, with old Ishmael and Katie both serving, old Ishmael faintly redolent of the big brick stable at the back of the lot. A long table, covered with satin damask, steel knives with ivory handles yellowed by age, a silver caster in the centre, a heavy silver coffee service at Adelaide's elbow, Mrs. Colfax bowing her head and saying: "For what we are about to receive, oh Lord, make us duly thankful." Mrs. Colfax indomitably carving, thin paper-like slices, Ishmael carrying the plates around, Katie following with the vegetables; Missie hungry and afraid to eat, watching the old woman, holding out her little finger. Adelaide asking:

"Will you have coffee, Missie?"

And Mrs. Colfax saying: "She's too young for coffee. Get her some milk, Katie."

After that an endless evening, Mrs. Colfax washing her hands under the stairs, knitting by the fire, Adelaide rolling spills, Missie sitting with her hands in her lap, waiting for she knew not what. Now and then a word.

"Mrs. Boroday must make her some proper clothes."

"I'll write to her, mother."

Again:

"You do not look like your father."

"Mother always thought I did."

"Well, you do not," said Mrs. Colfax, sharply.

Missie caught a warning glance from Adelaide.

In the long periods of silence, when the only sound would be the click of knitting needles, the rustle of Adelaide's papers as she rolled them, the hiss of escaping gas from a lump of coal in the fireplace, Missie's thoughts ranged far afield. She thought of Ellen on her wedding trip; of that mysterious relationship of hers and Tommy's. She was vaguely afraid for Ellen. Men were hard and cruel, and not to be understood. Suppose she had a baby, and then Tommy went off and left her? That was what Mrs. Kelch's husband had done.

"He just waited to hear it was a girl, and then he got his hat. And not sight nor sound of him for twenty years!"

But even that might be better than this, this sitting here in a dead house. When at nine o'clock she heard Ishmael putting the chain on the front door she felt that she was locked in for life; that she wanted to scream, to rush out and beat on the door with her hands. True, it had often been quiet at home. She still thought of the little house as home. But that had been only through the day. At nightfall it had wakened to noisy life. First there had been her father to come home, and later on Ellen and her mother; then the gas had flared, the mica windows in the stove had sent out a red glow, voices had lifted, Missie shrilly calling from the foot of the stairs:

"Supper, everybody! Mom, have you got the water pitcher up there? Bring it down with you."

Why had they brought her here? They did not want her.

Within a day or two she had an inkling of the truth. Mrs. Colfax said to her:

"I have had a letter from your father, Marcella."

Missie's face hardened.

"He is greatly relieved to know that you are here, with me."

"I don't see why he should be. He never worried about me before."

"That is no way to speak of your father."

"It's the truth, Mrs. Colfax."

Adelaide looked frightened, but Katie came in then—they were at luncheon—and nothing more was said.

It was that night after she was in bed that Adelaide slipped into her room, her finger on her lips.

"I'm glad you said that to-day about your father. She thinks the sun rises and sets on him. And the way he's treated her!"

"He killed my mother. If he hadn't left her she'd still be here."

Adelaide looked at her, and Missie sensed without knowing it the sex curiosity of a middle-aged single woman hateful and perhaps pathetic, but mainly hateful.

"You mean, she cared for him as much as that?"

Missie resented the look, the furtive question in Adelaide's eyes. She clenched her hands.

"She hated him," she said valiantly. "The very thought of him made her sick. But she had to work too hard. She——" She heard her voice begin to shake. "She just got tired."

Never! Never so long as she lived would she tell of Stella's tragedy. It was safe with her, and it was safe with

Ellen, too, for lying there in her big soft bed after Adelaide had crept out again, she knew that Ellen had never understood it. Ellen thought Stella had killed herself because of the trouble at the store. Only she, Missie, knew the truth.

But one result there was of that visit of Adelaide's. She knew now why she was there. Even there her ability to see both sides prevented any resentment on her part. She was there, not because she needed love and a home, but because through her this hard old woman could keep some contact with her son. Then, if that was it, she was not so hard after all. One could feel sorry for her. For there was no way of holding her father. She knew that better than anyone else ever could.

Chapter IX

Until she was a widow Sarah Colfax had never had the uncontrolled spending of a dollar. When William Colfax decided that he needed a house commensurate with his means, he bought his property, built his house and furnished it. Then one day he notified Sarah that it was ready to move into, and she moved in.

It was an ugly house, an expensive ugly house. Its library and hall were covered with brown wall paper in imitation of panelling and then varnished over, its mantels of black marble. And in the library was one set of bookshelves which were not shelves and books at all, but were painted on canvas glued to the glass doors, and behind those doors was William's private stock of liquors.

But it was a big house, with high ceilings, a centre hall, and behind the parlours a conservatory, now long emptied and abandoned, with an empty pool in the centre and a lady who, when one turned a valve, poured water out of the urn on her shoulder.

In its day, William's conservatory was famous, not because of its flowers, which were negligible, but because it was undoubtedly a conservatory.

He put in a bathroom, too, one which was heated from a storage boiler above the kitchen range, so that on baking days there was plenty of hot water, and on washing days none at all. Then he erected a high iron fence as a symbol of seclusion, and an iron deer for elegance; built a stable to house his wife's carriage—not that he cared whether she walked or rode, but a carriage was a symbol also—and the old side-bar buggy in which he went at seven o'clock, rain or shine, to his business, and for the Jersey cow which pastured in the back lot. And he installed his hideous furniture and some books in dull bindings; eleven volumes of the works of Thomas Dick, *The Christian Philosopher*, a great many sermons, Renan's *Life of Jesus*, a huge copy of *Josephus*, a set of the *American Senator*, being immortal truths uttered by divers legislators in long-forgotten debates, and for a touch of lightness and cheer, Carlyle's *French Revolution*.

Last of all he put in his family.

He was a hard man. His children hated him, his wife feared him. He did the family buying himself, stopping at the market stalls and haggling over pennies. But the baskets old Ishmael took back—young Ishmael then—were full and overflowing, for William Colfax was fond of his stomach.

At noon he came home to a midday dinner, and after it he stretched out on the hard leather sofa in his library and slept for an hour, with a handkerchief over his face to keep out the light. Like his son Lambert and the sheet later on.

But one day when Sarah went in the handkerchief was not moving with his breath. He left no great grief, a considerable property for those days, a widow who was too old to learn either how to handle or to spend money, and a family of children, now fairly grown, who had never known liberty and found it sweet to their taste.

He had been dead for fifteen years when Missie entered that house of his, with Stella's theatrical trunk to follow. That queer dead-alive house, where no servant ever raised a voice, where the very brooms were muffled in cloth, and where old Ishmael, when he was not driving, lived mostly in the front hall. When Mrs. Colfax was about—he did not mind Adelaide—he stood just inside the front door. When she was resting old Ishmael rested also. He sat on a hall chair, red plush with ball fringe, and sometimes he dozed. His head would drop forward; then the bell would ring or there would be some movement upstairs, and he would be on his feet again, the wide flat feet which turned out like a parrot's when he walked.

Old Ishmael was coachman-butler. There was always a faint smell of the stable about him.

William's furniture was still there, heavy, ugly, rather shabby; and William's carpets covered the floors. Old Ishmael was a dark island in a sea of carpets; the parlours, the library, the dining room, the hall stairs, were covered with carpets. Later on, on sweeping days, Missie was to see in the sunlight the masses of flocculent dust which rose from them. The servants swept, and then let it settle. When it had settled they brushed it off the furniture with dusters, into the carpets again.

And as her house, so was Sarah. It was a queer repressed life on which the girl had embarked; it hinted of old tragedies, it was filled with still living resentments. The house was always quiet, except when Adelaide dropped something. Missie saw, however, that she usually did this when she held something in her hands and her mother spoke to her. And Mrs. Colfax had learned this, so she generally waited until Adelaide had put down her tea cup, or whatever it happened to be.

Sometimes Missie watched them together, puzzled. Incredible that they were mother and daughter, that this old woman had brought Adelaide forth in agony; incredible too that this bringing forth had been the result of some mysterious relationship between this austere old woman and the elderly man whose portrait hung in the dining room. Impossible to believe that she had ever been young, that she had loved as Stella had loved, suffered as a result of that love.

She had nothing to do but to watch them. She learned that Mrs. Colfax was eternally washing her hands, that the mere necessity for touching a door knob sent her to soap and water. Also that she still regarded Adelaide as a child. She had even less liberty than Missie. And—perhaps as a result of that— she learned something curious about Adelaide, also.

Adelaide was afraid to cross streets. She would stand at the curb, hesitate, take a step out and retreat like a scared rabbit.

"It's all right now, come on."

"Just a minute, Missie! There's something coming!"

Sometimes, on bad days, she would not cross at all. They would walk around and around the block instead.

Even the sidewalks terrified her. Bicycles were ridden on the pavements, the streets being rough, and Adelaide would shrink back against the wall.

"They go so fast!" she would pant.

But it was the streets that really frightened her, the streets that later on Missie was to realize meant life to her, life and adventure. Adelaide, standing jerking on a corner, advancing and then retreating, was Adelaide confronting life and then withdrawing from it. She was too old. It only frightened her now. She could only stand at the curb and look on.

When Missie understood that she pitied her.

For two weeks then she strove to adapt herself. The small services she offered were refused. "Don't spoil the servants, Marcella." In the mornings she turned down her bed to air, opened the windows, and faced a day without interest and without hope.

Not entirely without hope, however. She began to count the days until Ellen's return. Never very close, Missie found herself now clinging to Ellen, waiting for her hard practicality, even wondering if Ellen might not take her away with her. And then one day Ellen came, and that hope died a painful death.

She ran down the stairs. Here was somebody dear and familiar, somebody who shared her memories, was a part of her past.

"Ellen!"

Then she stopped. Ellen was standing in the centre of the front parlour, carefully inspecting the mantel lambrequin.

"Well, of all the terrible things!"

She submitted to Missie's kiss, but with reservations; as

though she said: "Don't try any airs with me," and as though by depreciating the lambrequin she were depreciating the house, the people, all of Missie's new background. Missie chilled, but she smiled valiantly.

"How fine you look, Ellen."

Ellen cast a warning glance toward old Ishmael, more or less suspicious in the hall.

"I bought a few things at Saratoga," she said carefully.

They sat down, Ellen spreading her new finery with an air, and Ellen in calling costume that day was something to wonder at and to admire. High on her head was a large feathered hat, a wide blue figured silk dress with a train spread its six yards of hem on the floor, and over this, the climax of her magnificence, was a short velvet cape. Added to this was the dignity of the young matron and a resentment of the size of the room, of the size of the house, of Ishmael in his striped vest standing on his flat feet in the hall. Ellen was remote, formidable, affected.

"Well, my dear, I hope they are making you comfortable."

"I'm all right," said Missie dully. "How's Tommy?"

"Quite well. He's making money; lots of money," said Ellen distinctly. "We are thinking of building a house."

Suddenly Missie got up and closed the door on Ishmael.

"What's the matter with you, Ellen? You'd think we were strangers."

"That darky was listening," said Ellen calmly.

Things were better after that. Missie admired her clothes, her new chatelaine bag which, hooked into her belt, carried her purse, a small silver elephant for luck, a combination folding toothpick and glove buttoner, a powder box, one to hold car-fare with separate places for nickels and dimes. And as Missie enchanted inspected it, some of Ellen's affectations dropped away. She was happy. Tommy was very good to her, and generous. He was a "good provider." Missie listened. Her mind was back again, busy with the little house, with Stella, with Harry Sloane; but Stella was dead and

Harry had never cared for her. And now Ellen was gone too, busy with her new life, self-absorbed.

There was a short silence. Ellen twiddled the trinkets on her chatelaine. "I asked that darky for *her*, too. And he told her. I heard him rap on her door."

"She rests in the afternoons, Ellen."

"Do you mean she won't see me?"

"I can go up and ask her."

She rose, but Ellen caught her by the arm.

"Don't you move," she said. "She needn't put on any airs with me. I gave you up to her against my own natural feelings, and now if she thinks she's too good to treat me civilly in her own house, I'm too good to stay here. She's got a daughter, hasn't she? Why doesn't she come down?"

"She hardly ever sees any one, unless Mrs. Colfax does."

Ellen threw back her head and laughed unpleasantly.

"Oh, she doesn't, doesn't she? You're a nice little liar, Missie! And you're a Colfax, too. On their side already."

"Honestly, I mean it, Ellen. She——"

"Tell that to the Marines," said Ellen furiously. "And you can tell the Colfaxes something for me, too. Tell them I'll never darken their doors again."

Missie watched wretchedly from the window as Ellen sailed down the drive. Opposite the deer she stopped and stared at it. Then she went on and out through the gate.

Missie thought of that visit when Ellen bought the Colfax place years later. Yes, she bought it. She tore it inside out, put a marble floor in the hall, and a staircase with a wrought-iron rail, had a decorator from New York and a landscape man for the grounds, and gave there her dinners, balls and garden parties. But there was a vein of ironic humour in the Ellen of those riper days. She left the iron deer where it was.

"My *dear*, how can you bear it?"

"I have a sentiment about it," she would say cheerfully. "It has been in the family for a long time, and I used to play with the queer old thing."

Chapter X

NEITHER her grandmother nor Adelaide ever mentioned Ellen's visit to her. She knew then that the slight was intentional, that by accepting Missie they had accepted nobody else.

She lived that queer drab life of theirs without protest, a life of the manner rather than the substance of things. The Colfaxes were not rich. The early Eastern oil fields on which old William had based his fortune were playing out, the railroads had cut in on his big river packet line. Even the food, served with state, was none too plentiful. The good old days of William's overflowing baskets were long past. Missie with her healthy young appetite often left the table hungry. She saw that Adelaide never sent back her plate, and so she did not dare to.

But she learned before long that Adelaide had a private vice of her own. At night, lying in her bed, she would hear her door open stealthily, listen to the creak of the stairs as she went down, and follow her mentally to the pantry. Adelaide ate in secret.

In the morning there was a rising gong, followed in due time by prayers in the library; the servants standing. There would be a rustle, she and Adelaide and old Sarah knelt in front of their chairs, the servants—who had no chairs—as best they could, and Sarah would read: "Since it is of Thy mercy that another day is added unto our lives——"

Another day. Who wanted another day?

There would be the odour of bacon and tea, the rather musty smell of the upholstered chair seat, the even mustier odour of the old black garments of the elderly women and somewhere above, beyond the ceiling and even the roof, a God of whom Missie had only the remotest knowledge; a God who knew everything, especially everything wrong, and who would assuredly punish unto the third and fourth generation.

After prayers Mrs. Colfax would go into the hall and wash her hands, as though even the touch of the prayer book had contaminated them.

Missie tried to please them, but there was often in her eyes the look found in the eyes of lost dogs and orphan children. She was still grieving for Stella, but it had become a dull ache for something loved and long since lost. On Sundays she went to church with them. She learned to kneel and get up at the proper places, and that ladies did not cough during the sermon, or sneeze. There were a great many other things that ladies did, or did not do. They spoke softly: "a low, sweet voice was a wonderful thing in a woman"; they did not swing their arms when walking, and they did turn out their toes; they did not blow their noses audibly, but wiped them—in private if possible; especially they were not supposed to know about babies. Even Adelaide. Adelaide too was sent out of the room when Katie came in to announce that her sister had had one.

Once in a blue moon there would be a letter from Lambert. Her grandmother would open it with shaking hands, adjust her glasses, read it carefully.

"Your father sends his love, Marcella."

Adelaide would watch, furtively, resentfully.

"She's sending him money," she said to Missie one day.

"My father?"

"Yes. She's made herself poor for him. She's always doing it. I can go ragged for all she cares."

There was a bond between Adelaide and herself, the bond of hatred for Lambert.

She did what she was told, made herself out of cambric the heavy closed drawers, the long-sleeved high-necked nightdresses which Adelaide cut out for her. She would sit by a window sewing—the house was hermetically sealed against fresh air—and lift dispirited eyes now and then to the street. Sometimes she would think she saw Harry Sloane going by, and she would colour, go back to her needle.

Ellen of course never came, but Missie guessed that Tommy was prospering. The safety bicycle was sweeping the country, as Tommy had predicted. Inns were being built outside of town, the Wheeler's Retreat, the Century Run, the Wheelman's Haven. The drop frame for women had come in; large portly women in full heavy skirts with baskets on their handlebars cycled to market, to the stores. Society had taken to it, gave bicycling picnics, made excursions. One or two brave women had had bicycling skirts made, an inch, two inches off the ground!

One day an intrepid creature in such a skirt rode in to call on Sarah, leaning her bicycle against the sacred iron deer. Sarah saw her from a window, and declined to receive her.

"There must be some one to uphold the decencies," she said.

So Missie reached and passed her seventeenth birthday. She was rather lovely. Her long soft hair was drawn loosely back to a knot at the nape of her neck, and her eyes were candid and luminous, her mouth wistful in repose. She had a wealth of love in her; sometimes it rose like a wave, and she felt she must liberate it. She would embarrass Adelaide by putting a young arm about her heavy waist, contemplate some advance to her grandmother and then lose her courage. Also she was becoming a woman.

One day the seamstress, Mrs. Boroday, fitting a basque on her, said with foreign frankness: "You're getting a bust. I don't know as I need to sew ruffles in this."

Missie inspected herself carefully in the mirror. With her disfiguring high collar gone, her white neck, her smooth young arms, she was gently alluring. But she shook her head.

"I'll never be pretty, Mrs. Boroday. My sister is the beauty."

"Some day some man will find you very beautiful," said Mrs. Boroday.

Only she said "zome."

Mrs. Boroday was a Russian, a worried looking woman with spectacles. Her husband had been exiled to Siberia as a nihilist, and had escaped. Now and then Missie saw him waiting at the gate for his wife; an enormous man with a black beard. He had a terrible fascination for her, this man who wanted to see the Czar of Russia dead, and who had plotted to that end. He would stand there, whittling at a stick as he waited. Then one day he sent her a spool box, made of cigar boxes neatly glued together to make drawers, all of it highly varnished. She was obliged to reassort her ideas of him after that.

It was through Mrs. Boroday that Missie learned that there was a secret in the house. She was pulling out basting threads one day, and the Russian woman was shirring ruffles. She pinned the long strips of material to her knee and ran her needle through with extraordinary rapidity.

"You'll be like your father, I'm thinking," she said. "I never saw the other one."

"What other one?"

Mrs. Boroday looked up sharply.

"You don't know, then. I thought Adelaide would have told you. She likes to talk. But if she hasn't it's none of my business. They're a close-mouthed lot about their own affairs, the Colfaxes."

But she said no more. She went back to the Romanoffs. "They'll be punished some day," she said somberly. "The Russian people are not all soft-headed fools." And she launched on a tale of a ball at the palace where fifty great palm trees, or perhaps it was a hundred, were brought from the Crimea to garnish the fête.

However, Missie was no soft-headed fool either. She was young and observant. It was not lost on her after that that once a week or so on their walks Adelaide would seek a mail box well out of sight of the house, and then lifting her dress skirt would extract from a pocket in her gray alpaca petticoat a letter. This, after looking up and down the street, she would deposit in the box. The whole process was one of secrecy and mystery; indeed on the letter days there was always about Adelaide an air of furtiveness in advance, an increased jerkiness. Spoken to suddenly she would drop whatever she held.

Then one day Adelaide had a cold, and her mother forbade her going out. Missie found her in her room, sneezing and weeping.

"It wouldn't hurt me. I could put on my rubbers."

"Why don't you go anyhow?" said Missie practically. "You're a grown woman, Aunt Adelaide. If you want to go——"

But the thought terrified Adelaide. She picked up a book, let it drop nervously to the floor.

"I only wanted to go to the mail box."

"Let me do it."

"She wouldn't like it."

"I can go out the kitchen way."

"You won't tell her?"

"Never."

Whereupon Adelaide dropped on her knees beside her bed and began fumbling with the carpet underneath. When she rose she had a letter in her hand. "Here it is. Put it inside your dress, Missie. You might meet her."

When she went out she heard another crash behind her; Adelaide had dropped her sewing box.

The next day Missie asked Mrs. Boroday a question.

"Who is Mrs. Cecily Stanwood?"

"And where did you hear that name?"

"I can't tell you that."

"Well, I can't answer you either. Only—I wouldn't ask your grandmother."

Missie dropped the subject. It had ceased to be important, for life, surging happy romantic young life, had begun for her. On that stolen errand the day before she had met Harry Sloane, met and talked with him. And there had been a new look in Harry's eyes as he gazed down at her.

"I hardly knew you; you've done something to yourself."

"I've put my hair up," she told him gravely.

"But you're prettier. You're awfully pretty. I mean it. Can I come to see you?"

"They wouldn't like it."

"Who are 'they'?"

She told him, and he seemed impressed. He knew of the Colfaxes, of course. Everybody knew of the Colfaxes. But look here, it wasn't possible that they would shut her up like that. Anyhow, she could get out. They could take some walks together. Now he'd found her he wasn't going to let her go.

And all the time her poor silly heart beating like mad, her colour like a rose, her eyes shining, her resentment gone. Gone too Stella's warnings, her precept and example.

"I'm coming around and ring the doorbell some night anyhow. They can't do more than throw me out!"

"Oh, please! Please don't, Harry."

"Some of these days you'll hear a scuffle and a thud. I'll be the thud!"

When she left him she had forgotten to mail her letter. She had to go back again.

Unimportant, after that catastrophic meeting, the letters to Cecily Stanwood. Missie no longer cared to go to sleep at night. She preferred to lie there in the darkness and dream dreams. She was in love; the sun rose, the birds sang, the dull daily life went on to that refrain. Each walk now was an adventure; every head that rose above its fellows might be his. Forgotten was the girl that night under the trees. There was only Harry, looking down at her with soft, faintly girlish hazel eyes, and saying more with them than his words implied. Saying she was pretty, fidgeting a bit with his hands, watching her.

Every night, her hair smoothed, she listened for the doorbell. She would watch the clock, seven thirty, a quarter to eight, eight, a quarter past. Adelaide rolling paper spills, her grandmother knitting, erect in her chair, a deadly hush over everything; and herself a tense young figure, her muscles quivering as the hands of the clock moved on, and at a quarter after eight drawing a long breath, shivering a little as if with cold, and hope gone again.

He never came.

Chapter XI

HER first Christmas with Sarah and Adelaide was uneventful. Sitting in her room Missie remembered other Christmases, Stella's Christmases. Nothing done until a day or two before; then a wild scramble. Stella coming in puffing, her arms full of bundles.

"If I catch you girls peeping under my bed there'll be trouble. Mind that."

A mysterious odour of evergreen when one opened the cellar door.

"Mom, can I go down and get some jelly?"

"You stay right here. I'll get it myself."

On the night before Christmas Stella's sewing machine would start. It was like her to dress the dolls at the last minute. It would start and stop quickly, as if it had sewed a very short seam, and the little girls would listen and know just what she was doing. Sometimes they could hear their father waken and grumble, and hear her replying sharply. And at dawn in their thin nightgowns the two shivering little figures would steal down the stairs to the cold parlour. There would be the tree, strung with popcorn and threaded cranberries and paper cornucopias filled with hard candy, and underneath would be the dolls, dressed and ticketed in Stella's writing: "To Ellen, from Santa Claus." "To Missie, from Santa Claus."

She made a pincushion for her grandmother, and since Adelaide was always losing her keys, a key rack for her. This last was very handsome. It consisted of a rolling pin, gilded and with small brass hooks screwed into it. When she had tied pink bows to each handle and a pink ribbon by which to hang it to the wall, it brought forth exclamations of delight from Norah, the housemaid.

"Well, now," she said, "if that isn't fine. It shines something wonderful, doesn't it? And it's useful, too."

Although her gifts were received with appreciation, there was little or no Christmas spirit in the house that day. Mrs. Colfax gave her a copy of Schiller's poems, and Adelaide gave her Pope; the total result of which was a dislike of poetry which lasted almost all her life.

The truth, as she was to know later, was that the two women were worried and anxious about money. The panic of 1893 was approaching, with its bread lines and its unemployed, cold and hungry, seeking shelter in the station houses, where they lay on the floor, covered with newspapers for warmth.

They had welcomed the excuse of Stella's death as offering them a year or so of seclusion. Queer that Stella, dying, had served them when Stella living had been an intolerable tragedy to them. They still had a few callers, elderly women in handsome calling costume, for calling was still a function. One dressed for it. They came in, portly figures or lean ones hidden under a vast redundancy of clothing. Wherever a silhouette threatened to emerge, save at the waist, it was hidden under shirrings, ruchings, ostrich bands, lace flounces. They sat for the conventional fifteen minutes, rose with all their encumbrances of clothes, trains, and card cases, and moved out with the overwhelming deliberation of battleships.

Yes, Stella's death had served Sarah well.

There was no entertaining. Now and then Mr. MacDonald came to dinner, bringing with him—he was always a few steps in advance of her—a thin colourless wife. She was extraordinarily thin, and was therefore supposed to be delicate. She apparently enjoyed her condition, carried small knitted shawls about with her, had Missie tuck pillows at her back.

"I am not strong, you know," she would say plaintively.

By her fragility she kept her husband under control. It was like a weapon in her hands against him. Years later Missie was to hear that she drank vinegar in secret, to reduce herself to the last stages of attenuation.

After dinner Mrs. Colfax and the lawyer would shut themselves in the library, and long and hard were the battles fought there.

"Just how much have you sent Bert this year?"

"Very little. But I cannot live here in comfort and let him suffer."

"You'll not be living here very long unless you let him stand on his own feet."

One night he tried to explain to her. The country was in bad shape; commercial and bank failures were increasing fast; railroads were crashing; gold was scarce; there was widespread fear as to the government's ability to redeem treasury notes in gold. But how was William's widow to comprehend such matters?

"What does Adelaide do with her bit of money?" he demanded finally.

"She puts it in the savings bank."

"Then tell her to hold onto it," he said shortly. "She may need it if things keep up."

But Adelaide, as Missie could have told them, was not holding onto it.

The winter was interminably long. At dusk, quiet enough before, the big house died before her eyes. Downstairs tiny blue gas points dimly lighted the parlours and the library; shades were drawn, the world was shut out. After a time she ceased listening for the doorbell at eight o'clock. She would sit quietly with her hands folded in her lap, and try to ignore the palpitating life outside; try not to think, or to remember.

One thing she had gained, however. Now and then she was allowed to visit Ellen, a not too conciliatory Ellen, but a happily married one. Already she was going to have a child.

"Tommy wants one," she said resignedly. "I think it's too soon myself. Under a year it's hardly decent."

Missie flushed, and Ellen laughed.

"You'll be having one of your own some day. Then you'll know what I mean."

She always hoped that Ellen would mention Harry Sloane, but she never did. And she herself could not speak of him. There would be a curious tightening of her throat when she tried, an almost physical constriction about her heart.

"Have you seen any of the old friends?"

"Old friends indeed! I never knew we had any."

And that was all.

One day when the spring had opened she was allowed to go to the cemetery alone. Old Ishmael drove her up, and sat dozing in the sunshine while she worked over Stella's grave. There was a small white head-stone. It said: "Stella Colfax. 1850-1892."

It surprised and touched her. They had not told her.

When she had finished she sat on a nearby bench and looked at it. Forty-two years! Would she live as long as that? How could she bear it if she did? At least Stella had lived, had savoured to the full this strange adventure called life; had laughed and cried, loved and suffered, passionately, with unction. For her, Missie, there would be only the husks of life; going on, drying up, perhaps like Adelaide finding her solace in little stolen meals, finally dying like that.

She clenched her hands.

She was still sitting there when she saw old Archibald Kennedy coming toward her, picking his way slowly among the graves. She had not seen him for months, and in the spring sunlight she was shocked to see how old and how shabby he looked.

"That you, Missie?" he said, peering at her. "I broke my spectacles awhile back, and for a minute I thought it was your grandmother. You sit like her." He lowered himself onto the bench beside her, and she saw the handle of a trowel protruding from his pocket. He wiped his forehead. "Thought I'd a little work on them to-day. They kinda sag through the winter. But *she's* stayed pretty good, hasn't she? I suppose they graded when they set up the stone."

"I'm glad they've marked the grave."

"Well, whether they like it or not, she was a Colfax at the end. And the Colfaxes mark their graves. "I'll bet—" he stopped and chuckled—"I'll bet she'll put a stone over me! And I haven't spoken to her for a long time. Not since you were born."

"Am I what you quarrelled about?" she asked, astonished.

"Well, it wasn't only that, of course, but it didn't help any. You see she'd doted on Bert. Adelaide—well, you know Adelaide; and as to Cecily——" He stopped, glanced sideways at her. "You mustn't sit like that, Missie. It's like her. Don't you get like her, Missie. Better get away, if that's happening to you."

"I couldn't hurt them, like that."

"Well, perhaps. And maybe you're safer where you are. It's a hard world for the poor, although the poor live, Missie. Don't you forget that. The poor *live*."

There was a silence before she spoke again.

"Mr. Kennedy, what about Cecily? They never speak of her."

He cleared his throat, hesitated, took off his wide hat and sat turning it in his hands. "I don't know that I ought to tell you. Still, you're almost a woman now. There's nothing wrong about Cecily; she's a good woman. Life played her a dirty trick; that's all. She ran away with a man, and he got killed before they were married. When her mother learned she was going to have a baby she turned her out."

"And the baby? Did it live?"

"Oh, it lived all right. Love children mostly do. They've got vitality. That's the great thing, Missie. Your mother had a lot of it. Yes, she lived. She's a grown woman by now."

He rambled on. Old William had been a hard father. He deserved what he got. Sarah now, Sarah would have been different, married to another man. But every man left his mark on his woman. Old William's mark was on Sarah. Old William was hard; used to lock Bert in at night, but Bert got out a window and down a tree.

"That's what started Bert off," he said. "He was all right when he was little. Too much scolding and praying and not enough living and loving in that house."

Before he went away he stood before her, hat and stick in one hand, his imperishable dignity not impaired by the trowel in the other.

"You're a pretty girl," he said. "Not as handsome as your mother, but still—— Don't you worry about things. Some man is going to want to marry you before long. Haven't you found anybody yet that you like?"

She hesitated, with that queer contraction at her heart. "No," she said slowly. "No. I never see anybody."

He turned away, turned back again.

"Tell me, does your grandmother still wash her hands every few minutes?"

"Yes, she does."

"Curious," he said. "Strange thing, that. She's done it ever since she put Cecily out of the house."

She smiled and waved at him as he went hobbling off, shabby, majestic old scapegrace that he was. When she drove away she could see him once more stooping over his graves.

Chapter XII

THINGS were not going any too well in the household. During the next year the household was cut down, and there were long and anxious conferences about taxes. Now and then came letters from Lambert, and there was more pinching, more anxiety. One day Mrs. Colfax demanded to see Adelaide's savings bank book, and Adelaide fled the house in terror and hid in the stable. Mrs. Colfax searched her bedroom systematically, washing her hands at frequent intervals. There was a deadly purpose about her, and a deadly certainty when she found that slit in the carpet and a letter ready for Cecily under it. Without scruple she tore it open and read it. Then she went into her room and closed the door.

At twilight Adelaide, terrified of rats, came back to the kitchen.

"I'm afraid to go up, Missie. Did she find it?"

"She found a letter, yes. But why worry, Aunt Adelaide? You've done the right thing. She's wrong. She's always been wrong about Aunt Cecily."

"What do you know about your Aunt Cecily?"

"All I need to know. And I'm proud of her. She went ahead and had her baby, and——"

"Hush! You don't know what you're saying," said Adelaide heavily, and went slowly up the back stairs.

There was, all that evening, a sense of impending drama in the house. Mrs. Colfax had her dinner on a tray and kept her door closed. Adelaide ate very little, although late that night Missie heard her as usual in the pantry. And then, as usual in life, too, nothing happened; nothing, that is, except that Adelaide sent no more money to Cecily.

The anæmia of the life was making its impression on Missie. She was growing silent, repressed. There was about her a sort of terrible patience. The three women were like spectators at a play. Along the street in increasing numbers went bicycles—Tommy was indeed prospering. Men drove tally-ho coaches and tandems, one horse hitched before another. There was even talk of a horseless carriage, a deadly and *bourgeois* contrivance which would never be practical. In New York an ingenious gentleman had made a list called the Four Hundred; Bohemia was a place—or a state of mind —where men drank beer and smoked cigars in the presence of ladies; depressed females confessed to having the blues, progressive euchre was the solace of the leisurely; political campaigns were marked by processions of gentlemen in tall white hats and cape overcoats, carrying torches smelling unpleasantly of paraffin; and a crazy man named Langley in the National Capital was claiming that some day men would fly in the air.

But none of this touched them.

One day the grocer told Missie that there was a new way to seal jelly glasses with wax, but Adelaide snorted and sealed the jelly as she always had, with a small circular piece of paper dipped in old brandy before she tied on the paper cover.

Adelaide had changed very little. "I've taken off my woollens, Missie. Don't say anything, will you? They're in your closet. She was a little grayer, a trifle more bristly about the chin, a bit more uncertain with her hands, but that was all. And Harry Sloane had dropped out of Missie's life as though he had never been. Sometimes she thought she saw him on the street, and she would hurry on, breathless, to make sure. But it was never he.

Ellen had had her child, a spoiled little girl, very blonde; and Tommy had bought a house. The bicycle had indeed swept the country, and Tommy now had a new vision.

"You wait!" he said to Missie. "These horseless carriages

mean something. Some day they're going to be practical, and then watch me! You won't see me for dust."

Ellen laughed indulgently. She was not in love with Tommy; Missie was sure she never had been. But he had gratified her still modest ambitions. She had her own house, carpeted with imitation Oriental rugs, panelled with imitation mahogany. Her parlour set was of blue brocade with a self-rocker, and she had bought an upright piano on the instalment plan.

"But you can't play it," said Missie.

"It furnishes," said Ellen complacently. "And when Clare is old enough she will have music lessons."

Queerly enough, at that Missie was back in the little house again, and somebody was playing Paderewski's Minuet: "Te tum tum, tumpety tum tum." She turned a trifle sick.

She faced her situation clearly. Neither Sarah nor Adelaide cared for her, or ever would. Such love as Sarah had in her withered breast was for her father, and Adelaide was secretly jealous of her; of her youth, of her slenderness, of her young eyes and her steady hands. Jealous of her when she served the arbitrary old woman in the cap who had never asked her to call her grandmother, jealous because she was Bert's daughter and sometimes looked like him.

But they needed her. She would always stay with them, never marry.

"Are you ready to lie down now, Mrs. Colfax?"

"What time is it?"

For Sarah lay down and rose by the clock.

One day Adelaide and her mother had words. Not much, for Adelaide was easily silenced. And that night Sarah unexpectedly announced that she intended Missie to make her *début* that winter. It was during dinner, and the MacDonalds were there. Missie went pale, Adelaide's heavy face flushed a dark crimson with anger, and Cornelia MacDonald drew her shawl around her shoulders and twittered like a gaunt old bird.

"How delightful! And so you will be a bud, Missie! And all the young gentlemen will be trying to pluck you from the Colfax stem."

Her husband scowled, but he looked at old Sarah, proud and indomitable in her chair, with that bit of duchess lace which was her cap rather like a crown, and he said nothing. He had never been able to control Sarah Colfax.

Cornelia MacDonald rattled on, in her thin high well-bred voice. She hoped Missie would keep out of the fast crowd. Yes, indeed, there was a fast crowd now; bicycles had done it. What could one expect with young girls wheeling in short skirts, three inches from the ground, and without chaperons? This thing of exhibiting the feminine limb——

Sarah scowled and Cornelia settled her plumpers,—the two cup-like arrangements of woven wire bound with velvet which were intended to give the impression that her Maker, in denying her other charms, had been lavish as to bosom— and smiled complacently.

Missie was miserable, and after the MacDonalds had gone she summoned all her courage:

"About coming out, Mrs. Colfax. I'd rather—I'd really rather not."

"Why not?" Sarah demanded tartly.

"I don't know anybody, and I can't dance. Oh, please, I'd rather not."

She was panic-stricken, her hands trembling, her body taut.

"You will have some dancing lessons. Don't be silly, Marcella. I have already written to your father."

She came out early in December. Sarah seldom went abroad now, but she took Missie to Carter's to select the material for her dress. It was of white silk with flounces of tulle covering the skirt, and the close-fitting bodice was cut to a modest point front and back. The cutting was a delicate operation. Mrs. Colfax did not trust Mrs. Boroday, with her foreign notions.

"Just a little lower, Mrs. Colfax. It is awkward, so."

"It is plenty low enough."

And so Missie's neck was allowed to show, but her lovely young bosom was neatly covered with white silk.

Missie was terrified. The extent of the preparations, the solemnity of the discussions, were portentous; the very gravity of the men who came to measure for the crash to cover the carpets, the enormous dignity of the caterer: "Yes, madam. I understand, madam"; the amazing necessity that the windows be washed on the very day of the party, although nobody could possibly see whether they were washed or not; the even more amazing sight of Aunt Adelaide being fitted with a lavender satin gown, long of train and short of sleeves.

Also there was much wrangling over the list. Sarah pruned it ruthlessly.

"Cut out the Weatherbees, Adelaide."

"But they go everywhere now, mother."

"Not everywhere, for they are certainly not coming here."

At the last moment the list was subjected to still further scrutiny, and Missie's first view of Wesley Dexter was as he sat in the library looking over it. He was in the thirties, a heavy man of middle height, rather inclined to stoutness, but with a handsome head. He had been suspect in his early years, but now people said he had "settled down." He was a fastidious man; later on Missie was to know and hate his fastidiousness, his emphasis on unimportant detail, was to recognize it as a part of an enormous egotism. His belongings, his surroundings, were the setting in which he saw himself.

But it was to this instinct for detail that he owed his social popularity. He had no background, no family, but he led cotillions, consulted with hostesses over favours, long and grave discussions which almost made of the favour table an altar and himself a high priest, and was an authority on lists.

"I know they're new people, Wes. But they seem popular, and they have plenty of money, apparently."

"Mrs. Hemingway hasn't asked them. Or Mrs. Colfax. You can afford to wait and see."

So now he sat in the Colfax library, secretly elated to be there, to be sitting across from Sarah, to be autocratically blue pencilling the lists of autocracy itself. Only once did he so much as indicate that he knew Missie was in the room.

"We need more dancing men, Mrs. Colfax. Perhaps Miss Marcella has some suggestions?"

Missie's heart began to beat tumultuously. Why not? Surely to suggest one person—it was her party after all. If only she could speak clearly.

"I know one young man."

Both heads turned to her. They said nothing, but waited in alert silence.

"I used to know him. I'd like to ask him. His name is Sloane."

"Sloane?" Mr. Dexter considered. "I don't remember any Sloanes."

"I don't think they go out very much."

"The only Sloanes I can think of in town are the florists," said Mr. Dexter, and smiled with amusement. "Well, I'll add a few names, Mrs. Colfax; all good families and dancing men."

Missie hated him; for that smile, for his complacency, for his black satin tie with the cameo pin, for his long well-cared for hands, like Lambert's.

When he had finished Sarah ordered in port wine and small cakes for him. Adelaide followed the tray, as though in her upper room some sixth sense had warned her of food below, but Sarah ignored her presence; offered her nothing.

Chapter XIII

ON THE day of the party she roamed about the house, panic-stricken and yet enthralled. The glass in the conservatory had been washed, and from huge closed vans the florist's men carried in great palms, tall rubber trees, oleanders, ferns. The pool was filled with water and around the margin were set pots of blooming plants. All over the lower floor and up the stairs men were nailing down spotless white crash, stretching it tight; and the family used the kitchen staircase so that nothing should dim its perfection that night. Missie dressed early, standing on a sheet in the centre of her room and later spreading it over a chair before she sat down. And then the bedrooms were put into immaculate order, so that Ishmael at the top of the stairs could direct the guests.

"Ladies this way, madam."

"Gentlemen in here, please."

The music came and took up its position in the back hall. From her chair with its sheet Missie heard it tuning up. All at once she felt unhappy and self-conscious; she did not want to go down the stairs. Who were these people? What did she care for them, or they for her? They were only coming to meet each other, to eat the Colfax food and drink the Colfax champagne, now resting in barrels of ice on the rear verandah. She could hear Adelaide moving clumsily about across the hall. She had pinned up her train and was smoothing the coverlet of her bed. From the huge front room came her grandmother's voice, high and querulous.

"Are you ready, Marcella?"

"Yes, Mrs. Colfax."

"Then see if the caterer's men are stationed in the hall. It's almost time."

She went down the stairs, shining white figure, long white kid gloves, white satin slippers, tiny lace fan with ivory ribs. The crash was smooth under her feet; the rooms strange and bare, shining white floors gleaming under the old glass chandeliers, mantels banked with flowers and vines; a subdued rattle of china and glass from the pantry, low voices, a caterer's man in a dress suit at the front door, another at the foot of the stairs. And in the door of the conservatory, his back to her, a young man in street clothes, hastily directing a rearrangement of the flowers around the pool.

He heard her and turned. It was Harry.

"Hello!" he said. "I hoped I'd see you before I had to get out. I say, Missie, you're beautiful to-night."

She could not speak. She could only look at him with those wide candid eyes which had so often shed tears for him. And he mistook her silence, stiffened, his smile fading.

"I've changed the pool," he said, his tone businesslike. "How do you like it?"

"It's lovely. I don't know . . ."

"I've gone in with my father," he explained. "I don't expect to stay, but while I'm there . . . It's interesting work," he said, with a faint touch of defiance. "To take an interior as ugly as this, and make it over, that's worth while."

"I'm sure it is. I never see you any more, Harry."

He smiled his old smile.

"That's not my fault, Missie."

"But it seems queer." She was fumbling for words, inarticulate, miserable. She felt she could not let him go like that; but that he would go; that there was no way to hold him. "I often wonder why I don't see you. All this time . . ."

He waited for her to finish, looking down at her with bright boyish eyes.

"I don't know many people," she finished lamely.

"You'll know everybody after to-night. Everybody who is anybody. You see, I'm not, Missie."

"I don't think that matters."

The man in the conservatory had gone. Suddenly Missie was trembling; there were tears in her eyes. "I've been so lonely," she said.

Pity or love, she never knew. He looked around quickly, bent over and kissed her. The next moment the door bell rang, and he was gone.

She stood beside her grandmother in the empty front parlour, her eyes like stars. Carriages drove up, handsome horses, two men on the box. The occupants stepped out onto the red velvet laid down the front steps, came in, went up, came down. They passed before her, shaking hands with her, with Stella's daughter. And she smiled and greeted them, with Harry's kiss still warm on her face. The noise was deafening. People shouted over the band and when it stopped were shocked to find themselves shouting. After the first half hour Mrs. Colfax had a chair brought, and thus enthroned greeted her guests.

"And this is Marcella."

They eyed her, these people, but they were not unkindly. After all, only half of her came from the gutter. The rest was Colfax.

After the reception came dancing. The young women carried their dance cards on their wrists. At the proper time young men claimed them, put white gloved hands lightly on their back, held them at a proper distance, and rotated slowly to the Blue Danube Waltz, being careful not to lift their feet as they circled.

And Missie danced, sweetly and decorously. Once she danced with Wesley Dexter, but he smelled strongly of champagne, and held her rather too close. When she looked at him, however, his eyes were not on her.

He hardly spoke a word to her that night. Looking back on that, as she did on so many things, she was to wonder just when he became really aware of her as an individual, as Missie Colfax.

At midnight Sarah gathered up her black train and went in state up the stairs to her bed. But the party was not over; a line of portly mothers and chaperons still sat against the walls, somnolently digesting Sarah's excellent supper, their elaborately coiffured heads occasionally nodding. They would have to sit there, they knew, until the small hours. They moved restlessly in their tight bodices, yawned decorously. Outside coachmen dozed on their boxes and grooms beat their arms to keep warm. And in the conservatory and on the mantels Harry's flowers began to droop.

It was four in the morning when the last carriage drove away.

Adelaide, her slippers in her hand, found Missie above near the door of the conservatory, her face rapt, her eyes shining.

"Did you like it?" she asked, her heavy face twitching with fatigue.

Missie had an impulse of overwhelming happiness and love. She put her arms around Adelaide's thick waist and kissed her.

"I'm so frightfully happy," she said. "It scares me."

And Adelaide, filled with her own small satisfactions that night, and knowing that an extra tray of the supper was waiting in her room, did not repulse her.

"You looked very pretty," she said. She glanced past Missie into the conservatory. "Sloane's did very well, I think. Don't you? The son has better taste than the father."

Old Sarah lay in her bed the next day, contentedly resting. The party had taxed both her strength and her financial resources, but she had her compensation; under her pillow lay a letter from Lambert.

MY DEAR MOTHER:

I am deeply grateful for what you are doing for Missie. Naturally I deplore the fact that I cannot do it for her myself, but I realize that you can give her what I never could, poise and training and other advantages. I can only hope that she will pattern herself on you.

Years later Adelaide showed her that letter. It could still anger her.

"Soft soap," she said. "He was taking her money and spending it on gambling and women, but he could always flatter her into believing that he was her angel child."

Missie went out a great deal that winter. Her invitations were stuck into the edge of her mirror, sat on the mantel piece. Adelaide chaperoned her, eating enormously, bouillon, creamed oysters, chicken pâtés, salads, ices. Sometimes she smuggled away little iced cakes, to eat in her room later. She grew stouter, her bosom was like a shelf. She had a new air of dignity, a vicarious maternity. Missie would lay her favours in her capacious lap, and Adelaide would watch and count them. When a nearby lap contained more than hers she would grow watchful and anxious. And this happened rather often.

For Missie was never a belle. She had a sufficient number of partners, but no clamouring circle of moustached young males ever formed about her. Once in a while she sat out a dance or two, and to cover the awkwardness she and Adelaide engaged in springly conversation; on such occasions, however, poor Adelaide would jerk more than ever, and one after another the favours would fall to the floor.

Sarah would be awake when they got home. Missie would take in her trinkets, her photograph frames, hand mirrors, fans, sachet bags, and Sarah would sit up in bed and handle them with her delicate old hands. The next day she would write to Lambert:

"Marcella is having a wonderful season. Her room is filled with cotillion favours, some of them idiotic, but all showing that the child is popular. I think she will make a good marriage. I hope so for your sake, and as things are with me now, I hope it will be soon. I am grieved to know that your new company has got into difficulties, and I enclose——"

On the evenings when she was at home Missie listened for the door bell. Surely now he would come. He had kissed her and she had let him do it. Men and girls only kissed when they cared for each other. He knew now that she cared; she had as much as told him so. When she had been out she would say to Ishmael the next morning:

"Did any one call last night?"

"No, Miss."

Perhaps he was waiting for a word from her. She lay in bed at night, and thought of that. There was a telephone in the house by that time; one had only to turn the handle and call a number, and there he would be. But although she knew the number by heart she never called it. Mrs. MacDonald was full of stories of forward girls who called up young men, and were laughed at for their trouble. Surely the first move should come from him. She had let him kiss her. She——

One night, going to a dance, she saw him. She hardly knew him at first; he was in uniform, standing near the old Armoury evidently waiting for a street car. She felt again that sickening breathlessness, that frantic yearning which the mere sight of him always aroused. But what could she do? Adelaide was beside her, breathing hard in her tight clothes, her shelf of a bosom rising and falling, the white feathers in her hair trembling as she twitched. Missie bent forward, waved a hand. But he did not see her.

She stopped asking Ishmael, but she took to lying awake too many nights. She grew thin, her colour began to fade, She would come home from her parties, hang up her dress, put away her slippers, listlessly hang her favours around her dresser or set them on the mantel, put on her long-sleeved high-necked nightgown, brush her hair and then crawl into her bed to lie awake long after Adelaide had sunk into stertorous sleep across the hall.

She had no one to talk to. Elien had been furious over the slight when she came out, and had definitely broken off their relations.

"You live your life, and I'll live mine," she said, standing over Missie with her baby in her arms. "If that stodgy old crowd thinks it's the only society in this town, I'm out to show them something different. There are people here who could buy them all out, lock, stock, and barrel, and never miss the money."

"It wasn't meant that way, Ellen."

"Then what way was it meant?"

"They have their own friends. Some of them are quite poor."

"Did you ask her to ask us?"

Missie hesitated. "I did mention it, but I couldn't say a great deal. I wasn't consulted, really. And they've been so kind . . ."

Ellen stared at her.

"You're like your father," she said cruelly. "You even look like him. But you can't soft soap me, any more than he ever did. He never fooled me for a minute, running around with other women while Mom was sitting at home! You've got bad blood in you, Missie Colfax. You'd better look out."

So she was cut off from Ellen. Now and then she saw her name in the paper. "Mrs. Thomas Wilkins entertained the Neighbourhood Euchre Club at her residence on Glen Avenue yesterday afternoon. Handsome prizes were awarded, and refreshments were served later. Among those present were . . ." It widened the gulf between them that Missie recognized none of the names.

And, although she occasionally went back to Grove Street, for she had more liberty now, she found that the street was constrained with her. It was of no use to try to bridge that gulf, either; the glamour of her life, the account of her *début,* all had passed into history. She was a romantic aloof figure, and she saw that when she tried to be friendly, they thought she was merely patronizing. Amazing that they could think that, incredible that they could not see below the surface to her real heart-hunger. She would leave the carriage and walk, and Mrs. Wilkinson would note it at once.

"You're not riding to-day."

"I like to walk. It's exercise."

She gathered that Mrs. Wilkinson might resent her having a carriage to ride in, but that she enjoyed the prestige of having it standing before her door.

But it was when she tried to talk of Stella that she met real obstruction.

"You'd better forget all that. You're young. What's gone is gone, I say."

"Do you remember when we moved in, how happy we all were? I often think about that first day. The men carrying in the furniture, and Mom—Mother—so excited."

"Yeah," said Mrs. Wilkinson, non-committally. "And now tell me about yourself. I suppose you'll be marrying a rich man now, Missie, and getting yourself a family."

"I don't want to marry, really."

"Tut tut. Look at Mary Selden over there. Nothing but an old mother and a piano. And I don't know which I'd rather see carried out first!"

She would go home again, with a sense of a door, an old familiar door, closed in her face.

BOOK III
Wesley

Chapter XIV

ONE night in Lent—it was typical of him to wait until Lent to do his courting—Wesley Dexter came to call. There had been other visitors, of course; young men mostly to pay their duty calls. On Sundays they wore top hats and frock coats, and sometimes a gardenia. They were making the rounds, Mrs. Colfax, Mrs. Hemingway, Mrs. Rodgers, Mrs. Thaddeus Jerome, *not* to be confused with Mrs. Robert Jerome, who was nobody. They never smoked on these occasions; there were smoking rooms in all important houses, and the delicate nostrils of gentlewomen were not profaned. They eyed Missie, who was pretty enough if not beautiful, but the shadows of Sarah and Adelaide were over them, and Missie puzzled them.

She had no coquetries, no lures, no wiles, even no small talk. They fidgeted with their hands and feet before these three women, before Sarah's cold austerity, Adelaide's jerky movements; had she been alone with them Missie might have made friends, even found a lover. But she was never alone with them, and none of them came back to pay the evening call on Missie herself which was the indication of personal interest.

She was rather flattered then when Wesley came. He was in the library, in dinner clothes, and his manner conveyed that an evening call from Wesley Dexter was no small matter, that it had importance, social value. He bowed deeply over her hand, kissed it lightly. He had learned that this was being done in Washington and New York, and he was starting a vogue for it. By and large, before the prosaic new century killed it, Wesley and his cohorts had thus saluted a number of bony blue-blooded hands, and not a few young ones.

He talked easily, mostly about himself; but his eyes roamed over the room. By his own efforts he had put himself into the position he held. He had worked and plotted since those long-ago years when he had sold newspapers. He was thirty-five now; nobody knew he had ever sold newspapers. He was prosperous in a small way, with more to come. But he needed background, solidity. What did it matter if it was a trifle musty, more than a little stodgy?

He had no illusions about himself. Already he was thirty-five, and taking on some of that flesh which was to become unwieldy corpulence in his fifties. The lengthy unbroken round dances of the period found him short of breath, perspiring. He carried two extra collars with him to balls, and sometimes, leading some agile figure of the cotillion, he was aware of his bulk, of his lack of grace, for which he substituted an impeccable dignity.

So he sat, in old William's sagging chair in the library, and eyed the room rather than Missie herself.

"All things considered, you have had a very good season, Miss Colfax."

And he pronounced these words like a god passing judgment.

"I haven't thought so, myself. You see, I am shy. In my childhood I met very few people."

"A *succès d'estime,* perhaps," he said. "But a very real one, my child. We—" he cleared his throat—"we accept people slowly, but once they are in, they are there for life. And of course, being a Colfax——"

He looked around the room, across the hall to where Adelaide's lambrequin showed in a pin-point of light from the heavy chandelier. Ugly, terrible, but dignified. Background. "Mrs. Dexter? Oh yes; she was a Colfax." And he looked at Missie. She had an air of good-breeding; her hands were fine. And she was gentle, amiable. There would be no money probably, but he could make money. He sat back, threw out his chest, strained the buttons on his waistcoat through sheer self-confidence.

He left early, but he came again. Soon it was known that Wesley Dexter was paying attention to Marcella Colfax. Occasionally they drove out in his trap, behind a high-stepping cob. He would draw up before the house with a flourish, short loose fawn-coloured top coat, tan gloves, bowler hat; the small groom who sat behind with his arms folded would unfold them, get down; the cob would fidget; "Whoa, Bill! Whoa, behave yourself." Missie would emerge, large flowered hat, elbow-length gloves, wide flounced skirts. The little groom would help her up, Wesley would swing the long whip, and they were off. On such occasions his scarf pin was a gold crop, his cuff links were horses' heads, and the way he held out his chest was vaguely reminiscent of Stella.

Missie did not know what she felt toward him. Not love, certainly, if what she had felt for Harry was love. Sometimes he bored her, occasionally he frightened her.

One night he came over and sat on William's leather sofa beside her. The weight of his heavy body on the springs threw her toward him, and she hastily drew herself away.

"You're a stand-offish little thing, Missie," he said. "Maybe that's why I like you. A man doesn't like his women too approachable, eh?"

Poor Adelaide blundered into the library just then, blushed darkly and beat a hasty retreat. He laughed.

"We seem to have disturbed her spinsterly calm!" he said. "I suppose if I had had my arm around you she would have fainted." But something in Missie's face warned him. He did not make the attempt. Not then, anyhow.

Sometimes she tried to think about him, to wonder what she would do if he proposed to her. But she could not think; all feeling seemed to be dead in her. One thing is certain. She never encouraged him; often she wondered just what in her had attracted him; and later on she was to find that the very qualities which had seemed to allure him were the ones that annoyed him most, her simplicity, her candour, and a sort of native honesty. She had never heard of consolidating a position.

He was tactful, however. He talked about indifferent matters. Golf had just come to America, and he was planning a golf club. One night he showed her a tentative list of members, and she looked to see if Harry's name was there. It was not, however. It appeared that golf was a very exclusive game. Not entirely exclusive, however. One day she saw in the paper that another similar club was being projected. Thomas Wilkins was one of the founders, and Harry was on the "greens" committee, whatever that might be. She put down the newspaper; she could see him, as once she had watched him from the kitchen window, flushed with exercise, tall, slim, laughing. She got up angrily. Would she never finish with that nonsense? Was she going to let it cloud her life and destroy it? Was she like Stella after all?

That day she felt a wild impulse to get away, to live her own life for once. Not Sarah's not Adelaide's, not Wesley Dexter's. Her own; to burst out of this environment which was sapping her will power and her initiative; to leave this deadly comfort and work with her hands, to feel the good fatigue of labour.

"I'm just common, I suppose," she told herself. "I'm not really a lady. I never will be."

But the impulse passed. She could not hurt them like that. They had been good to her, after their fashion. It would be a blow to her grandmother's pride that she might not get over; and she had had enough. All those children, and not one of them to be proud of. She was lost once more in the mystery of life, of Sarah conceiving in the arms of her husband, of Sarah bringing forth young. And now the husband was only mouldering bones under the earth, and the very children of his begetting had forgotten him.

It was about that time that old Sarah showed her a letter from her father:

"I am delighted to know of Missie's prospects. I trust absolutely in your verdict on the man, and I can only thank you, dear mother, for your kindness to my poor child. I know that it has taxed your resources severely, and that if another season can be avoided it should be. In case there is a marriage the early autumn——"

"But Wesley hasn't proposed to me," she said. She felt driven, harried.

"He'd better do it soon," said Sarah grimly, "or stop coming here. It is fatal to limit yourself to him, unless he is serious."

"Who else have I?"

"Whom else can you have, under the circumstances?" said old Sarah, practically.

Then one day a new pressure was directed against her from a new quarter.

Her grandmother had been ill for a few days and was keeping her room. Spring had come, but the windows of the big house still remained closed, and Missie, coming in from a croquet party, encountered in the hall a musty damp chill that made her shiver. Ishmael had driven around to the stable, and the hall was empty. She heard voices, however, from the front parlour, and hesitated.

There was a woman in there with Adelaide, and she was talking in low angry tones.

"I can't go on, and I won't, Adelaide. Bert's a man; he can look out for himself. Don't tell me she's not sending him any money; I know she is. I've seen MacDonald. And don't tell me any more about this girl. I've got a girl too. It isn't her fault that she's got no father. Better the way things are than to have a father like Bert, anyhow! But how do you suppose I've felt all winter? These parties, the money you're spending on her, and then to cut the little bit I've been getting! I tell you if there's a God, and he's to judge between me and Bert——"

Missie went straight in, her hands and feet cold, her face flaming. Adelaide was crouched in one of the low brocaded chairs, her poor head jerking, her eyes red and suffused; and before her, pacing up and down like some caged animal, was a tall still handsome woman; an aquiline woman, with her grandmother's arched nose and erect bearing. She stopped and stared at Missie.

"I'm sorry. I heard what you said; not all, but some of it. I suppose I didn't realize——"

"Missie!" Adelaide had found her voice. "Go right up to your room. This is not for you to hear."

Cecily smiled bitterly. "Yes, it is not for you. You might learn something about life if you stayed. And you will please tell your grandmother that I am here."

But Missie did not move.

"I have a right to speak too, Aunt Cecily. I don't want charity; I never did. I certainly don't want what belongs to you."

"Missie!" Adelaide cried.

"What I really want to do is to work," said Missie stubbornly, "but we don't do that, do we? So I daresay I can get married. We don't seem to make much of a success of that either, do we? But I can try."

Then she went out, leaving a stunned silence behind her.

She took off her things in her neat room and then sat down in her small rocking chair. Suppose she married Wesley Dexter, without love? She did not dislike him; she simply did not love him. She tried to see him in the unlovely intimacies of marriage, as she had seen her father; asleep in the center of a wide bed, the sheet drawn over his head to keep out the light, shaving before the mirror, blowing out his cheeks to shave the line between his nose and his mouth, the blond hair on his chest showing through his open undershirt; usurping the scanty cream for his own use; walking jauntily out of the house, always well dressed and handsome, to meet some other woman, while Stella waited for him and rocked away the hours.

Suddenly she realized that she was rocking in her chair, like Stella.

She had not seen Ellen in months, by that time, but the next day she took her courage in her hands and went back. Luck favoured her, for whatever Ellen's private indignation might be she had not failed to use the Colfax name as a stepping stone to place, and Ellen was giving a luncheon that day. The meal was over, and a neat servant was engaged in laying out the card tables when Missie rang the bell. Ellen, peering through the curtains, saw her and herself opened the door. Missie, braced against coldness, found herself kissed, being drawn into the parlour, introduced as "My sister, Miss Colfax" to well-dressed women still a trifle too conscious of their good clothes, their diamond rings, their polished finger nails. Ellen saying loudly, "Don't tell me you walked, Missie! Where's the carriage?" Ellen's child being caught up and told to "kiss her nice auntie" and the child setting up a wail at Missie's unfamiliar face.

Then a rustling, a subsiding into the chairs around the card tables, and Missie saying:

"May I talk to you for a minute, Ellen?" And Ellen, distinctly:

"You certainly may. I always say the hostess at a euchre party might as well go upstairs and wash her hair!"

Polite laughter, and then she and Ellen were in Ellen's bedroom, Ellen still amiable, gratified. "I'm glad you came just now. Those old cats will have something to talk about!"

When she told Ellen her problem, however, she perceptibly hardened.

"Don't be a fool, Missie. They took you; they owe you all they've given you. As to this Cecily, she's made her bed years ago; let her lie in it. Anyhow, it won't be long. I hear Wes Dexter is paying you attention."

"I think I can marry him if I want to. The trouble is—Ellen, I don't want to marry him. I would rather work."

"Work! What sort of work?"

"I could go to Carter's, like mother."

Ellen's face coloured. "Never!" she said shrilly. "Do you think I've lived that down for nothing? What do you suppose I'm trying to do, working my head off to feed and amuse that crowd downstairs? I'm going to be somebody in this town some day; I'm somebody now. Tommy's on the board of a new country club; your set's not the only pebble on the beach, and they'll find that out. And you're not going to shame me, Missie Colfax; you're not going to pull me down again. You marry Wesley Dexter. What does it matter whether you're in love with him or not? Men are all alike, after you get used to them."

"But suppose," Missie said, in a low voice, "suppose you care for somebody else?"

"Who else?"

"I don't think that matters."

"Has *he* ever asked you?"

"No." Suddenly she felt the desire to speak Harry's name, to unload herself of that absurd hopeless pain. "I'll tell you, Ellen. It's Harry Sloane. I know it's foolish, but——"

"Harry Sloane!" said Ellen queerly. Then she laughed. "Go ahead and marry Wesley Dexter, Missie. Harry's engaged to the girl in the blue dress downstairs."

Missie said nothing. She smiled rather grimly and went out of the room, and out of the house; and that night she accepted Wesley Dexter.

Chapter XV

LAMBERT came on for the wedding in the early fall. Save that he was slightly gray he seemed unchanged; as well dressed, as urbane, as meticulously polite as ever. There was a pitiful bustle the day of his arrival; his old room had been carefully prepared for him, his favourite foods ordered, and when the carriage drew up, his mother, tremulous and feeble, herself stood at the door.

"Welcome home, my boy. My dear boy!"

Missie was never so near to liking him as when he took the shaking old figure in his arms. If it was acting it was good acting, but she did not think it was. In later years she learned indeed that it was not; that his mother had held the one un-selfish love of his useless life. Her picture always stood by his bed.

For Missie he had an air of heavy joviality.

"And how's the bride? All happy, eh? Got a kiss for her old father?"

He almost forgot Adelaide, self-effacingly behind her mother, and jerking with nervousness. Missie, watching her, saw the dislike in her eyes when she turned her cheek to him.

"How are you, Adelaide? Still afraid to cross a street?"

Missie found herself a detached spectator. She was glad that he roused no emotion in her, for she knew now that emotion was a dangerous thing. When she did not feel she was strong; it was only when she felt that she was weak.

Later on he had to view the trousseau and the gifts. He had eaten an excellent dinner, produced an excellent cigar. But over the extent of the trousseau he grew faintly cold. Missie saw it, the other women felt it.

"Been spending a good bit of money, haven't you?"

"She is your daughter, Lambert. Things have to be the best we can give."

Adelaide spoke up: "Don't blame Missie, either. She didn't want anything."

But he ignored Adelaide, as always. "Still, mother, with things the way they have been——!"

"I sold the Pine Street property, Lambert. I hadn't meant to tell you."

"And spent it on this?"

"A good bit of it, yes."

His urbanity left him. Suddenly he was in a white fury. Missie never forgot that scene; the bed piled with the dozens of undergarments which Adelaide had so proudly laid out, the bright dresses over chairs and hanging even from the gas brackets; their long full skirts which swept the ground interlined with crinoline, the enormous balloon sleeves similarly stiffened. He caught up a white *mousseline de soie* with tiny pink roses outlining the neck, and carried it with him as he raged back and forth. The flimsy thing trailed, and Adelaide made little furtive rushes to get it from him.

They were crazy, all of them. Had she—meaning Sarah —no sense of property? She had mis-handled the estate any-how, she and old MacDonald between them. She ought to have a guardian. He would take the matter into court and have somebody appointed. He raved on, carried away by his fury, making threatening gestures.

Missie had been standing beside her wedding dress when he started, her wedding dress of white satin with its long wadded train lined with lace ruffles, its stiff high collar, its narrow pointed basque, and by it her veil, her slippers, her gloves. Her grandmother was cowering by the bed, Adelaide had ceased her furtive rushes and was shaking violently. And suddenly rage shook Missie, a common shrewish rage. Like Stella's. She advanced on him, her hands clenched.

"Get out of this room," she said, "and shut up. Stop this raving. Nobody's afraid of you; certainly I'm not."

"By God——!"

"By God yourself!" she said furiously. "You're a poor thing. They've given you all they have. All this is for you, not for me. You've lived off them all these years. If any one needs a guardian it is you. And now, this is my room. Get out of it, and don't come back."

He was shocked into speechlessness. Her grandmother was regarding her with horror, with dislike. Only Adelaide's eyes showed a faint glint of triumph.

"You are your mother's own child!" he said at last.

Her hands were trembling, but her voice was steady.

"And you are that mother's murderer," she said, in a voice that cut. "I forbid you to speak her name to me."

And then Mrs. Colfax crumpled up in a dead faint on the floor. Only years afterward was Missie to give Lambert credit for the gentleness with which he picked her up and carried her to her big walnut bed, that bed where so strangely he had been conceived and later, born.

Some time in the night, as he sat by her bed, he made his peace with his mother. Or possibly she bought it, at a price. And it was like old times to find him at least on the surface his urbane self the next morning at breakfast. Missie had not forgiven him, and she knew Adelaide never would. His own attitude to Missie was one of generous magnanimity. Let bygones be bygones.

"Marmalade, Missie?"

"No, thanks."

Adelaide sat, stiff and ugly, behind the coffee service. She broke a cup, spilled the coffee, twitched, scowled.

"My dear Adelaide, why not have it poured in the kitchen?"

She ignored him, sat like some squat ugly Buddha behind the urn, ate heavily, loathed him.

Later in the day Mrs. Colfax rose. It was she who showed him the gifts after breakfast: onyx tables, heavy over-ornate cut glass, marble clocks, the Dresden china lamps just come into fashion, the usual silver. Missie, passing through the hall outside her grandmother's sitting room upstairs, where the gifts were laid out, found Adelaide outside the closed door in an attitude of strained attention.

"He's got something out of her," she said, helplessly. "I know him. Last night he wouldn't let me in the room. If only you hadn't said what you did——"

"If I'd had a hatchet in my hand I'd have killed him," said Missie, dully.

She was bewildered, terrified. What about men, anyhow? What were these strange unfathomable creatures who ill-used and brow-beat their women one moment and were gentle and kind the next? What certainty had any woman with them? They kissed you and forgot you. They could, if one cared enough, kill you by neglect. And yet marriage went on, the race went on. The race went on.

She turned cold with fear.

And this fear was not dissipated when she found that Wesley and her father took to each other at once. They met as two men of the world, indulgent toward the fuss with which women surround a wedding, faintly supercilious indeed, and mutually understanding. There was even not so much apparent difference in their ages; Wesley was an old thirty-five, Lambert an eternally young fifty. Still, it came as a shock to her to have her father tell Wesley to call him by his first name.

"I'm no heavy father, Wes. I've been Bert Colfax to the men in this town for longer than I care to remember." And Bert he was to Wesley after that.

Missie surmised that Wesley found a mild gratification in that request, but also that he made certain mental reservations. She even overheard him forestalling any future attacks on the basis of this new relationship.

"We'll not be rich, Bert, you understand. I can keep up a decent establishment, but that's about all."

And her father, understanding, perfectly and slightly amused: "Always spend less than you make. That's the ticket. I never did, but then I never made anything!"

They understood each other. They were men.

Sometimes she went in alone and looked at her gifts. Perhaps she hoped that they would rouse something in her, something on which to build a new home, a new life. But they never did. She felt that they were not really sent to her. They came from Wesley's friends, or her grandmother's. Only one thing she really felt was her own; this was a large silver cake dish from Ellen and Tommy. For Ellen and Tommy had been invited to the wedding and were to sit "with the family." It was an ugly cake dish, even as such things went in the nineties, but as Ellen said, it had weight.

"Don't talk to me of design," she said, "give me weight in silver every time."

It was Wesley who had put them on the list. Tommy was doing very well. He had raised some capital and built a small bicycle factory. He was thrilled with it, with the crude metal in the yard, with the forging room, the drill room. He bought his steel tubing, but the rest he made himself. He loved the assembling, the annealing, brazing, polishing, enamelling. When a bicycle was finished, its enamel gleaming, its nickel plate glittering, he was like a young mother with a child.

He talked of spokes, sprocket wheels, cranks, hubs, cones, cases, as to-day men speak of carburetors and magnetos. He was looking forward to the time when Clare could have one; the smallest bicycle ever made. And he was making money. The streets were filled from curb to curb with bicycles, and some of them were his. Also, Tommy had a secret; in a back room at the factory he was experimenting with a small engine. He was secretive about it. He never told Ellen. Not for several years was he to tell Ellen.

So Missie looked at the cake dish, and thought of Ellen and Tommy. Of Stella too. How Stella would have loved it all! But she refused to think of Harry Sloane.

She tried hard to love Wesley. She had a fierce revulsion sometimes when he took her into his arms; there was always about him a definite aroma, of cigars, bay rum, Peau d'Espagne, a suggestion of good food lustily eaten, an atmosphere of self-satisfaction and possession that chilled her.

"I can't wait. I can't wait, Missie."

But there were other times when he came in tired and quiet; when he made no passionate overtures, and when she found that her own gift of silence, to sit quietly sewing while he watched her and said nothing, was comforting to him. He depended on her. She felt maternal then, strong and yet gentle. What she had she would give him, tenderness, care, rest and comfort. He was giving her all he had; she would give him all she could.

She saw that this marriage was bringing about a certain concord in the family. Old Archibald had been asked to the church; Ellen was mollified, even came in to see the gifts; Sarah sat long hours with Lambert, two spots of happy colour on her cheeks, and busy between whiles; consulting the rector on the ceremony, going herself to the rehearsal, distrusting the local milliners and having her bonnet sent from New York. For it was to be a high noon wedding; an innovation that, and Wesley's suggestion. It was more expensive, since it meant a luncheon for the guests at the house, but it seemed that expense was not to be considered now.

"We'll show this town something!" Wesley had said. It sounded like Ellen. More than once later on Missie was to consider what a pair Wesley and Ellen would have made, with their similar ambitions, their hard material philosophy of life.

And so the wedding day came. A cockade had been fitted to Ishmael's new silk hat, and a white ribbon tied to his new whip. The old carriage had been painted, and temporarily lined with white linen, for nothing must mar the purity of Missie's wedding gown. There were canopies over the front steps of the house and at the entrance to the church, and under these canopies stretched lengths of rich red carpet. A new florist had come to town and his roses and palms, and not Sloane's, decorated the altar and the house. The house that morning smelled rather like a funeral, and through that funereal atmosphere walked her father in a new frock coat, smug and prosperous, whistling the wedding march and rehearsing the slow march down the aisle with Missie on his arm.

And Missie was locked in her room, fighting the hardest fight of her life. In those early morning hours of preparation nobody had missed her. Already she had been manicured; her soft hair was dressed to receive the coronet of satin and white paradise which held her veil. Over the wedding undergarments of finest lawn and lace she had thrown an old dressing gown, and now she sat in the low rocking chair, doggedly rocking.

What ought she to do? To send for Wesley and tell him what she knew? But to do that, if she had no defence, she must be prepared to call off the marriage, and to call off the marriage now— It might kill her grandmother. And what defence would he have? He would deny it, of course; she might believe him or not, but he would deny it. Then what would have been accomplished? Nothing. Nothing at all. And there was no time to prove or disprove the statements in the letter, delivered by hand an hour ago by a ragged urchin, and giving no address.

Emily Beaumont! Then she must have left the stage and be living here. But of course she would have left the stage; she must be almost an old woman by this time. Curious, she could smell that dressing room now, the carbon from a defective gas jet, the heavy perfume, and a faint odour of perspiration from the clothing hung over the screen. "There's nothing sinful about the human body unless you make it sinful."

Pictures rose in her mind; she and Stella sitting on the bench in the park. "Your father's hard and cruel and bad.

He's got another woman." And again: "You can't trust them. They take everything and give nothing. That's men for you." She thought she had forgotten all that. During these years with her grandmother something different had been built up, a cult of the male. Men were fine and noble, if exacting. They did the world's work, and women were their handmaidens. And that was partly true. There were plenty of good men, men who frowned on infidelity. They had come to the house, deferential and loyal to ugly old wives. Their women were safe with them, safe and secure.

And then there were women who were not exacting, who had weighed the comforts of their lives against the weaknesses of their men, and chosen to be comfortable. Ellen would be like that. She was practical. She did not demand perfection. What was the use of demanding perfection?

She had burned Emily Beaumont's letter. It had been brief. She had always remembered Missie, and knew about her. Also she had tried to reach Mr. Dexter that night but had failed. There was a girl—nobody Missie would know—who was fond of Wesley, and she was threatening to go to the church and make trouble. Emily Beaumont herself meant to be outside, but she might need some help. And it ended:

"Don't think too much of this, Missie. Mr. Dexter never cared for her and she knows it. He won't ever want to see her again."

Missie knew why Emily Beaumont had failed to reach Wesley. He had given his bachelor dinner at the club the night before; and no doubt it had been a prodigal one. He might not have gone home at all. But he would be there now. She looked at the clock. Eleven. In an hour——

She was still rocking doggedly when Adelaide came in, a flushed happily excited Adelaide in a pale gray dress with the balloon sleeves which made her look as wide as she was tall, and with a small lavender bonnet perched high on her tightly pinned hair.

"Resting?" she asked. "That's right. I tried to sit down

myself, but I'm so excited——! Missie dear, you'd better start to dress. Here's the sheet."

She was bending over, spreading a sheet on the floor. Her stays were very tight; she breathed heavily.

"Let me do that. But first I want to telephone Wesley."

"You'll see him in an hour," panted Adelaide. "Anyhow you can't go down like that. You——"

But Missie was gone. There was no decision to make; she could not go back on them. All she could do was to warn Wesley; by doing that she was making herself particeps criminis—not that she used those words; he would know that she had married him knowing this thing, virtually condoning it. But what did that matter? What did anything matter now, save to get it over and hurt nobody?

The hall was empty when she rang up his number, and his own voice was irritable until he recognized hers.

"That you, Missie! What on earth——"

"Listen, Wes. Can you hear me?" She lowered her voice. "I've had a letter. There is somebody who is threatening to make trouble at the church. Somebody you know. I thought I'd better tell you."

There was a brief silence; then:

"That's nonsense. Who dared to write you a letter like that?"

"I'll explain that later."

"It's an infernal lie, Missie. There's nobody who has any claim on me."

"Well, I've told you," she said drearily, and hung up the receiver. There had been terror as well as anger in his voice. Bluster, that was what it was. It was true, the letter, and he knew who the girl was. If she tried to call him now she would find his line busy; he would be putting his friends to work to prevent trouble; his friends, men like himself who would protect him. Men of that kind always protected each other. When she turned around her father was in the library door, watching her. He had overheard and he had been frightened.

He was still pale. He wanted this marriage to go through. He wanted to walk down the church aisle with her before the world which had repudiated him, in his new clothes, with Wesley waiting, "Wesley Dexter, my son-in-law."

"Missie, I beg of you! Your grandmother——"

"You needn't worry. I'm going through with it."

His colour came back, there was even kindness and pity in his face. He could afford to be kind and pitiful now. And she waited for him, her face white, her wrapper drawn close about her young body.

"I heard that, Missie. You mustn't believe all the letters you get."

"This one was true, father."

He hesitated; queer, to see him ill at ease.

"Suppose it is," he said at last. "A single man has a good many temptations, Missie. Marriage makes all the difference in the world. You'll find Wes a good husband. Don't judge him yet. Give him time, anyhow." And he added, not without a grim humour: "I don't suppose that means much, coming from me, but if a man loves his wife—— You're a good girl, Missie."

He did not try to kiss her. She turned and went up the stairs to where Adelaide had laid out the sheet on which she was to stand while putting on her wedding gown.

Then, almost immediately, an organ was playing somewhere, her father was offering her his arm, one of the bridesmaids was straightening out her long heavy train. As she moved forward it seemed to drag her back. Her father looked dignified and handsome; after all, this was where he belonged, with these handsomely dressed people around him. He had never belonged in the little house. There was some devil of restlessness in him that drove him away from them, but also something that brought him back. He was not really wicked. Nobody was really wicked. Even Wes. God made them weak, and life came along and was too much for them. The church looked lovely; the new florist was better than

Sloane's. Better than Harry. Harry would be standing and waiting like Wes before very long, while an organ played and——

She felt the ring slipped onto her finger. It was warm; the best man had carried it in his waistcoat pocket.

"With this ring——"

"With this ring——"

"I thee endow——"

"I thee endow——"

When they knelt she saw Wesley furtively pulling up the knees of his trousers.

Then it was over. The veil which had modestly covered her face was put back to mark her changed condition. She was a married woman; she was Mrs. Wesley Dexter. It was all over and nothing had happened. She was starting down the aisle again, but this time on her husband's arm; first her father and then her husband. Not wicked but weak. One leaned on them, and then they were not there. But then she was being silly. Ellen would tell her that. There was Ellen, looking very grand. She ought to smile at Ellen; every bride ought to smile.

She did it very well. If her smile stiffened as they approached the late-comers standing at the rear of the church, nobody noticed it. And who but herself could know that Wesley's arm tightened in its sleeve? Or that they both paused at the top of the steps and glanced at the curious crowd which stood in the street watching?

There was no disturbance. The hastily summoned body-guard had done its work well. She did not see even Emily Beaumont. There would be nothing for the reporters but that the bridal gown was of white Duchess satin, heavily embroidered in seed pearls. The carriage was waiting, old Ishmael was smiling. A policeman was holding open the carriage door. She got in, gathering her voluminous train and veil about her. Wesley got in, heavy, substantial, rather white. The carriage door slammed. Now she need not smile. But she could not stop; it was frozen there. Beside her Wesley was wiping cold beads of sweat from his forehead.

"Well, that's over."

"And without any trouble," she heard herself saying.

"Trouble? Oh, you mean that letter? Now listen, Missie darling, that letter was a lie. I have enemies; every successful man has enemies. Somebody was trying to stir up trouble, that's all. There wasn't a word of truth in it."

She did not believe him, but she put out the hand that wore his heavy gold ring and lightly touched his.

"Then we will forget it," she said simply. "I'll do my best, Wes, and if only you'll be honest and faithful——"

"Before God I will, Missie."

He bent over and kissed the ring. She saw that he was profoundly moved. Moved and—relieved.

Chapter XVI

PERHAPS it was as well for Missie that her honeymoon journey took her into the strange new world that was New York in the nineties.

She had no complaint to make of Wesley. Perhaps he had been frightened. He made things as easy for her as he could, respected her reserves, showed tact, gave to her new status as his wife a certain dignity. If his passion left her cold, he was not abashed. He knew women. Their passions were matters of slow growth; there were reserves, inhibitions. Not that Wesley had ever heard of inhibitions, but he was aware of them nevertheless.

He was complacent, self-satisfied. He even managed to give her an unexpected privacy. He had a way of taking himself away, downtown or to the lobby of the hotel, and letting her have the room to herself.

"Mustn't get tired of me right off," he told her.

She was grateful. She would bathe, and dress in those new clothes of hers which already she knew were not quite right, settle herself at the small desk and write her wedding notes of thanks, or stand at the window and watch the impressive traffic going by. If she thought at all it was to wonder that her marriage had changed her so little; that she was as virginal in heart as she had ever been. But she did not want to think. When she had extra leisure she wrote to her grandmother and Adelaide:

"The hotel is really wonderful. I could spend hours watching the women go by. Such clothes! Some of the veils are being worn loose now, Aunt Adelaide. They hang from the rim of the hat to the shoulders, but they look untidy to me.

"We have a delightful room, with a private bath. Just imagine! The walls are covered with pink satin and the furniture is as fine as any in a private house. I saw into a private suite the other day, and the parlour was furnished in gilt, even to the piano. It was quite regal.

"Wesley has bought me a watch at Tiffany's, with a diamond bowknot pin to fasten it to my dress. He is spoiling me, I am afraid." And so on and on.

During the day, then, she had plenty of distraction. She would stop on the street to look, and Wesley would catch her by the arm and good-humouredly pulled her along.

"These people will think you have never seen anything."

"But I never have."

It was all strange to her; the theatre coming into its own with Mrs. Fiske, Mansfield, De Wolf Hopper. Tall and even taller buildings rising so that if one looked up at the top, one might topple over backwards. Twenty-third Street the heart of the shopping district; the Waldorf-Astoria with Peacock Alley already famous and Oscar rising to autocracy. One day there was great excitement. A horseless carriage went up Fifth Avenue, ringing its bell vociferously. People crowded to the curb, horses reared and snorted. It was an ungainly thing. The crowd applauded and laughed.

"Ellen's husband thinks they have come to stay."

"Ellen's husband had better stick to bicycles, dear heart."

But often at night, with Wesley sleeping heavily beside her, she would lie awake after her old fashion and try to picture the future. Already she knew that they had no tastes in common; that he had none of the vague ideals and romantic stirrings which were her inner life. To Wesley, then and always, life was a matter of good food, good friends, good drink, success in affairs. His fastidious care of his body was that he might enjoy it. He was a frank and not unagreeable hedonist. And just now he was hers utterly. She knew that her ignorance amused and fascinated him, that her essential virginity thrilled him. Long after their relationship was fully established it still stimulated him to see her hair down her back and what he called the little-girl look about her. He was willing—it was even a part of her charm for him then —that she be passive in his arms, or even attempt to escape him. He would laugh exultantly, and perhaps let her go, but she learned in time that her evasions only excited him.

But how could she continue to hold him? She would not always have her youth, and what else had she to give him that he had not already had? Children? But he did not want children. He was too self-indulgent. And children did not always hold men anyhow. "Isn't that the way it goes? They get you, and you bear their children and lose your figure, and then——"

With the morning would come activity and an end to morbid terror. He would bathe and shave, calling in to her small good-humoured remarks. He was cheerful in the morning.

"Thank God you're a woman, Missie."

"Why?"

"Well, for more than one reason! But Providence didn't give you a beard that keeps on growing while you sleep."

"Suppose you had hair to do up, like mine?"

"I'd praise my maker, my child."

He was already a trifle bald.

She wondered why she did not love him. He was engagingly boyish at times. He would walk slowly behind her into the vast dining room, glancing to right and left, with exactly the proper air of slight ennui, as one who perforce dined in public but preserved himself haughtily from publicity. It annoyed him when she could not assume this attitude.

"Why should you scurry in like a scared rabbit?"

"I don't like people staring at me."

"Then why are we here? Why are all these other people here? To look and be looked at! We can get just as good food at half the price elsewhere."

He had bought himself a white silk waistcoat for his evening clothes. It was advanced, daring.

At the end of three weeks they went back home. Wesley had taken a house in a good neighbourhood, a tall narrow house in a row of precisely similar houses. It was a dark house with a basement kitchen; the food came up on a dumb waiter which no amount of oil could stop creaking, and never after could Missie hear a dumb waiter agonize without being immediately taken back to the innumerable dinner parties in that tall dark house; to listening for it and praying it to hurry before the delay roused Wesley's irritation.

For by that time she knew that he could be an irritable man.

"What the hell's happened in the pantry?"

"It takes a good while, Wesley. They are doing their best."

"You let them soldier on you. That's what."

She had two maids, substantial women whose very lack of grace annoyed him. And they were afraid of him. Long before Missie began to fear his angers these women were scurrying like frightened deer when he appeared. Even that first winter she sometimes found herself mutely apologizing for him, sitting at the table, when there were guests, with a smile on her face and her hands trembling. But when the food came his frown would relax. He would eat heartily, sit back, smile, be his handsome best.

They shared the same room, the same bed. He still laughed at her little girl horror of nudity; she unfastened her undergarments, slipped on her nightgown, stepped out of a little heap, chemise, drawers, petticoat. She locked the bathroom door when she bathed, that bathroom where he had installed a white enamelled tub.

"You're a prig, Missie. For a married woman—— "

"I don't *feel* married."

"Well, you are."

He would catch her to him, especially if he had had a drink or two. She never understood that, never understood that there were times when he felt the need of courage to approach her, and that liquor bridged the gulf. Not that she repulsed him. She was acquiescence itself. But deep in his soul Wesley knew that he had never touched her. It was a confession his pride would not let him make, even to himself.

He spent money recklessly. The house was well furnished. The back parlour was now a library, with hard tufted leather chairs, a sofa, a huge self-rocker. Adelaide's contribution to the beauty of the ensemble was a waste-paper basket of brown cardboard, the sides laced together with red ribbons tied into bows at the top. In the parlour was plush; red plush, a red carpet, red rep curtains hanging from poles. Wesley did the buying, and he liked red. Missie never sat there if she could avoid it.

He spent his money without consulting her, always with that sense of his power to earn more. He was one of the founders of the new Golf Club, an expensive matter. When opera made its first visit to the town in its history he was one of the exclusive list of guarantors, and it cost him a pretty sum in the end. One day a florist's bill came in, and she found that he had sent flowers to all the débutantes of the season. When she protested, her only protest, he was angry.

"I'm not asking you to pay for it, am I? And there are certain things people in our position have to do."

She said nothing more. She catered to him as well as she could, served the large elaborate dinner parties for which Wesley himself made out the lists, fed them the ten- and twelve-course dinners of the period, drove in expensive rented carriages to the dinners given in return—he had sold the cob —to the balls and Assemblies. And in private she wondered what it was all about. Was this then what life came to, after all? Where were they going? Where were all these people going? Surely, to eat, to drink, to dress, to sleep, that was not living. There must be something more, something just over the hill where she could not see it. Only what was it?

She found herself alien in Wesley's group of intimates. Nothing in her previous life had prepared her for them. After five o'clock the house was like a club. Men came in in numbers, drank high-balls and cocktails—going back to her tidy pantry to concoct new and mysterious variations of the latter— smoked Wesley's cigars and left behind them an aroma of stale tobacco and alcohol which no amount of airing seemed to remove. She moved in and out among them until she discovered that it did not matter whether she did or not. After that she stayed upstairs.

One afternoon her grandmother came to call. She was growing feeble that winter. It had come on her after Lambert went away. She had tried to keep him, but he had gone. It took Ishmael and Adelaide to get her out of the carriage and support her to the door. Missie was upstairs when the bell rang; when she got down old Sarah was standing in the doorway of the front parlour, her high-bred face disapproving and set. There was an uncomfortable silence within, and she was saying, in her high clear voice:

"No, thank you, Wesley. I shall not come in. It is too much like a bar-room."

There was nothing to do. Missie could not even ask her to the back of the house. She turned and went out again, leaning rather more heavily on Adelaide, and refusing Wesley's offer of help. When she reached home again she took off her gloves and washed her hands, carefully, methodically.

But the winter had one result. One day Ellen dropped in; only she had changed her name to Eileen now. Her hard prettiness attracted the men, and she enjoyed herself. She showed a new frivolity, a designed coquettishness, toward them. They were important men; their wives were "in society." After that she came often, and gradually she began to have her reward.

"Why don't you ask Missie Dexter's sister? She's amusing."

And sometimes "Eileen" was asked. Tommy too, of course, but Tommy never really counted. He was a money-maker. He had no graces, and it was too late to acquire them. He never even learned to wear his dress clothes as though they belonged to him; his coats always looked as though they were about to slip off those sloping shoulders of his. While Eileen danced he would stand against a wall somewhere, his pale blue eyes blank, his mind working. The horseless carriage was a practical thing. Some day somebody would invent a way to make them cheap, and then—— He would think about his engine, get out an old envelope and make notes on it.

Missie grew very thin that winter, and much of her elusive prettiness left her. During the day her high boned collars concealed the hollows in her neck, but in her evening dresses they showed painfully. Her eyes seemed larger, and there was a hint of tragedy in them. But of course there was no tragedy; who would have believed that Stella's daughter would reach such heights? Be well married, prosperous, important.

"Mrs. Wesley Dexter entertained at luncheon yesterday. Among the guests were the Mesdames Hemingway, Rodgers, Jerome——" And the list would contain all the important women, the ones who counted.

For the city was growing; Wesley's prosperity was only a reflection. It had been founded by tradesmen, living by barter and trade with the farmers. Its early aristocracy had been only its lawyers, its doctors, its clergymen. But now it had ceased to be a parasite, living on the surrounding country. It had roots of its own, mills, factories. It had classes also. True, only the upper class enjoyed life. There was nothing for the others. They could ride on a car for five cents, but where? The excursion boats on the river were crowded, dirty, sometimes turbulent. There were picnic grounds, with swings and merry-go-rounds, but these too were hot, untidy, noisome. And so far Mr. Wilkinson had been wrong; there were no playgrounds for the children. They played in the gutters, on the pavements, in untidy yards.

Sometimes Missie watched them, with a stab of pain.

There was still no pressure, however. True, the hours of

labour were long, ten hours. And wages were low; the immigrant trains disgorged day after day lines of cheap labour; men with bewildered eyes, women with kerchiefs on their heads and children holding to their skirts, stood in the station, gathered around their feather beds, their mysterious parcels, their tin trunks. But for the employers there was leisure. Business was unhurried. If not to-day, to-morrow.

One night the MacDonalds dined with them. Mrs. Mac-Donald was a sworn enemy of progress.

"A telephone!" she said. "Do you think I mean to place myself on speaking terms with anybody who chooses to call me?"

Queer to think that she was within the year to fall a victim to that progress she resented. And that Tommy should be the innocent agent of her death. Queerer still to think of her, drawing some ethereal shawl about herself in the strange democracy of heaven; having to mix with the spirits of quite impossible persons, where the last shall be first and the first shall be last. All queer, all of it.

Eileen—she was Eileen from then on—sometimes regarded Missie with a certain envy.

"Who would have thought ten years ago, Missie, that you would be where you are now?"

"Where *am* I? I often wonder."

"You've got what I have to fight for," said Eileen practically. There was no use being frivolous or coquettish with Missie, or even pretentious.

And it was Eileen one day who told her that old Archibald had sent a note to Tommy, trying to borrow some money.

"The old nuisance!" Eileen said. "Tommy's soft, but I told him not to send any. He'd only be back for more."

"He sent a note? Is he sick?"

"I don't know and I don't care. Too many pairs of shoes that I needed went into his pocket in the old days. Don't be silly, Missie. What is he to you? If his own sister will let him starve——"

"I don't suppose she knows."

Eileen dropped the subject. She was full of plans. They were going to build a house in the suburbs, and Tommy was going to give her a horse and trap. Tommy had bought a plot of land and was going to develop it. He thought the bicycle and the extension of the car lines would induce people to move out of town. And she had dropped the euchre club. She was playing whist now. Anyhow, those women were stupid, always pretending to be something they were not. By the way, did she remember the girl who was going to marry Harry Sloane? Well, he had jilted her, left her high and dry. Wouldn't you know he would do a thing like that?

Missie felt that old contraction of the heart. She steadied her voice.

"But why? There must have been a reason."

"He said it was because he wanted to study law, and it would be too long for her to wait. But she doesn't believe that."

"What does she believe?"

Eileen glanced at Missie, glanced away.

"She thinks he cares for somebody else," she said.

She felt no particular emotion after Eileen had gone. The thread between Harry and herself had been too definitely broken. But she missed her memories. He had stood for so much for so long a time, for blithe light-hearted youth, for romance, for impossible dreaming. She missed her dreams perhaps more than she missed him.

Chapter XVII

ONE day she got old Archibald's address from Tommy and went to see him. She found him with difficulty, and the change in him alarmed her. He looked infinitely old, and he looked ill-nourished. She had never known—never did know—why he had quarrelled with his sister, but she was resentful of his shabby little room, of his spotless worn linen, of his broken boots. He was feeble, too; it was with difficulty that he got out of his chair.

"Now this is an unexpected pleasure," he said, with some of his old gallantry. "I could wish I might receive you better. But—" he glanced around, at the litter, at the family pictures and the not so reputable ones—"what I have belongs to my friends. And how is Mrs. Wesley Dexter? She looks thin."

"She's been going to too many parties."

He inspected her from under his shaggy eyebrows.

"Don't let him eat you up, Missie. I know his type; strong as an ox, no nerves, no temperament. Full bodied, like old port. You can have too much port. How's your grandmother? Pretty lively?"

"She seems fairly well. She doesn't leave the house a great deal."

He showed a furtive anxiety when he learned she had taken cold.

"Keep her in bed if you can. But I don't suppose you can. She's an obstinate woman, Missie. We're all obstinate except you."

"Maybe I'm merely weak."

"Why?"

"I don't know. It's weak to drift along. I just let things

happen to me. Mom—my mother made a fight. And Eileen would if she needed to. She does it anyhow." She smiled at him, that twisted smile of hers with which she always deprecated herself. "Not that I have anything to struggle about, or to struggle for. Life has been very good to me."

Old Archibald cleared his throat.

"You're a woman," he said, "and you're soft. Fight 'em, Missie. You've got character. Fight your family if you have to. They're a domineering lot. I know them. Fight your husband too, if you have to. He'll think better of you if you do. My wife didn't, and I made a door mat of her; then when she was gone——"

He cleared his throat again, and Missie remembered him toiling over his graves. She shivered a little. Not that; oh never that. To fight, to be hard and selfish, and then to make one's atonement over a mound of earth, praying forgiveness with a trowel, shriving oneself with a rosebush, never.

Before she left he inquired again for her grandmother. She suspected a softening in him, an inarticulate desire for peace and reconciliation. But he said nothing more. When she offered him money he said that his old Masonic lodge was helping him, and that if she came again he wouldn't mind a bottle of Wesley's whisky, but that was all.

After that she went to see him regularly. She cleaned his room, took back with her his linen for washing, mended his worn socks. Now and then, too, she carried with her a bottle of whisky. Since he would drink he should have the best. But that was all she could do. Wesley was a true son of the nineties. His money was his. He earned it. His house, his servants, his wife, his money. She could buy the old man none of the small comforts.

She never knew why she clung to him, tended and cared for him. But then she never knew why she did a great many things.

The advancing spring brought her a certain relief. The endless dinners with their wines, their ritual of service with inadequate servants, the creaking dumb waiter, Wesley's quick irritable glances down the table at her, these were over for the season. And fewer people dropped in in the late afternoons. The golf links were ready, the new club house finished. And one evening Mr. MacDonald came to dine and brought with him a burly and dour-looking Scot, who spoke with an accent that left her helpless and in a language which was new to her, of greens and fairways and bunkers and pits, of niblicks and putters and cleeks.

They sat in the library later, on Wesley's hard tufted leather chairs, and pored over blue prints. Missie's head was aching. To the three men around the table there was no Missie; they were off in some man world of their own. But now and then Mr. MacDonald lifted his head and seemed to be waiting.

Then it came. From the pavement through the parlour windows came the delirious wailing of the bagpipes again. The Scot sat back, faintly amused, interested.

"That'll be Geordie."

"Eh, it's Geordie," said Mr. MacDonald.

Something caught at Missie's throat. She was a little girl once more, standing bare-headed on a curbstone, and before her strutted back and forth a magnificent creature from some strange and unknown land, making hideous entrancing sounds out of a plaid bag under his arm.

She burst into tears and left the room. When Wesley, astounded and discomfited, followed her, he found her face down on her bed, crying as if her heart would break.

"What's the matter? Are you sick?"

She shook her head.

"Then what's wrong?"

"I don't know. Nothing."

That angered him. He banged the door as he went out, and from the pavement still rose that raucous yet heart-breaking sound. She stopped crying, lay still. Did every newly married woman feel like this? Feel that life was over before it had begun, that no longer romance or adventure awaited, that she had reached the end of the road before she had even turned a corner?

She would have to explain to Wesley, but what could she say that he would understand? She had wept, not for herself, but for a little girl who long ago had stood on a curbstone, young and trustful and full of dreams which would never come true.

The next day she planted some morning glory seeds against the empty stable at the end of the lot. But the tall house shut off the sun, and the seeds only sprouted, turned yellow and died.

She felt better as spring advanced. The season was over, the house quieter, and her relations with Wesley had settled down into a humdrum cycle of daily life. If the compromises in any difference of opinion were chiefly hers, she was more or less trained to that; and she could not complain of him as a husband. He was unimaginative, his love-making purely amorous, but she felt that he was still being faithful to her. Like most women, she was intuitive in such matters.

He was growing heavier. That corpulence which was to be his the rest of his life was increasing. Sometimes he would have to borrow her button hook to fasten his stiff collar, and now and then she saw him stealthily inspecting the suggestion of a paunch in the glass.

"Got to get some exercise," he said one day. "This golf's going to be a great thing for me. It wouldn't hurt you either. Put some flesh on you."

"If it's to take it off you, how can it put weight on me?"

"You're a smart girl, Missie! With that brain of yours—— Where the hell's my scarf pin?"

"You put it back in the case."

He had innumerable scarf pins. The one he had bought for golf was a small mashie in gold, and his cuff links gold golf balls.

But those early days of the game tried him sorely. He was

a competent man; now he found himself, under the eyes of a patronizing Scot, struggling with the intricacies of a game that made him feel childish and inefficient. He would come home tired, and feeling that he had been tilting at windmills, but his pride was roused. Later on he became a scratch golfer; he had the coördination, the breadth of shoulder for the easy swing. But he was difficult and quarrelsome all that spring.

She was alone a great deal of the time. She had acquaintances but no friends; now and then a young woman or an older one called; they came in, silk linings rustling against silk petticoats. A man tailor had come to town; the tailor-made was the thing now. His coats were stiffly interlined with hair cloth. When they were taken off they were like plaster casts of the figure they had adorned. His silk-lined skirts trailed a foot or so on the pavements, and to hold them up there were cunning catches in silver. But elegant women let them trail, from carriage to door step, from door step to carriage. The ankles of the aristocracy were apt to be grimy those days.

Missie rustled down to see them. When they had gone she entered their names in a little book, and a week later she returned the call. She was twenty, and this was her life.

She rarely saw her grandmother or Adelaide. Now and then she prevailed on Wesley to go there for Sunday luncheon, but with difficulty. He had used them, he had consolidated his position, and now he was prepared to throw them overboard. She saw that, with those candid eyes of hers. Saw too that these women were lonely without her. They had not loved her, but she had brought them something. Now that final blooming was over. She ached with pity for them. Her grandmother looked older, more tremulous, and Adelaide's incoördinate jerking was more pronounced. She saw too that Wesley made them uncomfortable. He could afford to patronize them now.

She preferred going by herself, and it was on one such occasion that Mrs. Colfax sent Adelaide out of the room and then asked her bluntly if she meant to have children. She felt her colour rise.

"I don't know. Wes doesn't care for them."

"Probably not," said her grandmother drily. "He is self-indulgent. But you should have children, Marcella. That is the purpose of marriage; otherwise it is sinful. But you should have them anyhow. They—" she hesitated—"many a man has been held to his wife by his children. I am not judging Wesley. I daresay he is all that he should be. But you will not always be young."

"Sometimes I think I never was young."

She went away vaguely uneasy. Was she losing Wesley? She was maturing fast, and Stella's whisperings had a meaning for her now. She remembered Emily Beaumont's note, and knowing him as she did, she began to wonder if she had not been the anchor he had deliberately thrown to windward, to hold him from promiscuous association with loose women. Why else had he married her? He did not love her, in her sense of the word. He had no tenderness, no devotion. He made none but physical demands of her.

Suppose he had loved her? She thought about that too, walking home that day. She might have cared a great deal for him, if he had. She could care, she told herself. She had cared passionately for her mother, and there had been something deep and fine in the dreams she had built around Harry Sloane. But she must not think about Harry. Not now, not ever again.

After that she made an honest effort to care, to win him. It was a strange little drama that she played alone, with no one to see it. She made small timid advances to him, would touch his hand or stroke his sleeve. Sometimes he did not notice them. But once in so often he did, would turn on her, flushed, kindled, roused.

"You little devil! For all your quiet ways——!"

She began to wonder if all men were like that, but one day she watched Eileen, who wanted something at the moment,

lay her cheek against Tommy's, and saw his arm go around
her and his pale blue eyes soften. There was no passion there.
She began to see that there were certain spiritual values in
marriage and that Tommy had found them, even if Eileen
had not.

Wesley would never know that they existed.

She was restless that spring. She took long walks, mostly
alone. Sometimes she coaxed Adelaide to go with her, but she
was aware that her marriage had erected a gulf between them.
Poor Adelaide's eyes were full of furtive questions never
asked. She was filled with curiosities; sometimes Missie
found her eyes fixed on her, but she averted them quickly.
And Adelaide was abstracted, troubled, at times.

One afternoon Adelaide came to the house. She looked old
and tired, and her jerking was more pronounced than ever.
Fortunately there was nobody there. With the opening of
good weather the men were out of doors, bicycling, playing
tennis on private courts, driving their smart traps or struggling with the new intricacies of golf.

Adelaide wandered around the parlour.

"I was afraid you'd be out. It's a nice day. I saw a lot of
people at the Hemingways' tennis court."

"I play such bad tennis. I didn't learn exactly enough."

"I thought I saw Wesley there."

"Probably. He's trying to keep his weight down.

But her heart sank a little. Gus Hemingway had brought
home a new wife from Louisiana, a soft-voiced melting-eyed
girl who treated Gus with indolent scorn and all other
males with beguiling sweetness. She was a full-breasted
creature, opulent in her young curves, and Missie knew that
Wesley admired her. "Damned fine woman, Anna Hemingway," he had said. And, since Wesley was Wesley, the fact
that she was a Hemingway added to her attraction for him.

She forgot Anna, however, when Adelaide at last sat
down.

"Missie," she said, "have you any money?"

"Only the house money, Aunt Adelaide; and it is just enough."

"Could you get any from Wesley?"

She did not know. He was making money, she thought, but he was putting it into his business. And—what she did not say to Adelaide—he was parsimonious save where expenditure would show. What was the trouble?

Adelaide told her.

"We are behind in our taxes. I can't go to mother. I can't even tell her. She is getting feebler, Missie. I don't think I'll have her very long. And to lose the home where she's lived so long . . ." Adelaide's face worked, her chin quivered. She fumbled for her handkerchief. "She's all I have, Missie. I—I'm not rebellious, but if I'm left alone——"

She promised to see what she could do, and Adelaide left. But hitherto she had accepted Adelaide; now she began to think about her. After all, that was real tragedy; to be old and unbeautiful, living an empty life of vicarious existence; to have no one who cared greatly whether one lived or died, to have only further years to look forward to, and these empty ones—surely that was not living. It was only existing.

There was something of this in what she tried to say to Wesley that night, but it left him cold.

"I could have told you long ago that that was coming."

"Can't we do something?"

"MacDonald says they'll have to get out, or put a mortgage on the place. They have no business living there anyhow. Two women in that big place! It's ridiculous."

"Couldn't you take a mortgage, Wes?"

"I have other uses for my money. Look here, Missie, I haven't told you, but you might as well know. Your father's been after me too. I didn't marry your whole damned family, and the sooner they learn it the better."

Her colour rose, her hands trembled.

"I'm sorry. I didn't know."

But he was not easy himself. Not that he had any interest

in the Colfaxes; they had served his turn. But because he knew that their financial difficulties were already common talk. He could not very well let them be put out.

"Suppose I did take a mortgage?" he demanded truculently. "Do you suppose they'd ever pay the interest? They would not! There would be some hard-luck story or other, and where would I be?"

"They won't live forever, Wes."

"Adelaide's good for thirty years," he said brutally.

That night, stripped of his urbanity and his casual good humour, she felt that she hated him. Ultimately he did take a mortgage on the property, but she had reason to believe that he drove a hard bargain. He did not suffer, however. It was Wesley who, years later, sold the property to Tommy and Eileen, iron deer and all.

Chapter XVIII

SOMEHOW, somewhere in the first year of her marriage, the sense of her country began to invade Missie's consciousness. Perhaps it was old Archibald's incessant talk of the Civil War. He was full of tales:

"So we sat there, and what do you think those Rebs were doing? Singing, by God." And in his high old voice he would sing for her what he had heard, some never-to-be-forgotten night in his never-to-be-forgotten gallant youth.

"They were good fighters, those fellows," he said. "Right, too, according to their way of thinking. Slaves were property, and we confiscated them."

But he took an unctuous pleasure in that confiscation, nevertheless. "Served them right, Missie. Can't split up this union. United we stand, divided we fall. And never forget this. We're a great people. Pioneers, that's what we are. Even these immigrants, they've got the right stuff in them. It takes courage to start out for a strange land. Don't look down your nose at them, like your grandmother."

She listened. She hated war, all war. Why should men kill each other? Life was all they had. To throw it away——

"You liked it, didn't you?"

"Well," he said, "it's a sort of game. You get the other fellow or he gets you. Like baseball. Do you remember how your mother went to the baseball games? She was a handsome woman, Missie, and she knew it. Folks used to talk about her for going, too. Well, thank God we're progressive."

But at the house, too, the sense of her country began to creep in. This was the other side, however. Old Archibald had been one of its defenders; now came its exploiters, men

151

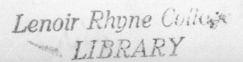

who talked of its natural resources as sources of revenue. They dreamed great dreams, these men, of development and the wealth to result from it, of steel, coal, and oil; of unlimited areas open to settlers, who had only to go there and dig their ploughs into the good warm earth; of immigrants settling on these lands, growing things, feeding the railroads which already were welding the country into a homogeneous whole.

She listened to them. They ate and drank and talked. Their faces flushed with excitement, they saw themselves rich, rich and powerful. Most of them added nothing to the country's productivity, but all of them were ready to fatten on it. Middlemen, brokers, bankers, promoters. Old Archibald in his shabby room waiting for his pension, and these others well fed, sleek, fat. Fat, like Wesley.

In August of that year she and Wesley went to the seashore. The seashore had become fashionable; it had for a time superseded those dreary mountain resorts where great wooden hotels, perched on some green height, spread their vast piazzas littered with rocking chairs, and thus brought nature comfortably to the indolent. Now the porches were abandoned, the cuspidors clean and bright, the bedrooms with their thinly mattressed beds unused, the croquet grounds grown up with weeds.

And, since the seashore was fashionable, Wesley went there. The Gus Hemingways had taken a cottage down the beach, others of their particular coterie were scattered here and there. At certain hours they met, the women in long skirted bathing suits, carefully corseted and stockinged. They bathed, dressed, drank cocktails together and then lunched. In the afternoons they slept, in the evenings they danced. Whole wardrobes were prepared for these outings, vast numbers of trunks were carried. Anna Hemingway was reported to have taken a dozen.

In this *milieu* Wesley was at his best. He swam well, he drank lustily, he ate a great deal. His jokes, not too delicate, kept the crowd in gales of laughter. He looked well in his bathing suit, too, although his waist line was creeping up. It was Wesley who organized the beach picnics and clam bakes, and Wesley who was the authority on that newly imported game called bridge whist. It was a strange formal game. The dealer bid, or failing to do it, "bridged" the bid to his partner who must name a trump suit. Then, amid laughter from the onlookers, the opponent on the left solemnly inquired: "May I lead, partner?" And the opponent on the right with equal sobriety replied: "Pray do."

The gay, tumultuous crowd sought amusement where it could. It hunted out shooting galleries and popped at clay pipes; it discovered obscure beer halls, sauntered in, the ladies lifting their delicate skirts above the sawdust and whispering comments behind their hands. And Missie, because there was nothing else to do, trailed with them. Always she was a little silent, a little aloof. Once when a band stopped suddenly she heard Anna Hemingway calling her the mouse. Anna was very polite to her after that, but the name stuck, and she knew it.

Gus and she sometimes sat together. He was a short man, very ugly, but with a charming smile. He had inherited money, and now he painted cows; his studio was hung with cows, and Anna had early named it the Stable. Nobody took his work seriously but himself; he would sit apart, saying little or nothing. Sometimes he watched his beautiful wife, and she would say: "Now hush! Gus is jealous, and he'll beat me when I get back."

Years later he did indeed beat her, and for cause; but in those early days he only sat and, Missie guessed, suffered.

She herself was miserable. She had not held Wesley, never would hold him now. Her little girl appeal for him was gone. If it was not Anna it would be somebody else. She grew quieter than ever, her hands often trembled.

One night Wesley brought matters to a head. She had been very silent all evening, and her remoteness continued after they got back to their hotel. Something had annoyed him, and he eyed her irritably as she set about her undressing.

"What are you sulking about now?"

"I'm not sulking," she said. "I just felt quiet."

"And why did you feel quiet?"

"I think," she said honestly, "it's all that noise. So much talking and everything."

"If you did some of it yourself you'd add a little to a party."

"I suppose I am not vain enough."

"And what do you mean by that?"

"You want their approval, don't you? You want them to think you're a good fellow, to admire you. Isn't that it? Well, you see I don't. Not that way."

He stared at her as though he had never seen her before. She had struck him in his weakest point, his vanity. She knew that his boisterous good nature in company was a part of that vanity, of his desire for approval.

"You're the hell of a wife," he jeered. "Just because I like people——"

"But *do* you?" She was not quarrelling. She stood by the side of their uncomfortable bed, virginal in her long white nightdress, her candid eyes fixed on his.

"Wes," she said, after a pause, "just why did you marry me? You knew what I was."

"Why does any man marry any girl?" he retorted. "The same old reasons, I suppose."

"But why do they marry one kind of woman, for certain qualities, and then want her to change? I sometimes think the very things you liked in me are the ones that most annoy you now."

"Oh, if you're going to argue——"

"I'm not arguing. I'm trying to think out loud, that's all. Wes, do you suppose that if we had a baby we'd be happier?"

"Oh, you're unhappy, are you?"

"I don't want our marriage to fail."

"It seems to me that's up to you."

She had hurt him. She should not have said that about approval, about being thought a good fellow. Her impulse was to go to him, to say she was sorry, to make once again her timid overtures toward peace. But she was afraid. She crawled into bed and lay carefully on the edge, so that the weight of his body on the springs should not throw her toward him.

The Anna Hemingway affair did not last long. One night —after they came home, that was—the door bell rang and Wesley went down to answer it. The maids had gone to bed. She heard a few words in an angry voice, Wesley expostulating, and then a heavy fall and the slam of the front door. When she ran down, terrified, Wesley was picking himself up from the hall floor and swearing furiously. Afterwards she knew that Gus Hemingway had knocked him down.

Strange quiet little man, with his charming smile, his painted cows, and his slow deliberate rages. Long years later she was to hear of him on the Argonne front. Clare, Eileen's girl, allowed there on her own tragic business, had seen him there in a Y. M. C. A. uniform. The enemy had been driven far back, and he was wandering over the bleak bare terrain. He had a musette bag over his shoulder, and he was searching the queer detritus of such places, the equipment abandoned before the charge; blankets, sweaters, old socks, rags for cleaning guns, even letters. When he found a letter he picked it up and put it into the bag.

He did not recognize Clare, but he seemed to think it necessary to explain what he was doing.

"There'll be a lot of them missing," he said. "If their folks get these letters back, they'll know where they were, anyhow."

Clare did not make herself known. She had an idea that he would not wish to remember, or to be remembered. And she had her own troubles to think of; tragic troubles, for Clare was looking for a grave.

That night at the house Missie found some raw beefsteak in the icebox and carried it up to Wesley.

"You'd better tie this on. You'll have a bad eye to-morrow."

He looked at her. His anger had gone; there was a boyish appeal for forgiveness in the one open eye he turned on her.

"Why should you care whether I have a bad eye or not?"

She made no reply, brought a bandage, helped him as best she could. And when she had finished he did one of the curious and touching things that men do. He caught her hand and held it to his lips. It brought tears to her eyes. Neither of them spoke. It was his plea for forgiveness, his promise of better things to come.

In two days he was able to face the world again. Gus Hemingway had gone to Europe, and there was talk of a separation, but nothing definite was known. On the third day Wesley brought home with him a diamond sunburst and presented it to her with a flourish. She saw that this handsome gesture of his was by way of evening the account between them, that he had written "paid in full" across it. But she wore the pin to please him. Anything to please him, to hold him.

By the following winter, however, she knew that she was not holding him. Her small tentative overtures no longer even aroused his passion. He was away from home a great deal; obscure business deals took him about the country. He came home, bathed and dressed, ate heavily, slept like a man exhausted. She dressed against these returns of his, wore her diamond sunburst, her watch with the bowknot, watched anxiously to see if he noticed, found that he did not, and went dully through the routine of her days. She was young, she had an enormous capacity for love, and she was left to stare ahead at nothing. Life was to be always like this; day after day, year after year, on and on for eternities of dreary time, until at last one joined the quiet sleepers on the hill.

Sometimes she felt that all the world was moving, and only she was standing still. The cable lines were being extended, some of the streets were being paved with Belgian block, telephones in private homes were common. Eileen's beautiful fair hair was dressed high off her face in a pompadour, the basis of which was a "rat" of woven wire, like Mrs. MacDonald's plumpers. And in that room at the factory Tommy was still tinkering with his engine. But the words "internal combustion" meant nothing to Missie, nor even to Eileen. Eileen was even impatient.

"Really, Tommy, the way your hands look is a shame. Either you'll have to stop playing cards, or stop this foolishness."

"It's a good sort of foolishness," said Tommy impassively. "It will make us rich, my dear."

And then one day he mounted his engine on a temporary body, little more to the eye than four wheels and a driver's seat, and took it out along a country road. It had no muffler. It was still a day of sparkers and mixers. Tommy, exploding along a remote lane, met Mrs. MacDonald driving in her victoria, a shawl over her wraps, another shawl around her knees. Very delicate, very haughty, was Mrs. MacDonald, seeking the far places where the street cars did not carry the rabble, or the street pavements of progress smack under her horses' feet. The top of the victoria was down; Mrs. MacDonald carried a tiny sun parasol to exclude her from the rays of the common autumn sun.

Then the horses ran away. They ran until they found a street paved with the new Belgian block, and there they threw her out on her head. One minute she was a lady, haughty and detached; the next she was thrust, willy nilly, into the vast concourse of the dead, forced to be one of them. No shawls even, no anything; taken naked into eternity.

Tommy had sputtered back after the team, and it was Tommy who found her. It was not the least ignominy of her end that he carried her into town, dead and all as she was, in the hideous contraption which had killed her.

It was months before he could look at it again.

But he went to Washington in the interval and applied for certain patents and he offered Wesley some stock in the new company. But Wesley declined.

"It's all right," he said. "I admit the automobile is here. But it's a luxury, and luxuries don't make business. Make safety pins and I'll buy stock, Tommy."

Alone, to Missie, he expressed his feeling about the automobile. It was just a trifle common; it would never take the place of fine big horses in shining harness, of the broughams and victorias and traps of the socially elect. Streets without hitching posts and watering troughs! Not in his time, or in hers. He went back and inspected the stable, where her morning glories had died.

"If all goes well, we'll have a carriage in a year or so. How would you like that, my girl?"

She did not care whether they had a carriage or not, but she pretended to be pleased. She was learning to pretend.

Tommy was not daunted. He went to Gus Hemingway, now back from Europe and living with Anna, but more detached than ever. And Gus bought stock. He went around to the factory and sat there day after day before he made up his mind. Then he went home and made a drawing—the one humorous drawing of his career—of a cow kicking over a milk pail as an automobile went by. He gave the car in the drawing a certain grace and dignity hitherto unknown, and strangely enough it was Gus's lines later on which first turned public attention to Tommy's machines.

Chapter XIX

APPARENTLY life was over for Missie Dexter. She had done her best, but her best was not good enough. She began to think of Harry again, still with that queer contraction of the heart; to dream of him was to escape. Life had trapped her, but if she could dream she was free.

She visited old Archibald, went to see her grandmother and Adelaide. Things were much the same there, save that Sarah was washing her hands more than ever; after callers had gone, after she had buttoned her boots, before and after food, after opening a letter. All day long she was running for water, for soap, for a towel. Her hands looked dry and withered. Doors were left open so she need not touch a knob. And Adelaide seldom went out. The increasing traffic had made the streets horrible to her; street cars and horses bore down on her from all directions, bicycles came at her with incredible speed. Better, far better, to sit in the house, roll spills, make cardboard wastebaskets, and at night steal down to the pantry and eat.

She was growing heavier. Mrs. Boroday sighed as she fitted the shelf-like bosom, those vast hips. She talked of Russia, and of the coronation of the Czar the year before.

"The little father!" she would say. "The little slave driver, say I. And don't you believe that the people went wild with joy. There's something coming to them. There has to be. Good folks starving, and the Czarina decked out with silver brocade and covered with pearls!"

But she did not say that Mr. Boroday alternated his wood carving with meetings of a highly incendiary nature.

Missie felt that whether she went or stayed away made little difference to Sarah or Adelaide. Sometimes she found her grandmother's eyes fixed with disapproval on her slim waist —she was very thin that winter—and she would flush. But they never mentioned Wesley to her. Relations with him had been definitely broken.

They were in financial difficulties, and no more checks went forward to Lambert. Once or twice he wrote Wesley, asking for a loan, only to be refused. Then one day that winter he telegraphed Missie to wire him a hundred dollars. The telegram was urgent and she went to Eileen.

"I have nothing, Eileen. If you——"

"Never," said Eileen furiously. "Let him starve. It isn't his fault we didn't."

But the moral pressure of that telegram pursued her. Wesley was adamant. She resorted to subterfuge, bought a dress, returned it, and asked to allow the charge to stand and the cash to be given to her. She did it through Mr. Taylor, and she told him her reasons. Mr. Taylor was willing to accommodate her; the store was not unused to such requests, at a period when few wives had any money of their own but unlimited credit. But he was shocked, also.

"It's not like you, Missie. You don't mind my calling you that, do you? Your dear mother—— But why do something that is not quite honest for—for a man who deserted you?"

"He's been sick, he says. And I can't let him starve, Mr. Taylor. For mother's sake, I can't do it."

She showed him the telegram, and he read it. She looked at him; he had dyed his hair and his long moustache, but they only served to make him look older. His frock coat was shiny, the silk facing was worn, his jauntiness was gone. Suddenly she was sorry for Mr. Taylor. Life had done things to him too. What had he to look forward to? A few more years of standing on tired elderly feet, a few more years of holding back age and decrepitude, and then what? A home for aged men, perhaps, or a little room like old Archibald's, stuffed with the memories of a lifetime of ineptitude.

She got the money and sent it, and that night she told Wesley. There was a violent scene; at one time she thought he was going to strike her. And he left her defenceless, for now that it was too late he maintained that he would have given her the money. She knew it was a lie, and that he knew she knew it; that his anger was because she had hurt him in his sensitive pride of place.

"My wife, my *wife,* resorting to a dirty dishonest trick like that! What do you suppose Carter thinks?"

"I didn't suppose you would care what he thinks. He is in trade, isn't he?"

But it appeared that while socially people in trade did not exist, the business world was different. They were directors in banks and what not; they granted or withheld "credit" whatever that might be, they served on the newly formed chamber of commerce; they whispered and society trembled. All this glory of being of the socially elect, then, was a factitious one. It was an empty gesture.

Wesley saw Mr. Carter the next day, and made his own explanation of the affair, but that quarrel marked a definite milestone in their relationship. There was often surliness in his manner to her, his suavity was thinner, his demands of her fewer.

She had lost him. Perhaps she had never had him. But she did not blame him; she was even sorry for him. He had married the wrong woman, that was all. He was not particularly happy; she thought sometimes, watching him in a crowd, that he too was lonely. As lonely as she was.

She did her part, sat, in the good clothes he bought her, at the foot of his noisy table during innumerable dinner parties, watched the service, listened to the eternal creaking of the dumb waiter; oysters, soup, fish, entrée, sherbet, roast, salad with game, dessert, coffee, cocktails, wines, liqueurs. But she felt frozen. At the end she would rise, and the women would leave. The men smoked and drank; when they joined the women they were plethoric and sometimes amorous. One or two of them even made advances to her; once a man next to her stooped for his napkin and caught her ankle. She paid no attention.

In the daytime she sewed, read, took her aimless walks, received calls and made them. She was twenty-two; her eyes and hair were still lovely, but her colour had gone. There was a wistful look about her; once or twice she found herself sitting opposite Wesley at the table and staring at nothing. When he spoke to her she seemed to come back from far away, yet she could not remember from where. Sometimes she looked at herself critically in the mirror, turning this way and that; she must not do that. It reminded her too much of Stella. Stella Colfax, 1850-1892.

Would she ever do that, she wondered? Simply come to the end of the road and lie down? There must come a time in most lives when the tired spirit flagged and longed for rest, or when the scale tipped, and effort did not balance with result. Did any one ever lie down to die, simply because there was nothing to live for? And she found herself crying, without knowing why she cried.

Late one afternoon in February she went to see old Archibald. She found him surrounded by newspapers, and in a state of great excitement.

"Well, they've done it at last!"

"Done what?"

"They've sunk the *Maine*. That pusillanimous bunch of politicians in Washington can't overlook that. The country won't let them. By God, the country has bowels, if those fellows haven't. McKinley! The poor spineless worm!"

"But just what——"

"War," he bellowed. "Good God, woman, don't you know what's going on in your country? We'll fight these damned Spaniards and lick the pants off them."

"War!"

Another war. Men killing each other. "If you didn't get them they got you." It was dreadful, of course, but it was far away. And it could not touch her. Woman-like, that was her first thought. It couldn't touch her. Then she remembered Harry; Harry in a uniform. Harry would go to this war. She went pale, but old Archibald did not notice. His knotted old hands worked, his eyes flashed. Those dirty Spaniards had thumbed their noses long enough at Uncle Sam. If he were twenty years younger, ten years, even——

There were tears in his eyes; not because there would be a war, but because he was too old to enjoy it. Men were incomprehensible. There was nothing mysterious about women. Women grew up, men never did. They were children, fighting, blustering, occasionally wistful children. And Harry——

She felt dizzy as she went down the stairs.

Then for two months nothing happened. Old Archibald waited in his chair and toward spring in his bed. Mark Hanna and McKinley were both holding out against the hysteria of the country, but old Archibald was counting on a young man named Roosevelt, Assistant Secretary of the Navy.

"He's got bowels, that fellow," he said. "He's a fighter, Missie. You keep your eyes on him."

In April war was declared, and things moved fast after that. Out in Texas this young Roosevelt had gathered together the strangest group of men that ever stood in shoe leather and was helping to mould them into a homogeneous mass. College men, cowboys and Indians, they flocked to this new adventure. In one of Carter's windows there was a dummy in the Rough Rider costume, and crowds stood there all day. All over the country men were preparing for war. They were gathered together, equipped for the tropics with heavy blue flannel shirts, with blouses and long trousers over which went their canvas puttees, with cape overcoats. Then they were put into trains and disappeared. Some few of them got to Cuba; most of them were held in camps that were pest holes, from Virginia to Florida.

But the crowds did not know this. The bands played gaily.

They played Good Bye, Dolly Gray, or There'll Be a Hot Time in the Old Town Tonight. The crowds cheered and waved their hands; the soldiers cheered and waved back. "Good-bye, Dolly, I must leave you——"

One day Missie stood in front of Carter's window, and felt a hand on her elbow.

"I thought it was you!"

It was Harry Sloane, looking down at her with his whimsical smile. She had thought she had schooled herself, but her heart gave the same familiar pang. She could not even smile back at him.

"You don't look so well, Missie. You're thin."

"I'm all right. I'm just surprised."

"And what do you think of all this?" He indicated the window.

"I suppose we have to fight."

"Yes," he said, gravely. "I'm going, you know."

She nodded. Her throat was tight.

"Better get it over and done with. It's been coming for a long time."

How little he had changed. She felt older than he, maternal; and she felt very young. Young and helpless.

"Why should you go?" she demanded, suddenly. "There are plenty without you."

"If we all said that, there would be nobody to go." He glanced down at her. "Missie, do you know what I was doing the night I read of your engagement in the paper?"

"How can I know?"

"I was deciding to beard the iron deer in his den, and ring your doorbell!"

The next moment, whimsical smile and all, he lifted his hat and left her.

One night very soon after that she stood alone on a bridge over the railroad cut and saw the troop train pull out. The car windows were full of boys, cheering. When the train had passed she still stood there. Long ago she and Stella and

Eileen had stood on this same bridge in the dark and waited
for something. There had been people everywhere, as now;
the embankments were lined, the bridge itself. She had
climbed the railings.

"Mom, make Missie behave."

"Get down, Missie. Be quiet."

She had dangled her button string over the edge. It was
late. She was very tired. And the people were quiet, quiet
and still.

"I want to go home, mom."

"Hush up, or I'll slap you."

"Here it comes," muttered the crowd. There was a slow
puffing of an engine; the men took off their hats, the train
moved underneath the bridge was swallowed up in darkness.
Missie felt the hot breath of the engine. It startled her.

"Mom!" she wailed. *"Mom!"*

Stella jerked her arm for quiet, and so it was that the
funeral train of the martyred Garfield carried along with it
Missie's first button string.

The brief war went on. "Not enough war to go round,"
somebody said. The ones lucky enough to get to Cuba had
their troubles; officers fighting for troop trains to get their
men to over-crowded transports, in mud and flies by the
millions. Fighting even for transports! And once aboard,
lying for days in a tropical ocean, with no cooking facilities,
until some canard of enemy ships was exploded. Then the
long heated journey, the landing of troops on a desolate
shore, the immediate movement forward into the jungle,
without transport or supplies, along trails known to the
enemy and under fire. And that enemy using smokeless
powder and not to be located, while every shot from the
American lines betrayed them.

No food, no shelter. Roosevelt and other officers riding
back and down, and bringing up food supplies. Heat, rain
and mud; bad uniforms and no tents. No field hospitals for
the sick and wounded, few ambulances. A bit of fighting,

heroic, high spirited, and then weeks of lying around in tropical rains, malaria eating them alive.

And Missie waited, without knowing for what she waited.

Better news from the Pacific, however; the white and buff fleet at Hong Kong having been painted the new battleship gray, it started south toward Manila; nearing their goal the ships stripped for action. Gratings, chests, even the wardroom chairs and tables were thrown overboard, the handsome mahogany partitions ripped out and heaved away. A trail of floating lumber marked their course. Men and officers stood or sat where they could. A fighting man, a harsh disciplinarian and fine officer named Dewey, faced his situation. He was far from his base, with only the routine supply of ammunition and not too much coal. He struck and struck hard. He was equipped for only that one blow, but it was enough. The Spanish fleet was quickly destroyed. When it was over he found that he had used only half his ammunition.

Three weeks later, and only then, did he know that he was a hero. His officers, reading the American papers for the first time, learned that they had conducted a Crusade, that Dewey was the great Crusader, an officer and a Christian; smashing at a blow the strangle hold of cruel Spain on the innocent Filipinos. And through the open hatch over their heads they could hear Dewey, after the manner of sailors, addressing his Creator but not in prayer!

When Missie learned that the local boys had not got to Cuba she breathed again. Harry was safe, after all. He was in a camp in the South, safe.

But the news was not so good, at that. As the summer went on typhoid was ravaging the camp. The bodies of men dead of it were brought back, and military funerals wended their way up the hill to the cemetery. The troops were dying like flies. There were no facilities for handling the epidemic; the field hospitals were unequipped for caring for its victims. And the men were dying, not only like flies, but because of flies. Camp sanitation was elemental; rains washed down the bare hillsides, flooded the latrines, washed out the refuse pits, and onto this filthy surface came the flies in uncountable millions. They spread germs everywhere; nothing was safe from them.

Tommy left the factory one day and went down to the camp. On the way back he stopped in Washington. The War Department was unhappy and therefore blustering.

"What the hell did these boys volunteer for, if they wanted feather beds?"

But Tommy had learned how to do things by that time. He saw the mayor, saw the city council. They had hospitals; he wanted these boys back, to be nursed and cared for. His sloping shoulders were stiff; his pale blue eyes hot. They listened to him, were convinced, agreed.

"I can't see why you're so worked up," said Eileen.

He tried to tell her, of men lying delirious, lips and teeth covered with sores, of occasional maggots, of no nurses but camp orderlies, often no bed pans, no charts, no ice bags. Philadelphia had already prepared a train to go South and gather up her boys. They must do it here.

She listened. It offended her sense of the niceties, that story, but she made no further objection. And in the end he got his train. He sent men from the factory to rip out the seats, installed cots and nurses; the baggage car was the diet kitchen and refrigerator room. He ordered milk, whisky, alcohol for sponge baths, sponges. He had his pick of medical men. He got a right of way for his train, pushed through madly, sitting on a box in the baggage car and checking over his supplies.

The day they started Missie went to see him.

"I suppose I can't go, Tommy?"

"Needing only trained help, Missie. I'm sorry."

"I would do what they told me. And I am—kind, Tommy."

He patted her shoulder. He loved Ellen—confound that "Eileen" business—but Missie often touched his heart.

"Sorry, Missie. It can't be done."

She went away again, a trifle dull, a bit apathetic.

The train arrived, loaded up. People cheered it along the way back, handed in flowers, fresh milk, fresh butter. The men on the cots raved; they thought they were in heaven. The baggage car issued its broths, its ice, its fresh cold milk. Each car was a ward, sweet and clean.

Missie sat at home and waited. Harry was down with the fever. Something of Stella's fatalism had descended on her, however. She was even aware that the Harry of her dreams and this tall young man with the whimsical smile were not the same. But as she had wept for the little girl who had listened to the piper, so many years ago, so now she grieved for the boy who had grown up and gone to a war.

And so, in August, she wept when she learned that he had died.

She felt loss rather than any wild grief, a curious sense of emptiness. On the day of the military funeral she stayed in the house and closed the windows, lest some strain of martial music come to her ears. She sat in the bedroom which was hers and her husband's and sewed doggedly. When Wesley came home he found her there in the hot dusk, her work in her lap.

"For God's sake! This house is like an oven."

She looked at him strangely.

"It's all right now. You can open the windows."

She saw him watching her at dinner, puzzled.

BOOK IV

Kirby Phelps

Chapter XX

WITHIN a year of the turn of the century now. Eileen wearing a turquoise ring surrounded by small diamonds, and patent leather shoes which "drew" in hot weather and hurt her feet, dressing up for evenings in Irish lace and exchanging her black lisle stockings for black silk ones; white fur rugs in front of the fireplaces, a new thing called a piano-player which one pushed in front of a piano and which hammered the keys with wooden fingers tipped with felt; old ladies still wearing caps and crocheted watch guards, but the younger ones wearing boas and tippets, and studying the Grecian system of physical culture to acquire grace; feathers, the demi-toilet, where a change of bodice transformed a costume into a dinner or theatre outfit.

A queer age, when Packard still meant a piano and Peerless an ice cream freezer. Only recently, two years before, the first moving pictures had been shown in New York, and the audience had leaped in alarm when a surf picture had shown it waves apparently about to sweep over it. Now out in a barn in Hollywood certain pioneers were making a picture or two, trying out the California climate.

A queer age, but withal an age of grace for women, of delicate trailing fabrics, of laces and flounces. Missie, with her soft hair piled high, a knot of tulle or a velvet rose in it, with her beautiful trailing gowns, her candid eyes, her sensitive mouth, her slender figure, Missie was very lovely at that time. Very lovable, too, had there been any one to notice it.

But there was no one. Even old Archibald had finally died. His mind failed him toward the end, and he babbled queer things, like the matter of the Five Pointed Star which became the Shield of David and the Seal of King Solomon. In a lucid moment one day he gave her his army sword in its battered scabbard. The Masons buried him, marching him in state up the long hill he had climbed alone so many years.

Missie had been startled to find that his death was a blow to her grandmother. After his death she and Adelaide helped Sarah up the stairs to the shabby room, now tidied by Missie's own hands, where the gaunt handsome old body lay on the bed.

Adelaide was jerking, but Mrs. Colfax was very still. There were none of the difficult tears of age. She sat down, her neat veil pinned under her aged chin, her indomitable figure erect, her face gray and pinched. And she looked at that dreadful room before she said anything. Then she spoke to the old man on the bed:

"I'm sorry, Archibald. I didn't know it was as bad as this."

Then she bent her proud old head and—maybe it was to bring sanctity into the place—she repeated the Lord's Prayer. "And forgive us our trespasses as we forgive those who trespass against us." Her voice never faltered.

When she had finished she took off her gloves, laid a hand on his cold forehead, and immediately went to the cracked basin and washed her hands.

Adelaide was blubbering, poor Adelaide whose very grief was unlovely. Missie wondered why she grieved; she had not liked the old man. Perhaps she wept for herself, for her own approaching loneliness, for her own fruitless years which could have but this empty end. Much grief was like that.

And so Missie was twenty-four. Some of the evanescent charm of her youth was gone, but there was a quietness and a steadfastness about her that were somehow beautiful. She had lived vicariously many lives, but never her own. There were untouched depths in her, of pity, of kindness, of generosity. She had asked only to be allowed to live and to serve,

and apparently her love was not wanted nor her service
needed.

Wesley was being unfaithful to her; she knew that now.
She suffered him on those rare occasions when he approached
her, but she no longer wanted to bear him a child. A child,
yes; she fairly ached for one. But not his child.

She had decided that after a visit one day to Mrs. Wilkinson.

Grove Street was changing. The trees which had given it
its name were dying off; some said leakage from the gas
mains had killed them; a branch of the cable cars now ran
where once its cobbles had echoed only to the feet of horses
and the milkman's bell; the laundry had gone, where so long
ago a girl had had her hand caught in a new machine for iron-
ing collars, a thing of two cruel hot rollers; and a new school
was being erected on its site, a bright, cheerful-looking school,
with wide doors and many windows, and a playground with
swings.

And Mrs. Wilkinson had changed also.

She was no longer the hearty rather Rabelaisian woman of
Missie's childhood. She had had some money in Pennsyl-
vania oil and now the oil was gone. She was taking in sewing.
The parlour was her work-room, and she apologized for it.

"Seems like I just can't keep the muss off the floor," she
said. "I clean up every night, but it's as bad again the next
day."

She had an Irish girl named Delia helping her to sew, a
silent efficient person. Mrs. Wilkinson confided to Missie that
she was queer.

"Always talking about freedom for the Irish," she said.
"Free! They're free enough around here. There's an Irish
cop on this beat, and the amount of lip I've had to take from
him is a caution." She lowered her voice. "There's a bad house
next door," she said solemnly. "Your old place."

"Surely not! Mr. Elliott——"

"Mr. Elliott's out for what he can get. I've told the cop; I said: 'If you don't believe me come and look over my fence. The yard's full of beer and whisky bottles. And those shameless hussies running around in their bare feet, and the Madam's got a voice you can hear a mile.' But they pay for protection. What's the use?"

Missie was horrified and sickened. She had invested the little house with a certain sanctity; it was as though she were its child, and now to find it debauched shocked her beyond words. Mrs. Wilkinson went on:

"They say the Madam's had a come-down in the world. Used to run a fine place somewhere. But what I say is, why come down on me? She's a big flashy woman, but I'm not afraid of her. Only yesterday I heard her in the yard, and I called over the fence to her. I said: 'Miss Beaumont, if you——' "

"Beaumont!"

"That's her name. Emily Beaumont. Well, I said——"

Missie got up.

"I think I must go. I'm sorry, Mrs. Wilkinson. I loved the house, you know. It's rather awful——"

Her face was frozen into immobility as she started back home. It was her first actual knowledge of vice. And she knew now that it was out of such a life as this, such a house—better perhaps, "a fine place," but equally sordid, equally sickening —that Emily Beaumont's letter had come the day of her wedding.

But what could she do? Stolidly, with something of Stella in the set of her shoulders, she went back to Wesley's house, to Wesley's bed, to Wesley.

She had made her contract. She would go through with it. But she would not bear him a child. She tended her house, her graves. There were a number of them now; Stella, Mr. Wilkinson, old Archibald and his family. And she watched over Wesley, made him comfortable, studied his tastes.

"You need some new socks, Wes. Shall I get them?"

"I'll do it. Never mind."

He was increasingly fastidious about himself; his underwear was the finest he could buy. He used heavily scented soaps, talcum powders. He had a vast array of ties, of scarf pins, of sleeve and waistcoat buttons. His pajamas were of heavy silk, his shirts were made to order. She closed her eyes to all this.

"What would you like for dinner, Wes. Anything special?"

"What's the use of asking me right after breakfast what I want for dinner?"

There was occasionally a smouldering anger in her, but she controlled it. And when the dinner came in she watched him, to see if he was satisfied, if she was doing her job, going through with it.

No Harry now; no dreams. Do the job, get on with it. Keep the contract.

Then one day Tommy invited her to the shop. He had made tremendous strides since that early engine of his on its grotesque *chassis*. He had built a real car this time, although still an experimental one. There was no talk in those days of quantity production, no vast assembling room. In a wooden shed built behind the repair shop and cluttered with machinery was the one car, and around it a group of men. Gus Hemingway was sitting on an empty box in a corner, and a tall man in overalls was adjusting something under the hood. Tommy was excited, prideful.

"Phelps, I don't think you've met Eileen's sister, Mrs. Dexter. How's it going now?"

They both apparently forgot her. It was a hot day, and the shop was blazing. Gus gave her his box and sauntered away; the engine was running without a muffler, and the noise was terrific. Suddenly she found the tall man in front of her with a glass of water.

"Thought this might help a little. We're not used to ladies here. We're apt to forget our manners!"

She liked him at once. Up to that moment she had hardly differentiated him from the mechanics about; now his cultivated voice identified him. He was the gas-engine expert Tommy had had working with him.

"Thanks. It is warm, isn't it?"

He went back to his engine, but once when some points of interest came up he took her over to the car again. He seemed to take her intelligence for granted; he even went to the trouble to explain the principle to her.

"I'm afraid I'm very ignorant."

"How could you know anything? As a matter of fact, these internal combustion engines are comparatively new to all of us. We are just feeling our way ourselves."

"Eileen says this will make you all rich."

"It may. I could use it if it came!"

He considered the question, rubbing his chin with a greasy hand.

"I'd like enough money to be independent. That's all money means to me, to have independence, to—to own my own soul. But you wouldn't understand that."

"Why not? I have been very poor."

He looked at her more intently. "I thought you were a Colfax."

"On one side. On the other I am the daughter of a burlesque actress whom my father deserted."

She was amazed at that impulse of honesty. Not in all these years had she so mentioned Stella. She found herself looking around to see if Tommy had heard, but Tommy was at the door of the shop; there was nobody near. Phelps was looking at her still more intently.

"You poor child!"

She was queerly emotional; quick tears rose in her eyes. "I shouldn't have said that."

"Why not?"

"I am prouder of being her daughter than of being a Colfax, Mr. Phelps."

"But you are having to be a Colfax these days, eh?" He

smiled down at her with his quick understanding. "That's a curious combination. And what has it done to you?"

"I don't understand you."

"What goes on inside of you? You must have two entirely different inheritances and training. Don't you ever fight with yourself?"

"I don't think about myself very much."

"Then don't," he told her. "It's dangerous business, turning one's mind in."

He was practical after that, showed her the engine, even tried to explain to her.

"You see, until now engines have been driven by steam, by power externally applied. Now we are burning our fuel inside the engine itself. And so——"

She listened to his voice, soft and kind. Something that had been hard and tight in her heart seemed to relax. She drew a long breath. What difference did it make that she had not the slightest comprehension of what he was saying? He was being kind, kind to her. She felt as though no one had ever been kind to her before.

She went home faintly exalted. It was a hot day in early autumn. She took off her dress, bathed, put on a thin blue silk negligee trimmed with flounces of white lace. She had been keeping it. Now for some reason she wanted to put it on; to be shimmering and fresh and cool; to be beautiful. She had no idea why.

She had not changed when Wesley came home. For some time now he had treated her largely as a part of his background; he came home to her as he came home to clean linen, to a good dinner, to a comfortable chair. But he eyed her with a certain appreciation that evening. She had a faint colour, her eyes were luminous.

He stood over her.

"Looking very pretty to-night, my girl."

He stooped—it was not as easy for him to stoop as it had been—and kissed her. And something in that gesture alarmed her; its easy possessiveness, the hand he placed on her bared arm. She got up, moved away. And he laughed a little, not annoyed. She was his. He had but to reach out and take her.

She waited until he had gone to his bath, then she tore off the blue gown. It was not for him to touch, to soil. And when he came back he found her in sober garb, regarding him with eyes that disquieted him.

"Wesley," she said, "I think I ought to tell you. I'm not sleeping well. I am going to move."

He was alert at once, suspicious, standing there in his undershirt, the buttons stretched tightly over the protruding flesh.

"Move? Where to? Out of the house?"

"Out of this room."

There was a rigidity about her that he did not like, a determination. What did she know? His mind was working fast, over this and that. Something must have slipped up somewhere. He picked up a shirt, began putting in the buttons.

"If you're not sleeping you'd better see a doctor."

"I shall try the other first."

She moved that night. Not far, only into the adjoining bedroom. Wesley, sitting and ostensibly reading in the library, heard her going back and forth. What did she know? What had slipped up? He got a decanter of whisky and some soda, and drank himself comfortably to sleep in his chair.

Chapter XXI

AFTER that she did not see Kirby Phelps for a week. He had apparently come into her life, served his purpose and vanished. The week was an uncomfortable one, for she had not only moved. She had locked herself in. One night she heard Wesley trying the door, but he went away quickly. She began to suspect that he was frightened, that he was carefully preparing a defence against attack, and that when she did not attack he was worried.

At the table she would catch him looking at her furtively. But as the days went on he gained reassurance. She was too matter of fact with him, he reasoned. She was honest, too; he knew that. If she had known anything concrete she would have said so. He eased a little. At the end of the week he bought her a bracelet.

"It's beautiful, Wes. Thank you."

He tested her, then and there.

"Don't I get a kiss for it?"

She understood, and there was pity in her; pity for his weakness, for his loneliness, for the hold of his flesh over him. She kissed him. But he could not let well enough alone.

"You've locked me out, my girl."

She looked him squarely in the eyes then.

"Are you sure it makes any difference, Wes?"

There was the issue, brought to the surface at last. And he could not face it. He muttered something, turned away. What did she know? What had slipped up?

It was the next day that Phelps came to call. It was a Saturday afternoon, and although such things as general Saturday half holidays were unknown, the prosperous business men were already using it for that new word in their vocabularies, "play." Wesley was at the golf club and Missie was alone.

She hardly knew him without his overalls. He was not handsome, but he had distinction, ease, poise. He sat in one of Wesley's over-stuffed, over-plushed chairs, and somehow it became pretentious and ugly.

"So you don't play golf?"

"I am not good at games."

"You ought to play good tennis. You have the build."

"I wanted to, dreadfully, when I was a little girl. There was a court near us. But naturally they didn't ask me!"

"Why naturally?"

And then she found herself telling him about that childhood of hers; the little house, the people who visited about on the front steps in summer but never came to them; Mr. Wilkinson and the morning glories. Small buried things that she thought she had forgotten. And he sat watching her, drawing her out. When she stopped she was ashamed.

"Why am I telling you all this? I haven't even thought of it for so long."

She was more withdrawn after that, but he appeared not to notice it. It was curious, he said, how people clung to their childish memories. He himself—— Perhaps it was because one would, if one could, always be young. Of course, sometimes it was because what came later was less pleasant. There were worries, frustrations——

"You are very unlike your sister."

"She is more practical. She is satisfied to live each day as it comes."

"And you are not?"

She pondered that, honestly.

"I don't know. I seem either to be looking back or looking ahead."

He did not stay very long, and when he had gone she felt that something warm and vital and kind had gone out of the house; she went upstairs and stood staring at herself in the mirror. Her colour had come back.

Afterwards Missie always thought of her life story as a triumph of the ordinary. It had all the usual elements, the boyhood sweetheart, the unfaithful husband, the kind lover. In a way it was not a story at all. It was life, life as millions of women live it. But it had its elements at that, its stark tragedies, its pathos, its bathos. That was life, too; not too consistent, not too good or too bad. Bearable, because of hope; and the thing hoped for not coming, but something different. Better or worse.

She and Kirby met occasionally after that at Eileen's. Tommy had built a new house in the suburbs. It had hardwood floors, and rugs, and a nursery for little Clare that was a model. Not that Eileen saw much of Clare. She was too busy.

It was a noisy house; Eileen was making her way by amusing people. In the afternoon it was like Missie's that first year, except that women came as well as men, women without their husbands and men without their wives. It was said that Mrs. Hemingway and the conservatives called her fast, but Eileen only laughed. Kirby Phelps seemed amused at these gatherings, but apart from them. He was a temperate man, and as the voices rose he would wander outside and stand on the wide verandah of the new house. On the few occasions when Missie went there he would take her with him.

"Come out and get some air. They'll never miss us."

Nor did they.

He would put Missie into a chair and talk to her. He had strange dreams; the horse was doomed, except for pleasure, men were going to fly in heavier-than-air machines. They would cross oceans, and set up new standards of time and distance; under-sea boats would be practical. Had she ever read *The Mysterious Island?* Well, read it; he would send it to her. Queer how every discovery was an idea first. Man was God's idea, when you came to think of it. First there was a vision, and then there was a fact. She would listen, try to follow him into this new realm of his. And from behind them through the open windows would be coming shrill voices, shrill laughter.

He was young—not thirty, to Wesley's more than forty— enthusiastic, lovable. Sometimes he would take an old envelope out of his pocket and with a few lines show her something. She wanted desperately to understand. She would look on anxiously. Suppose he thought her stupid? He was taking all this trouble with her, and she was stupid.

One day he said to her abruptly:

"You are not very happy, are you? You look as if you could be, but you are not."

"I don't know. I don't think about it."

"But I think you do. Is there anything to be done? You don't mind my asking that, do you?"

"You are doing a great deal. You are giving me something real to think about. And——"

"And what?"

She wanted to tell him that his interest in her was important to her, that the effort he was making was not lost on her, that she was grateful; more than grateful. But she had no easy speeches, like Eileen.

"You are being very good to me."

"Good to you! Good God! Do you suppose I'm being kind to you?"

"You are, whether you mean it or not."

Perhaps about that time he began to see that he was falling in love with her, for there came a long interval when she did not see him. Part of that time he was off selling stock in the new company and arranging for the building of a factory. And once he went to Washington; he had designed a powerful engine for a truck body, and was more interested in it than in the passenger car.

She found that while she missed him, he occupied her

thoughts even more during these absences. Like Stella, she built her house of dreams into a castle. She loved him; nothing else mattered. Then he would come back and there were the sordid facts to face. She was a married woman, in love with a man who still called her Mrs. Dexter, who told her his own dreams, great dreams indeed, but not for her. He had never shown her that he loved her. She was a shameless morbid creature who could lie in her bed at night and hug a warm secret to her breast, and who hated the daylight for the space it put between them; her husband moving about his room, the running of water into the tub, the odour of steam, of soap and of his big heated body when she followed him there; his wet towels on the floor, his razor drying on the window sill.

When she began to realize that this was love at last, she was frightened. She wept over it, prayed over it. All the sentiment which had clothed her virginal dreams of Harry Sloane, all the passion of her maturity, all the grief of her thwarted life went into that love of hers.

It was the great sex passion of her life.

Yet—such are the lives of women—these cataclysmic stirrings never showed on the surface. A few contacts which all the world might have seen, a sober going through of the days, even an attempt to be kinder and more understanding to Wesley, were all that marked it at least at first. If her hands grew cold under her tight gloves, if the pulse in her throat quickened under her high collar, who was there to notice it?

Whether the Kirby Phelps she loved so passionately was the man others saw, she neither knew nor cared. Just as in the end each individual creates the God he can worship, so she knew that every woman takes some man and builds around him the lover of her heart. Probably she recognized that he was of no heroic stature, no child of the Dragon's blood. But what did reach her was his kindness. He was kind to her. It touched her, made her heart swell. It was water on a thirsty land, it was a rock and shade in a desert. How could he know that she was dying of thirst and sun?

What was to come of it? She did not try to think. Once old Archibald had said of a man killed in battle: "That's the way to go. Have your big moment and then quit. That's all life is, Missie; a few big moments, and a damned long time in between."

But what big moment could there be for her?

She was never near to real beauty that winter. Kirby Phelps, watching her as he always did, wondered why she had not seemed lovely to him at first; sad and appealing she had been, but not beautiful. He had begun by feeling a great yearning, a pity; one day he realized that he was deeply in love with her.

He was an honest man; he liked to move and live in the daylight, and the first thing he did was to go to her. He was pacing the floor of the parlour when she came down, his hands in his pockets, his head bent. He wanted to know where he stood, what he was going to do. And he lost no time about it.

"Missie," he said, without sitting down, "do you care for me? Sometimes I've thought you did."

She looked at him with her candid eyes. She was not afraid with him. She could tell him anything and he would understand.

"I do care, Kirby."

"A great deal? I can ask you that, because I care so much for you."

"A great deal." Her voice shook. "A very great deal."

He hesitated, went to her, lifted her hand and kissed it. For all her directness there was something aloof about her, and the situation was too grave for light love-making.

"What would I better do? Go away?"

That frightened her.

"If you go away I shall have nothing left in the world. Nothing."

"But if I stay? That's worse, isn't it? You and I are not people to meet clandestinely."

"I've been very happy, just seeing you now and then. It was something to look forward to; something very precious, Kirby."

He was gentle with her. He tried to tell her that when a man loved a woman he wanted her; that he could not live on the bare bones of love, and when she understood him she coloured with distress. He saw that she was thinking of Wesley, of the animal urge in him; he knew Wesley and his kind, and he warmed with pity. "You poor child! You poor little girl!"

His arms ached for her. He put them around her without passion, and she let him hold her.

"It will be something to remember," she told him.

A rather pitiful little love scene, Missie drawing away, convinced of sin in that passionless embrace, Phelps more shaken with pity than love, but greatly loving nevertheless. And it got them nowhere. When he urged on her the right to happiness, to a divorce and a re-marriage, he could feel that she shivered. "It would hurt so many people," she said.

"Isn't it time to think of yourself?"

But he did not insist. He was a gentleman, and he was not any too comfortable, sitting there in Wesley's house and trying to steal Wesley's wife. He had his excuses, of course; he knew of Wesley's secret life. It was common talk. And he wanted marriage. He was no seducer. He wanted Missie as his wife, to cherish and protect.

When he went away nothing had been accomplished, except a clarifying of the situation between them. And life has its humours, if one can see them. That night at his club his bridge whist partner fell out and Wesley took his place. Kirby found himself saying gravely:

"May I play, partner?"

And Wesley with equal sobriety replied: "Pray do."

But there was nothing either humorous or playful in the

situation as it now stood between Missie and this tall young man who cared for her. As the weeks went on both of them felt the tension. They were conventional people, decent people. There was no security, no great happiness, not even much hope. Curiously enough, it was Missie who, knowing nothing of the outside pressure of public and private opinion, hoped the most. But even she was alternately exalted and depressed; she was even at times wildly jealous. One day she saw Kirby on the street with Anna Hemingway, and locking herself in her room, fell on her knees and prayed that she might keep him. Prayed and cried, abject, pitiable. And Kirby himself, waiting for weeks and nothing happening, found his own position untenable. He was having his own inner conflicts, his own jealousies.

"I can't go on indefinitely, Missie. And if you care for me and go on living with a husband— Have you ever thought how unbearable that is for me?"

"But I am not living with him."

He was more patient after that. He saw her now and then, at parties, at Eileen's. There were no secret meetings. There was a certain decorum, a gravity, about them when they met. They were no light-hearted lovers, but a man and a woman deeply in love and not too hopeful.

One day she told him that she wanted to tell Wesley. It startled him.

"It would be honest, at least," she said. "And he does not care for me. He might be glad to let me go."

"Not to another man," he told her grimly. "And if there is any talking to be done, let me do it. But you must be ready to take the step, Missie dear. It's irrevocable, you see."

She was afraid to have him do it. She knew Wesley, his violent angers, his sullen resentments. At the best there would be a brawl; at the worst— She did not know what to do.

Sometimes he sent her flowers. She would carry them jealously to her room, touch them, tend them. One day

Adelaide wandering in upset the vase, and Missie was suddenly angry.

"I'm sorry," said Adelaide.

She tried to pick them up, but Missie was before her. She would not let her touch them. It was as though Adelaide had desecrated an altar. And Adelaide stood by, furtively watching.

Through all of this Wesley came and went. He was still sullen, but he was less uneasy as time went on. She was not going to make a fuss, whatever she knew. And she would get over it. Women got over these things. Sometimes, however, he looked at her, as she moved about the house, sat across the table from him. She was devilish pretty these days, he thought. There was a new allure about her, the allure of the roused and passionately loving woman. He felt it without recognizing it. He began to make small advances to her again.

"That's a new dress, isn't it?"

"It's quite an old one."

"It looks different, or you do."

But he had lost his old self-confidence with her. He would remember the locked door and subside into sulky silence again.

His overtures alarmed her. She began to make her plans to tell him. She would rehearse the scene.

"It isn't as though you cared, Wes. There have been other women; there always will be other women with you. Don't argue. It's beyond that now. I'm letting you live your own life. But I have my rights, too. I want to be happy. I never have, you know. And now that I have found a good man who wants to marry me——"

She felt cool and capable as she rehearsed it.

But she never said it to him.

One night she left her door open, so that she might hear him when he came in. She meant to have it out with him then. But he was very late; she lay fighting sleep for hours, but finally she dozed off. When she wakened he was in the room, smiling down at her.

Chapter XXII

SHE was desperate after that, her position untenable, undignified, immoral. She needed help, but where could she go for it? Not to Eileen, so absorbed in her ambitions, so likely to resent any scandal which might thwart them. And Kirby was away again; not that she could have told him, but he gave her strength. For all his visions he was practical.

"Talk? Why should we care? We'll not be here to listen."

The automobile factory was to be on one of the Great Lakes. He was planning to live there.

And when she had mentioned her grandmother he dismissed her as easily.

"The world moves," he said. "The time is coming when even she will see divorce is more moral than marriage without love, Missie dear."

But she felt that Sarah and her kind were standing, in their own stiff-necked fashion, for something which had its value, for gentility, for that stoical pride which carried its griefs in secret and to the grave.

Missie thought of her grandmother, in those long hours when she sat alone and bewildered, of her indomitable body, so thin under its layers of clothing, its long woollen undergarment, its chemise, its corset cover, its flannel and white petticoats; of her thin white hands, of her long pale ears, of her rigid back; of her refusal to see that Adelaide was a mature woman, or that Lambert was other than a dutiful son. Of that strange habit of washing her hands, which she had begun when Cecily went away to bear a child; of old Archibald lying there, cold and handsome, and Sarah bowing her head: "Our Father who art in Heaven———"

She had survived him, big and strong as he had been. But women did live. They had enormous reserves, more reserves than men. They survived their men. All over the world were the Sarahs, lonely old women who had survived their men. Survived everything. She herself—she would live forever, on and on. She felt, for all her slenderness, a terrible inexorable vitality in her. Her mother had had it, too; had seen ages of unbearable time stretching ahead of her, and had refused to face them.

It made her desperate, that thought. She began to go to church again, seeking help there. But on her knees during the general confession, she would find herself trembling again.

"All we like sheep have gone astray——"

She felt like an adulteress.

One day she dressed carefully—Kirby was still away—and went to see Mr. MacDonald. She was shaking with fear, pale under her black tulle hat and the ermine tippet with which Wesley had repaid that open door. He was accustomed to paying for favours, was Wesley. But there was nothing formidable in the elderly man who sat behind the desk, untidy, uncared for, desolate, his empty sleeve tucked carelessly into his pocket. She felt a great wave of pity for him, and when she saw his eyes she had a burst of enlightenment. It was for the best that women survived. Old men alone, that was the greatest tragedy. They were so helpless. They looked out from wrinkled faces with the eyes of lonely small boys.

No, women had to survive them, to take care of them to the last, to hold tight to them at the end.

How could she talk to him of her own troubles, so trivial compared with death? The very effort he made to be casual made it harder for her.

"Well, well! And what can an old lawyer do for a prosperous and happy young married woman? How's Wesley? He looks well."

"I think he is. I don't see as much of him as I might."

"Well, that's to be expected these days. This drive **for**

success— He's a busy man. He'll go far, Missie." He cleared his throat. "Make him a good home, Missie. It's the woman who makes the marriage. That was your mother's mistake. She meant all right, but she nagged your father." He coughed again.

"There ought to be more to a marriage than that," she said, looking down. "There ought to be—loyalty, Mr. Mac-Donald."

He lifted a pen, put it down.

"You're young. By and large, a good many men wander a bit at first, but they settle down. They settle down, and they make the best husbands in the end. You——"

"And in the interval? I am not very happy, Mr. Mac-Donald."

That roused the Covenanter blood in him.

"Happy! We weren't put here to be happy. This new generation that is coming along, shouting its right to be happy, —it makes me sick! We're put here to do our duty, to take and carry on certain obligations, not to discard them. People come in here and talk to me about getting divorces! Divorce! What did that ever cure? If a human being fails in one marriage he'll fail in another. And marriage isn't only a civil contract; it's a religious one. It's a covenant with God."

She went away confused. With that terrible ability of hers to see both sides of a question she knew that he was right. But he was wrong too; he was both right and wrong. "Oh God, give me some help. Show me what to do." She walked along, tulle hat, ermine tippet, toes correctly turned out, her train lifted above the dust. Now and then she bowed to somebody she knew. Men took off their hats with sweeping gestures. That's Mrs. Wesley Dexter. Was a Colfax. Fine old family. Dexter's a coming man. Brother-in-law is Wilkins. Yes, the bicycle chap. Big man, Wilkins; head of the new Board of Trade. Coming man too. "Let me die, dear God, or else show me what to do. I can't go on, and I can't get out."

Two days later Sarah sent for her, received her alone in the great front parlour with the peacock lambrequin. Atropos she was as she sat there, the Inflexible One. And she began without preamble.

"I have no reason to love Wesley Dexter, Marcella. But I have reason to expect certain things from you. Mr. Mac-Donald tells me you have been to see him."

"I didn't know where else to go," said Missie simply.

"Does that mean that you are thinking of leaving your husband?"

"I don't seem able to think. Yes. I would leave him, if I could."

Mrs. Colfax glanced at the door.

"There is one word that I have never permitted in this house. That is divorce. I have never spoken to a divorced woman, and I never shall. I would not except my own grand-daughter; it would grieve me, but you must understand that, Marcella."

But after that ukase she was softer. Not gentle; she could never be that. But she sat back, twisting the worn gold band on her left hand. "I was not too happy in the early days of my own marriage; I had my rebellions. All young wives do. But I lived to be glad that no one but myself had ever known it."

She could be glad! Hard autocratic old William, Cecily, Lambert, Adelaide, and against all of them it was enough to have the consciousness of duty done. It was sublime. It was Spartan.

She sent Missie back in the carriage. It was very shabby now; it needed paint, and old Ishmael needed a new livery. The horses, too, were growing old; they looked bony, like Sarah herself; their feet slid on the newly paved streets. They moved slowly, cautiously, like old men at twilight.

Missie was very tired. She leaned back and closed her eyes. When she went home she wrote Kirby her first letter.

"I have been thinking things over. Maybe I am weak.

Maybe you will think I am ridiculous. But I think this is more than a question of Wesley and you and myself. I think God comes in too. I promised Him something, and now I am asking to take back that promise. I love you, I know I shall always love you. I did not believe that anyone could care as I care. I think maybe I have made you my God, and that is wrong. Indeed it is all wrong. When I think of all the people who would be hurt———"

There was more of it; she shed bitter tears over it, and had to re-copy it. She had never been able to write straight on unruled paper, and so, like Stella, she put a ruled sheet underneath.

But she never sent it. That night she fainted at the dinner table, and the next day she learned that she was to have a child. Wesley's child.

Chapter XXIII

KIRBY PHELPS came back triumphant from his long absence. The factory site was bought, the plans made. It was a great time in which to live, to be an engineer. A subway to be driven under New York City, rammed through the living rock; talk of a huge steel combine; new oil fields being opened up; skyscrapers thrusting up their stately heads; rumours of a new device for speech without wires. Not that he believed in that. It was ridiculous. But above all the automobile, steam, electric, gasoline. Still experimental, still to be tinkered with, improved, beautified, but come to stay. True, the country roads were still mud tracks in winter, thick with dust in summer. Thick with shed horseshoes, too. The nails tore into the tires, and farmers' boys stood about and jeered.

"Lend you a horse, Mister?"

But it had come. Sitting in the train he thought of Missie. He felt very happy, very tender, strong enough for both of them. He would marry her, and together they would face the future, that future which promised so much for an engineer. Why should not men fly? Take something on the principle of the box kite, put an engine in it, a propeller in the rear, like a ship. He watched the birds outside the window of the train.

When Missie learned that he was back she sent for Eileen, and Tommy brought her himself in the car. Not that first chassis of tragic memory, but the latest one. Tommy was thorough. He built, experimented, destroyed, re-built. Missie, white and sick, with her bloom gone and her eyes heavy with wakeful nights, had to go out onto the pavement and admire it.

Eileen followed her into the house. She had a brown veil tied over her large hat and a long duster over her clothing.

"Do you know what I thought as we came along? I wished Mother could have been with us. She'd have loved it, Missie."

Yes, Stella would have loved it. She would have loved the eyes turned on her; she would have sat up and thrown out her opulent bust, and missed no hint of the admiration she excited.

Eileen had removed her veil before the mirror. Now she turned and inspected Missie.

"What's the matter? You look sick."

"I'm going to have a baby," said Missie, apathetically.

"Well, it's time. Maybe Wes will settle down now. I must say——"

"Wes doesn't matter. Let him live his life and I'll live mine. Eileen, I want you to tell Kirby Phelps."

Eileen sat down suddenly.

"Missie Dexter! Are you trying to tell me that this is Kirby Phelps's child?"

"No." Her voice was still dull. "I want him to know that I am going to have one. That's all."

"What business is it of his?"

"I was fond of him, and he knew it. I wouldn't like him to come here now. It changes a good many things."

"What kind of things?" Eileen demanded, suspiciously.

But Missie was still inarticulate, vaguely protecting Kirby. "I don't want to see any one, really," she said. "I'm ill, for one thing, most of the time. I just want to get it over, the best way I can."

"Have you told Wes yet?"

"Yes."

"What does he say?"

"At first he wanted it interrupted. He's resigned now."

"Resigned!" Eileen's voice rose in scorn. "He'd better be resigned. If you weren't going to have a child, Missie, I'd tell you to leave him. What do you care if people talk? What do

I care? They're talking about me now! But at least they
know who I am, and some day they'll be fighting to get into
my house."

So Eileen would have helped her. But what did that matter
now? What did anything matter?

She was very ill. For days at a time she lay in bed, unable
to eat, to retain even water. She would lie there alone, dizzy
if she raised her head, unwilling to think, unable to sleep.
She had refused to move back into Wesley's room, or to ex-
change with him. What did it matter where she lay? Sometimes, to put herself to sleep, she found herself humming
over and over the opening phrases of the Minuet Mary Selden had played: "Te tum, tum, tumpety tum tum." She made
no sound, she hummed it to herself. It was like a drug, and
for a little while she would be back in the house on Grove
Street, putting up strings for morning glories, watching with
fascination while Mr. Wilkinson went down the street on his
visits to the slaughter house to drink fresh blood.

"It's not pleasant, but it stands to reason it's helpful."

One day Eileen came in and told her that Kirby Phelps had
gone away; he was to oversee the building of the factory.
Tommy couldn't go. He had started a bank, and he was to be
the president. He had a fine list of directors. "Now let their
wives snub me!"

But it seemed that Kirby had taken Eileen's news very
hard.

"I was sorry for him. He looked crushed," Eileen said.
"You didn't say he cared for you, Missie."

"He'll get over it. They all do, don't they?" said this new
Missie.

Eileen, however, did not tell her how Kirby had received
the news; how he had looked stricken at first, and how then
he had laughed. Had laughed until she was shocked, and then
had muttered something about God playing him a dirty trick
and bolted out of the house.

When Missie could think she wanted a boy. Women had

too hard a time. Life trapped them; they tried to get free, but before they could they bore children. Their features swelled, their breasts, their bodies grew grotesque and unbeautiful. They were ridiculous. She knew that the sight of her offended Wesley, his sense of the fastidious, of the beautiful.

She dared not think of Kirby at all.

She had not told her grandmother or Adelaide, but one day Adelaide heard and came flutteringly to see her.

"My dear child! Why didn't you tell us?"

"I don't know. It doesn't strike me as so important as all that."

"It's the most important thing in the world," said Adelaide solemnly.

"Why? Anybody can have a baby."

The child meant nothing to her. She was puzzled after that at Adelaide's tremulous excitement. She came often, moving clumsily about the room, setting things in order and talking about the child to be. It was a real child to Adelaide long before it was anything at all to Missie. She was filled with old wives' tales, queer superstitions. Once or twice Mrs. Colfax came with her, came feebly up the stairs and sat by Missie's bedside. She too wanted a boy, to be called for Lambert, and she told Missie that to bear a child was a holy thing, that it brought husband and wife even closer together, that it sanctified marriage.

Missie smiled faintly.

After a time she found that Wesley was not only reconciled, but that he was secretly proud. He even made an effort to be considerate. He was at home more, but he was poor company for himself. He did not read. He would sit down over a book and drop asleep. And at last he would give up the effort altogether; would tiptoe to her door, find her light out, and with relief go down again, get his hat, close the front door quietly behind him.

With the quickening of the child, however, she found herself changing. Her health was better, and she could think again. She knew that she still loved Kirby, probably always would. She was like that. But now she could think of him without agony. There was something at last to look forward to, something of her own. She jealously denied Wesley any part in it.

It was she and Adelaide who made the layette, the heavy flannel and white petticoats, the long-skirted dresses with their hand-run tucks and their lace insertions. The sleeves touched her heart, they were so small. Mostly her work was put away before Wesley came home, but one day he surprised her. He picked up a dress and inspected it, laid it down carefully, with a strange look on his heavy face. It was as though she had for a moment seen through the Wesley that was to the Wesley that might have been.

After that she was gentler with him, and she saw that after his fashion he was trying to be kind. At night sometimes he would walk around the block with her. It was dark and no one could see her. The arc-lights had vanished from some of the city streets, and some visionary had built a series of huge skeleton towers, sixty feet in the air. They threw a pale moonlight over the roofs and left the streets submerged, dim canyons walled with brick. She walked slowly and with difficulty; once her nausea recurred and she was ill. She knew that it sickened him, that he considered maternity an unlovely thing, that he was divided between pride and disgust.

She felt alone, save for the child. All her past was infinitely removed from her; Stella, old Archibald Kennedy, Harry, Kirby Phelps. There was no past, only the present to be lived through and the future to be awaited. She was like a woman listening for a sound.

And at last the sound came.

She suffered outrageously during the birth. Between the pains the doctor slept in his chair beside her bed. Once she rallied—in the middle of the night, that was—and saw Wesley in the doorway looking at her. She felt that he wanted to come in, that she ought to ask him to come in; but then the agony caught her again, and when it was over he was gone. Years later she was to think of that, of the pity in his eyes, the fear; and to wonder, had she been able to summon him, to hold to him, if it would have made any difference. She did not know. Perhaps not.

When at last they gave her the anæsthetic she talked feverishly. They were to let her alone. The baby was in the doctor's satchel out in his buggy. Please go and get the baby. *Please*. PLEASE. She ended in a scream.

Wesley heard that scream in the library. He was sitting sagged in one of his hard leather chairs, with a decanter and whisky at his elbow.

Chapter XXIV

WITHIN a month of Eddie's birth Missie felt that she had found the meaning of life. All that had gone before had been directed toward this one end, that she should bear this child.

She fed him from her own breast; he was always hungry. "A fine big boy," the nurse said. She was a very modern nurse. Each day she weighed and measured him. "He's a long child. He's going to be tall."

He would cry in his crib. Missie would pick him up, and he would stop crying, begin to nuzzle at her. When she lifted him she held the world in her arms. She would sing him to sleep, rocking back and forward, with a soft exalted look on her face, and once Wesley came in and saw it. He stooped awkwardly and kissed her.

He was trying hard, she saw that. He brought her more gifts; a bar pin set with pearls, a sealskin coat, and once again he tried sitting at home in the evenings, yawning over a book. But he loathed reading; he liked the company of men, men who played cards or talked business; or of women, gay sparkling women who laughed, who made it a business to amuse him. When the boy cried, the thin wailing sound made his very nerves twitch.

And often Missie took pity on him.

"Don't you want to go to the club, Wes? It's so dull for you here."

He would try to hide the eagerness in his eyes.

"How about you?"

"I'll be all right. I'll go to bed early."

He would affect reluctance, move slowly to get his hat,

his stick, his gloves. And outside on the pavement he would draw a long breath, hurry, almost run.

Yes, he was trying. During her convalescence she had heard much sawing of wood, hammering. She had asked no questions. But on the day she was to take her first airing it was no livery stable hack which drew up at the door. It was a shining new brougham, with a pair of handsome gray horses. Wesley was on the pavement, nonchalantly waiting, boyishly delighted.

"Well, how do you like it?"

She was moved almost to tears. He got in beside her; she felt the springs sag under his weight. Suddenly she put out her hand to him, and he took it awkwardly.

"Friends again, eh?"

"I'll do my best, Wes."

Incredible to think that, only a few months before, she had been hating him, planning to leave him. She knew, sitting there in the brougham beside him, that she could never love him as she had loved Kirby. But she was growing, ripening. There were still untouched depths of tenderness in her. There was still a chance that between them they could build their marriage into a success. It must be, for the boy's sake. He must grow up in harmony, in peace, in beauty.

And at that thought her breasts swelled, filled with the milk that was to nourish him.

"Why can't we be always like this, Wes? I'll try to do better, be more what you want."

"That's the girl." He squeezed her hand, let go of it, sat a little forward in the seat so as to be seen. "There goes Wes Dexter. New brougham, too! He's a coming man; making money hand over fist." He threw out his heavy chest, settled his tie, raked his hat.

"Best carriage team in this part of the state, Missie. And this boy knows how to handle them. I've bought some stock in Tommy's new factory, but nothing will ever take the place of this sort of thing."

She was happy for a year. She sang to the boy, sang about the house, sang over her sewing. She made him delicate little garments and planned his future. He was to be physically strong; he was to love the beautiful and the good, and he was to love his country. It was safe to love it now. People said there would be no more wars; that future difficulties would be settled by arbitration. That would be the great gift of the new century to the world, peace.

As she bent over her boy, or sat sewing and dreaming, there was more character in her face, but she showed the strain of her pregnancy and labour; she was thin and pale, and her waist was never quite to go back to its former trimness. When she was obliged to wean Eddie, her breasts for months looked sagged, almost withered, like the breasts of old women.

They had named the boy for her family, Colfax Dexter. Trust Wesley for that. But it was unwieldy for a child, and Missie called him Eddie.

She had not seen Kirby Phelps again. That part of her life was closed off, like a locked and shuttered room. She did not want to see him; it would be opening a door to emptiness. Nor did she want him to see her. She wanted passionately to have him remember her as the woman of that second blooming, to think of her always as young and lovely, and lovable.

But sometimes at night in her sleep she crept into that closed room, as the old Phœnicians crept to their dream chambers in the temple. She would waken with a start, a sense of guilt, and reaching out touch the child in his crib beside her. He was safety, he was reward, he was the gift of God to bring her peace.

Then, at the end of a year, she met Kirby once more.

Eileen had sent for her, sent Tommy's latest model car, for Wesley had the brougham. He often used it now; more than she did.

Years later Tommy was to show that early car at a motor show, to stand by and listen complacently to the comments:

"For heaven's sake! Look at the way they got in!"

For Tommy had built a *tonneau* to this car, with a door at the back, between the two rear seats, and a tidy flight of folding steps.

Let them talk. Let them laugh. Let them go out and laugh at the log cabins in the country, too. All pioneers are first ridiculed, then esteemed, then reverenced. He stood by and watched, jingling the money in his pockets.

"And no top! What did they do when it rained?"

"Used umbrellas, probably."

More laughter. But Tommy stopped jingling his money. He was remembering something. He was remembering Mrs. MacDonald and her sunshade. When he picked her up that day it had been lying beside her. Let them laugh. How could they know of the nights when he lay awake, his dreams turned into nightmares; when he felt that he could not go on?

Eileen was waiting for Missie. She had not changed with the years, Missie thought. But then she had not nursed Clare. She was pretty, an important young matron now. She had a "Buttons" to answer the door, a ridiculous child in a jacket to his waist and long trousers, who spent most of his time in the cellar reading dime novels. Beside the fireplace in the parlour sat her tea table. The tea table had reached the city, but not tea. Every house had its collection of cups and saucers and teapot. They sat in splendid uselessness beside every hearth.

Eileen looked at Missie as she sat down and took off her hat. She was tired; she was often tired now.

"Look here, Missie," she said. "How long are you going to drag along behind Wes? You can do one of two things with a man, follow him or go ahead of him. And Wes is ambitious. You can't go on being a mother forever."

"What do you want me to be?"

"A combination of housekeeper, mother, and mistress," said Eileen derisively. "That's what they want. You'll have to stick to Wes now, I daresay." She liked that word. She was learning, was Eileen. "And anyhow, why not? You've got everything, Missie. Who would have ever thought, years ago, that either of us would be where we are? I'm not as far socially as you are, but I will be. When you think back——"

"I don't like to think back."

"Well, I do. Every step up I take I say to myself, 'Pretty good, Eileen. And now for the next one.' And don't make any mistake. Wes has pulled himself up by his bootstraps, and he's holding on. If you don't play his game you'll lose him for good."

"He's doing better. We're getting along pretty well."

"There isn't any pretty well in marriage," said Eileen, practically. "It goes or it doesn't."

Then she turned and saw Kirby in the doorway. There was an instant's pause, then:

"Well!" she said. "And how's the inventive genius getting along? Here's Missie, too. Scold her for me, Kirby. She's in the house too much these days."

She shook hands with him, picked up a toy of Clare's, sauntered out of the room and up the stairs. She had no intention of being made uncomfortable, and there had been something electric in that second of silence. But after she had closed her door she sat down in front of her toilet table and stared at herself.

"What a lot of damned fools we are, anyhow," she thought.

Those two down there! It was funny, when you thought about it. She had a mild affection for Missie, and when she saw Kirby Missie had looked trapped. Well, life always trapped women, in one way or another. The thing was to know that ahead, not to be caught. She powdered her face viciously. She would never be caught. There was no man born who could make her look as Missie had looked.

Downstairs Kirby smiled as the door closed. Not his old whimsical smile, but the smile of a man finding himself ridiculous, and trying to make the best of it.

"Shall I call her back?"

She did not reply at once. She was looking at him carefully, gravely. She saw that he had changed; his eyes were not the dreamer's eyes of a year ago; they showed disillusion and disappointment. His movements had quickened, too, were nervous and wary.

"No. I shall have to go now, anyhow."

"Don't let me drive you away. Are you quite well again?"

"Perfectly well." She got up, reached for her hat. He saw then how thin she was, and he was quick to note the slight thickening of her waist, and to resent it.

"And the boy?"

"He is fine. I would like you to see him, Kirby."

And then he laughed, at himself, at her, at the trick he had been played. He saw her, armoured against him, fortified in her maternity, shut off in the world of mother and child. The child which should have been his. He had adored her. All that was best in him had gone into his love for her, and now she had turned it into a mockery and a jest.

Suddenly he saw that her hands were trembling. He took a step toward her, stopped.

"And he makes up to you for—other things?"

"For everything, Kirby," she said in a low voice.

He knew then that there were things she could not say to him, never would say. His anger died.

"Then what is best for you is best for me." He made a curious little futile gesture. "Of course you know that, Missie. I only want you to be happy."

She was still standing, holding her ridiculous hat.

"Try not to hate me, Kirby."

"I could never hate you. Why should I? I don't change as easily as that."

"You hated me a moment ago."

"I don't know where hatred ends and love begins, Missie. They are pretty close together. I think there is something in me that will always care for you. Maybe that's grotesque under the circumstances, but it is true."

Then, as if he had said either too little or too much, he turned abruptly and left the room, left the house. When Eileen came down she was still standing in the centre of the room, holding her hat.

Missie went back to her house, her boy, her lonely evenings. Electric lighting now; Wesley talking about a bathroom for the servants on the third floor. Wages for those servants going up; five and six dollars a week. Fitzgerald discovered by the literary and Omar being quoted by the elect. One night Missie read the book.

> "A moment's halt—a momentary taste
> Of being from the Well amid the waste,
> And Lo! The Phantom Caravan has reached
> The nothing it set out from.—Oh, make haste."

She put the book away, went back and looked at Eddie, asleep in his crib. Make haste? No, never. Let her hold to this hour, to her boy safely asleep, secure. Let Wesley make haste, if he would, drinking at his secret wells. Only let her sit quietly by this bed, holding to what she had.

Now and then she found herself thinking of Kirby. She was not afraid to think of him now. He could play no part in her life, but he had given her back her pride, her dignity. And, although she did not know it, his flat statement that he still cared for her had warmed and comforted her. He was to be a part of the background of her life, to be counted on. He was to ask nothing, to give everything. She would never be lonely again.

Chapter XXV

SHE did not see Kirby again for three years. Now and then she heard of him, of course. He was one of the first to make and drive a racing car; he took an automobile across the continent in fifty-two days.

"Got a charmed life, Kirby," said Tommy.

"Maybe he doesn't care," Eileen commented shrewdly.

But Tommy smiled at that. Women were incurably romantic; even Eileen. Men did not try to kill themselves in racing cars for the Missies of the world.

"Looking for thrills, that's all," he said. "If he kills himself we'll be out a damned good engineer."

But he had no use for Wesley, had Tommy.

"Fooling around with women again," he said. "I don't object to his drinking, if he wants to make a hog of himself. But this other thing—do you suppose Missie knows?"

"Any woman knows."

"Then why doesn't she get out?"

"She's got Eddie. Where's she to go? The Colfaxes have nothing. Unless you want her here!"

"I wouldn't object," said Tommy placidly. He might not see Kirby Phelps breaking his neck for her, but he was fond of her. "If it ever comes to a crash——"

But Eileen changed the subject. She had plans of her own. Already she and Tommy belonged to the new aristocracy of wealth. It smiled at the pretensions of the old families, rejected their standards of austere dignified living, demanded amusement and spent for it lavishly, showed a certain ostentation. But it was this wealth which was raising the cultural standards of the city, of the country. It travelled, collected, brought back to America not only works of art but an appreciation of them. It financed symphony orchestras in unlikely places, opera, picture galleries. Unlike the earlier generation it did not hoard; it spent.

And of this new aristocracy were Tommy and Eileen to be shining lights. Already they were planning another house well outside of town. They had fifty acres, and the plans included a swimming pool in the grounds. The planting was already going on, the excavation being made.

"We'll keep the town house," Eileen told Missie. "The country place is for the warm weather. And of course we can open it for Christmas and have house parties there."

Missie drove out there with her sometimes in Eileen's new electric, the children tucked in with them. Eileen talked, Missie listened. She had grown very silent, save when she was alone with Eddie.

Eileen drove. The seat was far back; she guided the little car by means of a long lever reaching from the curved dashboard. When they reached the property Eddie would trot about—he was four then—and bring Missie little pebbles, field flowers without stems. She would hold them carefully in her lap, as once Adelaide had held her cotillion favours.

She had lost Wesley again. She knew that. Out of the wreckage of her life this child, offering her tribute, was all she had. Eileen would talk, Missie would listen, her eyes on the boy. One day Eileen said that she and Tommy were going abroad.

"Come to New York and see us off, Missie. You need a change."

"I'm afraid to leave Eddie."

"Good heavens, what's your nurse for?"

She decided to go. She could get some clothes, fix herself up. Maybe if she did Wesley would stay around more. It was bad for Eddie, the way things were. Soon he would begin to notice.

She did not hate Wesley. She was often sorry for him. He was prospering, but she knew he was not happy. His infidelities were escapes from some profound inner loneliness which sent him into the back alleys of life after forgetfulness. That was her fault; she had not satisfied him. He loved life and the good things of life, gaiety and laughter, good food, good wine. He liked place, to be pointed out in a crowd. He was intensely physical; his body ruled him.

But whatever his sins of omission or commission, he had given her this child. She even felt dumbly grateful to him, but she would not tell him so. He would have laughed. She tried to show it in other ways, ordering his house as he liked it, his food, his drink.

"I hope the ducks are right, Wes. I told her how you want them."

He liked his ducks raw. He liked to cut into them and see the blue-red flesh, the juices flowing out.

And she never locked her door again. This at least she could do. But the boy's crib stood next to her bed; when Wesley wandered in it was to look at the child and to wander out again. They had settled down to a life together without love or passion, and apparently it was to go on forever.

In the end she agreed to go to New York with Tommy and Eileen.

She went to her grandmother's to say good-bye. Sarah was very feeble, in bed a part of each day. And old Ishmael was dead. The cow had gone, the horses. As she went in she noticed once again the dusty smell of old carpets long unlifted. Waiting to be summoned upstairs she stood at the window looking out. The iron fence, the deer, were unchanged, but beyond them the street had altered. There were bicycles, tram cars, an occasional automobile. Life was moving fast, speeding up. People even walked more quickly. "Hurry up, get out of the way. I've no time to waste."

When she went up Sarah was in her high-backed chair, a shawl around her old shoulders, and Adelaide was rolling spills. Spills! It took her back to the day she came; she felt young, uncomfortable again. More so when Sarah spoke.

"Sit down, Missie. I want to talk to you. Adelaide, you would better go out."

Missie threw back her jacket, drew off her gloves, braced herself. She caught Adelaide's eyes at the door. They were furtive, curious.

"What's this about your going to New York?"

"Only for a day or two. I need some clothes, and Eileen——"

"Eileen! Since when 'Eileen'?"

"Ellen wants me to see them off."

Sarah eyed her.

"Marcella, are you deliberately letting your husband go? Or what is the trouble?"

She flushed.

"I don't know what you mean."

"I am not so shut away as you seem to think. I have no reason to like Wesley Dexter, but I want to be fair to him. When a woman's husband leaves her for—pleasures of his own, it is the woman's fault."

"I suppose from that that people are talking."

She absently smoothed the gloves in her lap.

"Wesley married the wrong woman, that's all. I have tried, but I suppose it's fundamental."

"Nonsense! There is no such thing. Do you and Wesley have separate bedrooms?"

"I have Eddie. If he wakens in the night——"

"You have a nurse. What is she for? I was married twenty years and bore three children, and outside of childbirth I was never separated from your grandfather for one night."

"I think Wesley would be bored."

"Let him be bored," said Sarah grimly.

But she went to New York, nevertheless. She knew she needed a change. That old trembling of her hands had returned, and there were times when she wondered if middle age would find her jerking like Adelaide. When she saw Tommy and Eileen off she found herself queerly emotional on the dock, watching the ship slowly moving out into the river. Years later she was to wait for another ship to move down that same river, and to have again that sense of finality; the phantom caravan going on, and she being left. There were tears in her eyes when she turned away.

She found Kirby Phelps beside her.

"Missed them!" he said. "Well, since I have found you——!"

He looked older. There was a streak of white in his dark hair, but his eyes were still kind. He saw that she could not speak, and taking her arm led her out to a cab. "I'll take you to your hotel," he said. And only later, side by side and jolting uptown: "Missie, Missie! What has happened to you?"

"Nothing. Maybe that's the trouble."

She had no coquetry, no arts, even no desire to reclaim him. She was trembling, but she felt quite calm.

"Are you as lost as you look, Missie?"

"I have my boy. That's enough."

He had his old impulse to deny that for her, to take her into his arms and comfort her. Time had softened his hurt, but she still had the power to move him; he had been faithful to that memory of her. But he could not destroy for her what he saw was her only salvation. He sat back and folded his arms.

"Then you are indeed blessed among women," he said, rather quaintly.

He left her in the lobby of her hotel, and standing there, with his hat in his hand, he told her that he had never forgotten her, that he still cared, that she could count on him, always. She thanked him gravely, her eyes on his face as though she wanted to impress it on her mind afresh, or as though she were storing up some memory for the years to come. As indeed she was.

She went back to Wesley. She put on her pretty new

dresses, her smart hats. Mr. Gibson might have drawn her; she had the delicacy, the wistfulness that he gave his young women, the same proud little tilt to her head. But Mr. Gibson never saw her and Wesley did not notice.

One night she put on her prettiest wrapper, listened until she heard him come in, put out the lights, ascend the stairs. Then she went in to him, her long braids down her back, her eyes a trifle panicky. He had taken off his coat and was winding his watch. His paunch was very noticeable now, and his chin sagged over his high collar. She stood just inside the door.

"Do you mind talking a little, Wes?"

"What about?"

"About you and me. I've been thinking things over; I think maybe I haven't tried enough."

"Tried what?"

"Tried to make things better, between us. Wesley, would you care to have me come back?" She flushed uncomfortably. "To your room, I mean."

He looked at her suspiciously. Was there a trap in all this? But her face reassured him.

"It's pretty late to be talking about that, isn't it?"

"I want to do the right thing."

He had stopped winding his watch. Now he commenced again, methodically, deliberately.

"I haven't asked you to come back, and I don't intend to. It was you who took yourself away, shut yourself away, by God! If you want to come back, come. But come yourself, the way you went."

"And that is all you have to say?"

"That's fair enough, isn't it?"

"You don't really care, either way, do you?"

He looked at her; she was pale, and even with her braids the little girl look was gone. She was perhaps more appealing than she had ever been, but she had no appeal for him.

"Not enough to make any concessions," he told her brutally, and she went out again.

She made no further efforts of reconciliation. Perhaps
she did not know that that offering of herself to Wesley had
been defensive, that she still cared for Kirby and was instinc-
tively fighting it. But sometimes that summer in church her
thoughts wandered. She looked at the other married women
around her, kneeling and rising.

"Open thou my lips, O Lord."

"And my mouth shall show forth Thy praise."

Did they love the husbands who sat beside them, also kneeling and rising at the correct times? Or had some of them
found too late that they loved some one else? And what
about these men, so passionless and sober in their starched lin-
ens, their broadcloth? Were they faithful? What were they
thinking about, as they sat beside their wives? Business or
God? Or women?

Wesley's interests were extending. He was much more than
a middleman now; he was a director in Tommy's bank, in a
new insurance company, a stockholder in the bicycle business,
in the automobile factory. Tommy was carrying him up with
him. And some of Kirby's dreams were already coming true.
Men were flying; still experimentally, but conquering the air.
The idea had become the fact. One thought of a thing first
and then it happened. Man was God's idea. One must be
careful what one thought.

She tried not to be bitter toward Wesley, not to hate him.
She had been ready to rebuild their lives, but he had repudiated her. A little tenderness, an attempt at loyalty might even
then have brought her back, not to love perhaps, but to devotion and tenderness. They were not too old; they could still
build. But he had pushed her away.

They did not go away that summer; Wesley was too busy.
And the heat was terrific. It shimmered in visible waves above
the tracks of the street cars, and people dropped on the pavements as if they had been pole-axed. Even the nights brought

no relief. The tall brick house was breathless, torrid, and Eddie was ill; he could not eat, and in his fitful sleep he whimpered. Missie, hanging over him like a pale ghost, felt both her strength and her endurance failing, her nerves gradually getting the better of her. Eddie's doctor, looking at her, prescribed bromides she forgot to take. She felt always as though there was a tight band around her head.

The child was not critically ill, but she wondered what she would do if he died. She tried to pray, but she could not. There was no tender Saviour, but her grandmother's Jehovah, vengeful, lying in wait to punish. And she deserved punishment. She had not wanted Eddie, she had loved Kirby while she carried him. And God is not mocked.

The beginning of Eddie's convalescence found her collapsed. She dragged herself about the sizzling house. In the basement kitchen the stove had rendered the room unbearable, and the cook was sitting in the coal cellar fanning herself. Eddie was better, but pale and languid.

"Take your milk, darling."

"I don't want any milk, muvver."

By the end of the week she had reached her limit. Her request that she be allowed to take Eddie out of town had met with no response from Wesley, packing a bag for a weekend party somewhere. There began in her, with his departure, a slow smouldering anger and resentment that unknown to her was growing throughout all of that afternoon into the next day. Sitting over the child's bed she counted her money. She must get away, take Eddie with her. The house was crushing her, the heat was driving her mad.

She had not enough money. She was his chattel, his creature. It was his house, his child, his wife, his carriage, his horses. A furious hatred began to shake her, and all that Sunday while Eddie slept she sat and rocked, backward and forward, her eyes sunken and her mouth set. Something of Stella that was in her, something common and yet terrible, was rising to the surface.

And Wesley chose that night to attempt a reconciliation!

He had not been too comfortable during that interval. His mind was not subtle; it worked slowly, outside of business. And he was callous rather than cruel. Besides, he had had a hint or two lately. Tommy, about to sail, had said something.

"How old are you, Wes? Fifty?"

"Forty-three."

"Humph! You look older. Better try the domestic life for a while. No use wearing out a machine before its time."

And behind those quiet words of Tommy's there had been a threat. Tommy was carrying no dead wood. Push your share or let go, that was Tommy. Competition, speeding up, drive, those were the new slogans. He felt that he had coined them.

It was midnight when Wesley came in, cheerful, cool, magnanimous, and braced to his resolution by three or four highballs at the club. He noticed nothing strange about Missie, sitting rocking in the dim room.

"Come into my room," he said. "I have something to say to you."

The hall was faintly redolent of Scotch whisky as she followed him. She was fully dressed, queerly apathetic. And even then things might have been different had Wesley not closed the door behind her and tried to take her in his arms. She backed off. He was suddenly horrible to her, his mouth loose, his legs apart to steady himself. She warned him off, but he came after her. And then, with a cat-like gesture that might have been Stella's, she seized a poker from the fireplace and struck him with it.

He fell down and lay still.

She stood on the pavement, hatless, and breathed the night air. She was through. He would never take her back. Maybe she had killed him; well, she had warned him. Then she was dizzy, and she began to tremble again. She sat down on the doorstep; she thought, "I must get back and get Eddie." But she could not get up; she could not move at all. Some time later she heard movements within the house, slow careful movements. She felt that the door behind her was going to open, and that she must run, run fast and far. But she could not run. And the door did not open; she heard the bolt put on, and the slow movements again; Wes going up the staircase. She had not killed him.

Suddenly she knew that she had to get back into the house, back to Eddie. She was frantic; she rang the door bell, hammered on the door. Above she knew Wesley heard her, could even figure him, partially undressed, sitting on the side of his bed and listening. She even thought she heard Eddie. But there was no movement, only after a time the bell ceased to ring. Wesley had disconnected it. There was an air of finality about the bolted door, the bell that did not ring. Wesley was through, and he was telling her so. She was beaten.

With that knowledge she quieted, her Colfax blood came to the surface. She moved away down the street toward her grandmother's house.

Chapter XXVI

ADELAIDE was terrified. She stood in the lower hall in her dressing gown, her face working.

"But I don't understand it, Missie. Why would he lock you out?"

"I've told you. I struck him with a poker."

"But why on earth did you strike him? What did he do?"

Missie could not tell her. How explain to Adelaide the complexities which had lain behind that action of hers? The mental and physical revolt, following the smouldering anger of the day? And in Adelaide's eyes, for all her distress, she seemed to see once more a furtive curiosity that affronted her.

"I was angry, Aunt Adelaide. Let it go at that. I suppose I can sleep here to-night."

Adelaide was not so certain. She could slip Missie up to her old room, but Mrs. Colfax must not know about it.

"She's so feeble, Missie. I do believe it would kill her." She began to cry.

Up in Missie's old room she continued to weep, wept over the pillows as she turned down the bed, wept over the night-gown she brought in. "I did think *you* were fixed anyhow." And later on she said: "I can't think what possessed you, Missie. A poker! It's so undignified." She was worried too about Missie's lack of a hat. It seemed to epitomize the drama of the situation; to give it tragic finality. Missie hatted and gloved would have been comprehensible, but this bare-headed bare-handed young woman, with her soft hair blown about her face, looked like some bit of flotsam of the night.

When the room was ready she asked the question Missie had been expecting.

"You'll go back to him, Missie, won't you?"

"I'll go back to Eddie, if he'll let me. Not to Wes. He won't want me."

Adelaide sighed, "I hope you can fix it up. If you and Wesley separate, I don't know what we'll do. I suppose you know that we're behind again with the interest. The taxes, too, and now that they are paving the street——"

Suddenly Missie laughed hysterically. The walls were closing down on her again. What was the use? One did violent terrible things, escaped, only to find other walls, other prisons. Her laughter relieved Adelaide.

"I'm sure I don't see what there is to laugh about," she said, severely. "If Wesley turns us out——"

Missie went over and put her arms around the heavy figure.

"Of course I'm going back, if Wes will have me," she said. "Now just go to bed and don't worry. If the maids are curious, you can say Mrs. Colfax was ill in the night and you sent for me."

She crept into the wide bed, that bed where she had lain and dreamed of Harry Sloane. She felt like a child again, a child to whom life had done incredible things, and yet had left fundamentally untouched. She was a wife and a mother, but she was still the little girl on Grove Street. It seemed to her that this was one of the tragedies of all human life, that the body suffered, endured, grew old; but that the inner self changed hardly at all.

Some time in those hours before she fell asleep she allowed herself to think of Kirby. The mother in her had quieted with her decision to go back to Wesley; the night was cooler, the boy would be asleep. She could afford, in her emptiness, to turn to Kirby, to feel his arms about her, to remember the love and kindness which were hers for the asking. The very thought of him rested her. She closed her eyes and fell asleep.

But the night was not so kind to Adelaide. She lay in her bed and waited for the daylight making her slow painful de-

cisions, struggling to overcome the inertia of years of sub-
servience. She was not so certain that Wesley would take
Missie back, and if he did not, what would they do? She had
nobody to turn to, nobody. She thought with bitterness of
Lambert, a constant drain on their resources, of Cecily, ill
now and needing more than she could give her.

With dawn she was moving about her room, laying out
her bonnet, dressing herself carefully. Then she sat on the
side of her bed, waiting for her mother's bell and the day to
begin. She looked old and tired. When she found herself
shaking with anxiety she picked up her Bible and read the
Ninety-first Psalm. She was quieter when she put it down
again.

Missie was still sleeping when at eight o'clock she left the
house, and half an hour later she was standing outside Wesley's door, knocking timidly. She had been admitted to the
house, at least. The maid had stared at her curiously, but
otherwise everything seemed peaceful enough. In the boy's
room she could hear the nurse giving Eddie his breakfast.

"Now drink your orange juice first; that's a good boy."

Adelaide slowly climbed the stairs and knocked.

"Who is it?"

"It's Adelaide Colfax, Wesley."

He opened the door almost at once, an angry man before
she spoke. She saw his face, the blue ridge across his temple,
and her carefully prepared arguments died in her throat.

"If you've come from Missie you can go back to her again.
I've had enough."

She mustered her courage, followed him, closed the door
against the servants. She was jerking violently.

"Wesley, you must let her come back. You must."

"Why? So she can try to kill me again?"

"That was an accident, an impulse. I'm sure she's sorry.
Wesley, I can't keep her; I can't tell mother. It would kill
her."

He looked at her. She represented all that he detested,

failure, genteel poverty, ugliness, but she was a lady, and he passionately wanted to be a gentleman. His voice was more polite.

"I'm sorry, Adelaide," he said. "This has nothing to do with you, or with your mother either. There was no reason whatever for what Missie did last night, and no question of forgiveness."

And, remembering that magnanimity of his, he threw out his chest, felt outraged afresh.

"You won't take her back?"

"I am seeing MacDonald this morning."

He had only just thought of that, but it set her to trembling more violently than ever.

"And—Eddie?"

"She left Eddie here when she left this house. If she wants to go to law she can try it."

Adelaide had had no experience with the overstatements of humiliated and angry men. She went out blindly, mopping at her eyes, absurd even in her despair. Alone in Missie's room she packed a bag for her, got a hat, gloves. She wept over everything, dropped things, got down painfully and picked them up. All this time the hack waiting outside, Wesley's door shut, Eddie calling for his mother, and the steaming heat of a new day beating in at the windows.

When she got back it was to find that Missie was ill.

She was ill for three days, hidden in her room. She would make desperate attempts to get up, only to collapse again. Adelaide warned the servants, came and went. She brought broths, milk, fresh water; moving with amazing lightness for all her clumsy body. And on the third day, Missie being better, she told her in detail of that talk with Wesley.

Missie, however, was more hopeful. She had had time to think. Wesley would want no scandal, no divorce court. True, divorce was becoming more common; divorced people were not necessarily ostracized any longer. He might figure on that. But his life had been organized as he liked it; he had been comfortable, been free. If she went back, abased herself, promised to do better, surely he would let her stay.

She saw no irony in that attitude of hers. She was of the old *régime,* of a world where man was king. All about her young women were questioning the patience, the acceptance, the obedience of their mothers; were preaching revolutionary doctrines. But she did not speak their language. She had courage, but it was the kind of courage that endures, not rebels.

So, on the morning of the next day, still weak, she dressed herself and started back. She would plead, she would suffer any humiliation; but she must not lose Eddie. Her face was set as she left the house. Twelve years now since Stella had killed herself, eight years since her marriage, four years since Eddie came. She was twenty-eight as she went up the steps of Wesley's house that morning, her blue foulard dress gathered up from the dust. There was already a suggestion of the slender elegance that was to take the place of beauty with her as time went on. Her waist was small again, her breasts had regained their roundness. There was even pride in the carriage of her head.

But her eyes were the eyes of a frightened child as she rang the bell, her hands—that old trick of theirs—were shaking. When the maid opened the door she had difficulty in controlling her voice. She stepped inside, into her own house; the maid took the bag. Everything was quiet. It was strange, that quietness.

"Has Mr. Dexter left for the office?"

"Mr. Dexter's out of town, mam."

"Then I'll go up to Master Eddie."

The girl was watching her curiously.

"Master Eddie's gone, mam."

"Gone!" she said. "Gone where?"

"I don't know, mam. Mr. Dexter sent him and the nurse to the country somewhere."

She went upstairs, her mind obstinately refusing to work.

In the nursery she found herself doing small automatic things, picking up toys, gathering small garments and putting them away. She gave the wondering housemaid some orders, went downstairs where her bag lay in the hall, and picked it up. Twelve hours ago this had been her home, sanctuary for Eddie and herself. Now it was nothing to her. Eddie was gone. Wesley had taken him away from her. Where could she go? What could she do? She needed help, help and love. Somebody to care. Somebody to get Eddie back.

It was then that she thought of Kirby Phelps.

Chapter XXVII

SHE ate nothing in the train, scarcely moved, formulated no plan. She sat staring out, but the panorama she saw was not that of the fields, the towns, the cities. She was going back, trying to understand her catastrophe. Why had she struck Wesley? Of what use to build, to endure and build, slowly, painfully, and then destroy? What was it that made women do these things, have these emotional crises? They would go along quietly enough, work, build, bear and forbear; and then something would snap and it was all undone.

She had been crazy. Maybe all women were crazy sometimes. They were stronger than man, but they were less stable. Maybe that was because things mattered more to them than to men.

The heat was terrific. She had only one comfort: Eddie was in the country. She thought of him, picking his little stemless flowers, gathering bright pebbles. But she was not there to receive them. Her heart contracted, her hands clenched.

"Last call to dinner; lady."

"Thanks. I don't care for anything."

Kirby found her in the sitting room of an ugly hotel suite. She was wandering up and down, her bag on the table, not opened, her hat beside it. She did not even offer to shake hands.

"Don't be surprised, Kirby," she said. "Don't be surprised at anything. I think I am stark raving mad."

"Nonsense." He went to her and put his hands on her shoulders. "Steady now, Missie. I don't care what has happened, you are no more mad than I am. When did you eat last?"

"I don't know. This morning, I think."

"Then you're going to have something now. And not a word out of you until you have!"

That attitude of his, practical and unloverlike, helped her. She even smiled a little. He put her in a chair, hooked back the ugly Nottingham curtains so she could have air, sent for a waiter, and talked about trivial matters until he came. But he was confused, filled with pity and tenderness, puzzled. She had left Wesley, left her child, come to him. And he still cared for her. He had filled his life with other matters, but she had still that curious power to stir his heart.

She had come to him. Well, by God, he would keep her this time. They were still young. They could still build a life together. There would be a bad interval, and then——

When the waiter had gone he went over to her.

"Better now?"

"Quieter, yes. I was frightened."

"There is nothing to be frightened about, Missie. You are safe with me."

He stooped and kissed her, a brief reassuring caress, no more.

But she could not eat. She drank some coffee, got up.

"Let me walk around while I'm telling you, Kirby. It helps."

"Do anything you like. You've left Wesley?"

"He has left me, and he has taken Eddie."

"Left *you!*"

"I struck him. I told you I was crazy. I hit him with a poker and knocked him down. I thought I had killed him, and I didn't care. But I hadn't."

"That's a pity," he said drily. But when he saw that that shocked her. "Go on; then what?"

She told him, clearly enough but still moving about the room. Only when it came to her decision to come to him did he stop her.

"Just why did you come to me, Missie? Think that over as quietly as you can. Was it only because you needed help?"

She flushed, but she looked at him candidly.

"Partly that. Not only that."

"You still cared, then?"

"I have never changed, Kirby."

But when she came to Eddie her forced calmness left her. She became the mother again, desperate, trembling. She wanted Eddie, she must have him. He had not been well; the nurse was stupid and not very kind. Let him get Eddie for her, go back and find him, steal him. If he would do that she would promise to stay with him. She didn't matter anyhow. She would stay with him, love him, be his slave. He didn't even have to marry her."

He stopped her, angry for the first time.

"Don't talk like that. It's outrageous. Do you think you need to bribe me, Missie?"

"Then you will try?"

He made the same curious futile gesture he had made once before in Eileen's parlour.

"You see? It is help you want, not me, Missie."

"I have always wanted you."

"But you want your boy more."

"I want you both, Kirby."

He drew a long breath. He was puzzled, miserable. She was in no state of mind for argument, standing there watching him with terrified eyes.

"Isn't that possible, somehow?"

"We'll have to find a way, darling."

And with that reassurance she let herself go. She loved him. If he did not stand by her now she did not know what she would do. She had no place to go, no one to go to. "You won't send me back, will you?" She touched his sleeve, his hand, and with every tremor of her sensitive mouth he found himself weakening. After all, he loved her, and she had come to him. She was his. To send her back to the hell she had escaped was unthinkable. But he owed it to her to define her position for her. It would be a long time before she could get a divorce, a painful troublesome business. Could she put up with him until then?

"You know, Missie darling, that I want a wife, not a mistress. But I am a man. I want you; I always have. I think I always will."

When he left her she was quieter. She promised him to try to sleep, and he held to his attitude of tenderness without passion. But as he closed the door on her in that drab room he had a feeling of desertion. She would not sleep; she would lie there alone, agonizing. He made a move to go back, squared his shoulders, went on.

Until midnight he walked the streets. He had no belief that he could get Eddie for her. He saw Wesley, sullen and ugly, using his wealth to prevent that, to soil her and drag her down; and he saw her making her pitiful losing fight alone. Then what was he to do? Give her some good advice and send her back to that brute? Or hold her? Make her his and hold her, so that when the worst came she would at least not be alone?

At midnight he found himself across from the hotel, looking up at her windows. Her lights were going. She was not asleep; she was up there, brooding, maybe crying. If ever she needed him it was now. To hell with everything. He was going up to her.

And up he went.

She was in her nightgown, a thin dressing gown over it, her hair braided in its two long braids. She seemed hardly surprised when she saw him, went into his arms, let him kiss her eyes, her hair, her lips; even clung to him in a sort of desperation.

"Don't let go of me just yet."

"I'm not letting go, darling."

"I was afraid, Kirby."

"Afraid of what?"

"Afraid I'd lost you."

"You'll never lose me again, darling. You are mine and I

am yours. Always and ever, from now on, for life everlasting. Amen."

There was no atmosphere of assignation, no furtiveness. He told her that soon, please God, she would be his legal wife, and that now she needed him. He would take care of her. He would always take care of her, from now on. And when he had tucked her up in her white bed and kissed her, her eyes were serene.

"Am I being wicked, Kirby? It doesn't seem wicked, to be here with you like this."

"If you are wicked, darling, then so are the saints in heaven."

She lay still in her bed, listening to him as he moved about the other room. In the back of her mind pictures were forming out of her past; old Archibald holding his beer glass and saying: "We're a curious family. The men are too hot, and the women too cold. It's a bad world for women." Stella, during Lambert's disappearances, going around like a woman in a trance. "What do you want for supper, Mom?" "Oh, I don't care. You might open a can of tomatoes." The preparations for that meeting at Mr. MacDonald's office, Stella excited and hopeful, sewing the feather into her hat. "I don't look so bad now, do I?" You look great, Mom. Fine." Eileen smelling gas; the locked door, the policeman trying to break in, and Stella there, quiet and beautiful again. Then Harry Sloane, kissing her; the note from Emily Beaumont on her wedding day. And Wesley on their wedding journey, his easy passions roused by her little-girl look. She dwelt on that. After his fashion Wesley had loved her then. Then he had tired of her. Perhaps all men tired of their women in time.

She lay back, thinking of that. Another picture came to her. She and Stella were sitting on a bench by the river.

"Aren't we going home soon, Mom?"

"We're not going home."

"Not ever?"

"Never." And then Stella saying her father was a bad man, hard and cruel and bad, and that he had another woman.

"What for, Mom?"

And Stella laughing bitterly, and then turning on her fiercely. "Promise me you'll never be a bad girl, Missie." And herself shivering with cold, promising. Promising.

She sat up in her bed, stared at the door. This man in the next room, moving about—he was no god, able to turn wrong into right. He was a man like other men. Suppose she committed this sin for him, and then he tired of her, as Wesley had tired of her? How could she be sure? Did she even know that he could get Eddie for her? Eddie was not even his child. Why should he care about Eddie?

She was still sitting up in bed, her eyes wide and staring, when Kirby came in. And it was his first words which precipitated the crisis.

"You look like a little girl, darling."

Then the storm broke.

Throughout that insane hysterical night Kirby kept his head and his distance. At first he considered it the nervous reaction following her long hours of strain; later on he was to realize that it was far deeper than that, that a thousand early inhibitions, temporarily repressed by her desperation, were fighting him. She "wanted to be good." She didn't want Eddie to be "ashamed of her."

He was helpless. Indeed he saw that this attitude of hers was fundamental, a part of her. If she sowed the wind she would indeed reap the whirlwind. His great fear was that she would hate and loathe him later on; he fought hard against that.

"Try to get my attitude, darling," he told her. "I came to you with love, not—the other thing. I am no——" he wanted to say Wesley, but he did not. "I am no beast, no animal."

And he tried to explain to her the spiritual loneliness which lay behind the desires of men and women, the pathetic desire to escape it by physical union. "Not lust, but love."

Toward morning she was calmer. She told him little things about her life, things he had never known. It was a curious situation, but she seemed to feel no strangeness in it. What mattered to her was her essential integrity, and that preserved, he saw that it comforted her to talk to him of these small long-ago matters. One thing worried her. She was afraid he would think she did not care for him. Over and over she told him that she loved him, told him quietly but intensely. And she asked him to care for her as much as he could. She could get along better if she felt that he loved her.

"But what are you going to do, Missie darling? I can't let you go back like this."

She was not sure. She only knew she could not stay with him. She had come on an impulse. She had wanted him to help her get Eddie, and then to help her to rear him. "He will need somebody like you, Kirby. He's got to grow up decent and fine." He kissed her hand at that. But she saw now that she had gone about things the wrong way. She didn't want any scandal, for the boy's sake.

Toward morning, exhausted with argument and expostulation, he lay back on the other bed and fell asleep. He never knew that she sat brooding over him until daylight filled the windows. He was ashamed when he wakened to find her dressed, and her small belongings packed in the bag once more, but she only smiled at him gravely.

"I gave you a terrible night," she said. "You needed sleep."

And so she left him, going back to she knew not what. He wanted to go with her, but she preferred going by herself. Left alone, he was worried and despondent, blamed himself, wondered what she would do, where she would go.

But the great blow was that he had lost her. Whether by his own bungling or by that malicious destiny which had twice brought them together and twice separated them, he did not know. He had lost her.

Never had he loved her so much as now that she was gone.

Chapter XXVIII

IT WAS still early evening when she reached the house. A faint breeze had sprung up, and the front door had been set open to catch it. At once she knew that Wesley was dining in; there were lights in the dining room, the waitress in her black and white was moving about. She went quietly up the stairs, removed her hat and wrap, and came down again. There was no sign of Eddie. When Wesley came out she was in the parlour, standing by a window.

She heard him stop in the doorway, peer in at her figure in the dusk. His heavy figure almost filled the doorway; she could see that his head was thrust forward belligerently, and her hands shook. But her voice was quiet enough.

"Will you let me say something to you, Wes?"

"That depends on what it is."

"At least you'll let me say I'm sorry."

"Sorry for what?"

"For everything. If you'll give me a chance——"

He came in, closed the door deliberately, and advanced toward her with that heavy walk of his which was already that of an old man.

"Give you a chance for what? To try to kill me again? No, my girl, I'm not built that way."

"I didn't try to kill you, Wes. I don't know why I did it."

"Well, I do. You hate me, my girl. You've sat here with that holier than thou attitude of yours, and hated me. Too good to be my wife, weren't you? Too good and pure to live, that's you, Missie."

"I never hated you, Wes," she said, with quiet desperation. "Some of the things you did, perhaps——"

"There you go!" he said savagely. "How the hell do you know what I did? You don't know. You've been jealous, that's all. Jealous and filled with dirty little suspicions. And I'm sick of it and through with it."

That terrified her. "Listen, Wes," she said, "I have come back. I don't ask anything, except to be allowed to stay. I won't interfere with you. You say I always hated you. That's not true, but you have never really cared for me. I've known that since very soon after we were married. So I don't ask to come back as your wife. But I do ask to come back, Wes."

"Since there is no place else to go!"

"No, Wes." Her voice shook. "I want Eddie. After all, why shouldn't I have him? I haven't done anything wrong."

"You haven't, eh? And where have you been for the past thirty-six hours? Don't tell me you've been at your grandmother's. I happen to know better."

"I went to a hotel."

"A hotel!" He laughed. "Which one?" And when she said nothing he laughed again. "I've made it my business to know that you went to no hotel in this town."

"Does it matter where I went? I am here now, in your house. Where I have been is not important."

"It's damned important, if you're afraid to tell me."

"I'm not afraid."

He went to the wall switch and turned on the electric light. In the glare he saw that she was white but quite steady. He pulled himself together, dropped his bullying manner.

"Understand this, Missie. Before there is any talk of your coming back I intend to know where you have been. And I intend to check up on it, so don't trouble to lie."

"I never lie. When I found you had taken Eddie away and that you were consulting Mr. MacDonald, I had a right to seek advice too."

"And where did you go for this—advice?"

"I went to Kirby Phelps."

He was astounded; his heavy face sagged. He stared at

her as though he had not seen her before, had never really seen her before.

"To Kirby Phelps!" he said. "And why Kirby Phelps? With all the men in the world to draw on, why Kirby Phelps?"

"I needed a friend." She still kept her voice steady. "I knew I could count on him."

"Oh!" he said, "so you knew you could count on him! Why? Is he your lover?"

"Not in your sense of the word, Wesley."

"And in what other sense of the word does a married woman run off to another man? Tell me that."

"I have not violated any marriage vows. I will swear that, if you like."

But he paid no attention to that, threw it aside. So far he had kept himself fairly well in hand, but now he threw aside all restraint; his colour rose with his voice, his rage and jealous anger beat about her and silenced her. He called her an unspeakable name and saw her flush, but hold her ground. As he raved about the room his own past was the devil that scourged him; he had no faith in man or in woman.

"And now you want me to take you back," he finished, breathing hard. "You have a lot of courage, my girl. Men have killed women for less than you have told me."

"I have told you the truth. I have not been unfaithful."

"Did you go to his apartment?"

"No. He came to me at my hotel."

"And he's in love with you?"

She hesitated.

"That's all over, Wesley. I shall never see him again."

"So it's over! Then there was something to be over. Remember this; I can go back to that hotel and learn all I want to. They don't employ blind servants. If he spent the night with you I'll know it, and so will everybody else! You can swear to me until you are black in the face, my girl. It's the fact I'm after, and the fact I'm going to have. Phelps! By God, that's funny."

"I've told you the truth."

He walked to the door, opened it, turned to her with that outthrust head which was his fighting attitude.

"I'm through," he said. "If you want to fight me in the courts, well and good. But I'm through, once and for all."

"Wes! For Eddie's sake——!"

"You leave Eddie out of this."

He went out with a certain ponderous dignity, the picture of a virtuous and outraged husband. She stood there in the dark and heard him leave the house, then as quietly as she had come she went upstairs, got her things and went out again. She had lost her lover, her husband and her child.

She spent the night at her grandmother's. Adelaide, cutting cake in the pantry for her night lunch, heard her rap on the window and admitted her. They talked in the pantry, Adelaide stolidly munching cake.

"I'll have to stay just one more night, Aunt Adelaide. To-morrow I'll find a room somewhere."

"But where have you been?" asked Adelaide curiously. "Wesley was here yesterday, and the way he talked to me——"

"I went out of town. Did he say where Eddie is?"

"No, but he's got a trained nurse with him. I got that out of him. What is he going to do?"

"He's going to divorce me."

"It will kill mother," said Adelaide somberly, and cut another piece of cake.

She slept there, and in the morning Mr. MacDonald sent for her. He looked tired, tired and harassed. It seemed to him that for a long time now he had been struggling with this Colfax family, trying to solve the problems they created for themselves. Sometimes he thought about them. The world was moving; here and there were men who were asking why people did thus and so. What was the reason for this Colfax generation? Why Adelaide? Why Lambert? Why Cecily?

And why Missie? Perhaps one had to go back to old William and Sarah; to consider children born without love, reared without understanding. And to Stella, vulgar hot-blooded Stella.

But he said nothing of all this.

"I suppose you know why I have sent for you, Missie?"

"I can imagine." She tried to smile at him.

"I think he is wrong, and I have told him so. Just now he is an angry man, an injured man." He raised his one hand as she started to speak. "I understand that he may be in error, but I refer to his attitude of mind. He thinks now that he wants a divorce; personally I am not so sure. He has pride, and no man cares to let the world know that his wife"—he checked himself—"that his marriage has been a failure."

"You have only heard his story, Mr. MacDonald."

"I can guess the other. The point is this; these matters are not open and shut propositions. A man has a right to change his mind. What Wesley wants to-day may not be what he wants next week, or in three months from now. What you want to-day——"

"I only want Eddie. I will never change about that."

"So does Wesley."

"What does he care about Eddie?" she asked sharply. "He hardly knows him. He wants him out of revenge, Mr. Mac-Donald."

"Possibly. Still, the law would be likely to give him the boy, under the circumstances."

She went very white.

"Missie, what about this other man, Phelps? Would he marry you?"

"Yes."

"And he's a decent fellow? I mean, you could be happy with him?"

"Not without Eddie."

He sat back, looked out of the window. Just so had Cecily

sat there, refusing to abandon her illegitimate child and come home. Who had said that these Colfax women were cold? Cold? The very breath of living was in them.

"You see, Missie," he said gently, "there comes a time in the lives of a good many women when they have to choose between the child and the man they care for. It's so commonplace that we have ceased to see it as the tragedy it is."

She looked at him with her candid eyes.

"I don't think I matter enough to worry about. I am only thinking of Eddie. What would Wesley make of him? I'm fighting for him, not for myself. He has to have his chance."

"And if Wesley can be induced to some sort of *modus vivendi*, you'll agree to it? I mean, you are through with Phelps?"

She considered that.

"I shall always care for him, Mr. MacDonald. I can't help that. But I will agree not to see him, or to communicate with him."

When she went back she learned that her grandmother had heard her come in, and wanted to talk to her.

She went up the stairs, with Adelaide behind her. She felt terrified. She had always been afraid of this old woman, with her rigid back and her rigid code, and for the first time since she had fled to Kirby a sense of shame overcame her; she saw herself through her grandmother's eyes, a strumpet, a vile woman who had left her husband for her lover's arms. She was trembling when she entered the room. But she need not have been afraid. Mrs. Colfax, lying back among her pillows, old, emaciated, slowly dying, was a pitiable and not a menacing figure.

"Sit down, Missie," she said feebly. "Adelaide tells me you have been out of town. How is Eddie?"

Missie's throat contracted. "He is all right."

"I am glad you have your boy, Missie. A son is a great comfort. A mother and a son are always very close. When your dear father was a boy——" She closed her eyes. "Not that Adelaide hasn't been a good daughter," she added, as an afterthought. "Have you heard from your father lately?"

"Not for almost a year."

The thin chest rose and fell in a long sigh.

"He would be here if he knew," she said. "He had his faults, but he always loved his old mother."

"I think you are the only person he ever really loved," said Missie softly.

After a while Mrs. Colfax slept, and Missie slipped away. Adelaide went down with her. She was filled with resentment against Lambert. She had written to the last address they had, but they had not heard from him. "She wants him," she said. "Day and night she wants him. She doesn't care whether I'm around or not. After all I've done for her——"

Her eyes filled with tears. They ran down her cheeks, splashed on her shelf-like bosom.

"I suppose if Wesley divorces you he'll put us out," she said dully. "If he'll only wait till mother goes, I can manage somehow. I could go to Cecily, I suppose. She's sick too. I've had a letter from Grace. She's had to give up her position."

Missie stood listening to her. How absurd it was to think that any individual lived to himself alone. By the mere fact of being, other lives touched one, a dozen, a thousand. Move but a fraction this way or that, and they were affected.

"If only Eileen was here, Adelaide!" she said. "Now—I hardly know what to do."

"Go back home. He won't put you out."

But she shuddered at the thought. Eddie gone, the curious servants, Wesley living at his club.

"Do you suppose Cecily would let me stay there?" she asked suddenly. "I could look after her, and let Grace go back to work."

"She never liked you. But I could write and find out."

"Write!" she said impatiently. "There's no time for letters, Adelaide. What am I going to do to-day? Where am I going to sleep to-night? I can't stay here. I can't go to a hotel without being known, and—I can't go home."

Adelaide's slow mind was confused. She stood fingering the cards in the tray on the hall stand. "She never liked you," she insisted. "She was angry when you came out and Grace was having to learn stenography. And she hated your father."

"Why shouldn't she have hated both of us? Why shouldn't she have hated the world, for the way it treated her?"

"She did a wicked thing."

"How wicked? She ran away with a man she loved; he meant to marry her. And she had the courage to bear his child."

"I don't know what's come over you, Missie! I never heard such talk."

"Maybe I'm growing up, Aunt Adelaide. It's time I did. And I'm going to Cecily; she can only throw me out. And maybe I can help her."

And to Cecily she went that afternoon; sitting in a train once more, slender, well dressed, composed of face. Looking out and seeing nothing."

"Last call to dinner, lady."

"Thanks. I don't care for anything."

BOOK V
Cecily

Chapter XXIX

MISSIE never forgot her arrival at that house, or her reception there; the hideous industrial town, with its rows on rows of indistinguishable houses, the dirt and heat, the strain of the past four days, and then facing the blank façade of that small frame house, its shutters closed in spite of the temperature, its air of mystery and secretiveness. The cabman gazing at the number:

"Guess this is right, lady. They all look alike in this part of town."

The door opening after a long wait, and in the doorway a tall thin sulky woman, who eyed her without speaking.

"Does Mrs. Stanwood live here?"

"She does."

"You are Grace, aren't you? I am Missie Dexter."

And not a move of welcome from that thin figure, no stepping aside to open a path for her. A slight stiffening.

"What can I do for you, Mrs. Dexter?"

"You can let me come in, if you will."

Grace moving aside unwillingly, letting her carry in her own bag, leaving her in the dark room while she brought matches and lighted an unshaded gas jet, and then standing in that poverty-stricken place, bare of the slightest effort at home-making, and confronting her haughtily.

"And what brings you here, may I ask?"

"Your Aunt Adelaide thought you might need help, Grace."

"We need nothing. We are getting on very well. As well as usual," she added, bitterly. "I have no intention of being rude, but you cannot stay here. There is a hotel; not much good, but you could spend the night."

There was an air of stale cooking in the room, of old mouldy plaster, of soot from the mills. And the heat was stifling. Missie's head felt dizzy, her hands trembled after their old fashion. She longed to open the shutters, but she felt that they were never opened; that they symbolized the haughty seclusion with which Cecily faced her cutting off from the world. And Grace was moving toward the door.

"Don't put me out. Please! You see, I have no other place to go."

Grace stopped. Missie saw her inspecting her carefully, her expensive clothing, her white ungloved hands, her diamond-studded watch, Wesley's gift on their honeymoon.

"Where's your husband?" she demanded, with the abruptness which Missie was to learn was characteristic.

"I have had some trouble, Grace. Very grave trouble. If I could stay here for a little while I know I could be helpful."

Grace smiled ironically.

"You don't know what you're talking about. Can you cook and wash and nurse? That's what I've been doing."

"You forget that I was raised to work. And I think I can nurse."

"Nurse her! She wouldn't let you in the room. Where's your boy? You have one, haven't you?"

And then at last Missie broke down. All the strain and tumult of the past few days was in that outburst of hers. She felt driven, lost; she had been repudiated, not only by her familiar world, but by this strange half world of shadows and old griefs.

When she was quieter she found that Grace had gone, and overhead she heard her moving about, and voices. She stood there waiting. She had done her best. If they put her out she would go back to Kirby. She would know that it was meant. Suddenly she wanted them to reject her. If they did the onus was not on her. It was on God. He would have closed all the other doors. So she stood there, while upstairs the mystery that was Cecily determined her life for her. And at last she heard Grace coming down the stairs.

"Mother says you are crazy, like all the Colfaxes," she said. "But you'd better stay overnight. You can have my bed. I'm sleeping on the sofa in her room anyhow."

So there was no decision after all. That was the way He did things; He put people into certain positions and left it to them to work them out, and she could see God's attitude as well as her own. Could see both sides, as usual. She drew a long breath, picked up her bag, followed Grace up the narrow uncarpeted staircase to a room at the back.

There began then a curious interlude for her. She was neither asked to stay nor requested to go. Cecily, slowly dying in that upper room, ignored her presence in the house. Missie never saw her until she lay dead, stark and more mysterious than ever.

Missie worked hard with her hands that she might be weary enough at night to sleep; the door into Cecily's room remained closed; Grace came and went, still suspicious, slow to relax. It was as though each of the three of them lived her secret life in some shut-off chamber with thin intangible walls, and that Cecily's closed door, like the shutters of the house, was a symbol.

Twice a day the postman passed by. Missie invented small excuses to herself to watch for him, but he brought her nothing. It seemed incredible that she had lived so long and then with one gesture have lost all the life she had lived.

But little by little Grace began to relax. She was grateful for the new cleanliness and order, grateful for the chance to give her undivided attention to her mother. Missie saw that she loved Cecily passionately, defiantly, but that she was ashamed to acknowledge it. At night she slept on a sagging sofa in the sickroom, and at all hours Missie could hear Cecily talking.

"You're not getting any sleep at all, Grace."

"Oh yes, I am."

"But I hear her talking."

"She talks out loud, to herself. She's always done it." And when Missie looked puzzled: "She's had nobody to talk to for a good many years."

Poverty was apparent everywhere. One day Missie sold her watch and bought some necessaries; dishes and a tray for Cecily, delicacies, sheets. Grace eyed them.

"Why did you do it?"

"I liked doing it."

Grace walked out of the room, and closed the door behind her. But after that she was gentler with Missie, even—odd to think of Grace being kind—even kinder.

One day the postman brought a letter at last. It was from Adelaide. Eddie was well, but still away. Her grandmother seemed about the same, maybe weaker. They had heard from Lambert and he was coming home. He hadn't said when, but she had sent him money for his ticket. And she had seen Mr. MacDonald, but he had no news; only Wesley still seemed determined to get a divorce.

"I hope if he does, Missie, that he will wait until mother passes on. She keeps asking about you——"

At night she lay in her uncomfortable bed, making desperate plans, to the steady sound of that monotonous voice from the front room; Cecily thinking out loud while Grace slept, putting her case, presenting her defence maybe. Or not putting her case; restating her old angers, making a last clutch at old hatreds.

She would stay here while they needed her. Then she would go to Kirby, and together they would fight for Eddie. They might even steal Eddie. People did such things. They would steal him and hide away somewhere. In Europe, maybe. People did such things.

She would get out of bed, pad around the room in her bare feet, and all the while Cecily would be muttering in the front room. She was confused, unsure of anything. Unsure even of Kirby. She had rejected him, hurt his pride, made him ridiculous. Twice now she had done that. Men were sensitive as to their passions; perhaps because they felt themselves that nature had played a trick on them, made them absurd in love.

She would crawl back into her bed, able to see Kirby's side, Wesley's, Cecily's, but not her own.

She had been there a month, and Cecily was slowly dying, when Tommy came. Grace was out and Missie answered the door bell. Tommy was on the doorstep. He was clad in a long linen duster, revealing his sloping shoulders almost painfully, and in the street sat a car, covered with mud and already swarming with children.

"Hello, Missie," Tommy said casually. "Hey, you kids! Get out of there or I'll skin you. Quick now!"

Her first thought was of Eddie.

"Is there anything wrong, Tommy?"

"There will be if those youngsters do any damage. No, there's nothing wrong. I was testing my engine, and I thought I'd run in and call on you. That's all."

Already street doors were opening, windows being raised. There was a man with an automobile at the Stanwoods'. "Mother, hurry! Here's an automobile!" "Jim, wake up! There's an automobile outside." Like old Sarah's carriage the street thrilled to it, gained importance, dignity. "Willie, you come here and have your nose wiped before you go out. D'you hear me?"

Tommy, oblivious of all this, entered the house. With his pale blue eyes, while apparently seeing nothing, he was observing everything; Missie, big eyed and thin, the ugly poverty of the place, the odour of cooking and of disinfectants, the sheets hanging in the yard to dry.

"If you'll go into the parlour I'll come in a minute. I'm cooking."

"I'll go back with you," said Tommy.

But in the kitchen he had not much to say. He took off his duster, stood jingling the money in his pocket. He had seen

Eddie. He was fine, growing too. Going to be a tall fellow some day. Yes, they'd had a good trip. Eileen had bought a lot of clothes and jimcracks. No, he couldn't go back that night. To-morrow sometime.

When Grace came in he gave her no chance to be haughty. "You're Grace, are you? Well, let's have supper. Grace before meat, eh!"

He enjoyed his joke tremendously, and when Grace went upstairs he said she looked like a damned competent woman. He ate the simple meal with enjoyment, and later on insisted on bringing in the dried sheets.

"Used to do it for my mother," he said. "Where's the basket for the clothes pins?"

He left a curious sense of quiet and emptiness when he had gone. He cranked his car, climbed in, started the engine with a series of explosions.

"See you to-morrow," he called, and drove away.

The next morning evidences that he was still in town began to arrive. The first thing to come was a parlour set, including a self-rocker, of a vivid and intense blue. Following that came a hospital bed, soft mattress, pillows, blankets, china, odd chairs, cooking utensils, pictures, a new stove, a fern in a dish, canned delicacies, even a basket of fresh fruit. Fortunately Grace had had to go out. Missie, sitting confused among these riches, had a vision of Tommy, happy and active, darting into one store after another, jingling his money, ordering this, ordering that. Happy. Getting some fun out of his money at last.

In a few moments Tommy arrived himself, very dirty, rather breathless. In the tonneau of his car he had two workmen, and three or four rugs. He was relieved to find Grace not there.

"Come on, boys. Hurry up, or we'll get thrown out."

He had, it appeared, paced off the rooms the night before.

"Got to get all fixed up before Grace comes," he said to

Missie. "If I'm here she'll order it out. If I've gone she'll have to keep the stuff. I know her sort."

He was everywhere. On his knees, laying rugs; in the parlour doorway, squinting at his pictures on the walls. They were very bad pictures, very bright.

"Colour!" he said. "Colour's the thing and plenty of it. Some day I'm going to make coloured automobiles. You wait, Missie. I'll show them a thing or two."

Luckily, Cecily had had her opiate and was sleeping.

It was not until the house was in approximate order that he came to the real object of his visit. He had washed at the kitchen sink and was drying his face when he spoke.

"Sorry you've been having this trouble, Missie. Have you thought what it is that you want?"

"I can't have what I want, Tommy."

He put down the towel, coughed.

"I've talked to Kirby," he said. "Didn't want to butt in, though, until I knew what you wanted. If it's the boy——"

"It is the boy, Tommy," she said steadily.

"Then I guess I'll see Wes." He glanced at her, glanced away. "Kirby's a fine fellow, Missie."

"I know that, better than any one. But if I can't have him and Eddie too, Tommy——"

"It's the boy?"

"Yes," she said, with her throat tight. "Yes, it's the boy, Tommy."

He left almost immediately, giving a final satisfied glance into the parlour on his way out. "Cheerful, eh?" he asked. "Something to come home to! And tell Her Grace that these fellows are ordered not to take it back. That'll settle her!"

But Grace did not send anything back. She looked and listened, and then she went into that dreadful parlour and closed the door. When she came out she had been crying.

Only a few nights later Missie wakened to hear a queer silence over the house. Cecily was not talking. There were always silent intervals in that closed room, but somehow this one was different.

Missie sat huddled on the side of her bed until morning. She knew that Cecily was dead, that she had left this strange adventure called life for an even stranger one; and that Grace was in there alone, keeping her final vigil.

And she knew too that this phase of her own life was over; that now at long last she must cease drifting and commence to build her life. That she must take the materials she had at hand, her poor bricks made without straw, and out of them fashion something that would endure.

At dawn she went down to the kitchen and wrote her letter on the table there.

"I ask very little, really. I can only repeat what I think you know in your heart, Wesley. I did an impetuous thing, maybe a wrong thing, but I did nothing shameful. And I have a right to be with Eddie. If I come back I will promise to stay. I will make any promises you like, but I know Eddie needs me, as badly as I need him. You cannot hire a substitute to give him what I can give him.

"And as I sit here, with Aunt Cecily lying dead upstairs, I feel that life is too short for bitterness and hatred. It seems to me that even pride is a foolish thing. I have none now. I will do what you like, be what you like, only let us start again."

She put down her pen and sat, her chin in her hands, looking out the window into the dingy backyard. This was the way He did things. He held you back and let you see for yourself. There was no yes and no with God.

She was still there when Adelaide's telegram came. "Dear mother passed away quietly at two this morning." Missie put down the message. So they had gone together, this mother and daughter; kept some mysterious tryst in the night, met in some unknown rendezvous.

And this too He had done.

Chapter XXX

HER return to Wesley was arranged, rather like an armistice, by Tommy.

"Then it's all settled. Will you write, or shall I?"

And Wesley, sipping a whisky and soda—they were at the club—"You do it, Tom. I'm not much good on paper."

It was a queer homecoming, with Wesley in the parlour, half arrogant, half uneasy, with Eddie not back yet, a new maid carrying up her bag, and she herself, uncertain, in the hall. She had not been prepared for the Wesley she saw. He looked older, heavier, unsure; and his eyes, like the eyes of an unhappy boy, looked at her from the heavy folds of his face, from above the carefully adjusted Ascot tie.

"I can't very well welcome you home, under the circumstances," he said. "But I can explain a few things. Eddie will be back on Sunday. And I have new servants; the old ones knew too much. Also I want to say this. I think there has been no gossip. Every one has been away, every one who counts anyhow."

She hesitated. Her throat was dry, her hands shaking. He had suffered too. She had not thought of him as suffering. It was dreadful. All this anguish, and nothing coming of it. Nothing. But he misconstrued her silence. His voice hardened.

"Well, have you nothing to say?"

"I was trying to think what to say, Wes."

"You apparently wanted to come back."

"Yes. I am very glad to be back. Very—grateful."

Halfway up the stairs she stooped. They must do better

than this. He had tried to make it easy for her, had dressed
carefully, had probably even rehearsed that speech of his.
If she went down again——

She turned around, but Wesley was in the hall, putting on
his hat, straightening his tie before the mirror. His gestures
were complacent, with the complacence of a man who has
done his duty. He did not so much as glance at her, and so
she went quietly on up the stairs.

He did not come home to dinner that night, and she was
forced at last to accept his unequivocal attitude. He was
giving her a home but nothing else. Chains for her and freedom for himself.

She went into Eddie's room and sat by the window. She
was tired, but she was happy. Quite satisfied. She counted
the days until Sunday.

She went to see Adelaide the next day, an Adelaide in new
black which did not look new on her, a vague purposeless
Adelaide, who moved about the house, carrying things and
putting them down, and then forgetting what she had done
with them. Missie gathered that there would be very little left
after the estate was settled.

"One thing," she said. "I won't have to worry about Cecily
now."

Then she cried, softly and without hope.

Missie learned that Lambert had come back, but too late;
and that he had gone again, after seeing Mr. MacDonald
and failing to get a loan from him. But that he had ordered
extravagant flowers and a suit of black clothing for the
funeral, and had had both bills sent to Adelaide.

"I won't pay them," said Adelaide, through her tears.
"If I had what he got from mother, I'd be independent. Now
where can I go? What can I do, Missie?"

On Sunday Eddie came back. Her very heart turned over
with joy when she saw him. He looked well, handsome and
sturdy; he had grown, too. But she was shocked to find that
the reunion, for which she had sacrificed so much, meant

little or nothing to him; that he even felt strange with her. He seemed to remember his toys better. He was in a frenzy of excitement over his toys. He would pick them up and run to the nurse with them.

"Look, Miss Harris! I told you I had a train."

"Let's get your coat and hat off first, Eddie darling," said Missie.

"Miss Harris takes them off, she knows where to put them. Look, Miss Harris, I told you there was a caboose."

Missie was sick with disappointment and with jealousy of the smiling young nurse. After a while she gave up and going into her room, searched her face in the mirror. It was not a joyous face; it was sober, with faint lines already at the corners of the mouth. A thin face, not young, its radiance dimmed, its light gone out.

She turned away, a little sick.

After that she picked up the threads of her life as best she could. It was not easy. Wesley was drinking at night, and in the mornings he was irritable.

"I'll have to have some money to-day, Wes."

"Why the devil didn't you ask me yesterday? I don't carry money around with me."

"I put it off as long as I could, but now——"

"How much?"

"I shall need market money, and Eddie——"

"*How much?*"

She would tremble after he had gone.

Adelaide was still living at the old house, Tommy and Eileen prospering beyond their dreams. Trouserless natives in African jungles were riding Tommy's wheels. He had bought a small mill, was making his own steel, his own tubing. Eileen had a pearl necklace now, was blue pencilling her calling lists, already had her eye on the old Colfax place.

"How long is Wes going to let Adelaide stay there? It's ridiculous."

"He doesn't want her here, and where else can she go?"

A year, two years, going by; Eddie growing, watching his father, adoring him for his size, his strength, his casual caresses. Observant, too.

"What's the matter with daddy, mother?"

"Nothing, dear. Run back to bed. Daddy's not very well."

"Can I get into bed with him?"

"Not to-night, darling."

The instinct to protect them both, one against the other, became almost an obsession with her. Boys needed an ideal, something to live up to. She began, very deliberately, to build up for Eddie an ideal Wesley, the loving and generous father, the strong man.

"Why doesn't he come home? I want him."

"He's busy, Eddie. He has to work so we can have this nice home and everything."

"But I want him. I want to show him my Easter bunny."

The boy was headstrong and wilful at times. When he wanted things he wanted them desperately, and things were important to him. He was like Wesley in that. But having achieved them he was charming. There was something of Lambert in him then, in his smile, in his satisfied contentment.

She tried to fill her life with him, to make herself attractive to him. It was for him that she brushed her soft hair until it shone, watched her figure, her hands, her nails. When she was dressed for a party she would go in, and he would inspect her gravely. There was a new beauty about her, a great gentleness. She was gentle even to Wesley.

"Can I put your studs in, Wes?"

"No, thanks."

Sometimes she felt that her very gentleness exasperated him, but she was holding now to what she had; never again would she endanger it.

Now and then she heard of Kirby, but she never saw him. He was still racing. There were no speedways, no racing tracks. The route lay along country roads, with dangerous turns. Cars skidded in dust or mud, turned over and killed or maimed the drivers. She would lie in bed at night and see Kirby in these perils, and her body would be covered with a hot sweat. Then she would get up and look at Eddie, quietly sleeping, and her heart would settle down again.

One day Eileen rustled in and told her that Kirby had been hurt in a race, and that Tommy had gone to him.

Missie's hands shook, her throat tightened. Her voice sounded odd in her ears.

"Badly hurt?"

"We don't know. I'll telephone you when I hear, if you like."

All carefully casual, Eileen-ish; not looking at Missie, admiring her rings, talking to let Missie get her breath. But when she got up to go she did an unusual thing. She put her hand on Missie's shoulder.

"I think he'll be all right. Don't worry."

"I haven't the right to worry, Eileen."

"Don't be silly. What's that got to do with it? If I had my way you'd have the right."

"And lose Eddie?"

"Nonsense! Take Eddie with you. I know some things about Wesley Dexter that would take the wind out of his sails."

"It's too late, Eileen."

When Eileen had gone she went upstairs. She felt breathless and very tired. She felt like Adelaide that day in the old house; as though she had gone through life picking things up and putting them down, and getting nowhere.

She sat up that night until Eileen telephoned her. Kirby was better, was going to get well. Then she crept into her bed. She found that she was shaking again, but very calm, thinking clearly. Eileen was wrong; she had done the right thing. If she had the last two years to live over again she would not change them. But she could not sleep. After a while she got up and went into the nursery. Eddie was asleep;

sound and secure. Kirby was safe and Eddie was safe. She had so much to be thankful for. So much. So very much.

She had an impulse then to go into Wesley's room, to waken him and tell him: "I am glad to be here, Wes. Glad and happy. Can't we start again? I'll try harder. And I was never unfaithful, Wes. You know that, don't you?"

She got as far as his door, opened it. But Wesley was lying on his back, snoring heavily, and over the room hung the odour of stale whisky. She went out without waking him.

It was sometime after that that Tommy took over the old Colfax house for Eileen. "Something for her to play with," and being loath to throw Adelaide out, offered her an annuity for life. He was totally unprepared for the scorn with which she refused it.

"Why not? I can afford it, and you need it."

"That's not the question."

"Then what is?"

"The Colfaxes do not accept charity. They have a decent pride."

"Then to hell with pride," said Tommy. "If you'd rather accept Wesley Dexter's help than mine——!"

"If my niece offers me a home, that is her affair. And mine."

Her enormous bosom heaved, her small eyes defied him. And Tommy went away at last jingling his money furiously, sheepishly admiring.

"Queer lot, these Colfaxes. Got spunk, though. Missie too; lots of spunk. And Grace! Her Grace!"

He chuckled. He had never forgotten Grace.

So Adelaide came to the tall dark house, with Wesley ungraciously assenting. She moved in, bringing with her her mother's set of heavy walnut furniture and an incredible number of trunks filled with old clothing, hoarded without reason.

Missie tried to build her into her life, made her comfortable, was very kind to her. But from that time on Adelaide did her bit to complicate the situation, watched Wesley relentlessly, even attempted to undermine Eddie's confidence in his father. In her third floor front room there gradually developed the same odour of mustiness which had pervaded the old house. At night mice came to eat the crumbs from her surreptitious suppers; she set traps for them, and when she heard one snap she would get up and taking out the small dead body, would lay it carefully on her hearth. Sometimes by morning six or seven little corpses would be lying in a row.

Wesley did not like her, did not pretend to.

He would eye her at the table.

"Don't hurry, Adelaide. There won't be another meal until bedtime."

And Adelaide would retort angrily: "If I ate as much as you drink, Wesley, there would be reason for remark."

Missie would sit quietly, listening to them, listening to the creak of the dumb waiter, waiting for them to finish. And they would eat on and on, concentratedly, their heavy figures bent forward, their eyes on the food.

To that group was to be added another before long.

One day Missie, coming into the house, saw a strange and rather shabby overcoat and hat in the hall.

"Who is here, Pauline?"

"A Mr. Colfax, madam. He is up with Miss Adelaide."

So her father had come back. She stiffened a little, went up to her room, removed her hat and wrap. Why had he come? Did he hope to stay? She would fight that. She could cope with Adelaide when it came to Eddie, but not with her father, that dangerous irresponsibility of his, his facile gift of lies, his attraction and his cynicism. Her face was set when she went upstairs.

Adelaide was sitting uncompromisingly in a chair, and on the floor was Lambert with Eddie, exploiting a new toy he had brought with him.

"Five cents on the red horse," he was saying. "Put up your money, son."

He looked sheepish when he saw her, got up, dusted his knees.

"Well, well!" he said. "And here's your mother come to scold us. Women are the devil, Eddie!"

He kissed her. She saw that he looked older, very shabby but somehow natty.

"Why didn't you let me know, father?"

He smiled.

"I came on impulse," he said. "And I didn't trust Wesley's hospitality over much. I rather fancy he'd have damned his immortal soul to keep me away."

"Run downstairs, Eddie," she said hastily. "It's time for your supper."

Adelaide had not moved. Her small eyes, filled with hatred, were on Lambert.

"Teaching that child to gamble!" she said. "You're old enough to know better."

"Always gentle and sweet!" said Lambert. "Family affection's a great thing, Missie."

He stayed for months.

Eddie adored him—there was much of the boy in Lambert, the incorrigible boy—adored him and imitated him, ripped out a good round oath now and then, copied his tone in speaking to Adelaide, swaggered like him. While he was there Missie's peace was definitely gone.

It was not only Eddie. Wesley was barely civil to him, and between him and Adelaide there was open warfare. Late one night she heard a scuffle and a shriek from the pantry downstairs. It was Adelaide's voice. When Missie went down Lambert was leaning against the doorway in his pajamas, a revolver in his hand and a sardonic grin on his face.

"I thought I heard a burglar," he said. "But it was only Adelaide rifling the refrigerator as usual."

Adelaide was crying, with a slice of bread and jam still clutched in her hand.

Missie never believed the burglar story.

It was after he had been there for three months that he took sick. He had been both eating and drinking unwisely; Missie guessed that good food and drink had been luxuries to him for some time, and on top of it he took pneumonia. She relieved the nurse, for he would not have Adelaide in the room, and it was when he was convalescent that she had that conversation with him about her mother.

He was willing to talk; he had always liked to talk. His marriage had been a mistake, an impulsive thing. He had stuck it out as long as he could, but there were "fundamental differences." When he left for the last time he was relieved. He felt free. He had played poker on the train that night and lost almost all he had.

"And you felt nothing? You had no regrets at abandoning her?"

"You want me to say that I had, my dear, don't you? Well, I am no hypocrite. God forbid that I should speak ill of her now, but you have lived your life and made your own mistakes." He eyed her shrewdly. "No, I had no regrets. Of course, when I heard——"

She looked down at him, so tidy, so unregenerate in his soft bed. What had he done when he heard? What had he thought? How much guilt had he felt? But as it turned out, he had felt none. He had chosen to believe that Stella had died because she had been caught stealing a black silk dress.

Well, maybe that was life. Strip off the armour of self-delusion, the shams and hypocrisies, and what was left? A cringing soul, unable to bear the truth about itself, covering itself fiercely with denials.

Chapter XXXI

TIME moving on now, relentlessly. Eddie going to dancing school in a blue Norfolk suit with a white collar, carrying his pumps rolled up in paper; Mr. MacDonald a judge, addressing graduating classes. "The ways of America are the ways of peace." Tommy building automobiles in quantity, growing richer all the time, carrying Kirby up with him, and Wesley. The leisurely days gone; talk now of drive, of efficiency, complaint of pressure.

Sometimes when Wesley came up the stairs he was breathing hard; he ate, drank, smoked and worked too much, and while Tommy and Kirby were sleeping he was leading the new gilded night life of the town.

He was a tired man, prematurely old. Sometimes Missie thought he felt this. He would make an effort to talk to the boy, but his attention would flag. Now and then on Sunday afternoons they walked out together, Wesley in his dark morning coat and striped trousers, his top hat, gloves, and stick; Eddie circling about his pompous figure like a puppy. But Wesley was too old; he could not relax, had forgotten how to be young, and Missie felt the tragedy in this, but she could do nothing.

She had accepted her life. At night sometimes she dreamed of Kirby Phelps; that curiously faithful heart of hers would not let go of him. But when she saw him, as now she occasionally did, there was no attempt on his part to remind her of that brief episode of theirs. Sometimes she thought he brightened when he saw her, but that was all. He never sought her out, never tried to see her alone. But he had lost his whimsical smile; he was a sober man now, meticulously go-

ing ahead with his business, still driving a racing car occa-
ionally, tinkering in odd times with a new motor for aëroplanes.

"Clear crazy," Tommy said. "Says the mails will go by
air some day! Says somebody will fly across the Atlantic, too.
Wants me to make the damned things, by heck!"

Just how much she had built on Kirby she did not know
until she lost him. Lost him, ironically enough, not by death
or tragedy, but to another woman. After the fashion of her
kind she had believed that his feeling for her had been as
enduring as her own, as able to live without food. She had
held him, more or less loosely, but still she had held him, for
years. He was something fine and dependable and faithful,
always in her mind, a part of the background of her life, her
release in sleep.

And then, not brutally but as gently as he knew how, he
took himself away. It was not easy for him. She still made
her queer call to him, perhaps because he had never possessed
her. Indeed, he was never entirely able to forget her. But
he was living a barren life. He resented the lapses into which
he was occasionally driven. He looked on men like Wesley
with loathing, and he began to be afraid.

One cold January day Missie took the carriage—Wesley
still considered motors *bourgeoise*—and drove out to the
country club, and with her chinchilla coat drawn about her,
walked over the frozen links. The club had grown, the links
were already in the championship class. All around, on the
hillsides, were large country estates. It was the thing to do
now; Tommy and his kind had made it possible. There were
even paved roads. Strange how life moved on. She thought
of that as she walked. She was thirty-four. Soon she would
be forty. When she looked at herself in the mirror she could
see no change. She still saw the Missie Colfax of her girl-
hood. But Eddie was growing up into a new world, a world
that had outstripped her. The thought frightened her. She
would lose him; he would go on and she would stand still.

When she went back to the clubhouse Kirby was there, sitting alone in a big chair by the fire. He did not look up when she approached. He was gazing somberly into the fire, his fine head drooping, but he gave no impression of relaxation. There was an intensity of gaze, a certain rigidity of body. Her old breathlessness came back.

"Kirby."

He seemed to return from some remote place, turned slowly, looked at her.

"I was thinking of you, Missie."

He got up, drew a chair for her. But he did not sit down. He stood looking down at her, at the firelight on her face and quiet hands. He seemed at a loss for words, and Missie too, was silent. Always, when they met now, there was this pause between them. It was as though their separations tore down the wall between them, and when they met it rose again. Perhaps too there was always with the passing of the years a faint shock, a furtive endeavour on the part of each to re-build the other, to reconstruct the ideal.

"What were you thinking?"

He hesitated.

"I was wondering if you could see my feeling for you, what it is and always will be. And yet try to understand something I want to say."

"I can understand anything from you, Kirby."

He looked at her, ran his hand over his hair.

"I wonder if you will. You see, I don't want to hurt you. If you were different, and things had been better for you; or if I were different——"

She looked up at him with her candid eyes, tried to smile.

"I wouldn't have you changed, Kirby."

He sat down then, but he did not look at her. He fell back into his old position, head drooped, hands extended on the arms of the chair, holding on to them.

"Let me put my case, Missie," he said. "I have loved you long and well. I have—reverenced you. I loved you too well to try to keep you when you came to me. I knew you wanted your boy; you are that sort. No lover, no husband, could compensate you if you lost him. And I have lived on the husks of love ever since. Don't misunderstand me, I am no plaster saint, but I have done my best."

He paused, but she had nothing to say. She was waiting, with the terrible patience of women, for what was coming.

"I am over forty. Men don't fall in love, real love, very easily at my age. Don't misunderstand that either, Missie. I have not fallen in love. But what am I to do? I am not a promiscuous man. Like you, I have a curious quality of faithfulness——" He did not finish that. "If there was any hope I could wait indefinitely; if I thought that eventually you would leave Wesley. But I know you will not do that, for Eddie's sake."

"No," she said.

He stirred restlessly, sat up.

"I have found a woman who cares for me," he said, almost abruptly. "And I need a home, a home and children. I am lonely, Missie."

Once more she had the queer constriction, the sickening breathlessness. She wanted to shriek aloud that she was lonely too; to beat her hands on his chest and implore him not to desert her, not to take away her dream once more; to beg him to stand fast and save her from all the empty years to come. But her lips were stiff. She could not move them.

"Does that shock you, Missie? Or hurt you? God knows I don't want to hurt you."

She stirred a little, found her voice.

"No," she said. "It is very natural. I am glad you are being honest with me. After all, I can give you nothing."

"You have given me a great deal, for a long time."

"Is she—young?"

"In her twenties. She is rather like you."

She flushed, but she was still outwardly quiet.

"I am not committed. I know, as a man does know those

things, that she is willing to marry me. But I wanted to see
you first. I wanted to know if there was any other hope, and
I wanted to be honest with you."

"I never had any hold on you, Kirby dear. You have always been free."

"I have never felt free, nor wanted to." Then he made a
last impulsive gesture to her, caught her hand and held it to
his cheek. "If I had only kept you, my darling, when you
came to me!"

Some inkling of her tragedy must have come to him when
he touched her hand, icy cold as it was. But her eyes were
steadfast, her face quiet.

"I want you to be happy," she told him. "And I cannot be
selfish. I have had you to myself for a long time."

She left him composedly enough, went home to her house,
to her life. To Wesley and Adelaide and Eddie, to the week of
grand opera with the newly rich occupying the boxes in full
dress, and the old families in demi-toilet in the orchestra, to
Eileen in a tiara, pretending to like Wagner and Tommy
peacefully sleeping, having guaranteed a thousand dollars
for his nap; to giving endless dinners, listening to talk about
woman suffrage and the Pankhursts, even to talk about divorce. Divorce had come into the open now. "The purpose of
marriage is the protection of the idea of the family. Even if
the incident of happiness is lost, duty remains."

Gus Hemingway listening to that and watching Anna
across the table, Wesley gay and heavily flirtatious, Adelaide
eating and spilling food on her dress. Cocktails, sherry, champagne, liqueurs; the voices rising, a fuddled gentleman running his hand amorously over Missie's bare arm.

And Missie at the foot of the table, watching the service,
listening to the creak of the dumb waiter.

They were cheery enough now, these men who surrounded
Wesley. Old Archibald's young man with bowels was gone;
after riding hard after railroads, corporations, trusts. No
danger now of a fellow going to jail for pursuing ordinary

business methods. Construction now, a tariff board, parcel post, arbitration. Coming on, the country. No more wars to disturb peace. Peace conferences; The Hague. No more wars.

They never noticed, these men and their women, that Missie's faint smile was a fixed one, and that when they spoke to her she seemed to come back from some far place.

But after they had gone she would trail upstairs in her long soft dresses and go into Eddie's room. Sometimes she only stood and watched him; sometimes she knelt and prayed. And her prayers were queer things; for peace, for happiness for the boy, and breathless little apologies that she could be sad when she had so much. So very, very much.

She never knew that they were queer.

She heard nothing from Kirby. The winter dragged on, and spring came. There had been no announcement, nothing. Then one night in May she went into Wesley's room to open the window.

She stood there, breathing in the early summer night. Adelaide ought to have her windows up; she would go up, but what was the use? Adelaide hated fresh air.

As her eyes grew accustomed to the darkness, she saw that a man was standing quietly across the street. For a moment she felt that their glances crossed, that the eyes in the shadow below were fixed on her intently. Then the figure moved away with quick nervous footsteps. Kirby's walk. She waited breathless until he reached a street lamp, but he did not pass under it. She could not tell whether it was Kirby or not.

She went back to her room and sat down. She felt very tired. She thought: Thank God Eddie would be a man. Men could shape their own lives; most of them lived for the day, thought in terms of actualities. They left patience and endurance for women. Patience and endurance were not virtues in a woman; they were necessities, forced on her. Perhaps some day things would change and women would renounce them. They would rise up and say: "We are not patient. We will endure no more." Then what would happen to the world?

The next morning at breakfast Wesley opened an envelope, stared at the contents and then grinned as he passed it to her. She was aware of his eyes on her as she took it. It was an invitation to Kirby's wedding.

"What is the custom under such circumstances?" said Wesley, still watching her. "Does one send the usual silver?"

"I should think we would send something very nice," she said evenly.

"Why? To show we don't give a damn?"

She did not answer. She was glad that Kirby had sent the invitation; glad that he was so honest. In effect he had said to her: "See, now, I want you to have this. It is important to me that you have it. Between us there can be nothing underhanded."

That day she selected a wedding gift, being very careful about the engraving. Just before she left, however, she asked the clerk for a glass of water. When she drank it he saw that her hands were trembling.

Chapter XXXII

WHEN Eddie was thirteen he went away to school.

The night before he left Missie sat preparing his outfit for him. She sat as Stella might have sat, doggedly sewing tapes bearing his name on his towels, his blankets, his stockings; writing his name on his handkerchiefs and sheets with indelible ink, and setting the marking with a hot iron. She sewed and pressed, and as she finished she piled the things up neatly.

She was through, now. She had done her part. Henceforward other people would guide Eddie. Yet how short a time she had had with him; it was only yesterday that she had shouted that the baby was in the satchel, and now here she was, alone again. One paid a price for security, and then there was no security. One loved, and as if that were a signal, the thing one loved was taken away. She had no confidence in life that night. She called the roll of the years, and saw one after another the milestones which had marked it. Little joys, great griefs, that was life.

When Eddie came in, however, he found her placid, her hands working busily.

"Gee!" he said. "I feel rotten about leaving you."

"You'll be home often, and I can go on. You'll write regularly, won't you?"

"I sure will. Say, mother, old MacDonald had the piper again to-night. It seems funny it's the same one he had when you were a little girl."

"Why?"

"Well, you'd think he'd be dead by now, wouldn't you?"

How old she must seem to him, and how young she felt! As though she would live forever, on and on.

He did not notice her silence, but he hung around her all the evening.

He was very long as he knelt down by his bed to say his prayers that last night. He was not a little boy any more. She knew, as she listened, that she was passing another milestone; that never again would he kneel there while she sat by: "God bless daddy and mother and Adelaide and grandfather."

He always put Wesley first. That was her work, was what she had built.

"Daddy and I have been talking about Christmas." "Daddy has been studying your school report, dear." "Daddy thinks you might like a party on your birthday."

The rugs lifted, a piano and a violin, and an early supper of creamed chicken and ice-cream. She would hover over the table, helping to pull the crackers, adjust the paper caps, distributing the ribbons of the Jack Horner pie. And when it was over she would hurry to get the house in order before Wesley came back.

"What's all the mess about?"

"I told you, Wes. Eddie's had a party."

"Dirty little devils!"

But when Eddie gravely thanked him for the party he ironically accepted the thanks.

"Had a good time, eh?"

"Fine, daddy."

Sometimes he would glance at Missie. What was she getting at? Was she trying to win him back through the boy? The idea flattered him without touching him; unconsciously he would straighten his tie.

Late that last night she went into Eddie's room. He was sleeping soundly, a handsome boy, with Wesley's head and Lambert's long slim body. She wondered what that queer mixed heredity would do to him. What had she given him to offset it, she with her own weaknesses, her lack of heroic stature.

She had tried; taken him to church with her, for she

wanted him to have a God, not the Jehovah of her grandmother, but a loving and understanding one. On Decoration
Days he always went with her to fix her graves. She seemed
to have a great many of them now. But here too she was
careful. He was to have no horror of death. One day there,
however, he frightened her. They had watched the soldiers
coming up the hill, had listened while the local soprano,
elderly and just escaping the high notes, had sung the Star
Spangled Banner, and had stood still while the despairing
finality of "taps" was sounded.

"When I grow up," he said, "I'm going to be a soldier."

She was standing by Harry's grave. Suddenly she was back
once more on the bridge over the railway embankment, the
crowd cheering the troop train pulling out, somewhere far off
a band playing. "Good-bye, Dolly, I must leave you——"

She leaned over, picked a dried leaf from the grave.

"There are other kinds of courage than the courage to
fight, Eddie."

"What?" he said. "Making money and sitting around
clubs?"

It was then that she had decided he must go away. He was
growing up. It would be easier at a distance. Clare, Eileen's
girl, had already gone. She was a pretty child, spoiled and
headstrong, and Eileen had shipped her off with relief.

But Missie was different. She held off for a while. Then
one day they took a drive into the country. Wesley had abandoned the carriage at last, and bought a limousine. They had
a break-down, and the chauffeur hailed a passing car. Not
until it had slowed up did she see that Wesley was driving it,
and that there was a woman beside him. He recognized the
car at the same moment and muttering something, drove on.
But Eddie had seen him.

"Why, it's dad! It's dad, and he didn't know us!"

"Never mind. There will be another car along soon."

"Who was with him, mother? Who was the lady?"

"Perhaps it was Aunt Eileen."

"It wasn't. I never saw her before."

She glanced at Adelaide, but Adelaide was looking straight ahead.

Then at last she knew that he must go.

She saw him off with a smile that next day. He was gone. He would come back, from school, from college, but he would never be entirely hers again. She went back to the house, to Adelaide and Wesley, to Eileen's occasional visits, and to such dreams as remained to her.

She lost weight that fall. In evening dress her collar bones showed painfully, and there was a flat opaque look in her eyes for the first time. And as if their common loneliness brought them together, now and then Gus Hemingway came in to see her. He would wander in, sit almost speechless, go away. He was still painting cows. Sometimes he looked as if he wanted to say something important, but he never did.

"It's a queer world," he said once.

"Maybe we make it queer, Gus."

"I don't know. Everybody in it is alone. Some people can't stand it; that's why they go in crowds. But they're alone just the same."

For a few months he wandered in and out, always with that look of something to say, and never saying it. Then he drifted away. She wondered how she had failed him. Perhaps she had no gift for friendship.

That fall she had a talk with Wesley. It was not easy to talk to him. For years now their relationship had been limited to the surface affairs of their common life. She had given his dinner parties and consolidated his position, had eaten his food and worn his clothes, had protected Eddie from his weaknesses, had paid her penalty with her head high, but with an inward humility.

But as Christmas vacation approached she took her courage in her hands and went to him.

"Eddie will be back on the twenty-first, Wes, and I think we ought to have a talk first."

"What about?"

"About you and me, and this house. He has been away to school. He will have learned—things. He'll only be here for ten days, Wes, and I would like things to be happy for him."

"Happy! Go as far as you like."

"It isn't a question of me." Her colour rose, her hands trembled as they always did. "Wes, one person can't make a home. It takes two."

"You've got Adelaide!" He still resented Adelaide.

But when she said nothing he softened his voice.

"What do you want me to do, Missie?"

"Just to be careful. A boy needs to look up to his father. It isn't enough that you are successful; he needs more than that. He's not a baby any longer. And he's fond of you, Wes. I've never interfered with that. You must give me that credit. He thinks you are a great man."

"And I'm not! I suppose that's the inference?"

"No. But there is a certain amount of illusion in all hero worship. I want him to keep it as long as he can."

But he understood her. He went on with his shaving, puffing out his heavy cheeks to let the razor slide over them, careful not to meet her eyes in the glass. He was fifty-two; his good looks were definitely gone, his hair was graying rapidly. She felt a wave of pity for him that day. It was not his big lusty body which ruled him now, but something rather pathetic, a refusal to admit approaching age, a desperate clinging to youth and the illusion that he could buy romance and love.

"You can count me in. I'll do my bit."

A few days after that he called her into his room. The summons startled her; it was an unwritten law that she never enter there while he was present. He was standing on the hearth, near that very poker with which she had struck him, and he held a parcel in his hand. It was a gold watch for Eddie, marked inside the case, "To Colfax Dexter from his father," and the date.

Wesley was watching her, half sheepishly.

"Got to keep up the illusion, you know."

It almost destroyed her. She knew then that she could have loved him. This warmth of the heart was not what she had felt for Kirby, but it was love of a sort. There was one Wesley that she hated, and one, boyish and furtive and deeply hidden, that she could have worshipped. Perhaps even then, if she made a gesture of peace——

But she was afraid, and the next moment he had slipped the watch back into his pocket.

"So you think he'll like it?"

"Like it? He'll be frantic about it, Wes."

She saw that for some strange reason her approval had been important to him, and that night she thought over their married life, without bitterness. If she had married him when she was thirty she might have held him. As it was, she had had nothing to give him but her youth, her passionless immaturity, and before she ripened he had tired of her.

That night she was glad that she had built up for Eddie the super-man who was not Wesley. How she had worked over those letters. "Your father is too busy to write just now, but he sends his very dearest love." "Did you know that father won the local golf championship last Saturday? He was up against terrific competition, too." "Do be careful not to get into debt, Eddie dear. Your father works very hard, and he has been so generous with you." And apropos of some scrape or other: "Your father is so proud that you went to Mr. Stuart and told him. I read him your letter, and he was so pleased."

And the boy had responded. Once—that fall—a newspaper editorial had suggested Wesley for Congress, and she had cut it out and sent it on. He had shown it all over the school, proudly.

So Eddie came home. He had grown that fall, was broader in the shoulders. Little girls called him on the telephone, and he would assume an air of boredom and carry on long endless disjointed conversations with them. In the afternoons he went out to parties, innumerable parties. He was too old to be taken now; the car drew up at the door, Eddie gave a final touch to his tie in the hall mirror, went out, and the car drove off.

While he was gone Missie mended his clothes, sorted them —he seemed to have brought back a variety of garments, mostly not his own—and in the evenings sometimes they went to the movies. Adelaide loved the movies. She who had never lived could now sit in a chair and live vicariously the lives of thousands; she would weep copiously, laugh until her vast bosom rose and fell like a tide, and nibble candy out of a box on her lap.

And Wesley was indeed doing his bit. During that week at least those secret haunts of his saw him no more. He had bought a small pool table for Eddie, one that folded away when not in use, and in the evenings he taught him the game.

"Watch this, son!"

When it was bed-time Eddie would gravely consult his new watch, and sometimes they went up the stairs together. Father and son. Missie, waiting below to put out the lights, would thank God for that week of peace and security.

But it was not to last.

Chapter XXXIII

NEW YEAR'S EVE Wesley telephoned that he would not be home for dinner. Eddie was disconsolate.

"Business!" he said. "Who attends to business on New Year's Eve? I'll bet he's at the club."

But Missie felt that he was not at his club, nor among the revellers anywhere; that he was shut away somewhere, close and warm, and happy as she had never made him.

After Eddie had gone to bed she thought about that second establishment of his. He had maintained it, she felt, for a long time. It must be almost like a marriage, that relationship. She imagined that, after a while, it *was* a marriage of sorts; Wesley going in, reading the paper in dressing gown and slippers, resting, relaxing. Nothing too much expected of him; no particular effort, everything designed to his comfort. In such a life the man was king, and Wesley liked to be a king.

She moved about the room, packing Eddie's trunk, thinking as she worked; people lived their lives, suffered or were happy or both—mostly both—and out of this living they built character. But when the building was over, they died. Then why the building, unless one went on in some other existence, some active pragmatic world? What use was character in the heaven of tradition, where there was no sin and no temptation?

She was very tired when she went to bed. She never heard the telephone, or Adelaide finally creaking down the stairs to answer it. The first thing she knew was when Adelaide pounded furiously at her door.

"Missie, Missie!"

She crawled out, unlocked the door. Adelaide was in her nightgown, jerking violently.

"Missie, Wesley's been hurt. His car turned over on the Hopeville Road. He's at Saint Barnabas Hospital."

Missie caught at the door for support.

"How badly hurt?"

"I don't know. He's unconscious. That was a reporter on the 'phone. He says there was a woman in the car, but she got away. They've got her muff, and he wants to know if you were with him."

"What did you say?"

And suddenly she saw in Adelaide's twitching face a malevolence which horrified her.

"Say! I said you were here, where you ought to be. If Wesley Dexter thinks I am going to whitewash his sins——"

"You fool!" Missie blazed. "You ungrateful hypocritical fool! You can live in this house, eat Wesley's food, and then betray him. What about Eddie? Do you want him to learn in the morning that his father's been out with a prostitute?"

She had Adelaide by the arm, was shaking her. And Adelaide was frightened.

"What can I do?"

"Do? You can pack your trunks and get out, or you can get that newspaper and lie to them. I'm not here, do you understand? You've looked in my room and I'm not there. It was I with Wes. Now do it, and do it quick."

She gave Adelaide a push that almost knocked her down and sent her blubbering along the hall. And perhaps not a little of the success of that night's ruse was due to the fact that Adelaide was undeniably crying when she got the newspaper office on the wire again.

Missie did not wait to listen. She was throwing on her clothes, planning, plotting. Almost before Adelaide had rung off she was in the street. She had to think now, think fast.

What would a dazed woman do? She had walked a block before she remembered that she carried her chinchilla muff in her hands. She threw it away. She was thinking clearly now; something of Stella's fighting quality was rising in her. She had been in an accident. She was still dazed. Then she could not go to Saint Barnabas. She would go to a police station. But suppose the other woman turned up somewhere? She would have to take a chance on that. Anyhow she had run away. She would hardly turn up now.

She was a long time in finding a police station. She was cold and very tired when she wandered in, and her face was ghastly. The sergeant on duty stared at her. She was shaking so that she could scarcely speak, and the incoherence of her story gave it validity. Somebody put her in a chair, somebody else was telephoning. "On the Hopeville Road. Yes." And then—"At Saint Barnabas, eh? All right."

A police car took her to the hospital. Everything was all right. Eddie could read the morning papers now. She had lied, but a lie was a sin of the flesh. It was buried in the grave. If Wesley died perhaps his sins too would be buried in the grave; there were two sorts of sins.

She was very tired now, shaking all over. Maybe she would always shake now, like Adelaide. Picking things up and dropping them. What did it matter whether you dropped them or just put them down again?

The officer helped her up the steps, and took her upstairs. There was a door, and two or three men standing outside of it talking to a nurse. Reporters. Well, there was no scandal for them now.

"The gentleman's wife," said the policeman. "She was with him, and she's still dazed. Better look after her."

Wesley was in bed. He looked enormous on the high flat mattress. There was an *interne* with him, and another man. He was moving, his eyes were opening. The doctors looked serious, but not grave. He was not going to die.

"All right now, Mr. Dexter?"

"Where am I?"

"You're in a good place. Don't try to talk yet."

He lay still. His eyes moved over the two men, to the ceiling, the walls. He raised an arm, grunted, dropped it. Then he saw Missie. He lay looking at her and she saw dismay creep into his face. If he could be frightened he could understand her. She went over to the bed.

"I'm all right, Wes. I wasn't hurt at all. I was dazed, that's all. I ran away. I'm sorry."

His mind was functioning slowly. He still stared at her, at the dirt on her face, at her general disarray. He looked puzzled.

"But I thought——"

"Don't think," she told him sharply. "Just lie still and rest. We are both safe, and that's all that matters."

He closed his eyes, and after a minute or so she saw him smiling faintly. He understood. He could even see a certain humour in it! Well, let him think it was funny. Perhaps it was.

He was quite conscious before she dared to leave him. He seemed, oddly enough, to be glad to have her there. She even thought he was grateful. But what could he thank her for? It was not easy to break the silence of years, to admit the other woman in words.

"I'm all right now, Missie. You'd better go home and get some sleep."

"I'm going now. Wes, you won't see any reporters, will you?"

"Hardly."

She looked down at him. He had put her out of his life as coldly and as definitely as he knew how. She had no reason to care whether he lived or died. But there was something tragic to her in that big body lying there, in the blotched swollen cheeks above which his eyes looked up in a sort of mute appeal. Impulsively she bent down and kissed him on the forehead.

"Don't worry, Wes. Everything is all right."

She turned away quickly. She never saw the slow flush that suffused his face.

So that was over. Picking things up and putting them down again. Nothing changed. Eddie back at school; Adelaide sitting in the movies and living vicariously a thousand lives, or nibbling little cakes in her room and setting traps for the mice who gathered the crumbs, an Adelaide now, however, nursing a grievance, often sulkly, never quite forgiving. Tommy at last turning over the old Colfax house to Eileen, and Eileen tearing it limb from limb, but saving the iron deer. Women saying, "My dear, how can you bear it?" And Eileen replying cheerfully: "I have a sentiment about it. After all it has been in the family for a long time. I used to play with the queer old thing."

Tommy bringing Grace on, taking her into his office as a secretary, alluding to her as Her Grace. "Damned competent woman, Her Grace." And Wesley going on much as usual; not fundamentally changed by his mishap, but showing a more conciliatory attitude. There were fewer outbursts from him when things went wrong, when a button was missing from his shirt, or the soup was too salty. There was less autocracy in his slamming of doors, not quite so much patronage toward Adelaide.

But Wesley was Wesley. Missie knew that he would not alter. When, a week after his return from the hospital a jeweller's messenger brought her a handsome string of pearls with a diamond clasp, her first impulse was to hand them back to him.

"You cannot pay me for what I did. Keep gifts like this for your other women."

But here again her dreadful capacity for seeing both sides of any matter made her hesitate. She did not want the pearls, but she felt that the giving had some private and personal significance for him; that it had hurt his pride to rest under the shelter of her protection; that by paying her, after his own fashion, he made a gesture of freedom again.

She wore them down to dinner that night, wore them with a black frock which set off their size and lustre, and she saw relief in his face. He had not been certain, then.

"They are lovely, Wes."

"Glad you like them," he said briefly.

He was more cheerful that evening than she had seen him for a long time. He was satisfied. He could write paid across that account, too, and forget it.

Spring came early that year. On Decoration Day she was early at the cemetery. She moved from grave to grave with a trowel, setting out her plants. Always she fixed Stella's grave first. When she had finished she heard the sound of martial music, and watched the soldiers march in; the National Guard, very young, very stiff; that men who had been boys in the Spanish War but who were men now; and last of all, coming slowly, pausing for breath on the hill, old, feeble, hardly able to carry their precious tattered flags, the veterans of the War of the Secession.

Her throat contracted, her eyes filled with tears. It was the march of the ages; youth, middle age, age. The young men fought wars, and those who survived grew old. Nothing could stop the passage of time. She saw them moving about; they put a small cotton flag and two geraniums on Harry's grave.

"How many you got there, Bill?"

"Six."

"Well, two here then."

She went from the cemetery to Mrs. Wilkinson's. She had been quietly paying her rent for her for some time; paying it to Mr. Elliott. Mrs. Wilkinson was sick, and Delia was carrying on the dressmaking for her; that strange Irish woman who talked of Ireland as Mrs. Boroday had once talked of Russia, in terms of bloody revolution, yet who served and nursed the sick woman in a very passion of gentleness.

Emily Beaumont had gone long ago from the house next

door. There was an elderly German couple there now, very quiet.

"You ought to look over the fence, Missie. He's strung up morning glories again, like you used to."

Downstairs she stopped to talk with Delia. Delia had had a letter from home that morning. Things looked black in Ireland. "They'd better watch out," she said. "There's a big war on the way before long, and if England thinks the Irish are going to fight for her she'd better give them something to fight for."

She went to the corner and paid Mr. Elliott his rent. Mr. Elliott had prospered. He had a big store now, white tile, white paint, clerks in white coats, and he himself sat in a glassed-in office. He had a chain of smaller stores throughout the city, each of them as sanitary as an operating room. When she left him she had already forgotten Delia's words, but as she started back home she heard the beat, beat of drums as the veterans came down the hill.

She went on with her building. When Eddie came home, a few days later, she pleaded a headache so that Wesley would meet him at the train. She heard them come in, talking together cheerfully, as man to man.

"And then listen, father. The next fellow up was Red; you know, I've been writing about him. And he——"

The boy's eager young voice, Wesley's deep one. She felt a grateful swelling of the heart. The family group, the home had been preserved. Behind him all his life Eddie would have this warm sense of homecoming.

When she met him at the top of the stairs there were tears of happiness in her eyes.

"Eddie darling!"

He threw his arms around her. He was tall, taller than she was. His arms were strong, young and strong. Here was her world. She asked nothing else. It was enough. It was too much. It frightened her.

BOOK VI

Missie

Chapter XXXIV

MISSIE was still under forty when the European war broke out. She had no prettiness, but a fine evasive beauty. Her hair swept softly up and back from her wide forehead, the forehead that Kirby Phelps had loved. She was still slim. Her hands were beautiful, her eyes were as candid as ever, but not so luminous. They were the eyes of a woman looking out on a world which puzzled her.

On Sundays she went to church. On other specified days she attended to charities, went to hospital board meetings.

"Relative to the new refrigerator for the diet kitchen, I am authorized to say——"

All around her were other women, women like herself; protected, well-dressed, well-housed women. The matron sat a little aloof, ready to be interrogated. She was a little elderly woman with her hair parted in the centre and drawn smoothly back. She had been a hospital matron for a long time. She must have seen many tragedies, but they had left her quiet and serene.

"I would like to say that the new washing machine provided by this board is proving highly efficient."

Now and then strange noises, painful noises, penetrated to the dignity and decorum of the meetings. Then the matron got up quietly and closed the door. Nothing unpleasant must disturb the equanimity of these protected women; life must not come too close.

Sometimes Missie looked about her, at those fine thoughtful faces under the handsome hats. Why were they all here? Because they were needed, or because they wanted to be needed? Who was ever to know about women? They wanted so much; they wanted youth and love and beauty. They dreamed impossible dreams of love, and wakened one day to find themselves old beyond romance, to gaze at haggard faces in their mirrors, and to know that the best that they could ask of life was to be needed by somebody.

"The net proceeds from the country fair held at the estate of Mrs. Thomas Wilkins will be devoted to a new sterilizing plant. I suggest that a rising vote of thanks———"

When the meetings were over Missie would go home again, to Adelaide and Wesley. Eddie was still away, almost ready for college, and Adelaide was more and more aloof. Missie was very lonely much of the time. Her own life seemed incredibly narrow. Wesley had finally tired of social life; he protested over dinners, got himself into his evening clothes under protest. He still ate and drank heavily, but without zest. He went out less at night alone.

Eileen told Tommy one night that Wesley was a sick man and didn't know it.

"What's the matter with him?"

"Hardening of the liver, I imagine. And the menopause. Don't you suppose men have a menopause? Well, they do, His nerves are bad, and he's bracing them with alcohol."

"He's making a lot of money," said Tommy mildly.

"And he's drinking a lot of liquor," said Eileen.

"You can't stop him doing that."

"Well, you might suggest that he leave the pretty ladies alone for a while. He'll have a fit some time in the wrong establishment, and he won't like that."

"I don't imagine he'd care to have a fit anywhere, my dear."

Both Tommy and Wesley were making a great deal of money. The demand from Europe for practically everything was enormous. Companies that had been almost moribund put on new life, new companies were formed, sent their agents abroad, brought back orders and prospered. Tommy's engines were hauling soldiers, food, guns and ammunition; one of his shops was making shells. And Kirby Phelps was building experimental aëroplanes, carrying his own engine. Special wood was being cut on the Pacific coast, special kilns being developed for its drying, so that Kirby's engine might be carried safely aloft.

First the idea and then the fact. All of Kirby's dreams coming true, save perhaps one; men flying, ships under the sea, automobiles as common as once Tommy's bicycles had been.

But Eileen was right. The strain was telling on Wesley. He spent more and more evenings in the library. He had commenced collecting books in fine bindings; he liked the sensuous feel of fine hand-tooled leather, but he read very little. He had collected some of the more decadent of the classics, and with one of these on his knees he would sleep through the evening. Sometime later Missie would go down and rouse him, and he would climb ponderously up to bed.

She thought that perhaps he had wearied of his old life. There were times when she roused him, before full consciousness was restored, when he would smile up at her boyishly, and that smile, on that prematurely aged face, touched her.

"Don't you want to go up now, Wesley?"

The smile would fade, he would lift himself slowly.

"All right. I'll put out the lights."

But one night she went down, and found him trying to put an unsteady arm around a frightened parlour maid. The girl left the next morning, and Wesley sent an English butler to take her place. Missie wrote Eddie:

"Father has installed an English butler. He will probably be able to handle the old dumb waiter better, but he is a very grand person. His name is Hobbs!"

She thought Adelaide suspected something, however. It was a relief therefore when one day she opened Missie's door, put her head in and then sidled through. She had a letter in her hand.

"Missie, I've had a letter from your father. He's sick, Missie. He's been sick for months. He says he is not going to get well."

Suddenly Adelaide was crying, slow awful tears. She made no attempt to wipe them away. "I've hated him, Missie. It's dreadful, my own brother. And now he is dying."

"He may not be. You know he never could bear to be ill."

But Adelaide was certain. Moreover, she was moved by the instinct of martyrs. She would have to go to him and take care of him. He was all she had. And Missie saw that it would be better for her to go, that at last even Adelaide found that she was needed, and that for all her tears it was meat and drink to her.

Missie helped her to pack that afternoon. She took an incredible amount of stuff with her; she would wander around uncertainly with something in her hand, eliminate it finally, and then desperately catch it up and put it in one of the trunks.

When she had finally gone Missie settled down to her lonely life. Once she had liked to sleep, to dream. While she was awake she had shared the world with others, when she slept it had been to enter a world of her own. But of what could she dream now? Of Kirby Phelps, with another woman in his arms? Of Wesley and herself locked up together, growing old together, and Eddie out in this young man's world which moved so fast, so terrifically fast.

Sometimes then she resorted to that old trick of her pregnancy, and hummed the Minuet. "Te tum, tum, tumpety tum tum." She sang it to herself, over and over. And once again it was like a drug. She could sleep.

Two months after Adelaide's departure Wesley collapsed. They found him lying on the floor of his private office, unconscious, and called her by telephone.

"What is it?" she asked. "What sort of an attack?"

"It's hard to say yet. The doctors want to know whether to

bring him home or take him to a hospital? He may be sick a good while."

"Then bring him home."

When the ambulance drew up she was ready, the bed turned down and hot-water bottles in it. But never in all her life was she to forget that slow progress of the stretcher up the staircase, the delay in rounding the corner, Hobbs's voice: "If you'll raise the corner, sir." Then the tramping of feet in the upper hall, the flushed faces of exhausted men, and that inert body, a fleck of foam about the lips, which was Wesley.

It was apoplexy.

She had a few brief moments alone with him, somewhat later. The doctors were consulting in another room, the nurses had not yet arrived. She stood over him in an agony of pity, and at last she thought he was conscious. She knelt down beside him.

"Wesley dear, can you hear me? You are going to be all right. We'll have the best doctors, everything."

She thought his eyelids flickered.

"And listen, dear. I'm sorry. Sorry for everything. I'll stick by, my dear. I'll help all I can."

She was not sure she had reached him. He seemed far away and alone in some distant land of the spirit.

For weeks he lay there, inert. Eddie came home. He hung around the door of the sickroom, asking his worried questions, watching every one who came out for some answer to them. Eddie was difficult. He was resentful, without knowing why he was resentful. His god had been stricken down and he was furious at the injustice.

"But why? Why?" he demanded of Missie. "He was as strong as an ox. Where's the sense of it?"

"He had been working too hard. This war——"

"I wish the damned war would get over. Killing good men because they try to send the things it needs!"

Missie suspected him of wandering off to weep in secret

his shamefaced boyish tears. She had indeed built, built with a vengeance.

There were endless telephone calls, flowers, notes of inquiry. She found that Wesley had been very popular among men; that surprised her a little. They came in, and she went down to see them. They were constrained and stiff, but anxious. One day she found Judge MacDonald. The old Scot was in the library, inspecting Wesley's books.

"I'd keep that young man of yours out of here, Missie," he said. "How is Wesley?"

"There isn't much change from day to day."

He sat down across from her, eyed her.

"There comes a time in many a woman's life, Missie," he said ponderously, "when she is glad she has stayed by the man God gave her. I think you are glad now, aren't you?"

She coloured faintly.

"Very glad. If only I could do more——"

"You will have plenty to do. The doctors tell me he will probably live, but that——"

"His right side is paralyzed, Judge."

He cleared his throat.

"Well, men have lived a long time like that, lived to bury the women who cared for them. I don't think it will be easy, Missie, but I'm counting on you. You have plenty of spirit. You are not Stella Colfax's daughter for nothing."

Eddie went back at the end of six weeks, went rebellious and protesting. The atmosphere of the house was not healthy, and he had nothing to do but brood. One day she found him in the library reading one of the forbidden books, and that day she made up her mind.

"I'm not a kid, mother."

"You're not a man yet, either."

"If father thought those books were worth buying——"

"He bought many of his books for their bindings."

After Eddie had gone she went in to see Wesley. The room was dark, save for a light behind a screen, where the night nurse sat reading. She sat down beside the bed. He was not asleep. He lay there staring up, a shrunken, lonely figure. She was not even certain that he realized she was there.

"Are you comfortable, Wes?"

He nodded slightly.

"You know that Eddie's gone? He came in, but you were sleeping."

She had leaned toward him, and now she saw that he was grasping with his one good hand. He moved it slowly, painfully, until it touched her shoulder. Then he patted her. Her throat tightened. She caught the wavering hand and held it between both of hers.

"We are seeing this out together, Wes," she said huskily.

Chapter XXXV

WESLEY was a rebellious sick man, given to furies which his thickened speech obstructed, so that in those early rages he would pick up whatever was nearest at hand and fling it. Nurses came, endured it as long as they could, packed up and departed. He called them outrageous names and then, the outburst over, would lie back and look the apologies he could not bring himself to make.

And money flowed in, ironically and uselessly. Judge Mac-Donald brought him papers, and he learned to sign them with his left hand. The right was almost useless. He would never walk again, or if he did, it would be with a dragging foot. Eddie, coming home for his mid-year's vacation, would sit for hours rubbing the bad leg and arm. He had big strong hands, as tender as a woman's.

"See what you can do with it now, dad."

Mostly Wesley would make his effort, but there were periods when he felt the futility of it all, when he drove the boy away. His speech was clearer by that time.

"Let me alone, can't you? The trouble's not there."

"Still, if we keep the muscles exercised, dad——"

"Get out when I tell you. If I can't have anything else I can have peace when I want it."

The two would stare at each other, oddly alike, both angry. Then Eddie would slam out of the room, to come back later, apologetic, sheepish.

Missie was relieved when he went back to school. The life in the house was not normal. One night she found that he had got out of a back window and taken out the car, and she did not know what to say to him.

286

"But why did you do it, Eddie?"

"I guess I just wanted to. What's all the fuss about, mother? I didn't hurt the old car."

"Suppose you'd hurt yourself?"

"But I didn't!"

He kissed her, smiling. As if that settled it, as if by that gesture it was finished. Like Lambert bringing Stella a box of candy, like Wesley giving her pearls.

She felt helpless, as all the Colfax women had felt with their men.

One day that spring she heard from Eileen that Eleanor Phelps had borne a child, a daughter. She realized then how complete was the break between Kirby and herself. A man might marry a woman while carrying another image in his heart, but when that woman became the mother of his child the image faded. She felt that this was a tragic matter for her, the sort of thing at which the gods laughed, but when that afternoon while Wesley slept she got out an old picture of Kirby and looked at it, she was shocked to find that it roused in her no emotion whatever; that this man, between whom and herself there had been a basic attraction so strong that she had wrecked her life for him, was now nothing to her. She saw no irony in that, however, no mockery. *Tout passe,* as Eileen would say. Eileen had picked up a bit of French.

She put the picture away again, giving it decent interment, as one might who wishes no haunting ghost to walk; closed the drawer, turned the key on it, and had a queer sense of dreariness as she did it.

But she had no time for brooding; the problem of Wesley began to obsess her. There was no resignation in him. He would lie for hours, brooding, and she wondered if his mind was affected. One early morning he drove both Missie and the nurse out of the room. He had been in a sullen mood for days. They stood outside, uncertain what to do, and he suspected that and yelled to them.

"Don't stand whispering outside that door. Get the hell out of there."

They went away, dominated by this helpless man, uncertain what to do next, and they only went back when they heard a heavy fall. They went running, to find that in some miraculous fashion he had dragged himself out of bed and locked the doors. Missie called, but there was no answer. Then she heard slow painful movements, as of a man pulling himself across the floor. The nurse was banging at the door.

"Telephone for a locksmith," Missie said, and ran down the stairs.

Wesley was dragging himself toward the window. She knew that as surely as she knew anything. She ran out onto the pavement and stood looking up. An early milkman driving past eyed her curiously, but she never saw him. The windows were open, and in a moment she saw Wesley himself. He had dragged himself to his feet and was standing there, looking down at her.

"If you do it, Wes, I'll stand underneath you," she called clearly. "You will fall on me."

She saw him waver. Then there was a crash somewhere in the house, and she knew that they had broken down the door.

The next day, over his furious protests, she had iron bars put across the windows.

By spring he was better, mentally and physically. He was still irritable and sometimes sullen but he was certainly sane, and he was able to be moved into a wheeled chair. One day she ordered an elevator to be installed, and only told him when the workmen arrived. She had expected an outburst from him, but he surprised her.

"Not a bad idea," he said. "If I can get out of this cursed room I'll be more normal."

After that they would wheel him into the hall, and he would watch the work. He was not cheerful; he was still irritable, unreasonable, sometimes violent; but he was better.

She was able to write to Eddie:

"Father is really wonderful. He was not quite normal when you were here, but he is so much better. He is even attending to business in a small way, and he is learning to write with his left hand. He feels that the war may go on for a long time. He has so many friends, all clamouring to see him, and I hope they can soon. He is much more patient, and——"

Patient! Wesley!

He was increasingly dependent on her, hated to have her out of his sight; and in return for that dependence she forgave him absolutely. But sometimes she thought, as they sat together shut in that room, that they were like two derelicts, flung together by chance and clinging each to the other in a sort of desperate loneliness.

He was much thinner. With the loss of weight some of his good looks had come back. He would sit in his wheeled chair, his fine head outlined against the window, and she could see how like him Eddie was. The slight droop of his features on one side was hardly noticeable now.

One day he found that he had some motion in the right leg. The arm had been improving for some time. There was a strange look in his face when he told her.

"Have you ever faced the fact, Missie, that I may get well again?"

"I pray for it every night," she said simply.

He looked at her.

"Why? You never cared about me."

"I could have cared, Wes. I could have loved you very dearly. But you didn't want me to."

"And now you're only sorry for me!"

She considered that.

"No," she told him honestly. "I do love you, Wes. I think there is a kind of devotion that comes to people who are together for a long time. Devotion and tenderness. Even if things had been all right between us, I think perhaps that is where we would be now."

She felt that he had something to say to that, that with this new hope of recovery he wanted to reassure her, to promise her a better life and a happier one. But he had never learned to put his tenderness into words. His passions, yes; his tenderness, no.

"You're a good woman, Missie," he said.

She thought about that. Men were strange; they followed women who were not good, gave themselves to them, sank in the mud with them. But their high praise, the praise they reserved for their deeper moments, was for the good woman. Their harlots they could call as they liked, could lavish the entire vocabulary of passion on them. But their wives and their mothers were "good women."

"I have always been a good woman, Wes."

He nodded. He believed her at last.

One evening she read to him for an hour or so after he had been put to bed. She did not think he was listening, but she knew that the sound of her voice soothed him. When at last she closed the book he reached out his hand to hers, and carried it to his lips.

"You have been a saint from heaven to me, my girl," he said. And he added softly. "*My* girl. My dear girl."

They were the last words he ever spoke. He had another brain hemorrhage in the night, and two days later he died without recovering consciousness.

She sent every one away that night and sat with him. He looked young again and very peaceful. She did not cry. She sat quietly beside the bed, her hands in her lap, and watched him.

Where was he? Alone in some outer darkness, frightened, waiting for a light? Confused, perhaps, not realizing what had happened to him. Perhaps not even very far away. She looked around the room. Suppose he was there, wanting help, needing reassurance, depending on her still?

She spoke, not to the bed but to the room.

"It will be all right soon, Wes," she said. "Just a little while now and you'll be all right. And I'm standing by, dear." And after a minute she added, "I do love you, Wes. Never forget that, my dear, wherever you are."

Suddenly she was stricken with grief for him, for herself. They had come very close during those last days. If it was the crowning irony of her life that now she should grieve for him, once more she did not see it so. She wept for their lost years, for pity, for desolation; that life should separate people and only death unite them. His sins against her she forgave freely. They seemed unimportant now. The weaknesses of the body, the sins of the flesh, what did they matter now? How trivial they were, seen in the light of the spirit; as it came from God so it went back to God, clean.

Toward morning she heard Eddie sobbing, and went in to him.

"Why should you cry, Eddie darling? He is so well and strong now, so—like himself."

"He was such a man, mother."

"So he is still," she said steadily. "Better than ever. Not burdened with his body, that's all."

Chapter XXXVI

FOR weeks she seemed unable to rally herself. Eileen was impatient with her; drove her out, took her to see the old Colfax house, now in the hands of builders and decorators; the Louis XVI drawing room, made out of the old double parlours, the Italian Renaissance library, the Jacobean dining room—trust Eileen to be thorough—and her own boudoir upstairs where old Sarah had sat stiff-backed for so many years, now done in Empire with slender curved gilt chairs, delicate brocades.

In her deep mourning Missie looked incongruous. Eileen found her once standing in the doorway of the remodelled conservatory, now furnished with Italian garden furniture.

"How do you like it?"

But Missie seemed to come back from a far distance before she answered.

"Why on earth should she miss him?" Eileen demanded of Tommy. "You'd think it would be a relief. He dissipated himself into his grave. He treated her like dirt for twenty years. And just because he soft soaped her at the end she misses him! I'm going to talk to her."

"I wouldn't if I were you."

"Why not?"

"Facts don't mean anything to her. Let her alone."

"Let her think Wes sprouted wings at the end. And so go on grieving forever!"

He turned on her almost savagely.

"For God's sake let her have something. Let her have her decent grief, anyhow."

He was rather silent after that. He had been a faithful husband to Eileen, and a loving one, an indulgent father to Clare, but sometimes he wondered about them both. Was he anything more to them than the source of all good things, the "good provider" of his early days? He gave them everything they wanted, paid their innumerable bills without question, and in return they gave him something, but just what was it? It was not love; it was even at times faintly condescending.

"Don't be quaint, old dear. This is the twentieth century."

He did not blame them entirely. He had had to be away a good bit. His interests were scattered, the factory, the different shops and mills. He had grown very rich. Once in a while he went to the bank with Grace to glance over his holdings; Grace had the vault opened, the boxes were spread on the table in the small room, and together they would meticulously check against the typed lists. And somehow at those times he was once again Tommy Wilkins, and this spread of heavy parchment paper was unreal. It was paper only.

But he began to understand why certain men of his acquaintance had second establishments hidden in obscure corners of the city. He wanted quiet, and his house was never still. Suppose he found some calm and quiet woman, to whom he could talk? A still room somewhere, with an open fire, and his slippers and dressing gown there. An open fire, not cluttered about with tea things and gossiping women, or with half-fledged youths who drank his old whisky. A few books to read, maybe aloud, and no effort·to be made. It would be restful.

Sometimes his pale blue eyes rested thoughtfully on Grace. He had been attracted to her from the first, and she was a quiet woman. She liked to read, too. But he never got any further than that.

He was co-executor of Wesley's estate, along with the Judge. Missie would be well off, very well off. Now if only the money didn't spoil the boy——

One day he said that to her.

"You'll want to keep a stiff hand on Eddie, Missie, when he comes into his share."

"I'm not afraid of Eddie, Tommy."

"Money goes to the heads of most of us, my dear."

"I have talked to Eddie. He feels that it is a sort of trust. You see, he worshipped his father. Wesley was always an ideal to him. A very fine ideal."

She gazed at him with her candid eyes, and it was Tommy who broke away, fumbled with the papers he held. No, he knew nothing of women! Was she deluding herself, or was she telling him something, something he ought to know? He felt that she was telling him something.

Eddie was in college now, Missie quite alone. The house was quiet, always in order. In the evenings she put on her soft black dresses and trailed down to dinner. Hobbs pulled out her chair, she sat down, the dumb waiter creaked. She ate very little. When she had finished she went quietly into the library and sat in one of Wesley's chairs. Sometimes, when the evenings were cool, she drew a small black lace shawl over her shoulders.

Every Sunday she carried flowers up to the cemetery and put them on Wesley's grave.

Early that spring she made a journey to see her father. Lambert was in his seventies now, with a frail old body which hardly lifted the bed coverings, but he managed a certain jauntiness when he saw her.

"Don't be too optimistic, Missie! I'm good for ten years yet."

But his lips were blue and his breathing difficult.

She stayed a few days, living at a hotel. Adelaide was nursing him with a perfect frenzy of self-abnegation, but Missie saw that she worried him. Her incoördination annoyed him, her very solicitude irritated him.

"Damn the woman, I wish she'd let my pillows alone."

Before she left Missie installed a pretty young nurse, and

—the incorrigible youth of the man!—he sent her out to buy him some silk pajamas. When the nurse had been there rather less than an hour Missie overheard him telling her that she had beautiful eyes.

Adelaide cried when she went away.

"It's dreadful to see him like this," she said. "He was always so gay and so happy."

So gay and so happy! Going deliberately down the street, leaving Stella to worry about the food and the rent. Going blithely out of the house for good. "I'll send an express wagon around." Playing poker that night on the train, when Stella lay dying in the back room. Cheerfully leaving Eileen and herself to starve. Neglecting his dying mother. And now living—and dying—contentedly on Missie's bounty, trying to flirt with the nurse, openly jeering Adelaide about her breadth of beam, the spots on the bosom of her dress.

So gay and so happy!

And while she called the roll of his sins she was sorry for him. It was a pity that those who loved life could not hold to it. But what was there so precious about mere living? Was it fear that there was nothing beyond that made it so terrible to them? The dread of extinction? But extinction was not painful. The dead could not lie in the grave lamenting that there was no immortality.

She went back home again, and even into her seclusion there penetrated the prospect of war. She tried to shut her ears to it, but it penetrated through the walls, into Wesley's study where she sat writing her letters to Eddie. "I'm afraid I have no news." She would sit and think. What would interest him? What would he want to hear? "I saw Mary Elizabeth the other day, and she asked for you." Mary Elizabeth was one of the little girls who telephoned, a slim quiet girl with big eyes, very soft, very feminine. "She looked quite pretty, I thought. Now about your having a car there——"

She would write, and through the walls would come the growling of an angry nation. She could not shut it out. Often it made her hand shake so that she had to take a fresh sheet and begin again.

When he came home for his spring vacation the tension relaxed somewhat. He was normal and cheerful, and he never mentioned war. The house bloomed again, his maleness brought it to life, as Lambert had once vitalized the little house on Grove Street. Doors banged, the telephone rang, there was a smell of tobacco, of cakes baking in the kitchen. Food was important again.

"Is that steak too rare, Eddie?"

"I like it this way."

He was like Wesley; he liked rare meat.

"What shall I order for your dinner?"

"Good heavens, mother, I've just had breakfast!"

He was very gentle to her, very kind. She bloomed for him that spring, her third blooming. He told her how pretty she was, and so once more she brushed her soft hair until it shone, ordered her delicate clothes. But in the evenings after dinner he would fidget about the room, and after a time she would say:

"Don't you want to go out, Eddie? It's so dull for you here."

He would try to hide the eagerness in his eyes.

"How about you?"

"I'll be all right. I'll go to bed early."

Like Wesley so long ago he would affect reluctance, move slowly to get his hat, and outside on the pavement he would draw a long breath, hurry, almost run.

He and Mary Elizabeth were always together, when he was out of the house. She was a demure little mouse of a girl, very thin, hardly pretty. But to Eddie, who had known her all his life, she was suddenly the flower of beauty, the joy of spring. He took immense trouble with his dressing when he expected to see her, and came back slightly strutting and given to long abstracted silences. Once Missie found him reading a book of poems. She pretended that she had not noticed.

And the rumbling went on. After Eddie had gone back she could hear it better. The house was so very quiet. She would sit in Wesley's library, and it seemed to pour in through the walls and beat upon her ears like a drum. War. War. War.

One evening Hobbs came in to tell her that he was leaving.

"Leaving? Why, Hobbs? Aren't you happy here?"

"Very satisfied, madam, but it's time I went home. They're calling up men of my age now." And he added: "They've killed off all the young men. It's our turn now."

She felt sick. Shocked, too, for there was blood-lust in Hobbs's respectable face.

It was the next day that war was declared.

She watched Eddie's letters after that. She thought they showed constraint. But she still had hope. He was not yet eighteen, and now that America was in, the war would be quickly over. Six months, maybe. Things were moving fast; Congress voting a war credit of seven billions, lending three billions to the Allies, passing a Draft Act. Ten million men to be drafted. They would not need Eddie. What would they want with Eddie?

One day she found Mary Elizabeth waiting for her. The girl's eyes were swollen, her thin body taut as a string.

"They won't take Eddie, will they, Mrs. Dexter?"

"No, indeed. He's too young."

"But he looks older."

She worried over that. She began to be afraid, terror stricken. Once more she was a woman waiting for a sound, and at last the sound came.

"Darling mother: I hate to write this letter. Not because I am afraid you won't approve, but because I know it will hurt like sin. You have been so wonderful, mother, and just now, too, when you are missing dear old dad so fearfully.

"But I can't sit back now when we are going in at last. You wouldn't want me to, and if dad were here I know what he would think. He would be proud to have me do my bit. I couldn't be his son and not fight, mother."

There was more, much more. But the gist of it was that he had lied about his age and had already enlisted. When she received this he would be on his way to camp.

She sat still for a long time, with that letter in her hands. So this was what it had come to; all this living and suffering, the tremendous sweep of one human life, its endurance, its weaknesses and its strengths, now narrowed down to a pin point; to one boy in ten million men.

Chapter XXXVII

TEN million men to be drafted; brought in from heaven only knows where, their cards filled out, passed to the medical examiners. "Two grinding teeth on each side above and below, providing they meet." Scales, more cards; naked bodies, black and white, sweating with nervousness. Bits of humour.

"Say, boss, I can't go. My wife needs me."

"What for?"

"I carries the washing for her."

Or:

"I wish you'd look at this man, doctor. His pupils are irregular."

"Irregular! You fool, he's got a glass eye!"

Tommy volunteered his own offices, own staff. The big men of town came in, sat down at desks, lost themselves in seas of paper. Still a paper war; nothing else ready, no lessons from the past of any use. Tommy sending in lunches from the club, working late at night, weeks on end. Then at last after weeks of labour the cards ready; "Get them in here, somebody"; shuffling them about on a table, drawing one here, one there; the first draft. Life or death for thousands on the turn of a card.

One night the work was done. Tommy's big limousine was waiting, the cards, in great packages, were ready. He went alone with them to the Post Office, handed them in to the Registration desk to be sent to Washington. He was gray with fatigue, covered with sweat.

The clerk looked at the first package.

"Ten cents for registration," he said.

"Ten cents hell!" Tommy bellowed. "It's cost me a million dollars to get those ready for this Government. Now it will take them as is, or you can burn 'em up."

And he stalked out.

Camps sprang up over night, cheerful camps, filled with boys. War was a new game, life had been reduced to its elements, was care free. They were fed, drilled, cared for. They had no responsibilities, and the regular life and the exercise agreed with them. They resented the discipline but thrived under it.

Eddie was very happy. He ate enormously, slept on his narrow cot the heavy unbroken sleep of youth. In the daytime he dug trenches on imitation battlefields, practised bayonet drill on imitation enemies. Into a trench and out again. "Have at you, Heine!" "That's the way! Give it to them!" "Right in the belly, by God!" Sweating, dirty, grinning. Little jokes. Meals in towns. Pretty girls.

"Hello, sister. Aren't you kinda lost around here? If you want a guide——"

At *reveille* he would heave up his blankets, grunt, groan, yawn.

"Who the hell wants a war, anyhow? They can have mine."

But sometimes at sunset, during retreat, with the band playing and the flag slowly moving down, he would feel a little tightness of his throat. Then he would stiffen his shoulders and stare ahead.

He had a faint look of Missie then.

Missie was very quiet that fall. She seemed unable to adapt herself to war. Other women were doing it, she knew; telling themselves that war was noble, heroic; putting on pitiful little airs or pride: "Yes, Jim's gone. He was one of the first to volunteer." Then going home to sit alone in some upper room, perhaps with childish garments on their knees, old forgotten toys.

But she could not do that. There was a terrible revolt in her, bitter, implacable. War was useless, damnable. Sometimes she sat in the rocking chair in the old nursery, and rocked doggedly back and forth. What had happened to God? Where was He? On what other business, that He could let this war go on? And there were times when she felt that she must go to some one, some one high up, and get Eddie back.

"He is under age. He lied about his age."

"My dear lady——"

"You don't want children. There are plenty of men. Take men. Not little boys."

One day she found herself rehearsing that out loud. Like Cecily.

It was years now since she had seen Kirby. He was in Washington, something to do with aviation; very restless too, according to Eileen, wanting to fly, to fly and fight, but too old. Not old, at that, but too old.

"Anyhow, he's pretty well cracked up," Eileen had said, lighting a cigarette. Yes, Eileen smoked now. She said it quieted her nerves. "Too many racing accidents."

Missie was sorry for him. He should have had his chance, she felt; his one big moment, as old Archibald used to say. She thought about him sometimes. Was he happy? Had she done him any harm? She could see his side of things so well. He had been faithful to her, as men view such things, for a long time; and he had finally married without love. Like herself, like Wesley. Did he ever blame her, she wondered.

But apparently Kirby did not blame her. One day, when Eddie had been three months in his camp, the parlour maid announced a Colonel Phelps calling. It took Missie a moment to realize that it was Kirby, another moment or two to still that ridiculous shaking of the hands. It was not this Kirby who disturbed her, moving restlessly about the drawing room in his neat uniform, a trifle gray now, a bit stiff in one knee from some old accident. He was a ghost, a substantial ghost, but a ghost nevertheless, like Harry, like Wesley, only he was living and they were dead.

Just what he felt she did not know, standing there in that

room where once he had held her in his arms. He was remembering, perhaps.

"Do you care for me? Sometimes I've thought you did."

"I do care, Kirby."

"A great deal? I can ask you that, because I care so much for you."

"A great deal." Her voice shaking. "A very great deal."

When he heard her on the stairs he shook himself, threw away his cigarette.

"Well, Kirby! And how fine you are in uniform!"

"Bit of nonsense, really," he said. "I'm a non-combatant, you know."

God, how little these unawakened women changed! There, in that dusky room she was the Missie of years ago. How still she was, too. Eleanor was never still; she made him feel tired and old by comparison.

But he was not a sentimental man, not any more. He was a business man, a business man in a uniform.

"I've only just learned about Eddie, Missie. He's too young, isn't he?"

"Yes. He said he was older."

He made an impatient gesture.

"It's ridiculous. This war doesn't want boys. It's man stuff. If you want him back there may be some way to arrange it. I don't know, but I could try."

Her heart leaped, then settled down with heavy painful beating.

"Would that be fair to him, Kirby?"

"I don't know what you mean by that. He ought to have a good thumping. He's all you have, and he knows it."

She made a small gesture, as if she were putting something away from her.

"I couldn't humiliate him," she said. "He would hate me for it. And maybe it will be good for him." She coloured faintly. "He has my father's blood in him, and also——" she stopped. "Also mine."

"Yours."

"I'm weak, I've just drifted. I'm no mother of kings." She smiled at him. "His father was strong; not always right, perhaps, but strong, and Eddie knows that his father would have wanted him to go."

He stared at her. Did she believe that? Had she really built up a defensive wall against the memories she must have of Wesley, or was she living up to all this damnable propaganda about mothers in war? Take their boys, if it had to be done, but why demand that they smile? He moved, got up.

"That is, of course, the proper attitude." He picked up his cap, stood turning it in his hands. "Only don't think you're weak. You're strong, Missie. Quiet and strong."

"You don't know."

"I think I do." He looked around the room, back to her. "Missie, suppose I had kept you? Never let you come back. Made a fight for Eddie. Have you ever thought about that?"

She faced him steadily.

"I would not change my life, as I have lived it, in any particular, Kirby."

"It has satisfied you, then?"

"I have had a great deal. Toward the end Wesley changed, Kirby. He began to care for me; I know that. He was very gentle, very dependent." Her eyes filled with tears. "When he died I missed him. I missed him dreadfully. And now my father is dying."

Suddenly he was possessed by a dreadful impatience. He knew all about Lambert Colfax. What was the matter with this woman, that she could forget the wrongs these two men had done her, and mourn for them? She *was* weak, after all, weak and sentimental; a pale woman in a black dress, tending the graves of people who had ruined her life, shedding tears over them! And he did not know that his anger was jealousy, jealousy of these dead people for whom she wept and prayed. Jealousy of that past of hers, marked like milestones with its graves.

They had left their mark on her, all of them. Only he, who had loved her long and well, had failed to mark her. His vanity was hurt, his sex pride outraged.

When he reached the street he found that he had left his gloves behind. He swore and went on.

As the weeks went on Missie was more and more alone. She seldom saw even Eileen now, but Eileen was busy and happy those days. She had had no boy to give, and now the Red Cross work had broken down the last social barriers. The war would end, but she, Eileen, would go on, splendidly, and gloriously.

Already she was calling by their first names women who had never invited her to their houses.

"Ready for lunch, Fan? Let's run over to my place. I daresay there'll be something."

There would be "something"; beautiful food, an air of solidity and dignity.

"I see you still keep the iron deer."

"Yes. It's quaint, isn't it, the dear old thing!" She would gaze at it fondly.

In her Red Cross veil she looked spiritualized, exalted.

Tommy was still working. Now he was selling Liberty bonds, on the streets, in theatres between the acts; the orchestra wailing "It's A Long Way To Tipperary" or "Over There," and Tommy standing waiting, jingling his small change nervously, clearing his throat, squaring his sloping shoulders.

"Ladies and gentlemen, I don't suppose I need to tell you why I'm here to-night——"

One day he told Missie that Mr. Boroday was back in Russia, a big man in the Revolution. Missie had a vision of him there, big and black bearded, sitting in the seats of the mighty, whittling at a piece of wood perhaps, and passing sentences of life and death.

It was Tommy who told her when Eddie's division was sent to the port of embarkation. He had a way of knowing things.

He was in with the Government now; very thick with the Government. He could walk into the office of the Secretary of War with an easy air: "Good morning, Mr. Secretary,"— as though he had never repaired bicycles. "That tire's about wore out, son. Twenty-five cents." As though he had never wailed to a mandolin on the front steps on Grove Street, and been insulted by Lambert.

So it was Tommy who told her one day to go to New York, and managed to get twenty-three and a half hours' leave for Eddie, to coincide. She sat in the train, planning how they were to fill the time. She made dozens of little plans. And in the intervals she thought of what she was to say to him. Not too much; no preaching. Just a word or two about certain types of French girls, and about drinking.

"You know how your father would feel."

She found, however, that Mary Elizabeth was there. All that day they were a party of three. She was not resentful, but she looked defeated. She was almost too weary to dress that night, but she did. She put on a black dinner dress and Wesley's pearls, and they dined at a restaurant, with dancing. She sat at the table and watched them dancing together, Eddie big and strong and protective, Mary Elizabeth small and very feminine.

Sometimes she saw him lowering his head to the girl. Whispering.

"I adore you."

"Don't. I'm afraid I'll cry."

The band playing, Missie in her black and pearls sitting alone, Eddie in his uniform feeling every inch a man, Mary Elizabeth grave, sedately dancing.

"You'll write often, darling, won't you?"

"Every day of my life."

He had a cocktail or two, and the room swam in a glamorous haze. His hold on her tightened. He was a man, going away to a war.

"I'll come back an officer, honey. A cooty loot."

"I'm sure you will, Eddie."

"Insignia and boots and everything! Sam Browne belt, too. They wear them over there."

"Just so you don't forget me."

"Forget you! Darling!"

Missie watched them, sitting erect in her chair like Sarah. She was rather lovely. Men looked at her, but she did not notice them. She was bracing herself; in an hour now, or less than an hour——

When she found that her hands were trembling she held them in her lap. Now and then she smiled, to relax her frozen muscles. That was what women did, wasn't it? They sent their men away with a smile. "When you say that, smile." That was in a book. What book? What good were books? They were never honest. They never told you what life was; that it was something that led you on to some unknown goal, and when the goal was reached it was no goal at all, but a closed door.

"We'd better go back to mother, honey."

"Just another minute, Eddie."

It was time to go. Eddie was paying the check. It was his party. Mary Elizabeth was shaking; her face was very white. A great wave of pity for her swept over Missie. How young she was to have to suffer, as young as she had been when Stella died. She slipped an arm around her.

She talked feverishly in the cab. Mary Elizabeth was staying with friends, and she and Eddie dropped Missie at her hotel. Missie had hoped perhaps that they would alter this, that his last farewell would be to her. But they accepted it, and after all, why not? They were young and desperately in love. Let them have those last few moments together.

"Good-bye, mother dear."

"Good-bye, Eddie. God bless you."

"I'll be all right, mother."

"I know you will. Don't worry about me. Good-bye, dear."

He kissed her. She smiled up at him, then she turned and

went in. Inside the doorway she staggered, and the porter caught her.

"Better sit down a moment, lady."

"I'm better now, thanks."

She turned and looked out at the street. The taxi had gone.

She had told Eddie she would stay until she felt sure he had sailed, and so she did. At last, however, she felt that she could go; that during one of those endless nights he would have marched down the silent streets to his transport. The gates to the dockyard would have opened, the men would have filed between the sentries; there would have been the shuffle of many feet, the creak of accoutrements, the muttering of voices, the tramp-tramp up the gangways. Then the casting off, the stealthy movement of the ship out into the river, until it slid out of sight in the mists of dawn.

She packed that night, and at last she crawled into her bed. It was done, irrevocable. He was gone. Nothing could call him back now.

She lay there, adjusting herself to that. He was gone, and she had sent him off with a smile. If there was no real peace in her, there was stoical resignation. She had done the hardest thing in her life; nothing else compared with it. But it was over. Thank God it was over.

At midnight there was a knock at her door. She got up, turned on a light, threw on her dressing gown, and opened it.

Eddie was in the doorway. He was in full equipment, with knapsack and blanket roll, with a steel helmet on his head and a rifle in his hand. She put her hand to her throat.

"Took a chance on your still being here!" he said gaily. "I had to do an errand for the captain, so I thought I'd come up and show off. We're sailing to-night."

She backed off. Suddenly she began to cry, terrible crying. She could not control it. It frightened Eddie.

"Stop, mother! For heaven's sake! I'm so sorry. I'm so sorry, mother."

At the distress in his voice she stopped. Perhaps nothing

else would have stopped her. She sat on the edge of her bed, drying her eyes, trying to smile at him.

"I'm all right now, Eddie."

"That's the stuff! That's the girl! You'll go to sleep now, won't you? After I'm gone?"

"Of course I will."

He picked up his gun. She forc   herself to look at it, at the helmet, at the whole equipment for killing, and having looked she could not take her eyes from them.

"It seems such a lot to carry, Eddie!"

"I'll tell the world!"

Her calmness satisfied him. He walked to the mirror, put on his helmet, gave it a tilt, came back to her.

"Sure you're all right?"

"Of course I'm all right. You surprised me, that's all."

"I'll be back, you know. With bells on."

"Of course you'll be back."

At the door he stopped, turned and looked back at her.

"You'll sleep now, won't you? Sure?"

"Yes, I'll sleep. Good-bye, and—God bless you, my son. My dear son."

When he had closed the door she stood for a long time, staring at it.

Chapter XXXVIII

EILEEN had bought the house on Grove Street for the Red Cross. Then one day Mrs. Wilkinson died and Delia went back to Ireland, and she added that house too.

Missie went to work there. She sat all day, among the other women. To her they were all mothers, and the flimsy piles of dressings that rose on the tables were the barricades they were erecting—all they could erect now—between their boys and harm.

She was forty-four as she sat there—"Fold D. B. over J. K. toward G. H."—very gentle, very tolerant, very silent. Sometimes the noise made her head ache, but she stayed on. It never occurred to her that Eileen and her kind were working there for what they could get out of it, Eileen for place, others for vicarious excitement. Not all, of course; not even a majority. But they were there, as they were everywhere; Clare lounging in in uniform—she was driving for something or other—smoking incessantly, proud of her putteed legs; shooting past indignant policemen, finally having a bit of an accident and Eileen coming to work afterwards with the air of one who too has suffered.

"I must not complain," she said sweetly. "The child was doing her duty, and—I have no boy to give."

The next day old Mrs. Hemingway heard of that, and left cards at the Wilkins house for the first time.

When Missie went home in the evenings it was often to find Mary Elizabeth there. The girl was thin and tense. Missie was always tired, but she would take her in, try to talk to her. She wanted to go upstairs, to lie on her bed and close her eyes, but she would do her best.

309

"He said he would write every day, Mrs. Dexter, and now——"

"All the mails are very slow, my dear."

Missie would sit there trying to make talk; between her and this girl of seventeen there was a gulf neither could bridge, but she felt that Mary Elizabeth was dumbly reaching out to her. She must not fail her.

"That's such a pretty dress!"

"Is it? I got it because Eddie liked blue."

Eddie, always back to Eddie, and Missie's feet aching, her body weary, her very soul.

"Would you like to stay to dinner?"

"I'd love to, if you don't mind."

Endless meals, Missie and Mary Elizabeth and two ghosts at the table. Once Mary Elizabeth began to cry.

"Every time I look at Eddie's empty chair——"

"Stop it!" said Missie sharply. "Don't talk like that. Don't be a little—goose."

Sometimes she did not go home. She evaded the girl. And as work piled up occasionally she spent the night in the little house. She had had a cot bed placed in Stella's old room. She would move about the building in her white uniform with her blue veil, clearing up the day's disorder, preparing for the next day. But after she had lain down it was full of ghosts; it was as though all the lives lived there had left their imprint on it; Stella, the girls who had lived their casual days and nights there when it was a brothel, the old German, torn between two loves. She could hear Stella's rocker, light laughter, sighs and groans. But when she slept it was to dream of Eddie in a trench, with shells bursting around him. Or he was crawling out over the lip of the trench with his gun in his hand, bayonet fixed, eyes staring toward an enemy that waited to kill.

She always saw him alone. It was Eddie's war. Eddie was fighting the war.

When the Armistice came and she knew he was still safe,

she could not believe it. She felt numbed, beyond emotion. In the afternoon she filled the car with flowers and went up to the cemetery. It was as though she was telling her graves something.

She did not go alone to see Eddie come home. Bands playing, flags waving, triumphal arches in the streets. Mary Elizabeth begged to go with her, and because she knew it would please Eddie she took her. Tommy got them passes to the pier. Wonderful Tommy. "That's Tom Wilkins. You know, the Wilkins car. One of the first in the business. Vision, that's what he had." Missie was still in black, for Lambert had died, but she made herself as smart as possible, wore her pearls, her little pin with one star. Not gold, thank God. Thank God, not gold.

But beside Mary Elizabeth's joyous youth she felt old and faded.

She stood on the pier, waiting. The Committee was there, a crowd of other people, also admitted by the Tommies they knew. She was alone most of the time, for Mary Elizabeth was too impatient to stand still. She had worked her way to the platform at the end of the dock, and was in momentary peril of being shoved overboard.

The transport was in the river. Tugs were slowly nosing it about. Its rails were crowded with men in uniform. They all looked alike. They were a sea of young faces, tanned with the winds of France, bronzed by its suns. They were waving and cheering, and the people on the dock were waving and cheering also.

Mary Elizabeth was shrieking and crying at the same time.

"Eddie! Eddie Dexter! I'm here, Eddie."

"We're all here," yelled the doughboys. "We're all here, sister."

They were not all there, but they could forget that now. They were young, the war was over. Why worry about what was past? There was the future, the glorious future.

"Stand back, please," said a policeman to Missie. "Get back there, everybody."

Ropes were being stretched. The crowd fell back. Missie could hardly breathe. He was coming. Eddie was coming. The war was over, and he was coming back to her. In a few minutes, a half hour, an hour, she would see him. All her life seemed to have been pointed in this one direction, that this day, this minute, she should be standing on this pier in the cold, waiting for her son to come back from a war. It was the answer to everything.

As she stood there she was undistinguishable in the crowd. All the living she had done to reach this moment was obliterated. And around her and in the surging street outside, were dozens of other women, each with a life story behind her, and each forgetting that story in the triumph of this moment which was its culmination.

Not that she thought of that. She was thinking of Wesley as she stood there. She wished that he were there, to see his son returning in glory from the war. But she had forgotten Wesley too, as he was. What she remembered was the Wesley she had built up for Eddie, the strong man, the decent citizen, the patriot. Her eyes filled with tears.

"He would have been so proud," she thought.

She stood there alone in a new world. Behind her loomed the city to which Wesley had taken her on her wedding journey, but a new city now, of skyscrapers, of subways, of a railroad tunnel under the river. From curb to curb its streets were filled with automobiles. Over the bay flew aëroplanes, triumphantly swooping down, the pilots waving to the transport, the soldiers waving back. A new world, but not hers. Eddie's world. A world for the young, for those who could run, not for those who stood still. She could not run any more. She was very tired. The cold penetrated to her thin body and made her shiver.

They were warping the ship in. The noise of the crowd was deafening. Somewhere a band was playing "Hinkey

Dinkey, Parley Voo." Everywhere people were waving little flags, little cotton flags. Little cotton flags like the ones the veterans put on the soldiers' graves on Decoration Day. What was she crying about? She must not let Eddie see that she had been crying. She had been crying when he went away. She thought of that night, of Eddie in the doorway, the fighting man, wearing and carrying the insignia of war. Of war and death.

"Stop, mother, for heaven's sake! I'm so sorry. I'm so sorry, mother."

Mary Elizabeth came back to her, charging through the crowd like a young fury.

"They're putting down the gangways," she shrieked. "It'll only be a minute now. Only a minute."

She held Missie's arm and jumped up and down. "I can't wait. I can't wait. I think I saw him. He waved at me. It looked like him anyhow. I've yelled until I'm hoarse. Listen how I croak. Hurrah! *Hurrah!*"

The crowd was yelling again. With a rattle of chains the gangways were being lowered into place. A group of staff officers came down. There was some delay after that. The January wind was cold, the crowd grew impatient.

"Hurry up there. Let's go. Let's go."

"Let's go," shrilled Mary Elizabeth, holding tight to Missie's arm.

Missie looked at her. How young she was, and how frankly ardent. She must not care too much if Eddie's first look was at Mary Elizabeth. She must not be jealous of this child. He would know that she, Missie, was always there behind him, ready to be called on when she was needed.

Mary Elizabeth got out her vanity case.

"I've cried all the mascara off my eyelashes," she said. "I must look awful. Do I look awful, Mrs. Dexter?"

"You look very beautiful, dear."

Mary Elizabeth powdered her smooth face, coloured her pink lips. Beside her Missie felt old and ugly and drawn.

Eddie would not think she was pretty now; he used to tell her she was pretty, but that was long ago. He would come along and kiss her dutifully, but his eyes would be on Mary Elizabeth.

"They're coming now, Mrs. Dexter. Hurrah, they're coming."

Missie found she could not speak. Her hands were shaking, there was that old constriction about her heart.

Down they came, grinning, slightly sheepish. The crowd went crazy. They came and came, in dozens, in hundreds, in thousands. The gangways shook, the dock vibrated. A woman fainted. Men shed shameless tears. And at last Missie saw him. He had grown; how big he looked, how strong, how wonderful. Her boy. Her grown son. Eddie, Eddie.

He came on, looking right and left. He did not see them. Don't let him pass. Stop him quickly. Stop him, somebody.

"Eddie! Eddie!"

The line stopped. He saw them. He saw them both. He looked at her, at Mary Elizabeth, at her again.

"Mother! Mother darling!"

He held her in his arms, his strong young arms. He held her as if he would never let her go. And beside her Mary Elizabeth stood waiting. She knew that her time would come, that eventually he would turn to her. She stood by, waiting, her hand touching the sleeve of his worn khaki coat.

Chapter XXXIX

A YEAR later Missie was sitting in church. The organist was playing softly, and at Missie's elbow was a great stand of white chrysanthemums, tied with tulle. She was glad they were there; they protected her. But when Eddie came out she moved a little, so she could see him. She did not see the procession as it came up the aisle. She saw only Eddie.

"Dearly beloved, we are gathered here together in the sight of God——"

She was standing up. The incredible thing was happening. Eddie was being married. She leaned rather heavily against the pew ahead, tried to listen.

"Colfax, wilt thou have this woman to thy wedded wife— and forsaking all others, keep thee only unto her, so long as ye both shall live?"

Eddie's voice was clear and calm as he replied. Deep, too. He was a man now. Not a boy. Never again a boy.

"I will."

Missie did not hear all the service. She was busy with her memories. But when the organ pealed out she came to with a start, and she smiled at them as they passed her. She was very calm and quite lovely at the reception later. It was a handsome reception, with plenty of champagne.

She waited there until Eddie had gone—Eddie and Mary Elizabeth, of course—and then she went back home to her quiet house.

She was not unhappy. She had developed a philosophy of life by that time.

She knew how women deluded themselves, believed as they climbed each hill that they would find the Promised Land

waiting on the other side. And that there was no Promised
Land, unless it lay in some vague hereafter.

She took up her life again, but she felt older. Much older.
One night during that time she looked in her mirror, and
she saw that something had happened to her throat. She had
seen it happening before to the throats of women, especially
of unloved women, but now it had happened to her. It was
the throats of women that died first. With men it was the nape
of the neck. It withered, or it grew heavy; men wrote their
lives there, where they could not see what they had written.
But with women it was the throat.

She bought a little jar of cream after that, and at night
she rubbed her throat, as if she would rub away the years,
erase her life; and in the mornings she would look, and there
was her past again, etched as in copper, permanent, betraying. She took to wearing soft tulle scarfs in the evenings, and
sometimes when people looked at her, she would draw a fold
across, under her chin.

Fortunately she was busy. She was giving her house to
Eddie and Mary Elizabeth. She had refurnished it for them,
and was taking the old Colfax place herself. Eileen and
Tommy were going to New York, with Palm Beach in the
winter and Newport in the summer. Tommy was going to
play now, to try to get some good out of his money; sitting
on a beach, gambling at Bradley's with yellow chips, a thousand dollars on the turn of a card. Like the cards on the table
during the draft, only then it was life and death. Making out
checks or pocketing his winnings.

"Lunch money! Come on, folks!"

Nothing to do now but play; waking up in the morning
to face a day filled with trifles, keeping a man, by Eileen's
orders. Shouting at him irritably: "For God's sake get away.
I can hold my own pants."

Nothing could polish Tommy. But also nothing could stop
Eileen.

Eileen was not so pretty as she had been; her fair hair was

frankly bleached, her figure growing heavy. There was something reminiscent of Stella in her now. She weighed herself where Stella had measured; it was her full breasts that she constricted, her hips, where Stella had laced in her waist; but when she came home now, from parties or bridge, she would take off her stays and binders, kick off her high-heeled shoes, soak her feet in hot water.

"One thing trouble has done for you, Missie," she would say. "It's kept you thin."

She envied Missie her tragedies, because they had saved her figure.

Adelaide was greatly excited at the prospect of the change —Adelaide was with her again—but Missie moved somberly about. It was she now who picked things up, put them down again. Before they left she went into Wesley's room, newly furnished for the young people, and stood there looking about her. The big bed on which Wesley had died was gone now. "My girl; my dear girl." Her throat tightened, there was the old constriction about her heart.

She had moved before the children came back from their wedding trip, but she was never quite at home in the rejuvenated old house, among Eileen's florid furnishings. Adelaide loved it. She would clump about, leaning heavily on her stick—she had a bad knee—and criticize Eileen's taste; and at the same time she was secretly proud of her grandeur. One day she said:

"Why on earth don't you get rid of that old deer? Nobody has them now."

"I like it, Aunt Adelaide," she shouted. Adelaide had grown very deaf. "I always felt that it stood for something."

It seemed dreadful to her that Adelaide wanted to get rid of the deer.

She settled down as best she could. It was like old times to hear Adelaide at night furtively making her way down the back stairs. In the daytime she received her callers; they came in limousines now, sometimes with two men on the box. Or she went to her hospital board meetings, the matron watching the door, reading her reports:

"The corner stone of the new research laboratory, donated by Mrs. Dexter and to be known as the Wesley Dexter Laboratory, will be laid next week. It is hoped that the members of this board will attend."

She listened to that, greatly moved. It was to be Wesley's enduring monument, his name was to be carved in stone over the door. Nor did she see any irony in that, in thus cannonizing him. She only hoped that Eddie would be back, Eddie and of course Mary Elizabeth.

They did not get back, however. It was a rainy day, and Missie stood alone under her umbrella—Adelaide's rheumatic knee had kept her at home—and she thought it went off very well. All except Judge MacDonald's speech; he could have said more, a great deal more, in his eulogy.

If she was not happy, she was apparently contented. She was forty-five now, her hair not quite so lustrous, her skin still clear but faintly lined. From a little distance she had a deceptive appearance of youth; close by she showed the years she had lived, the tears she had shed. But the children in the children's ward at the hospital called her the beautiful lady. She went there rather often, always a trifle shy with them but gentle and tender. Sometimes when the nurse was out she would talk to them. It was like the old days with Eddie; they would lean their small warm bodies against her.

"Tell us some more. Some more!"

The nurses would find her flushed and smiling, but she would stop when they came in. They made her self-conscious, as though they had guessed some secret hope of hers.

Before Eddie brought his wife home she had everything in readiness. She went over the house again. It was in beautiful order, servants installed, flowers everywhere. With her own hands she made up the two beds in their bedroom, put on the fine linen sheets, the soft blankets. If she felt any resentment at those two beds, at the trick that life played all mothers, using them as long as they were needed and then casting them off, she made no sign. When they came home she was there to welcome them, but she did not stay.

"You must have your first meal in your new home alone," she said, smiling at them. "I'll be here often enough. Don't worry."

They let her go, politely sorry, self engrossed. Eddie closing the front door, taking his wife in his arms.

"Home, darling! Our very own home!"

They had already forgotten her.

She gave a ball for them soon after that. She could do that now. Her life was set, and theirs. They were safe, all safe. Her mistakes, such as they were, were buried in her graves, and along with them her passions, her wild griefs. Nothing could happen now. She saw the years going on, inexorably but peacefully. They would have children and she would live her vicarious life in them. That was her dream. Then one day in the fullness of time she would lie down to rest, and she would not get up. She would keep a rendezvous, like Cecily. She thought of that quite calmly.

So she gave her ball. There was no Wesley now, sitting in William's library making out lists, but a social secretary, an efficient young woman, very businesslike. She checked off the names in a copy of the Social Register. Now and then Missie objected.

"I don't like that Jerome girl, Miss Henderson. She's— well, she's dreadful."

"She goes everywhere, Mrs. Dexter."

"Not here, please."

She spoke a little like Sarah then, but she did not realize it.

The house looked very lovely the night of the ball. She had had Sloane's decorate it. Perhaps she was thinking of that when, before the first guests came, she went into the conservatory and found a young man working over the fountain.

He looked up when he heard her.

"I've changed the pool, Mrs. Dexter. How do you like it?"

He thought she looked at him queerly. Then she turned and went away.

The ball, however, went off splendidly; Missie inside the door, like Sarah so long ago; Mary Elizabeth beside her in her wedding gown; Eddie big and handsome, happy, boisterous; like Wesley, only taller. The brasses in the band blared, voices shrilled, young people came in eagerly, occasionally forgot to greet her, rushed into the hurly burly.

"There he is! I told you he'd be here."

By midnight they had forgotten her entirely. Adelaide was still there, her stick beside her, her vast body sunk in a chair. She was waiting for supper. Missie was very tired. She slipped quietly up the stairs, so quietly that the couples sitting there moved over automatically, engrossed in themselves, not even recognizing her.

There was a bench at the top of the stairs, and she sat down there. Just below her two young people were talking.

"It's a good party."

"Pretty fair."

"Look here, tell me something. Wasn't there a scandal once about Mrs. Dexter?"

"You're in the lady's house, my child."

"Don't be silly. Wasn't there?"

The youth yawned.

"Nothing much. She ran away with another man once. That's all."

"Honestly?"

"So they say. Before my time, though. How about another whirl before supper? Got to do something to raise an appetite."

When they had gone she went dully into her bedroom. As she moved about, taking off her finery, she could hear the blare of the brasses below, laughter, the sound of china in the pantry, the voices of waiters. Her hands were trembling once more.

She saw that her safety, so dearly bought, was no safety

at all. This new generation, so outspoken, so cruelly frank, held it in its irresponsible hands. And she had no defence. Suppose Eddie learned it? What could she say for herself? Defend what she had done at the cost of what she had built?

For the first time since Wesley's death she saw him clearly again, not the Wesley she had canonized, but Wesley as he had been, selfish, sensual, hard; driving her off and then virtuously refusing to take her back. A hard man, a cruel self-indulgent man.

But Eddie would never believe that. It was too late, even if she told him, and she would never tell him. Let him think of her what he would, but let him keep what she had built. She could not debase the dead. She sat down before her dressing table and automatically rubbed the cream into her neck, and all the time she was thinking, plotting. Nobody would tell Eddie, except Mary Elizabeth. Then, if she was kind to Mary Elizabeth, very kind——

Suddenly she realized that her security, her very life itself, might lie in Mary Elizabeth's small carefully manicured hands. She lay in her bed later on, thinking about that. So small, so young and inexperienced, to hold so much; like Mr. Boroday, whittling somewhere in the seats of the mighty, and passing on matters of life and death.

And below her the drums beat and throbbed, so that her bed seemed to quiver. It was some time before she knew that she was shaking.

Hours later she heard the party breaking up, heard Adelaide's stick on the stairs, heard Mary Elizabeth cautiously open her door, look in.

"May I come in? I was afraid you were asleep."

Missie rallied herself.

"Of course. Come in."

She came over to Missie's Empire bed, sat down on it, radiant and flushed. She did not see Missie staring at her hands.

"I wanted to thank you," she said rather breathlessly, "for the wonderful party. It's a perfectly huge success."

"I'm glad. If it has made you happy——"

"Frightfully happy."

Eddie came in then, and sat down beside her.

"You're a grand old girl," he told her, affectionately vernacular. "But if I were you I'd give Adelaide a pill. She's eaten up the works."

She lay back on her pillows, even laughed a little. How silly she had been! She was safe, and so were they, safe and happy. Nothing could happen.

But she could not sleep. She got up at dawn and stood by her window, looking out, and something odd about the old iron deer caught and held her eye. Some exhilarated youth had placed on its head a tall silk hat and left it there. Its dignity was gone. It looked what it was, a pathetic survival of a bygone age.

Chapter XL

ADELAIDE died early that winter. One morning the cook found her in the pantry, stretched out on the floor stiff and cold, with the crumbs of a night lunch all about her, and little marks where the mice had been nibbling at them. As she lay there she was enormous. Missie, crying over her, over that vast body which had never lived, never adventured, felt a dreadful pity for her, embarked now alone on the great journey. She brought a pillow and placed it under the heavy head, as though she would soften things for her.

With Adelaide gone Missie was very much alone. She lived very quietly. Now and then she found herself unnecessarily washing her slim white hands, where now the veins began to be somewhat prominent. When she noticed it she would dry them quickly, smile rather wryly. On Sundays the children came in to luncheon, but they seldom stayed for long. They were restless, filled with energy. They telephoned the moment they were in the house, getting up tennis games for the afternoon, motor parties.

"What a lot of work in order to play!" she would say to them.

Eddie was faintly impatient at her grief for Adelaide.

"She'd lived a long time," he said.

And she could not explain to him that this was her grief; that Adelaide had lived so long and so little. There was something masterful about Eddie now; masterful and a trifle hard. He was a man of family. Every day he went to the office which had been Tommy's, and pushed buttons and used the telephone. When he dictated his letters it was Grace who took them. Once or twice at first she had called him Eddie, but that

323

was bad for office discipline. He had had to tell her about it. But sometimes, looking up suddenly, he caught a faint mocking smile about her lips, and it annoyed him.

"This family stuff——!" he said to Mary Elizabeth. "Mother's always carried the whole damn family. It makes me sick."

Mary Elizabeth, however, liked to think that Grace was there, and not some demure little stenographer who would use her wiles on Eddie. She was very jealous, was Mary Elizabeth; jealous and possessive.

But as time went on the Sunday luncheons with Missie grew less and less frequent. They would call up, apologize, make excuses. She understood, as she always had understood. They must be free. And because she never had been free she made no demands, showed no resentments. Their world puzzled her, with its brutal frankness, its cynical rejection of romance, its material philosophy. It seemed to have passions, but no heart. And its passions were apparently without depth, were reduced to physical acts hastily consummated and carelessly forgotten. She recoiled from it; it was a world Wesley would have understood, but she could not.

She missed them. The growing gulf between them and her frightened her. It was as though they thought she had never lived, felt nothing, knew nothing. Yet, she thought, to have been born, loved, married, borne a child and been widowed, was to have known all of life but death.

It was Judge MacDonald who told her one day that Eddie was like old William. He came in now and then; he was feebler than ever, his eyes still looked out from his wrinkled face like those of a lonely boy. He liked to come. She was gentle with him, gave him the soft food his ancient teeth required, let him put pillows behind her, as if in memory of that peevish incredibly beloved and long lost wife of his. He was still shrewd, however.

"But William was hard," she said. "A hard man. Eddie——"

"The youth of to-day is fairly hard, Missie. Hard as to its elders; it reserves its compromises for itself."

She did not believe him, but the next Sunday when Eddie and Mary Elizabeth came to luncheon—they still came, although less and less frequently—she found Eddie asleep on the library davenport with a handkerchief over his eyes to keep out the light. She put her hand to her slim throat, where now in daytime she wore a black velvet band, and told herself fiercely that old William had been honest and upright. Hard, yes, but better that than softness like Lambert's or weakness like Wesley's.

When she went back, Mary Elizabeth looked at her suspiciously. She was very jealous of Missie. She always suspected her of stealing off for some secret rendezvous with Eddie, of using her influence to undermine her own. At night she would ask casually:

"Was your mother in the office to-day?"

"No. Why?"

"I just wondered."

Her jealousy frightened Missie. It made her constrained with Eddie, and time did not help it. Two years, three years, and still the small furrow between Mary Elizabeth's eyes when she found them alone together.

"I'm not intruding, am I?"

And Missie looking guilty, colouring faintly, making her ineffectual protest.

She still heard now and then from Eileen. Eileen had been to Paris and had had her face lifted. "I hardly know myself," she wrote. "It is really wonderful, and such a comfort. No bother now about having to be massaged. Tommy doesn't like it, but then of course he wouldn't. Says it's not moral; and that it's like living with a strange woman. Can't you hear him?"

Eileen was very happy, apparently. Now and then she cut out accounts of her parties and sent them on, and Missie dutifully read them. She felt no envy, but sometimes she wondered

about Tommy. Now and then she saw him. He was less talka-
tive than he used to be, and he did not jingle his money any
more. Eileen thought it a vulgar habit. It was four years before the blow fell. She had lulled herself into a sense of false
security. She no longer avoided Kirby. When he came to town
he would drop in to see her, and she looked forward to his
visits. She had never heard that a dead passion makes a live
friendship; she only knew that his coming warmed her, that
he alone was unchanged in a changing world. Between them
there need be no secrets, no reserves. When he dined with her,
she would dress carefully for him, wrap her soft gray or
lavender tulles about her throat, go down happily to greet him.
And as before he would tell her his dreams; strange that he
still had dreams. Zeppelins it was now, carrying freight and
passengers across the seas.

"Did you ever read *The Night Mail?*"

"No."

"I'll send it to you."

There was no question of sentiment between them, but she
knew that she gave him something he sadly needed, peace and
an old loyalty.

"You don't mind, Missie, do you? I can talk to you. I
always could."

She let him talk. She would knit or sew by a lamp and let
him talk; his plans, his hopes, his frustrations. He unloaded
himself on her, and she took the burden and carried it for
him. Perhaps after all this was the answer to many things,
to have a friend at the end. She was grateful to him. His
visits were something to anticipate. She planned the food
carefully. She made little mental notes.

"I must tell Kirby when he comes."

If Kirby's sentiment for her held anything deeper she
was never to know it. Sometimes he would fall quiet, staring
at the fire. Perhaps he was thinking then of how pleasant this
was, he and Missie together there; of her long understanding silences, her quiet capable hands, her kind eyes, her shy

smile. His passionate days were over. He could hardly remember them, with their violences and bitter angers. He had
reached the age of sentiment, a good and lovely woman, a
friendly hearth——

It was so he was sitting one night when Mary Elizabeth
came in and found him there, relaxed and at home. She gave
them both a queer little look and backed out again.

"Mary Elizabeth!" Missie called. "Come back. Come in,
child."

"It wasn't anything," she said from the doorway. "I was
just going by."

She would not come in, and Missie knew then that she
knew. Her peace of mind was definitely gone. Sometimes
when they were alone together she would find the girl's eyes
fixed on her, studying her, perhaps trying to reconcile her with
some flaming and passionate picture of the past. When she
looked up Mary Elizabeth would hastily avert her eyes.

She never told Kirby, but from that time on the sword hung
over her. Some day, some time, Eddie would know, to his
bitter shame and anger. When that time came she prayed that
she might be dead. One did not hate the dead.

Perhaps she was not entirely normal after that. She moved
about much as usual, going beautifully dressed and groomed
through the routine of occasional dinners, charity, afternoon
concerts. She would sit at the concerts and try to understand
them, but the new modern music puzzled her. It made her
think, but it did not make her feel; and all around her were
other lonely women like herself, filling in time, not understanding the music but reluctant to have it end, to leave these
other women, as lonely as themselves, to go out to their handsome cars and drive home to their empty houses.

But her health was not good. She was tired for no reason,
nervous, emotional. Sometimes, for no cause whatever, her
body would turn into fire, her delicate face would flush. She
would feel suffocated, have to open a window to breathe. She
knew that all women reached this final hill-top, only to gaze

into the empty valley beyond toward the sunset. But she was no longer sure of herself. She had curious obsessions, and she thought of Stella rather more than she should.

One day Judge MacDonald told her that the piper was dead.

"Aye," he said. "I've outlived them all, although only God in His wisdom knows why. Even you, Missie, you've outlived a good many."

"Yes," she said, with her throat tightening.

"It's a strange adventure, living," he said. "Perhaps Browning is right, and we never know what it means until we die."

She thought of that, too, when she was alone.

The burden was growing unbearable. One Sunday she said impulsively that she might go abroad. Perhaps she hoped they would protest, but there was a sudden brightening in Mary Elizabeth's eyes, and Eddie was robustly encouraging.

"Why don't you, Mother? You need a change."

She put her betraying hands in her lap.

"I mean, to stay. Not forever, of course, but for a year or two."

"Better and better!" said Eddie. "Who deserves it more?"

She longed to cry out to them, to ask them to need her, not to let her go. But already they were planning for her.

"You'll love it," Mary Elizabeth told her. "You'll find plenty of other women over there, too. Women like yourself, you know; free to do what they like."

She wanted to cry out again at that, to say that she would not join that army of unneeded, unwanted women, wandering drearily through foreign picture galleries and cathedrals and shopping for little gifts to send back home, gifts with which to purchase remembrance at a price. But she said nothing. When they left it was settled that she was to go.

She went about her preparations methodically. Fortunately Kirby was busy. She wrote him that she was going, and he wrote back that he would see her off. She sat with that letter in her hands, thinking of the time she had met him on the pier when Eileen and Tommy had sailed.

"Are you as lost as you look, Missie?"

"I have my boy. That's enough."

She got up and threw open the window. She felt that she was suffocating.

She bought her trunks, prepared to close the old house. A day or two before she was to start she visited her graves again, carrying flowers with her. The ivy on Harry's mound covered it now, was trying to cover the headstone, and that pale green moss which appears only on the graves of the aged was over her grandmother and old Archibald. Stella Colfax, 1850-1892. Only forty-two. She was older now than Stella when she died.

She went home again. She was in a mood of quiet desperation, afraid to go, afraid now to stay. And the next day, the day before she was to leave, the final blow fell.

Eddie knew. In some quarrel between them, in some moment of jealous anger, Mary Elizabeth had told him. It was still new to him when he came. He was still burning with anger, against herself, against his wife. If he had spoken about it it would have been better, but he said nothing. And she could not ask him. He was armoured with self-righteous fury, hard, aloof. He would not even look directly at her. He got out the labels and tags, the steamship tickets, her letter of credit, and put them on the table.

"Everything's here, I think."

She looked them over, her hands so uncertain that she dropped some of them.

"I don't see any ticket to New York, Eddie."

"I have that. I'm going on, of course."

She was stunned. To have those two meet on the pier was unthinkable. There was something ugly in Eddie just then, something sinister. Anything but that. She steadied her voice.

"I have a friend seeing me off. An old friend, Eddie. If I had known———"

"Who?"

"Kirby. Kirby Phelps."

And then he swore.

"Kirby Phelps!" he said. "Well, he's not. I won't have it. I won't have him hanging around you. God Almighty, hasn't he done enough to us?"

He flung away from her and ran out of the house.

She did not go down to dinner that night. At eight o'clock Talbot brought up a tray. She heard him coming, the faint clinking of china and glass, the careful footsteps. Just so must Stella have heard her, long years ago. She sent him away, wondering, and sat on in the darkness. She was not thinking, only suffering. But her senses were alert enough. She was listening, waiting. Surely Eddie would come back. He could not leave her like this. He was not hard or cruel. He would come back, and she would tell him; tell him carefully, so as not to hurt Wesley. She must think how to tell him. Only, she could not think.

By midnight she knew he was not coming.

She got up then, moving heavily about the room. If he would not come to her she would go to him. He would be up still, unhappy, desperate. She might quiet him, so that he could sleep. She let herself quietly out of the house, and the night air refreshed her. She felt almost strong now, full of courage. She would tell him, and he would understand. He was no child now; he was a man. He would understand.

It was midnight when she reached the house. It was dark, and his bedroom windows above were opened for the night. He had gone to bed. Even now, while she stood there, he was sleeping. He was not agonized, for her or for himself. He could leave her like that, and then sleep.

She went on, apparently objectiveless. Some time later she found herself before the little house. After a moment she fumbled in her bag, found the key, and went inside. Automatically she closed the door, turned on the electric light in the hall, entered the dark office. She sat down there, very tired, very haggard, and looked around her. In her strange state of mind, however, it was not an office now, but the old parlour. There was the hard rosewood chair where Sarah Colfax had sat, not touching anything, the jet bugles in her bonnet quivering, her dolman rigidly fastened; the old sofa where Eileen had sat after Stella's death, her head on Tommy's shoulder, crying, while Missie washed and ironed her handkerchiefs.

She was confused, sitting there. She seemed to be herself, but she seemed to be Stella also. Stella listening, and Mr. Taylor in the hall.

"You're not to worry, mom. You're not to worry about anything."

And Stella's voice, flat, ugly.

"Tell the old fool to go away."

After a while she got up and moved slowly through the house, still seeing it not as it was but as it used to be. From that window she had watched Harry Sloane playing tennis. Outside in the dark was still the fence where she and Mr. Wilkinson had planted the morning glories. In the dining room Stella had stood in her new black silk dress.

"How does it look, Missie?"

"You look wonderful, mom."

She would have to stop this. It wasn't normal. She would have to stop it and go back home. But she did not go. Instead she went up the stairs. At the door to the back room she stood still for a moment, then she opened it. Just so, probably, had Stella stood, more than thirty years ago; stood and held the knob, hesitated, listened, maybe trembled. She went in, turned on the light, closed the door, looked about her.

There between the windows had stood the old washstand, with the splasher over it; "Cleanliness is next to Godliness," embroidered on it in red. The washstand with its basin and pitcher.

"Using the cake bowl! What's your basin for?"

"I haven't any. It's broken."

"Then you broke it, you dirty slut."

Over the washstand the gas bracket. It was still there, the bracket. Missie sat down on the cot and stared at it. How easy! And no one thought ill of the dead. They forgave them. Stella had known that. Odd to think how once she had thought this room was haunted; how it had frightened her. It was a good room, quiet and shut away. It was sanctuary and peace.

She got up, moving toward the gas bracket like a woman walking in her sleep. But once there she hesitated. Then she made an odd futile gesture and turned the stop-cock.

When she had gone back to the cot she lay for a time with her eyes open, staring after her old fashion at the ceiling. She was very tired. The bed felt soft beneath her. Once she raised her head. The gas must be flowing now, but it was very slow.

She felt nothing yet. She felt filled with vitality, that terrible vitality of women. Women always had it. That was so they could survive their men, hold on to them to the last. But she was not doing that. She was letting go, letting go of Eddie. He had not wanted her, or needed her. He would be sorry now.

Suddenly she sat up. What was she doing? Leaving him to think that he had driven her to this! It was cruel. She could not hurt him so. She understood Eddie. He was not hard, he was only young. She would get up. In a moment she would get up. Just now she felt dizzy, dizzy and weak. She lay back again. Just a moment to rest, and then she would get up.

But the dawn found her still there, that same dawn which found Eddie tossing on his bed, and Mary Elizabeth sunk deep at last in sleep. Eddie had seen Grace, had talked to her. Soon he could get up, get up and set things right again. His heart warmed. He felt magnanimous, gentle, loving. Perhaps she need not go abroad; she had not seemed to want to go. He could turn in the tickets; there would be a forfeit, but after all——

He looked at his watch.

Missie lay very still. Now and then she moved a little, but that was all. The air in the room was rather heavy, but the crowning irony of that gasless bracket she had not yet discovered. She lay relaxed and quiet, her face strangely young. She was dreaming, and in her dream she was a girl again, watching for Harry Sloane. There was even a faint smile on her lips.

"But you're prettier. You're awfully pretty, Missie."

As the sun rose it turned into burnished copper the tarnished gas bracket, through which no gas had flowed for many years, and beat pitilessly on her throat; that throat on which her life was etched with fine lines, and in which now the pulse was still throbbing, throbbing with the terrible vitality of women.

THE END